THE NOBLE AND THE NIGHTINGALE

What Reviewers Say
About Barbara Ann Wright's Work

Lady of Stone

"Yet another stellar read from Barbara Ann Wright, *Lady of Stone* is a wonderful blend of magical fantasy and lesbian romance that had me eager to find out how it all ends, and yet reluctant to have it end."
—*Beauty in Ruins*

Not Your Average Love Spell

"Barbara Ann Wright mixes so much into her story—romance, comedy, drama, action, adventure—that it threatens more than once to collapse under the clash of themes, but those clashes and contrasts only serve to make it stronger and more engaging."—*Beauty in Ruins*

"…a solid little fantasy tale with a lot of really cool elements…Wright plays to all the tropes…in a way that keeps the story fresh while preserving the surprises. …As for the romance, that was surprisingly sweet and amusing, with four women at the heart of the story who are entirely likable…the spark of attraction and the emotional connections are undeniable."—*Fem Led Fantasy*

"…a great story filled with magic, wondrous creatures and adventure but what I really enjoyed about the book was the way that the characters grew. …It is a great thing to read in these trying times and I took hope from it. The story pulls with enough magic to feel like a fully fleshed out fantasy world while keeping our heroes relatable and engaging. …I give it a full hearted thumbs up and you should definitely check it out."—*Paper Phoenix Ink*

"I thought this was a fun and entertaining adventure read…the fantasy aspects are very approachable. …The way the whole plot unfolded just felt different and I loved that. What also really impressed me was the amount of action this book had. It was one thing after another after another all keeping me completely glued to the book...I could not stop reading."—*Lez Review Books*

"The adventures, as mentioned above, were plentiful. There are pirates and warriors, a yeti, giant spiders, a possible dragon, lizard people, and in general, a lot of tough-headed knights. The plot was definitely interesting, with a lot of twists and turns. The writing was seasoned with beautiful writing and truths. I highly recommend this book to lovers of fantasy and to those that want characters to be challenged to deconstruct what they know and learn how to live together. It's a beautiful book!"—*The Lesbrary*

"[*Not Your Average Love Spell*] is an entertaining...romantic fantasy adventure comedy? (I'm not sure how to categorise its Venn diagram of subgenres, either.) Starring an agoraphobic witch; a bright, curious, talkative homunculus; an archivist/scholar with a revolutionary bent; a knight who—at least initially—believes wholeheartedly in her order's mission to stamp out magic; and an invasion of genocidal warriors, *Not Your Average Love Spell* takes its characters on an entertaining ride and delivers all of them a happy ending. (Except for the genocidal warriors. Their happy ending would be terrible for everyone else.)"—*Tor.com*

The Tattered Lands

"Wright's postapocalyptic romance is a fast-paced journey through devastation. ...Plenty of action, surprises, and magic will keep readers turning the pages."—*Publishers Weekly*

House of Fate

"...fast, fun...entertaining...*House of Fate* delivers on adventure." —*Tor.com*

Coils

"…Greek myths, gods and monsters and a trip to the Underworld. Sign me up. …This one springs straight into action…a good start, great Greek myth action and a late blooming romance that flowers in the end…"—*Dear Author*

"A unique take on the Greek gods and the afterlife make this a memorable book. The story is fun with just the right amount of camp. Medusa is a hot, if unexpected, love interest. …A truly unexpected ending has us hoping for more stories from this world."—*RT Book Reviews*

"The gods and monsters of ancient Greek mythology are living, breathing entities, something Cressida didn't expect and is amazed as well as terrified to discover. …Cressida soon realizes being in the underworld is no different than being among the living. The heart still feels and love can bloom, even in the world of Myth. …The characters are well developed and their wit will elicit more than a few chuckles. A joy to read."—*Lunar Rainbow Reviewz*

Paladins of the Storm Lord

"This was a truly enjoyable read…I would definitely pick up the next book. …The mad dash at the end kept me riveted. I would definitely recommend this book for anyone who has a love of sci-fi. …An intricate…novel one that can be appreciated at many levels, adventurous sci fi or one that is politically motivated with a very astute look at present day human behavior. …There are many levels to this extraordinary and well written book…overall a fascinating and intriguing book."—*Inked Rainbow Reads*

"I loved this. …The world that the Paladins inhabited was fascinating…didn't want to put this down until I knew what happened. I'll be looking for more of Barbara Ann Wright's books."—*Lesbian Romance Reviews*

"*Paladins of the Storm Lord* by Barbara Ann Wright was like an orchestra with all of its pieces creating a symphony. I really truly loved it. I love the intricacy and wide variety of character types…I just loved practically every character! …Of course my fellow adventure lovers should read *Paladins of the Storm Lord*!"—*Lesbian Review*

Thrall: Beyond Gold and Glory

"Once more Barbara has outdone herself in her penmanship. I cannot sing enough praises. A little *Vikings*, a dash of *The Witcher*, peppered with *The Game of Thrones*, and a pinch of *Lord of The Rings*. Mesmerizing. …I was ecstatic to read this book. It did not disappoint. Barbara pours life into her characters with sarcasm, wit and surreal imagery, they leap from the page and stand before you in all their glory. I am left satisfied and starving for more, the clashing of swords, whistling of arrows still ringing in my ears."—*Lunar Rainbow Reviews*

"In their adventures, the women must wrestle with issues of freedom, loyalty, and justice. The characters were likable, the issues complex, and the battles were exciting. I really enjoyed this book and I highly recommend it."—*All Our Worlds: Diverse Fantastic Fiction*

"This was the first Barbara Ann Wright novel I've read, and I doubt it will be the last. Her dialogue was concise and natural, and she built a fantastical world that I easily imagined from one scene to the next. Lovers of Vikings, monsters and magic won't be disappointed by this one."—*Curve*

The Pyramid Waltz

"…a healthy dose of a very creative, yet believable, world into which the reader will step to find enjoyment and heart-thumping action. It's a fiendishly delightful tale."—*Lambda Literary*

"Barbara Ann Wright is a master when it comes to crafting a solid and entertaining fantasy novel. …The world of lesbian literature has a small handful of high-quality fantasy authors, and Barbara Ann Wright is well on her way to joining the likes of Jane Fletcher, Cate Culpepper, and Andi Marquette. …Lovers of the fantasy and futuristic genre will likely adore this novel, and adventurous romance fans should find plenty to sink their teeth into."—*Rainbow Reader*

"*The Pyramid Waltz* has had me smiling for three days. …I also haven't actually read…a world that is entirely unfazed by homosexuality or female power before. I think I love it. I'm just delighted this book exists. …If you enjoyed *The Pyramid Waltz*, *For Want of a Fiend* is the perfect next step…you'd be embarking on a joyous, funny, sweet and madcap ride around very dark things lovingly told, with characters who will stay with you for months after."—*The Lesbrary*

"Chock full of familiar elements that avid fantasy readers will adore…[*The Pyramid Waltz*] adds in a compelling and slowly evolving romance. …Set against a backdrop of political intrigue with the possibility of monsters and mystery at every turn, the two women slowly learn each other, sharing secrets and longing, until a fragile love blossoms between them…"—*USA Today Happily Ever After*

For Want of a Fiend

"This book will keep you turning the page to find out the answers. …Fans of the fantasy genre will really enjoy this installment of the story. We can't wait for the next book."—*Curve*

"A fun, unique story with a distinctive world. This series doesn't imitate other popular fantasy novels. It stands on its own. The writing is well paced and Wright incorporates a more modern or colloquial language which makes the books easy to read. Overall, *For Want of a Fiend* was an enjoyable read and I think you would like it if you are a fan of books like Game of Thrones or a TV series like Reign."
—*Lesbian Review*

"If you enjoyed *The Pyramid Waltz*, *For Want of a Fiend* is the perfect next step. If you haven't read either, know that you'd be embarking on a joyous, funny, sweet and madcap ride around very dark things lovingly told, with characters who will stay with you for months after. The plot still moves at a fast clip. Characterisation continues to deepen—and I love that. I love seeing a passionate, adoring romantic relationship flanked by friendships."—*The Lesbrary*

A Kingdom Lost

"There is only one other time in my life I have uncontrollably shouted out in cheer while reading a book. [*A Kingdom Lost*] made the second. …Over the course of these three books all the characters have blossomed and developed so eloquently. …I simply just thought this whole novel was brilliant."—*Lesbian Review*

The Fiend Queen

"After reading this series Barbara Ann Wright has made my favorite author list. Her writing always seems to sweep me away to another world. The pacing, characters, and language were all perfect. …I am so addicted to Fantasy now. I knew fantasy was one of my favorite genres but it was always hard for me to come by a consistent source of fantasy books. After finishing the series A Pyradisté Adventure I knew that I had found a diamond. I can't wait to read the rest of Barbara Ann Wright's works. …Read it! I am obsessed and I don't know how I will ever want to read a non-fantasy Lesfic ever again. I literally felt drunk off the series. Even after I was done with this book I thought about it constantly for at least two days."—*Lesbian Review*

By the Author

The Pyradisté Adventures
The Pyramid Waltz
For Want of a Fiend
A Kingdom Lost
The Fiend Queen
Lady of Stone

Thrall: Beyond Gold and Glory

The Godfall Novels
Paladins of the Storm Lord
Widows of the Sun-Moon
Children of the Healer
Inheritors of Chaos

Coils

House of Fate

The Tattered Lands

Not Your Average Love Spell

The Sisters of Sarras
The Noble and the Nightingale

THE NOBLE AND THE NIGHTINGALE

by

Barbara Ann Wright

2021

Credits
Editor: Cindy Cresap
Production Design: Susan Ramundo
Cover Design By Tammy Seidick

Acknowledgments

Thanks to everyone at BSB, from Cindy and Stacia, who make sure I don't write crap, to the many writer friends I've met along the way.

Thanks to the Beavers and Writer's Ink: Angela, Deb, Erin, Matt, Natsu, Sarah, and Trakena. You are so far above other writing groups, it's really not fair.

Thanks to all my readers and anyone who reached out. I hope you like Sarras because we're going to be here awhile. ;)

As always, thank you, Mom. You're the reason I'm here both as a person and as a writer.

Dedication

To Angela, for always volunteering her home
and her critiquing skills.

PROLOGUE

Bridget froze as she heard barking.

Dogs. She was finished. Why did they have to use the damned dogs to track her?

Peering around a tree, she tried to ignore her icy-cold hands and searched for signs of pursuit, but she couldn't see anything through the mass of pine trees and dense undergrowth of ferns and thorn bushes. Her pilfered trousers hadn't protected her legs much, and if that wasn't uncomfortable enough, she'd picked the coldest, wettest day of the year so far to escape. If her luck wasn't going to hold for better foliage and milder weather, she should have expected it to collapse in other areas as well.

Like hunting dogs.

She imagined Baxter's wrinkled face scowling at her. "Run, you lumbering ox," he'd say, "or brambles won't be the only thing tearing your trousers!"

She took to her heels again, hoping the soldiers of the Firellian Empire and their stupid dogs would be thrown off by the rain as much as they were no doubt annoyed by it. Ah, yes, having her pursuers being nicely irritated when they caught her would be a continuation of her lucky streak all right.

All worth it not to live a lie anymore, not to kill anymore.

She laughed at herself as she ran. The first part was a bit of bullshit. Any life she had from now on as an ex-spy for the empire would be as much a lie as the countless assignments she'd completed.

Well, yes, damn it, but it would be *her* lie. And after long enough, it could become the truth.

As for the killing, well, she'd do her best.

The barking turned into howling. Closer now. They'd found her scent. Bridget cursed. The soldier's coat she'd stolen had long ago lost its buttons, and she gave up trying to hold it tighter around her. She pumped that arm as she ran, clutching her mandolin case with her other hand.

Any truth she'd ever find in the future had to have music in it.

The sound of the Kingfish River had been a murmur for the past mile, but now it grew to a roar, drowning out the sounds of pursuit. At least she was still headed in the right direction. This far downriver, she should be well out of the rapids but still high enough to be carried swiftly away.

Forcing down her fear, she repeated Baxter's last words to her in her head. "Once you hit the water, ducky, you've got around twenty minutes before you get so stiff, you can't move." He'd shaken a long finger in her face. "No more than twenty, mind. You'll drown before you freeze to death, but as you'll be dead, I doubt that will be much of a comfort." Then he'd given her a rough hug and had practically shoved her out of his office. He probably thought that saving her from a long good-bye made up for training her as a spy in the first place.

It didn't, but she still counted him as a friend. Sort of. And he went up in her estimation when she broke through the trees and saw a large bundle of broken branches sitting on the muddy bank of the swiftly moving Kingfish River.

Bridget sprinted for the bundle, recognizing it as the old spymaster's trick for disguising a small, overturned boat. She caught a hint of shouts coming from the trees, and her heart pressed into her throat.

With shaking fingers, she secured her mandolin case under the oilskin tarp fastened inside the circular boat on the bottom, so it would hang over her head as she floated. The case fit next to a pack Baxter had supplied when he'd hidden the tiny craft.

"Thanks, Bax," she whispered as she lifted the boat and hurried toward the river, keeping it the wrong way up so it would cover her. "Just another tangle of branches and flotsam hurtling downriver in the early fall. Nothing to worry about. The traitor probably drowned. Let's all go home."

If only.

Now to actually get in the damned river.

"Here's to the devils." She plunged in, not letting herself think.

The cold hit her legs like a hammer, and she sucked in a breath so hard, her chest ached. Any later in the year, and this would be unthinkable. It was pretty difficult to think of now, but as she waded up to her chest and lowered the boat over her head, she could think of little else.

The current grabbed her, yanking her away, taking her breath again. She curled her hands around the oar wedged over her head and picked her feet up, letting the river have its way.

Twenty minutes, Baxter had said. That was the same as singing, "Break Not My Heart, O Lady Fair," five times or so. Even fifteen minutes should carry her well out of sight of this batch of pursuers or any others who'd made it to the river. She could force herself to concentrate that far.

Bridget sang through chattering teeth, searching her body for sleepiness or a pull like invisible weights on her limbs. Nothing. She was wide-awake and taut as a board. Maybe Baxter had been wrong about the temperature of the river at this time of year. She felt no hint of his ultimate sign of danger, a creeping, unexplainable warmth.

Hell's teeth, that would be a relief.

She began the song again but hesitated. Was this the second time through or the third?

Blasted cold. It was the third. Definitely. The first line was… was…

Bridget growled and shook her head. Damned song, she knew it by heart. It had four refrains. Or was it five?

Something *thunked* into the boat. She gasped and swallowed a mouthful of water, freezing her tongue, her teeth, her chest, too cold to taste of anything but ice.

Now she knew what winter tasted like.

Bridget laughed, swallowing more water, now lulled by the river within her as well as the one without.

Damn it all, when had she gotten so sleepy?

That meant something, an important something.

If she'd been at home, Baxter would have been shouting at her, but she couldn't hear him. Again, strange. She usually carried his voice wherever she went. He was father, mother, teacher, judge, confessor. "All the gods in heaven, and all the legions in hell," he'd said when her training had begun.

Another *thunk*. Bridget's eyes went wide as she pulled her chin from the water. It wasn't so bad, really, not anymore. Baxter had been wrong and not just about the cold. She'd had parents beyond him. She looked up and caught sight of the mandolin case.

Clear as glass, she heard him again. "If you drown, the only thing you have of your mama will wind up at the bottom of the river."

By the devils, it would not.

Bridget forced her limbs to work past the invisible weights. It felt like dragging a plow just to move her arms. With a grunt, she turned the boat over in one shaky motion, glad she'd practiced it so many times in Baxter's bathhouse that she could do it in her sleep.

Too soon to show herself to any potential hunters? So be it. She was getting out of this cursed river now. Besides, it didn't matter if anyone saw this face. Only Baxter had ever seen her without a disguise. She'd take off her makeup and prosthetics, and they'd never track her by looks.

She was babbling in her head, wasting time. "Get in," she tried to say, but her teeth were clamped so hard, their grinding drowned out the river. She pulled up on the boat but slipped back into the water, her limbs like liquid, too.

She tried again, failed again.

"Get in, damn you." One more pull, and she could be safe and away, ready to show her actual face to the world.

And if the soldiers were waiting and shot her full of arrows, well, she wouldn't be cold anymore.

Bridget threw her head back and laughed as she pulled up a third time, imagining Baxter goading her, calling her names, signs that he actually liked her.

"Damn you, too, Bax!"

One final shove, and she was up, in the boat, safe.

Sort of.

"There's more to do, ducky," the Baxter in her head said, but he sounded as smug as she felt.

Bridget didn't bother to look toward the bank. She stripped as quickly as she could while lying on her pack and case, cast the stolen uniform into the river, then pulled a blanket from under the oilskin and wrapped up in it. Branches and clouds rushed past overhead, and she smiled when the sun caressed her through a gap in both.

Luck was taking a turn.

Chapter One

Adella was determined not to lose her temper this time, but the Firellian ambassador seemed equally determined to touch every single nerve in her body.

Ambassador Lancel de Maupassant was an oily little man, and not just because of his personality. His salt-and-pepper hair shone with some kind of grease, his mustache curled up at the ends with it, and his pointed goatee fairly dripped. Adella supposed the purpose was to make him shine like a jewel in the candlelight, but he only oozed like a pantomime villain.

He and his aides lined one side of the large table in the gilded meeting room. They were all as pale as fish bellies, but Adella couldn't really fault them for never seeing the sun. That was an ambassador's affliction, one she shared.

"Clause one hundred and four," de Maupassant said, his quick smile displaying a gold canine.

"Has already been covered," Adella said.

De Maupassant's black eyes shifted to her, as did those of Dolores Vega, Adella's superior, but Adella would not be one of those secondary ambassadors who never spoke their mind. It was her brashness that had gotten her this coveted position at thirty-four, and she wasn't going to shut up now.

"Your *aide* is correct," de Maupassant said, inclining his head. "But there are several clauses we should like to reopen."

We indeed, as if he was an oligarch and had the right to the royal plural. The Firellian Empire didn't even employ multiple ambassadors. Who was this *we*?

"Ambassador del Amanecer is correct, however," Dolores said. "Clause one hundred and four has already been argued to the satisfaction of both parties. Reopening those issues is a step backward." She waved a hand heavy with jewels, a flash of wealth, before touching a lock of gray hair that had been left to coil over her right shoulder. The gesture drew the eye to the elaborate curls and braids atop and behind her head, a coiffure also bedecked with gems and the large silver pin denoting her status both as noble and an ambassador, another reminder that the people of the Kingdom of Sarras had deep coffers.

Compared to her, de Maupassant's velvet clothes and hat seemed like rubbish. But quite a few baubles caught the light as he spread his hands, too. "Perhaps we should adjourn before tempers begin to fray." He smiled Adella's way, and she nearly dug her fingernails into the varnished table, the same show of temper she'd displayed at the last meeting.

Her aide Juno tapped her knee lightly, reminding her that the meeting wasn't over yet.

"Of course, if you're tired, Ambassador," Dolores said, and before de Maupassant could argue his vigor, she waved to her aide, who leaped to open the door. "The sentinels will show you to your rooms."

De Maupassant and his delegation stood and bowed, and Adella's side of the table did the same. She heard one of de Maupassant's aides mumble in Firellian amidst the shuffling of departure. "Keeping diplomats under guard is an insult."

She nearly threw her pen at him, nib first. A country that never allowed any foreign diplomats inside its borders was an insult. If the Firellian Empire admitted ambassadors, Adella and Dolores would be there now, and they'd no doubt have guards, too.

Of course, if the empire wasn't also known for employing more spies than soldiers, there wouldn't be as much need for a round-the-clock guard here in Sarras.

When the Firellians had gone, Dolores turned to Adella. Her aide Cristoff drifted to the other side of the table and began tidying wineglasses and bottles. Juno joined him, and they began a quiet, we're-not-eavesdropping kind of conversation about the weather.

"Adella," Dolores said, her voice quiet and even. "Tell me what I'm about to say."

Heat filled Adella's cheeks, and she resisted touching the smaller badge in her own hair, a nervous habit acquired when she was promoted to secondary ambassador. She did *not* need its reassurance. "That I should keep my temper in check."

"Is that not the same counsel I gave after our last meeting?" Her gray eyes weren't hard or unforgiving, merely patient, but it was a weighty kind of tolerance, the fortitude of mountains.

"It is…serrah," she added hastily, hoping the respectful term of address would garner some goodwill.

It got a ghost of a smile. "You're not a trainee any longer, Adella. What is an ambassador's greatest weapon?"

"Patience."

Dolores nodded and clasped her hands in front of her gray, impeccably tailored gown. Its simple silhouette flattered her spare frame, the lace neckline falling around the edge of her shoulders. The silver thread running through the fabric was another reminder of wealth and power. "Patience is the river that wears down the stone."

Adella gnawed her lower lip. "What if I played fire to your water? I could make them angry and off guard, and you could provide the calming influence they will open up to."

"And when I retire? You will burn out of control." Dolores gave her a wry smile as she gathered her papers. "You can hardly expect the secondary you select to play your patient counterpoint and lead the discussion." She stepped toward the door before tapping Adella's bare shoulder with her pen. "And stop biting your lip."

Adella chuckled, gathered her own papers, and swept her long skirt around her chair as she followed Dolores into the halls of the Bastión, the seat of government power in the Kingdom of Sarras. She breathed in the smell of wood polish, paper, and an aged smell that reminded her of old leather. Whether she was walking inside the halls or viewing the four-story bulk from outside, it never failed to make her proud.

She smiled at the sight of carved woodwork and intricately painted ceilings, at the portraits of ancestors from every noble family in Sarras, including her own. As always, sadness followed pride. She and her sisters were the last of the del Amanecers.

But they would leave their mark.

Adella shook both thoughts away. "You will stay here forever if I have anything to say about it, serrah."

Dolores smiled over one pale, freckled shoulder. "You did not tell me you were some sort of supernatural creature, Adella. If you have the considerable power to extend life, could you not also give me a back that aches slightly less?"

Adella paused at the door to Dolores's office. "Consider it done."

With a laugh, Dolores waved her across the hall. "I want an annotated report of that meeting within the next two hours." She drew herself up, though she only reached to Adella's nose, and Adella had never considered herself tall. Still, Dolores had a presence that loomed. "Make a special note of every instance which required more patience on your part."

Adella managed not to sigh as she bowed with one hand angled across her waist. When Dolores went inside with Cristoff, Adella crossed the hall to her own office, Juno on her heels.

"I didn't think it went that badly," Juno said as she shut the door. Her blue gown was plainer than Adella's cream-colored affair, but it was well-made and entirely suitable for the cousin of a noble family. The badge in the two simple plaits that circled her head like a crown was the merest bit of sparkle amid her dark hair.

Adella was tempted to pull her own elaborate hairdo apart, but she didn't want to have to bribe Juno to wrangle the mess into shape again. That wasn't her job, and they already had plenty to do.

Not even bothering to sweep her skirt to the side, Adella collapsed onto the leather cushion in her desk chair. She didn't care if she wrinkled anything. "Dealing with that oily tick of a man is like chewing glass."

"Have you ever considered another profession, serrah?" Juno's dark eyes twinkled.

Adella considered scowling but chuckled instead, so happy her aide wasn't a fawning sycophant or a tradition-bound twerp. "I've met several ambassadors from the other blasted countries Sarras trades with. None of them are like that man. If the Firellian Empire let us inside their borders, we wouldn't have to deal with de Maupassant, either. He'd be working with the Sarrasian ministers just as Dolores and I should be working with the Firellian ministers in the damned empire." She swiveled her chair side to side and glared at nothing.

Juno sighed. "It would be nice to get to snoop around the empire."

"I would not snoop."

"Certainly not," Juno said with a straight face. "You would never."

"Quite," Adella said with a sniff.

"You would just turn a blind eye while I did so."

Adella swallowed another laugh. "Are you quite done being cheeky? Can we get on with writing this report now?"

Juno readied her pen at her own small desk in the corner. "Whenever you like."

The sooner they did it, and the sooner Adella added her own thoughts about patience, the sooner they could leave work for the day. She could let the greasy smiles of de Maupassant and the mumbles of his aides drift from her mind as she began the short walk home through the square, past a certain corner, where listening to one particular street performer had become the highlight of her days.

An hour later, they'd nearly finished the report, but something about it didn't sit right. Adella frowned and chewed her lip until Juno tutted at her.

"If that's all, serrah, you have but to sign it. I'll hand it over across the hall, and you can probably still catch..." She lowered her head when Adella glanced at her, but her smile was hard to miss. "Whatever or whoever you would like to see before it gets dark."

Adella sighed. She'd told Juno about the singer on one occasion, but some of her admiration must have showed in her face. It was Juno who'd told her such street performers were called nightingales, which was charming, but Adella often thought of them as troubadours, characters from old tales who were known for being great lovers as well as great musicians.

A nice fantasy to waste time with...but not at the moment.

"There's something wrong with the report," Adella said.

"Wrong?" Juno glanced down at where she'd been writing. "I've written everything exactly as you've said it, serrah."

"No, Juno, your work is impeccable, I'm sure. It's not just the report. It's the entire negotiation, this whole visit. These are minor trading disputes, unworthy of a visit at all. Couriers could have carried these messages back and forth, and no great upset would have come from the time lost."

"It would with all the renegotiating the Firellian ambassador seems inclined toward," Juno said with a snort.

"That's another thing, our lack of progress. Surely de Maupassant has better things to do than argue about the total weight of fish that can be taken from the river by any one boat at a time, especially when the increase we proposed is not that far above the terms that were already in place." She stood and began to pace behind her desk, the doubt in her building now that she'd voiced some of her concerns.

"And these interruptions." Adella tapped her chin with one finger. "I will admit, I shouldn't have let my annoyance show, but what kind of ambassador calls a halt to a meeting because a junior clerk gets a bit testy?"

"You're a secondary ambassador, not a junior clerk."

Adella waved the comment away. "I read every report concerning de Maupassant before his arrival. I would expect him to ask for my removal before calling a halt to the proceedings. This, all this"—she picked up a handful of paper from her desk and waved it around—"is all…shit."

Juno gaped.

"Busywork," Adella amended, but her anger was up now, and theories were flying through her mind. "He's keeping us busy, but why?"

"Why?" Juno asked, leaning forward, face as intense as if she was watching a play.

"I don't know. Perhaps he's trying to lull us into a stupor so he can sneak some other proposal past us. He could be waiting for information about another of our neighbors, and he wants to be here to see how it affects us, how he could turn it to the empire's advantage. He could be trying to distract us while the empire prepares to invade, for all I know."

"It's far more likely to be something in the realm of your first guesses," Juno said with a smirk common to folk from the border towns between Sarras and the Firellian Empire. They took their duty to maintain the walls and natural earthworks very seriously, and they'd never been breached. The only time the soldiers of the empire had set foot on Sarrasian soil, they'd had to capture part of the Kingdom of Othlan to the east and come in from the side.

"Well, whatever he's up to, let's lay it all before Dolores, and then we can go…home." Adella ignored Juno's grin and marched past her and across the hall. With Juno standing behind her, she presented the report and told Dolores of her suspicions.

When the tale was done, Dolores sat in silence for a few moments and frowned softly at her massive desk with its intricate carvings. The light coming from the windows had faded into evening. All the nightingales would have flown.

"Interesting," Dolores said, breaking Adella's reverie. "There may be something in it."

Adella waited for more, some command to action. When nothing came she asked, "What do we do?"

"Do?" Dolores lifted a hand. "We watch and wait. What else would you have us do?"

Adella fought the urge to cry, "Why are you asking me?" Dolores was the senior; she should know. "Something," she offered lamely. Heat suffused her cheeks, and she ducked her head.

Dolores chuckled softly. "I will think on what you've said and add it to my own thoughts. But we are not alone in caring for our homeland. We have guards along our borders and ambassadors in other kingdoms, all of whom would warn us of danger. As for de Maupassant trying to sneak more important provisions past us, well, we must be vigilant. Do not bother yourself yet, my dear. You will find that most of these negotiations are no more than what they seem: boring posturing. As for the others?" She shrugged. "We must wait and see. We cannot shake the answers from de Maupassant's mouth."

A pity.

With a sigh, Adella nodded. "I know you're right."

"Good." Dolores sat forward a bit. "You can return home with a lighter heart, yes?"

"Yes." Adella tried not to make the word sound too morose. "Shall we walk out together?"

"I've a while longer yet. I was just getting to my mail."

Adella leaned forward, craning her neck at a stack of envelopes to Dolores's left. "Any missives from our neighbors warning about Firellian trickery?" she asked, only half joking.

"I think not, though I do have one from a certain border town." She peered around Adella. "Roundtop is your family home, is it not, Juno?"

"It is, serrah," Juno said softly, her eyes wide.

"And Elena Garza is your…"

"My mother, serrah." Now she'd gone pale, too.

"Bad news?" Adella said softly, taking Juno's hand.

Dolores shook her head. "If it were bad news, she would write to Juno herself, I think. More likely, this is a mother fed up with a daughter who doesn't write home often enough, so she appeals to the superior of her daughter's superior." She lifted a silver eyebrow.

Juno swallowed, and pink suffused her pale cheeks. "I have… neglected her a little, serrah."

"You wouldn't be the first."

Adella fought the urge to laugh. Elena Garza must be quite a woman indeed and not only because she caused such anxiety in her daughter. It took courage to write to an ambassador demanding news of one's wayward child.

"I'll take it, serrah," Juno said softly, stepping forward.

Dolores pulled the letter back. "Oh no. It's been a long time since I had to answer to a mother for the conduct of a young lady. The fact that this is business instead of pleasure will not affect my nostalgia."

Adella couldn't contain a small chuckle at the thought of Dolores having to defend her intentions to the parents of many a lady in her younger days.

Or even now, for that matter.

Now Adella was blushing, too.

"We'll be off, then," she said brightly, towing Juno with her toward the door. "Good night, Dolores."

Her laugh followed them into the hall.

When the door had shut, Adella rested a hand on Juno's arm. "I'm sure it will be all right."

Juno nodded but still looked a bit miserable. Adella thought to invite her for a drink, maybe cheer her up, but Juno shook her head and seemed to rally. "Go on, serrah. I'll tidy the office and lock up. Night has yet to fall."

Her nightingale might still be playing. Adella didn't even bother to argue. "Thank you, Juno." Guilt pricked her as Juno began tidying papers, still looking maudlin. "Maybe—"

Juno put her hands on her hips. "Clearly, I need to walk you out." With a smile, she took Adella's arm and walked her to the cloakroom at the front of the building. "Be off with you," she said.

Adella took the kindness offered, grabbed her cloak, and hurried toward Bastión Square.

CHAPTER TWO

Bridget hesitated to put her mandolin in its case. The other nightingales had either already left or were packing their instruments and putting their coats on, but Bridget didn't want to go without seeing *her*.

The nobles and other worthies of Sarras were easy to spot. She'd learned of their lavish clothes and intricate hairdos during her tenure as a Firellian spy. She'd even seen some in smaller Sarrasian towns, but those paled in comparison to the notables in the capital city.

The city, which was also named Sarras, just like the country. And they used serrah as a polite term of address for everyone, another word that sounded like Sarras and meant something like "citizen." Bridget sighed as she laid her mandolin in its case. Why couldn't people so imaginative in dress and form put a little more effort into all areas of their culture? Their buildings also lacked grandeur, at least on the outside. All made of the same gray stone, all squat and dull save for the occasional pillar or statue, they lacked the spectacle of Firellian architecture. Even the square she performed in seemed dull, with foot upon foot of slate tiles and a single fountain with four stone lions vomiting water all day.

Baxter would have scowled at her. "All that effort to escape, and she's *bored*," he'd say.

Yes, she should be thanking all the gods and devils for that. And Sarras wasn't without a few points in its favor. The buildings might be dull, but they seemed impregnable, not that she had to test that now; evaluating defenses was part of her old life. In the three months since she'd arrived in Sarras, she hadn't once considered going back to the empire, even if her nostalgia for the minarets, buttresses, spires, and multicolored stone of the city of Montagne Noire sometimes got the better of her. And even if her old instincts never seemed to leave her.

Like noting how difficult it would be to do some breaking and entering.

Movement from the corner of the square caught her eye. Night was falling, and traffic had faded to nearly nothing, taking any chance at tips along with it, but Bridget was glad she'd waited. The buildings of Sarras might not be beautiful, but the women certainly were.

This one in particular.

Adella del Amanecer. Bridget had learned her name the day after first seeing her pause to listen in the square. One pint of ale to a fellow nightingale had done the trick. Adella was a noble, a diplomat, a blond-haired, blue-eyed goddess with skin so pale it seemed luminous and a figure to make hourglasses commit suicide in envy.

Why she didn't use a carriage was anyone's guess. Her elaborate gowns must be heavy. The weather had to play havoc with the pearls in her coiffure, but she walked every day, her only concession to the weather being a voluminous cloak for snowy days and a wide parasol when it was wet. Her skirts usually concealed her feet, but when she'd held them out of a puddle one day, she'd revealed stout boots instead of dainty shoes.

Beauty, intelligence, and foresight? It was all Bridget could do not to fall at her feet in worship.

Now, here she came, later than usual, but her eyes lit up as if happy to find Bridget lingering, too. And her course didn't change, even though Bridget had packed her mandolin. Maybe she hoped for a private performance at her home.

Gods, if only.

"Good evening," Adella said when she was close enough. She had stress lines around her eyes and a small hunch in her shoulders that might not be coming from the chill in the air, but she smiled as if shaking off her worries.

Out of all the times Bridget had imagined them speaking, a simple "good evening" had never occurred to her. It was always more like, "Follow me to yonder inn, peasant, and service me roughly."

Bridget ducked her head and hoped the dusk hid her smile. "Um, hello, serrah."

"Adella," she said, placing a hand on her bosom right where her cloak opened and just where her dress dipped to show her cleavage.

Bridget told herself not to stare. "Bridget." She didn't stutter, at least, having at last gotten used to using her real name.

And then…silence.

Bridget waited. Adella was a diplomat. She had to have something to say or could figure out a conversational topic easier than Bridget could. Or maybe that was just when she was at work, and she didn't like to talk when off duty. Right now, she seemed…lost.

Bridget knew the tension from a demanding job when she saw it. That had been her face and shoulders all through her twenties. If Adella didn't want to make decisions once her work was finished, that was one service Bridget was happy to provide.

One of many, but she didn't let herself get carried away.

"Let's get a drink," she said, making it a statement instead of asking a question. It was harder to refuse that way. She smiled widely as she picked up her case.

Adella's instant of hesitation turned into something like relief. "I suppose I have time," she said, the dimples in her cheeks beyond charming. "The Crown has an amusing little chardonnay." She went pinker. "Or so I've heard."

Bridget couldn't help a chuckle as she gestured at her own clothes, a dark blue jacket dotted with colorful patches and brown trousers with ragged hems above old boots. "Sadly, I am not up to the dress code of the Crown, serrah."

"Ah." Adella flushed and glanced around as if searching for a way out.

Bridget sensed this whole daydream falling apart. Baxter would say, "Don't think, dummy, act."

"Come on. I know a place." Bridget slipped her free arm through Adella's and began walking. Adella gave a little laugh and went along. "I'm not sure what chardonnay is, but if you're looking for amusing, there's a gin cocktail at the Donkey's Rest that'll have you smiling in no time."

Baxter would have been proud.

Adella had a little smile on her face as they walked across the square and down the cobblestones of Mercy Street, one of Sarras's main thoroughfares. The happy look slipped a little when they turned down a narrow brick lane that connected the spacious and affluent Oligarch's Ward with the narrow, crowded Trade District.

Bridget patted her hand. "Don't worry. It's not far, and we're not going near the Tides or Haymarket." Both were even more crowded and far seedier than here. The residents of the Trade District might be poorer than Adella was used to, but they took great pride in their homes, washing their stoops and making sure only the best washing was left to dry on the lines overhead.

The embarrassing stuff with holes in it was hung up inside.

The Donkey's Rest was a riot of light and noise in the falling darkness. A crowd had already gathered outside the front door, laughing and drinking and smoking cigars which Serrah Nunez didn't allow indoors. A few turned to give Adella curious looks, but they'd had nobles in before. Bridget paused under the streetlamp with them and slapped a couple of backs, calling a greeting, and they turned back to their own conversations.

"You've been here before," Adella said.

"I rent one of the attic rooms with another nightingale."

"Do they give you a discount for bringing in the people you pick up in the square?" She had a teasing look in her eye, one that bloomed into her extraordinary, dimpled smile when Bridget winked.

"Having never done so until tonight, I wouldn't know. I get the occasional free drink when I play." She led Adella through the few patrons clogging the door, but conversation became impossible in the sudden noise.

Bridget's roommate, Videl, was playing on the tiny stage, and her lively fiddle music had a few patrons dancing between the small tables that crowded the floor from the stage to the bar across the back. The large chandeliers and wall sconces glowed with light. Every table held at least one patron, all with glasses or decanters, and most people wore uniforms or livery, though with the top buttons undone.

Adella's smiling look faded as she glanced around the room, no doubt noting the lack of available seats. Bridget winked again and led the way down the side of the room, nodding to the servers as she passed. The crowd didn't know the secret spots available to those who lived here and who brought back the occasional date.

Bridget had told the truth before. She'd never brought anyone from the *square*.

A curtained alcove stood near the bar. Bridget paused before it, gave a wave to Serrah Nunez behind the bar, and drew back the heavy red velvet, revealing a little table and two chairs. It was a monarch's nest, a holdover from an older time that had always been reserved for royalty back when Sarras had not only a monarch but one who wanted to drink with the people.

That was probably how they'd ended up being overthrown.

Serrah Nunez's little nest was reserved for staff and residents, and the servers were ready to get pushy to keep it that way. They'd all used it a time or two if only to duck away from the patrons for a moment.

"A perk of the job?" Adella asked as they sat.

Bridget partly drew the curtain, blocking some of the noise. "You're very astute." One of the servers dropped off two gin cocktails and departed quickly, causing Adella to raise one perfect eyebrow. "When they're busy, they assume I want my usual."

"And that your…companions want the same?"

Bridget sighed. If this sort of thing continued, Adella was going to think her some mad seducer with a routine. She pointed to the glass. "I can get you something else."

"Not until I try it." She took a tiny sip and seemed pleasantly surprised. She gave another of those world-weary sighs and sagged. She undid the cloak clasp on her right shoulder and let the heavy garment rest on the back of the chair. Bridget shed her jacket, too, as the room was much warmer than outside, thank the gods.

Adella turned her head slowly as if stretching tired muscles. Bridget wished they knew each other well enough for her to offer a massage for those silken shoulders.

"Well," Baxter would have said, "no time like the present to make friends."

"Long day?" Bridget asked.

Adella nodded slowly and sipped her drink. "One of those that comes with a problem you can't solve, and you just have to wait and see if it works out."

"Oof." That described much of her former life as a spy. "But you can't keep from worrying about it at the same time."

"You've got it."

Her training wanted her to offer to listen, to help, to groom this possible source. She told that part of her mind—a part Baxter had created along with his words of *wisdom*—to shut up. She was curious because she was interested and wanted to listen because she already cared about Adella a little. She couldn't help but care about someone whose job seemed to be devouring them bit by bit.

"You work in the Bastión, right?" Bridget asked.

Adella nodded.

"Then I don't suppose you can tell me about the problem and share the worry?"

With a sad smile, Adella shook her head. "But thanks for the offer." She leaned forward and rested her chin in one hand. "Tell me about you."

Bridget opened her mouth, her cover story lined up neat and tidy behind her tongue, but she had to close her teeth before the lie escaped. It was now a sad fact of life that no matter where she went or what she did, her past had to remain a lie. It kept her up many a night. She thought she could escape the empire and make her own truth, but she would forever have to cloak herself in falsehoods or spying still.

At least her personal ban on killing had worked out…so far.

She'd told some people the false story of her past, but she couldn't bear to say it to Adella's earnest face.

"Are you all right?" Adella asked, frowning. "I really didn't intend to pry."

"No, you did nothing wrong." Bridget wished she could use Adella's words and say she simply couldn't speak of her past, but that would only invite curiosity. She decided to walk the thin road of truth, as Baxter liked to say. "I haven't had an easy life, and talking about it sometimes causes me pain." When Adella put a sympathetic hand on hers, Bridget was shocked to feel tears prick her eyes. "Usually, I throw out a joke and a half truth, but I don't want to do that with you, so I'll say that I'm happy now, living by my music. I've got no kin, but I've plenty of friends, and I have my health." She lifted her glass. "And I enjoy getting to know beautiful women whom I bring in from the square, along with taking advantage of any discounts they might bring with them."

Adella ducked her head and chuckled. She clinked her glass against Bridget's, but she had a shrewd look in her eye. "Why give me the truth instead of the joke and the half lie? Because of my so-called beauty?"

Bridget didn't miss how her half a truth had been turned on its ear. Adella didn't seem to miss much, nor would she be blinded by compliments or led by the nose.

Baxter would have said, "Walk away." But as Bridget looked into Adella's eyes while the candle made them sparkle like bright blue jewels, she would have replied, "Not for all the bounty of heaven."

What came out of her mouth now was, "Because of your boots."

Adella sat back, eyes wide. "What?"

"I have always admired a woman with sensible taste in shoes. And you walk every day, shunning the conveyances of your peers. You like to do things your own way, and you make sure you have the right tools, like those boots. You're the kind of person who deserves the truth."

After a moment's stillness, Adella threw her head back and laughed, a full-throated guffaw that had Bridget joining in and feeling joy from her crown to her toes.

"To boots and beauty," Bridget said, lifting her glass again.

"Thank the gods you added beauty on its own," Adella said as she touched glasses once more. "It is certainly not part of my boots." She sparkled like a diamond, her cheeks flushed with laughter or gin and maybe a smidge of desire. She sipped her drink with a flirty look over the rim, and Bridget had to stop herself from leaping the table and kissing her.

As she drained her own drink, Bridget asked herself why she hesitated. Adella was no green girl who seemed ignorant of seduction. Her gaze was full of invitation, and no doubt she knew her own limits and would let Bridget know them, too. Still, Bridget stayed put, not even sliding her chair closer so she could slip an arm around Adella's shoulders or more easily hold her hand.

She couldn't do it, not when that space was already occupied by the lies she would eventually have to tell.

CHAPTER THREE

Adella would have been sliding one foot up and down Bridget's long, muscular legs, but she couldn't risk a loose hobnail from her boots snagging on Bridget's trousers. If she'd known her evening was going to be this flirty, she would have crammed some shoes in her reticule.

It wasn't the only change she would have made if she had the evening to do over again. She would have found a way to say the truth: the reason her family had no carriages or conveyances was because they'd had no money since her parents died and not because they shunned such conveniences. But no, pride had gotten in her way. Again. And it felt as if she'd told a lie, which was no way to start a relationship, especially when the other party had already made a pledge to tell the truth.

Then there had been a moment when she'd been certain Bridget was going to kiss her. She'd tensed, ready to feel Bridget's mouth on hers, to nibble that full lower lip, perhaps to feel that tall, slender body pressed against hers. Then the moment passed, the heat in Bridget's eyes dimmed, and Adella had been disappointed but also a little relieved. She didn't want to have her omission of truth rewarded.

Bridget ran a hand through her short dark hair, the cut wildly different from anything seen among the nobility, but it showed off her cute ears, high cheekbones, and the line of her tanned neck. Much of her hard life must have been lived outdoors.

No, Adella couldn't pry, even hypothetically. If Bridget's past became important between them, it would come up naturally.

Still, her curiosity was piqued. And once that happened, she rarely let things go.

She tried to bury the thought in laughter and chitchat. Bridget had natural charm as well as a musician's grace. Adella had admired her hands before, but her slender fingers were even more exquisite up close as she gestured with nearly every word.

Adella wondered if she would be as animated during lovemaking. Heat began to build in her core, both at the turn her thoughts had taken and by the interest flickering in Bridget's deep blue eyes. They seemed almost purple in the candlelight.

At a lull in the conversation, their gazes locked. Now was Adella's chance to make a move if Bridget wouldn't do so. But… suppose Bridget *didn't* want her? A thousand personal faults went through Adella's mind. Her confidence plummeted. The moment passed again.

She sighed. No wonder it had been so long since her last love affair.

"Are you thinking about going back to work and all its problems tomorrow?" Bridget asked.

Gods and devils, she noticed how late it must have gotten. "Um, yes." Well, now she was. "I'd better go. The Bastión waits for no one, as they say."

"Apt, since that's where the tax collectors work."

Adella laughed, reluctant to leave and not just because Bridget drove all thoughts of work from her mind. Well, Bridget and three gin cocktails. She'd have to get some gin for the house, though her sisters would give her grief for eschewing wine for something cheaper. Well, Gisele would tease her lovingly. Zara would be confused because Adella had told her to try to maintain their wealthy image when they could.

Bridget stood, and Adella followed. Butterflies filled her. What happened now? Most of her affairs had been arrangements of convenience rather than lasting interest, and as much as she wanted Bridget to invite her to stay the night, she wanted to drag out their experience and indulge in some romance.

No, that was foolishness she didn't have time for.

But she *wanted* it.

Ignoring her butterflies, Adella fumbled in her reticule and laid a few coins on the table.

"No, I'll see to the drinks," Bridget said. "Remember my discount."

"That's a tip for the servers, then," Adella said with a smile.

Bridget closed her mouth and smiled slightly. "They'll appreciate that." She followed Adella to the door. The fiddle player had gone, and most of the patrons had cleared out. Adella had no idea when bars in this part of the city closed, but this one seemed well on its way. A few people lingered in the street, and a few cabs waited, too, the pairs of horses shifting and stomping in the chill air.

Adella donned her cloak and turned as she pulled the hood up. Her heart thumped, and warmth spread through her as she wondered if Bridget would overcome her reluctance enough for a good-bye kiss.

She could do it herself with a little courage.

She was about to lean in when Bridget nodded down the street. "I'll get you back to the square, then you can lead the way to your place."

Well! Some of Bridget's charm went out the window with that straightforward self-invitation to Adella's house, but it was good to know they were both attracted. The loss of romance hit a bit harder.

Adella's rush of emotions must have shown in her expression because Bridget went as red as a beet. "I only mean to walk you home, serrah," Bridget said, eyes wide as saucers.

"Oh." Adella covered her mouth, stifling a humiliating giggle, of all things. When she got her breath back, she said, "But if the streets are too dangerous for a person alone, you mustn't risk them either." Bridget swallowed visibly, and Adella realized her words sounded like an invitation, too.

Though a far more artful one.

"I mean to say, that is…" Adella blinked. What had she been trying to say? Right, danger. "You shouldn't return here alone, not that you should stay with me. Though, of course, you'd be welcome." She felt heat in her cheeks this time, and another giggle was on its way up her throat. She spoke quickly to smother it. "We have a spare room…not that I wouldn't want to share with you. I mean, I do find you charming and attractive. It's only…" Gods and devils, she was making it worse, and she talked through difficult situations *for a living*. Poor Bridget looked as if she didn't know which way to turn.

Adella supposed she could run away.

If only she knew the way home from here.

Or she could find her damned brain and backbone again.

Adella took a deep breath, vowing to avoid gin to her last days for making her so silly. "I would like to see you again, Bridget, and I don't wish you to come to harm on the streets alone. Kindly forget everything else I said."

Bridget chuckled. "Forgotten. How about you take a cab?"

No doubt the best solution.

Adella paused. Did she have enough coin? Probably not. A cab could get her closer to home, at least. Only Zara would fret over the expense, but Adella didn't have her skills with a blade or Gisele's magic, so they had to give her some slack.

"I know you're used to traveling by foot," Bridget said as she led the way to the cabs. "But surely you can take the easy way once."

Adella felt the weight of her reticule and wondered how much distance it represented. "I suppose." The coins inside jingled, and Bridget turned, glancing at the purse before realization bloomed across her features.

Oh, shit. Now she'd guess that Adella's family had no money, but surely that wouldn't matter to her. Would it?

If it did, better to find out now before hearts became involved.

"What was I thinking?" Bridget asked. "Since you don't take cabs, you probably don't carry the cash for them, eh?"

It was on the tip of Adella's tongue to correct her, but the words got stuck.

"Smart of you to go out with only the money you think you might need." Bridget dug in her pockets, bringing out several large coins.

"No, you can't," Adella said, guilt fighting with pride. "I won't let you pay, I—"

Bridget turned so quickly, Adella had to back up a step. "I asked you out, Adella, and I kept you out late. Please, let me send you home in safety. To do otherwise is more than my honor can bear."

She looked so serious and stricken that Adella was forced to nod, though she suspected a bit of teasing mixed with the fine words.

She gave her address to the cabman, and Bridget paid the fee. Adella stepped toward the doors but turned at a slight pull on her arm.

Bridget cupped her cheek, her hand blessedly warm. Before Adella's brain had time to ramble, Bridget pressed their lips together. Adella melted, keeping her face tilted upward as her thoughts blew away, and she leaned into the soft contact. A flash of an earlier fantasy came to mind, so she opened her mouth to suck on Bridget's lower lip.

Bridget made a small noise of pleasure and shifted closer. Adella imagined the heat of her body through their clothing and pressed even deeper into the kiss. When Bridget drew back, it felt like a dash of water. Adella fought the urge to throw caution to the devils and invite Bridget home.

Where she'd see that most of the furniture had been sold, and they didn't use the top floor because the attic was in danger of collapsing on it.

Now that was a dash of water. Of the icy variety.

The cabman cleared his throat, telling them he wouldn't wait forever, payment or not.

"Good night, Adella. I'll see you tomorrow?"

She nearly floated into the cab. "Undoubtedly. I look forward to it."

Bridget kissed the hand she rested on the outside of the door. "Say hello to your spare room for me."

Adella kept her laugh in and lifted her chin imperiously. "That was among the words I kindly asked you to forget." When Bridget grinned, Adella sat forward quickly, pecked her on the cheek, and waved her away as she banged on the roof of the cab. "Good night." Then she was away, waving and watching Bridget's lovely face become lost to the gloom.

Even if there were still secrets between them, the evening had been a rousing success.

The ride home was swifter than Adella expected. She tried to calculate how late it was. Dawn had not yet broken, but most of the windows of the grand houses in the Oligarch's Ward were dark.

Del Amanecer House, her family seat, had a candle glowing in the sitting room on the ground floor. Only one because Zara hated to waste them, but she still wanted a way to welcome Adella home.

Or so she could have a more comfortable wait before pouncing.

Adella liked to think her parents would have done the same if they'd lived past her teenage years. She had a speech lined up in her head as she unlocked the door and slipped inside. She was the eldest. She needed no excuses. She could do as she pleased, and Zara could let her worry about the cost.

The words died on her lips as she turned into the sitting room to find Zara asleep on the one remaining settee they'd kept for visitors. All the other ground floor rooms—save the kitchen—sat empty behind closed doors.

"She fell asleep waiting for you," a soft voice said from the grand stairs in the foyer.

Adella only jumped a little, used to the way Gisele moved like a cat. She'd always been good at sneaking around. Adella backed into the foyer as Gisele walked into the meager light. She looked like an amalgamation of her older sisters. Her dark hair, a copy of Zara's and their father's, stood out against her white nightshirt. Her rounded features and the dimples when she smiled were more like Adella and their mother. Like Zara, Gisele's eyes were also dark.

And they missed nothing.

"You were at a bar?" Gisele asked with a sniff. "Did you have fun?"

"Yes, thank you." She didn't ask how Gisele could tell where she'd been. With her extraordinary magical talent, she was often hired out by the mage's guild, sometimes as a spy hunter. Even without the magic, she deduced more than most people observed. But when Adella noticed her cradling one hand and favoring her right leg, she was reminded that some gifts came with a price.

Adelle hugged her gently from the side. "The pain keeping you awake again?"

"Don't fuss. You know as well as I that there's nothing to be done for it." She returned the hug to take the bitterness out of the words, then blew a raspberry against Adella's ear to cut the sweetness.

Adella remembered to leap away from her rather than risk pushing her over. "Shush. You'll wake Zara."

"Gods forbid," Gisele muttered, her tone angry.

Adella sighed. "You've been fighting." She hung her cloak in the closet near the door. "About the same thing as always?"

Gisele deepened her voice into a mocking tone. "Why continue to use magic if it causes you such pain? If you'd but stop and recover your strength, you could easily get a position in…"

"The scouting division of the oligarch's army," they finished together.

Adella rolled her eyes. "Zara found her calling and can't imagine any other."

"For *anyone.*"

"Why did you even bother to answer?"

Gisele put her good hand on her hip. "Because I've found my own damn calling. So I called her a stupid, pushy, stubborn asshole."

Adella leaned her head back and closed her eyes as she tried, yet again, to think of a way to permanently mend the fence between the two. "This is why I can't have a life," she mumbled. "Then what happened?"

"She said if I were anyone but her sister, she would challenge me to a duel."

"Gods and devils. You two—"

"She *shoved* me, Del."

Now that was a surprise. The threat of a duel was to be expected from someone who'd been born as old-fashioned as Zara, but to shove their infirm baby sister… "Did you fall? Hurt yourself?" She looked Gisele up and down, focusing on the favored limbs. If Zara had caused that pain instead of the magic, Adella was going to instigate a few duels of her own.

"Well…no. It was more like a push than a shove, a little one, but still."

Adella crossed her arms as Gisele avoided her gaze. Zara had probably grabbed her upper arm. She loved dramatic gestures. Adella's anger expanded to include both of them. "And how did you respond?"

Gisele played with the strings of her nightshirt, staring at the ground. "Lit her trousers on fire."

"Right." She marched past Gisele and into the room where Zara still slept.

"Just the cuff," Gisele said from behind her.

"No wonder you're in pain if you're throwing magic around for no reason." She shook Zara. "Wake up."

"I had a reason!" Gisele cried from the foyer.

Zara blinked sleepily. She yawned before standing. "Del? What's going—"

Adella held up a hand to shush her. "Gisele, get in here."

Zara stood, stretching. When she saw Gisele, she frowned hard. They both began talking and pointing at each other.

Adella stomped, and the thump from her boot boomed in the carpet-less room. "This fight is over. Shake hands and apologize." As usual, she had to stomp once more to quiet them again. "Are you adults, or shall I continue to treat you like children?"

They glared at each other but still shook hands and mumbled apologies. It would do. For now.

Adella took up the candle. "Upstairs, now, both of you. We all have duties in the morning and people relying on us." The first would motivate Zara and the second Gisele. Adella simply longed for her bed.

As they trudged up the stairs, Zara asked, "Where were you, Del?"

"At a bar by the smell of alcohol," Gisele said.

Zara half turned. "I hope you didn't walk home alone."

"I saw a cab pull up," Gisele said with a note of amusement in her voice.

"A cab?" Zara's tone held recrimination.

Adella wasn't having it. "Keep moving." But she could tell by the way they glanced at each other that the tide had turned against her. "You can berate me over breakfast and not a moment before."

The mischievous look on Gisele's face and the accusatory one of Zara's as she saw them to their rooms said it wouldn't be a breakfast to look forward to.

CHAPTER FOUR

Adella had lucked out at breakfast. Zara woke her at eight like normal, but she'd been so tired that she'd washed and dressed too slowly to eat before it was time to leave. If Zara hadn't accepted the task of keeping them all on time—and therefore commandeering the last clock in the house—and hadn't bullied everyone out of bed, Adella might have sent word that she was too sick to come to work, something she'd never done.

Of course, she rarely had anyone to stay out late and get sick with.

Now, Adella raced out of the house after Zara had already left and while Gisele called a hasty good-bye from the kitchen. She usually didn't go to work until a little later, saying that she hoped that the spies and criminals she was sometimes hired to hunt never figured out that mages liked to sleep late. If they knew, dawn to midmorning would become prime time for espionage and crimes serious enough to consult the mages' guild.

Adella slowed her stride even though it meant she'd be a few minutes late. She'd spent too long on her hair to damage it through haste. She smoothed the skirt of her light green gown, lamenting the fact that she hadn't had time that morning to switch out the trim or move the buttons to a more fashionable place on the sleeves. Those who couldn't afford new gowns every season had to rework what they had.

Luckily, she and her sisters made enough money to pay for food and necessities. Everything else had gone to either the enormous death duties paid when their parents had died or to the repairs that kept the house intact. But Adella had fulfilled her parents' wish that the family keep the house, at least. And maybe one day, she could finish the remodeling that would prevent it from collapsing around their ears.

Maybe she could even afford a new dress now and then.

As usual, the square before the Bastión stood empty of nightingales this early in the morning. Most people were probably too grouchy to tip well on their way to work. Disappointment threatened, but Adella told herself not to be silly. She wouldn't have had time to stop and chat with Bridget anyway. Perhaps she could sneak away at lunch.

Perhaps they could kiss good-bye again. And hello. And halfway in between to keep things interesting.

The thought made her hum as she entered the imposing comfort of the Bastión. A glance at the clock above the steps told her she had still gotten here before Dolores. She had just enough time to work with Juno and Cristoff to prepare the agenda, and Dolores would never know she'd been late at all.

Juno waited in Adella's office, two mugs of coffee at the ready. Adella took a grateful sip as she sat at her desk. "Did Ambassador de Maupassant call for another meeting today?"

"I don't know, serrah. Cristoff hasn't come in yet to unlock Ambassador Vega's door so we can sift through her messages."

"Strange." Adella frowned. Maybe he'd had a late night, too. And Juno only had the key to this office. "I have her spare…somewhere." She dug through her drawers and handed it over. While Juno went across the hall, Adella began to flip through her own messages which, as usual, had been dropped through a slot in the door.

She tossed them in all directions as Juno screamed from the hall.

"Juno?" She hurried around her desk, kicking one of the legs in the process. With a curse, she half spun and grabbed for the doorjamb. Juno ran into her, and they had to embrace to keep from toppling.

"What is it?" Adella asked, keeping hold of her, her own heart picking up speed.

"Ser…serrah…" Spittle flecked Juno's lips, and her eyes were so wide, the dark irises seemed lost in the white. Adella smoothed a few strands of hair off her cheek, but Juno panted with harsh little breaths, eyes straying to Dolores's open door. Adella let go and stepped in that direction.

"No," Juno said in a shrill whisper. "No, serrah, no, no!" But she backed into Adella's office, her hands up as to ward off devils.

Adella's heart now thundered in her ears, but she made herself keep going. If there was something dangerous in there, it would have come out already.

Or so she told herself. She walked slowly, ignoring questions from down the hall where others had come out to see the fuss.

Adella stopped in the doorway, finding nothing amiss in the chairs, the desk, the window. Dolores's messages crinkled underfoot before giving way to the rug. Adella took a deep breath and stepped farther in. If this turned out to be about a spider or something, she would give Juno such a dressing down that—

A pale arm extended along the floor from behind the desk, the fingers curled against the rug as if pulling toward the window.

Adella couldn't breathe, tried to speak, but her mouth had turned to sand. Still, she made herself take those last few steps. As an orphaned teenager, she'd had to investigate many a scary sight or sound for her sisters' sake. She could do this, too.

"Dolores?" she whispered, but she knew she wouldn't get a response. She leaned over the desk. Dolores lay prone, her head turned to the side, pale eyes and mouth open and shocked. Her other arm was folded beneath her, a hint of her hand showing just where the blue and cream carpet bore a ghastly scarlet stain.

The world tilted sideways. Adella staggered back, swallowing her rising bile. Voices came from the hall. Concerned faces swam in and out of focus in the door. Adella had to get away, to run and hide as she'd always wanted to when she'd patrolled the house for burglars or ghosts. She stepped toward the door and grasped the jamb, ready to push past the gawkers and bolt.

Juno's bleak face peered at her from the back of the crowd. Tears glistened on her cheeks. That wasn't right. If she wanted to rise through the ranks in government, she had to learn to conquer her emotions.

Dolores had said that many a time.

And the best way to teach was by example.

Adella took a deep breath. First lesson: one must create the space one needed, if only in one's mind. She held up a hand to halt the questions and took another breath. "Fetch the sentinels. Dolores Vega is dead." When they stared, she drew herself up and did her best to incorporate the authority of her office into her stare. "I do believe I just said that the ambassador to the Firellian Empire is dead. *Fetch the sentinels.*"

A few people hurried off. Second lesson: each task had to be seen as nothing more than a series of steps. That was one step down. Now for the next.

Adella held the door against prying eyes and intruding feet. It wasn't enough that Dolores was dead. The blood might mean she hadn't died a natural death. An accident? How? Falling on her damned letter opener? She'd never been clumsy, and she wouldn't take her own life. That meant…

Gods and devils, a murderer in the Bastión.

For all her thoughts about suppressing her emotions and despite the faith shining in Juno's eyes, Adella would have fallen if the doorjamb hadn't been holding her up.

When Bridget saw the square was more crowded than usual, she cursed, thinking she was missing one of Sarras's many festival days. She would have been here early if she'd known. She already planned to be at the square at dawn and long past dusk on the oligarch's shared birthday celebration a few weeks from now. A musician could make a bundle from the throngs of partiers and their alcohol-inspired generosity.

But no one was laughing or carousing today. Everyone clustered in little groups, speaking in low voices and casting nervous glances at passersby. Bridget crossed to where some of her fellow nightingales stood together. They weren't even bothering to play for the nervy crowd.

"There you are," Videl said, breaking out of the group. She'd been up and away before Bridget had even awoken. "Did you just get here?"

"I had a late night. What's up?"

"I had a damned late night, too, and I wasn't the last person to hear there's been a murder in the Bastión."

Tightness seized Bridget's chest. Adella? What were the odds? No, no it couldn't be. Could it? What if Firellian hunters had found Bridget, had seen her with Adella, and then—

Baxter would have said, "Get ahold of yourself. Use your head for more than a hat rack."

She took a deep breath. "Who?"

"I heard it was someone important," Videl said.

"One of the nobles," another singer said as the group shifted. Bridget couldn't remember her name.

And her heart wouldn't stop pounding for her to try to remember. "Which one?"

"I heard it was an oligarch," the singer said as she twisted the blond braid that lay over her shoulder.

"Don't be stupid," Videl snapped. "The sentinels wouldn't leave everyone standing out here if an oligarch had been killed."

"Oh yeah?" Tomas, one of the tambourine players, crossed his arms and lifted one dark eyebrow. "What would they do instead?"

Videl blinked her pretty blue eyes, then shrugged. "Round people up or something."

Tomas snorted, and he and the others fell to quiet bickering about assumed procedures in the case of murdered leaders.

Bridget nearly yelled at them to shut up. "Does anyone know any actual facts?" she asked loudly.

"Why do you care so much?" Tomas asked.

"Oh gods." Videl gasped. "You brought a noble to the Donkey last night."

The group scrutinized her anew. "Did you...kill her?" the singer asked, then turned bright red when Bridget glared.

"Sure," Tomas said with a smirk. "Bridget took a noble to a dive bar in a dark, crowded part of town, then afterward, sneaked with her into the heavily guarded, well-lit Bastión to murder her."

Bridget was glad she hadn't had to say it. But relief bloomed in her from Tomas's words. "Did anyone say when it happened?"

"Last night," Videl said. "Or so one of the cleaners said. They found the body this morning."

The ice around Bridget's heart began to melt. Adella had been with her most of last night. But by the devils, what if she'd decided to go back to work instead of home?

"I'm sure it wasn't her," Videl said softly. "She looked much too smart to…" She paused, no doubt sensing the lack of sense in her words. For once.

"Look," Tomas said, nodding toward the Bastión. A ripple went through the square as everyone turned.

A group of people in the crisp, dark blue uniform of sentinels came down the wide steps of the imposing hulk of a building. They surrounded a few others dressed in the scarlet livery of the oligarchs' staff. Those carried a cloth-covered stretcher between them.

Bridget's chest tightened again. What if that was her? They hadn't known each other well, but that made it worse. It meant that a wealth of possibilities had died along with a light as bright as Adella.

Another figure followed the stretcher, this one in the black and gold robes and elaborate headdress of the mages' guild. The mage turned halfway down the steps and held out a hand, beckoning someone forward.

Another person stepped from the shadows of the columns.

Adella.

Bridget breathed out slowly. She started walking in that direction as Baxter said, "You won't make it. Don't draw attention to yourself."

But Adella looked so small and pale, as if she'd suffered a shock while wearing her mother's clothes. And Bridget could help, if only with a comforting hand, and they'd kissed and promised to see each other again, and—

"Hold it," a stern voice said.

Bridget blinked at a humorless looking fellow in the pale gray uniform of the city constabulary. A ring of them separated a crowd of nobles at the feet of the stairs from the regular riffraff gathered behind them.

"I need to get through," Bridget said.

The constable nodded at her mandolin case. "Got an important concert in the halls of government today?"

"No, I…" She forced herself to be calm, to look relaxed. The more composed she seemed, the easier it would be to get what she wanted. She took in the constable's smirk and the slightly cruel gleam in his blue eyes. He wouldn't be motivated by pity, and there were too many other constables nearby, including a grouchy-looking sergeant, to offer him a bribe.

Time to find another way.

Bridget shrugged. "There's a noble in the crowd there who might want to…have me nearby in this time of crisis. That's all." She kept her eyes half-lidded and wet her lips.

The constable snorted. "A nose-in-the-air rich piece having some scruffy nightingale like you on the side? Don't make me laugh."

His language was a little coarse. That was good. She could be crude, too. She leaned closer and gave what Baxter called her best smolder. "I could do more than make you laugh, thief catcher, were I so inclined. My noble doesn't keep me around for my music." She smiled slowly. "And she's had me on more than just one side."

His ears went a little pink, and his lips parted, his entire posture saying he'd love any smutty details if nothing else.

Bridget glanced around as if to make sure no one was listening before she offered those details, but she really wanted to make sure the sergeant was watching. Oh yes, that hatchet face had turned in her direction, and its expression said he ate dereliction of duty for breakfast.

Perfect.

"Which noble?" Bridget's constable asked breathlessly.

"I can't give you a name," she said teasingly. "How about a list of birthmarks and favorite positions?" She eased to the side, forcing the constable to look away from the sergeant. Staying a little low, she leaned in as if to whisper in his ear.

"Durango!" the sergeant bellowed on cue.

The constable turned, belting out a squeaky, "Yes, serrah!"

Bridget eased behind him at the same time and into the crowd on the other side. She stepped through in a sliding method Baxter had called a slither, where the spy tapped arms or shoulders, causing their target to turn one way while slithering past the opposite side. It worked well, and within moments, she was near the front of the crowd. The stretcher had been loaded into a hearse, and two sentinels took their places on the back while two others sat behind the horses. A few more had turned to where Adella was still speaking to the mage.

Bridget paused. The sentinels wouldn't even bother to engage her in conversation. They'd just clap her in irons if she tried to get past. She kept her gaze locked on Adella and held back the urge to wave, silently pleading for her to turn, turn, turn—

She finally did, and her face seemed to light up when Bridget caught her eye. Bridget couldn't keep from beaming as Adella gestured her forward. She passed the sentinels with an ease she never would have accomplished on her own.

She had a thousand questions for Adella but restrained herself to, "Are you all right?"

"Yes. Well, no." She sighed and mashed her lips together until they went white. "Sort of. I'm happy to see you." She squeezed Bridget's arm and smiled. The mage cleared her throat, and Adella's smile turned a little wry. "Bridget, allow me to introduce my sister Gisele."

Bridget turned to a young woman with the same friendly face as Adella. She smiled from under a headdress that made it look as if she had two twigs sticking straight out of her hair, except the twigs were made of gold and had jeweled ornaments hanging off the ends. The chain that hung across her forehead had little gems dangling from it, too. Those were something like trophies, if Bridget remembered right, and Gisele had quite a few for being so young. Bridget bowed, but any charming words died in her throat as one memory in particular assailed her. The central ornament of Gisele's headdress had two small gold sections, the lower one only awarded to spy hunters.

CHAPTER FIVE

The entire morning had become a chaotic whirl in Adella's mind, a parade of faces, many of whom she couldn't remember. Dolores's staring eyes had kept popping into her mind behind those faces, making her flinch.

Now she was standing on the steps of the Bastión, breathing deeply in the fresh air, and it had helped clear her mind a little, just as Gisele's presence did.

And then Bridget had appeared like a calming wind. She'd smiled comfortingly when she'd first shown up, but now she stood rather stiffly, no doubt uneasy under Gisele's scrutiny or from standing in the eyes of a crowd when she wasn't performing.

At the realization that they were currently being observed by much of the city, Adella let go of Bridget's hand. When Bridget glanced over, Adella whispered, "I'm not embarrassed. I just don't want to share you with a bunch of nosy busybodies." And the nobles who also worked for the government were even busier at being nosy than most.

Bridget gave her a tight smile, but it seemed as if she understood.

"What now?" Adella asked Gisele. "Are you going with…" She couldn't bring herself to say, "the body." "Her?" She nodded toward the hearse.

"Now that I've finished with the room, yes. I just wanted to dawdle as long as I could to avoid taking the rest of these wretched steps." To most, it had probably appeared as if moving around the room was all she'd done, her investigative powers being mental and affecting her senses. Adella knew better. The magic she'd used in the office had taxed her, and she'd done a lot of kneeling besides. Gisele had been reading the auras of those who'd recently visited Dolores. Everyone left a colorful trail wherever they went, but only mages could see it. Gisele had matched the auras of Adella, Juno, the cleaners, and an abundant remainder that were probably from Cristoff. She'd found no others, but she'd also said that a good mage could disguise someone's aura.

"Doesn't matter," she'd said, nodding to Adella. "I'll sniff them out, fear not."

Adella squeezed her arm again now, as proud as she was worried. "Thanks, baby sis."

Gisele made a little growling noise, a warning to not get too sappy, or she'd do something embarrassing.

Adella sighed, well-acquainted with that noise.

And the sort of things that came after it.

Still, Gisele gave her a sympathetic look. "You'll be all right? Going home?"

"Gods, no. I'm now the ambassador to the Firellian Empire, lucky me." She sighed, feeling anything but fortunate. "There's a lot to do."

"Don't worry. You'll be aces. You always are." Gisele winked, then glanced Bridget's way. "Now that you have plenty of help, you'll be even better."

Adella felt too tired to be embarrassed, but her cheeks warmed anyway. "Go earn your keep, charlatan."

Gisele grinned as she started down the stairs. "Love you."

"And you. Mind your feet."

Gisele barked a laugh but made it downstairs unaided until she reached the carriage that waited behind the hearse. She let a sentinel hand her inside, the only assistance she usually allowed. Adella was glad the mages' guild had their own carriages so Gisele didn't have to walk the city in pain.

She touched Bridget's hand again. "Would you like to come in?"

Bridget seemed to start out of a dream. "Do you want me to?"

It was at the front of Adella's mind to say no, to point out that Bridget surely had more important things to do than comfort her. She didn't want to be needy, but gods and devils, she was also too old to pretend she didn't want help. "Yes, please."

"Let's go." Bridget's smile was warm, and she proved adept at steering them through curious crowds, politely repeating that the ambassador had important business, and if anyone needed to converse with her, they would have to make an appointment.

The excuses seemed to confuse everyone, stopping the nosy spectators in their tracks. Adella clung to Bridget's arm, and they soon made it back to her office with only a little fuss. She shut the door on the world and leaned against it. When Bridget offered the further safety of her arms, Adella took a step forward, but a sniffle from the corner made her turn.

Someone was on the floor. Adella's heart leaped into her throat again, and she began to back away. "Who—"

"Serrah?" Juno stepped into the light of the candelabra on the desk.

Adella took a deep breath as her heart settled again. It wasn't another body. Everything was all right. "Juno, what were you doing on the floor?"

Juno nearly leaped into her arms. "I'm sorry, serrah. I've been hiding like a coward. I kept bursting into tears when the sentinels questioned me. They think it was Cristoff that…" She mashed her lips together and pulled on a strand of hair that had escaped her crown-like braid.

Adella nodded. She'd also considered Cristoff as the murderer, but she didn't want to say so now. Juno and Cristoff were friends, perhaps more, and she clearly didn't consider him a killer. But if he was innocent, what had become of him?

In addition to her untidy hair, Juno's face nearly shone with tears and was red and puffy even in the meager light. She had a handkerchief balled in one hand and couldn't seem to stop sniffling.

Adella's heart went out to her. "You're in no state to be here, Juno. Go home."

"No, serrah, I can't leave you alone." She cast a hopeful glance at Bridget, though.

"I'm not alone, as you can see. Go straight home. And try not to worry about Cristoff. The authorities will find him." What they might do with him depended on what he had done. She took Juno's chin in hand. "If he contacts you, come straight to me. I'll help him." Help him speak to the sentinels, but she didn't point that out, either.

Juno nodded miserably but hurried out, sniffling loudly as she went.

Adella rubbed her temples, wondering if she'd ever be at peace again, and when Bridget's arms went around her, she nearly fell into the embrace.

"You're a good boss," Bridget said into her hair.

"She's easy to be good to." Adella wrapped her arms around Bridget's trim waist and breathed deep. She had a mildly spicy scent, like herbal soap. "I'm sorry our second date isn't up to much so far."

"Meeting the family so soon is a bit much."

Adella snorted, though the day hadn't had much humor in it.

"Based on what you said to your sister about being the new ambassador to the empire, I take it the woman who died was…"

"Dolores Vega, the primary ambassador. Well, the former…" Adella took a deep breath, so close to falling apart.

"So you were the secondary ambassador."

"Yes." But at this moment, she didn't want to be anything other than the person standing inside this pair of strong arms.

"Gods and devils, Adella. I'm so sorry your promotion had to happen this way."

"Thank you." She swallowed several more times, but her tears wouldn't stay down much longer. "She was my friend. I just…keep seeing her." Her hard-won control finally fled, broken by Bridget's kind words. She tried again to hold it back, but why? She'd taught Juno all the lessons she needed to, had walked the house for ghosts, and now she could let her fear out.

And let Bridget see how emotional she could be?

Well, she'd already admitted she was tired of pretending.

"If you don't leave now," she managed, tears clogging her throat. "You're going to see how ugly it looks when I cry."

Bridget's chuckle moved through her. "Fire away." Her grip tightened, and she sounded a little choked, too. "If I join you, we'll scare any visitors together."

Adella tried to laugh, but Dolores's smiling face flashed in her mind's eye again, and she sobbed as if the world was ending.

While Bridget cried in part for Adella's pain, it was mostly her own frustration that brought tears to her eyes. Here she stood, an ex-spy for the Firellian Empire, with a woman she liked immensely, who also happened to be the new ambassador to said empire.

Because the old one had been murdered.

Oh, and said woman she liked had a sister who was a spy hunter.

Even Baxter was speechless.

She needed to leave. Not just this office with its piles of juicy secret documents or even the Bastión with its full document buffet. She should leave this city, maybe the whole country. If her past became known, she would be the prime suspect for Dolores's murder.

Adella stepped back and wiped her eyes. "I'm sorry to go to pieces like that."

"Think nothing of it." Bridget had become a master of replying to conversations while not really listening. She wanted to pay attention to Adella, for many reasons, but she was already three steps into an escape plan.

First, she needed to get out of this intricately decorated potential trap and past the highly trained guards who watched all the exits.

"She was such a good mentor, a good friend. I don't know what I'm going to do without her," Adella said.

"I'm so sorry. It's never easy to lose someone but especially someone who filled so many different roles in your life." She kept her tone sympathetic. Easy to do because she actually felt sorry for Adella climbing the career staircase because of a murdered friend.

But she couldn't focus on that. Not when she had to get out of town. Right. She had a little money saved. She could ask her friends for a loan. She might even pay it back someday. Renting a horse would be trickier. She wouldn't be returning it, and she didn't want to avoid being hanged for spying only to be pursued for thievery. Maybe she could leave the horse at a border town, and it would find its way home eventually.

"Oh gods, I suppose I'll have to plan the funeral." Adella shuffled some things on her desk. "Dolores has a sister, but she lives…" She opened and closed a few drawers. "I know I have that written down somewhere." She didn't look ugly at all, just tired and vulnerable and heartbreakingly sad.

"I'll help you," Bridget said.

Her escape plan came to a screeching halt. Where the hell had her brain come up with that? Baxter would have been appalled.

"Bridget." Adella pressed her hands over her heart, her eyes shining with gratitude. "We barely know each other. I can't ask you to give up your time with—"

"You don't have to ask." What? She told her mouth to shut up, but it just kept saying the wrong things. "I like you, Adella, and you're in a tough spot. I want to help."

Adella came around the desk and hugged her again. Bridget called herself a fool in her own voice and Baxter's. She should have made some excuse and bolted, should have been halfway to the Donkey's Rest by now. She should not be looking into Adella's bright eyes and listening to Adella say, "I like you, too," and then gently kissing her.

But that was what she was doing. Adella's lips were as soft as she remembered. She went a little weak in the leg department as Adella swept a hand through her hair. How easy it would be to forget everything except this kiss.

"Thank you," Adella said when they broke apart.

"You're welcome."

As Adella sat at her desk and reviewed all she had to do, Bridget slumped in the smaller chair and marveled at herself. She knew what she had to do, and still she sat there.

Baxter would have broken in at last with, "Well, ducky, what more have you got to lose? Your life, yes, but that was always on the line. Any country in the world would execute an ex-spy, including your own."

That was true. Sarras wouldn't give her the chance to stress the *ex*. She might claim to be a defector, but that probably wouldn't help. How much more danger could she be in than she already was?

With a diplomatic murder next door? Plenty.

Baxter would argue that being near the heart of the investigation might be safer. "The spy hunter's gaze will be turned out, not in." And as she'd thought earlier, the Bastión wasn't exactly easy to get into. The murderer had to be someone with access.

Adella paused and gave her another grateful smile.

She returned it, telling herself she could also get Adella to safety if suspicion fell on her, and the sentinels thought she might be a secondary ambassador who'd do anything for a promotion.

Baxter, always willing to argue the opposite side, would say, "But you also endanger her by sticking around, you lazy ass. Do you think the Sarrasians will believe she hasn't been working with you as a spy? They'll think you turned her."

Well, Bridget would help her escape, then, too. They could flee together, go somewhere far away. Like a deserted island. They'd eat coconuts and make love in the surf.

If Adella didn't kill her for telling lies and destroying their lives.

Well, she hadn't lied. Yet.

And she hadn't destroyed anything.

Yet.

"I have a few hours of work before I can leave," Adella said. "I can't take an entire day off to grieve." She seemed to shrink again. Another round of tears might wash her away. "No doubt you'll want to find something else to do. We can meet up later."

Bridget didn't detect any insincerity or manipulation in her words. She was going to let Bridget walk out now without a hint of rancor. And Bridget could take the opportunity to choose the best path for both of them, to make the safe, intelligent choice.

And break both their hearts.

"Do you want me to stay?" Bridget asked.

Adella ducked her head, but Bridget still caught a hint of pink in her cheeks. "Well…"

"I'll stay." She called herself a fool a thousand times, but Adella gave her another smile, this one with full dimples.

She wasn't going anywhere.

Chapter Six

Adella's more suspicious nature wondered what Bridget wanted from her. The parts of her that believed in goodness and needed someone to care for were already in love. The rest of her hovered between intense interest and cautious optimism.

But with Dolores's murder, the suspicious parts of her had become louder. Helpful, sexy women didn't usually fall into her lap like this, and her diplomatic training warned against people who might try to use her for political reasons.

Or for access to higher-level staff whom they could kill.

She told her inner naysayer that was a bridge too far. Bridget couldn't have gotten in the Bastión without an escort, and one of the oligarchs' physicians had said Dolores had died well before dawn, when Adella and Bridget had been together.

Still, there was no harm in finding out a little more about the person currently sacrificing her daily income to keep Adella company. Every part of her wanted to know Bridget better, after all.

"What's your family name?" Adella asked.

Bridget looked up from where she'd been writing at Juno's small desk. "Leir. Why?"

"It just occurred to me that I didn't know my knight's full name."

Bridget's crooked grin brought sighs from the one part of Adella that wasn't suspicious at all: her often ignored libido. "Knight? If we're talking old stories, I'm more of a troubadour."

Just as Adella had always thought. "Those don't have to be separate people. There was one troubadour who hid his sword in a guitar."

Bridget frowned in distaste but still looked lovely. "I think that would ruin the sound. Anyway, I'll be whichever you want." As she winked, Adella curled her toes inside her boots.

Ugh, her boots. Bridget might admire them, but Adella wished she'd worn more attractive footwear. And her face probably looked a mess, maybe even her hair. Juno's heartbroken appearance came to mind, and Adella fought the urge to hide under her desk and fix herself up. The only mirror hung on the right-hand wall. She'd have to get up to look, and she was too embarrassed to tackle her toilette under scrutiny.

She nudged the candelabra a little farther from her face. "What's, um, what's that you're writing?"

"Just tinkering with a new song."

"Oh?" Gods and devils, she hoped it wasn't about her or at least about how she looked right now. Maybe she could sneak a peek at herself in the back of the coffee spoon. "Play some for me?"

Bridget looked away as if she felt a bit shy, but she took out her mandolin. "All right, but it's a work in progress, so be gentle."

Adella's libido took over, adding a bit of a purr to her voice when she said, "Of course."

Bridget glanced at her again, and the crooked grin was back. "Gentle at first, I should have said."

Clearly, Adella's libido didn't give a damn what she looked like because its plans for the future did not include surreptitiously looking at herself in spoons. Its plan was: one, leap over the desk; two, have sex with Bridget; three, repeat.

Luckily for the rest of her, Bridget began to play.

Adella reached for the spoon as Bridget's eyes closed, but as the melody filled the office, and Bridget sang, Adella froze to listen.

She sang about finding beauty everywhere in the city. Her husky voice captured the pain of poverty and all the raptures of love for two young people. Adella became caught in their story, in a life so different from her own. Her family might not have riches any longer, but they still had status and opportunity. If she and her sisters sold their house, they could have…

She couldn't get carried away. Parental wishes and pride meant something to every family in Sarras. And this was just a song.

A beautiful one. Adella applauded softly when Bridget finished.

She bowed from her chair. "Thank you. As I said, it's not finished."

"It's fantastic. You play very well."

Bridget ducked her head and set her mandolin down almost reverently. "I should hope so. I've been playing nearly all my life." She stroked the mandolin's neck. "My mother taught me. This was hers."

The sadness in Bridget's voice said they had something in common. They'd both lost mothers. "It's beautiful. I'm sure she'd be proud of your playing, and that you kept her instrument."

"Always." Bridget gazed at it lovingly, and the air in the room grew heavier.

Adella tried to shake it off. "Is your song based on anyone you know?"

Bridget shrugged. Her face still held some of the peace it had while she'd played, but she still looked away. "Bits of many stories, mainly other nightingales. We all mix up one another's tales." Her eyes caught the light, and her expression smoldered, almost predatory in the best way. "When they find out about you, it'll really inspire their creativity. I know it's inspired mine."

Adella's mouth went dry as Bridget rose and stepped around the desk to lean against it. She only had to bend a little and flash that rakish grin for Adella's libido to shove all the other Adellas aside and take the reins.

Bridget tried to lose herself in the vibrancy of Adella's kisses, her passion obvious in the way she combed her fingers through Bridget's hair.

But the lies between them kept coming up like a self-raising wall.

No, she could ignore them, damn it.

If she and Adella were close enough, there wouldn't be room for anything except the heat between them. She pulled Adella up while leaning back, pinning herself between Adella and the desk. Crushing her close and kissing through her moan, Bridget wrapped one leg around Adella's skirt while giving her rump a squeeze.

She made a delighted little noise and thrust her hips forward, displacing Bridget's other leg until she stood between them. It was Bridget's turn to moan as her insides filled with liquid heat.

Adella pulled back slightly. "Did I hurt you?"

"No, it was a good noise," Bridget said breathlessly. "So good." She pulled Adella back in, reaching inside herself for the place where passion blocked out thought, but Adella's words beat through her brain and let a bit of Baxter in.

"Maybe she didn't hurt you, but you're gonna hurt her, and you know it, especially if you bed her before she knows the truth."

She nearly growled at him to shut up as Adella began pulling at the ties of her shirt. But he wasn't really there. It was her conscience speaking. If she and Adella made love with all these secrets between them, there would be no going back. And she couldn't even make herself feel better with the fact that she hadn't actually told a falsehood.

Because she hadn't told the truth either.

"Wait," she mumbled, cupping Adella's cheeks and stopping their kisses. "I have to tell you something."

"Now?" Adella's amused, incredulous expression quickly gave way to a look of worry. "Gods, it's…" She stepped back. "I'm not repulsive or anything right now, am I?" She seemed far too serious to be joking, so Bridget coughed through a snort.

"No, you're beautiful. You never stopped being beautiful." But she didn't let Adella kiss her again. "It's about me."

Adella's happy smile faded to a curious one, but it wouldn't stop there. She'd be angry next, maybe fearful. She might want to call the sentinels. Gods and devils, what if Bridget had to restrain her to get her to listen? What if something went wrong?

"Tell me," Adella said, stroking her hair. "Is it about…" Her eyes flicked toward the door, and Bridget knew she meant the murder.

"No, nothing to do with that. It's…my past." And all the words were right there, but they wouldn't come, and she realized she'd never admitted her former profession, not even when it had been her current profession. "It wasn't exactly…" She tried coming at it from another direction, but it was slippery.

Adella's eyebrows rose. "Law-abiding?"

Well, in this country, it certainly wouldn't have been. "Right."

"And now?"

"Yes, all law-abiding now." But there was more stuck halfway up her throat.

Adella's dimples knocked Bridget for a loop again. "That's all right, then. Everyone has a past. You're very sweet to be so worried." She came in for another kiss.

Bridget leaned away as her passion snagged on something, refusing to return. "Hang on. What makes you think I was a criminal?"

"I…don't know. You seemed so reluctant that I thought—"

"I must have broken the law?" She told herself not to take it badly, to take the out she'd been given and be grateful, but her pride had been nicked. She'd been living a blameless life in Sarras. She'd been careful to give that impression, too, and she was damned good at getting people to think of her the way she wanted.

"Not a really bad criminal," Adella said. "A thief perhaps." She frowned and looked away as if she knew that was still insulting. "Anyway, you already said that was your former life, so—"

Bridget crossed her arms. "What about me says, 'maybe a thief,' past, present, or future?"

Adella laughed, but it had more than a hint of exasperation. "Can we forget all this and start again? I meant no disrespect, truly."

And Bridget might not have taken any if she wasn't already tied up in knots, sexually frustrated, and trying to do the right thing. Not to mention, she always feared the word "spy" was somehow tattooed across her forehead, along with "untrustworthy." It irked her.

"Something about my looks?" Bridget asked.

Adella moved out of reach and leaned against the wall. "I would not presume someone to be a criminal by looks alone."

Oh, that was quite haughty. Bridget had played haughty before, but she hadn't enjoyed it. She preferred simple, to the point. "My profession? Have I gone from troubadour knight to rogue? Plenty of thieving bards in storybooks."

"No." The word practically had ice dripping off it.

Baxter would have cringed. Icy didn't exactly bring out Bridget's best side. She crossed to where her mandolin rested. If simple questions wouldn't give her the answers she wanted, perhaps crude ones would. "Do I smell like a criminal? Kiss like one?" And she so wanted to make a joke about how her lovemaking skills should be a crime, as they made everyone else seem inferior, but she couldn't say it. She felt as if she'd started down a dark path and couldn't find her way out.

"Now you're just being silly," Adella said.

One more turn into the dark; she hated having her feelings dismissed. But she bit her tongue at last. Even if she couldn't find her way back, she could stop where she was.

"I'm sorry," Adella said. Perhaps she also saw the need to stand still. "I don't know why I guessed about your past, honestly. I...I will think on your question and try to give you an answer. Please, Bridget." And the look on her face begged forgiveness.

Bridget had to step forward and take her hand. "I'm sorry, too. It seemed you, uh, struck a bad chord in me." Adella still looked worried, so Bridget had to drown out Baxter's reassertion that she could still walk away with, "I'm not going anywhere, Adella."

She smiled as if relieved and already halfway to love.

With an obvious criminal.

Bridget buried that thought as Adella gathered a few papers. "Walk me home?"

"Absolutely." But the part of her that was still knotted and offended said a walk would be all Adella was getting until she answered the question.

The sexually frustrated part of her called her names that would have made Baxter blush.

Adella called herself a fool a thousand times over even as she wasn't completely sure what she'd done wrong. If she hadn't already been grief-stricken and under strain, she might have apologized immediately, but instead, she'd bitten back.

And even though she felt badly for doing so, she remained, well, peeved.

Why had she made any guesses about Bridget's past at all? And what a guess! She'd felt a little nervous when they'd gone to the Donkey's Rest last night. She'd rarely left the Oligarchs' Ward in the whole of her life, and though she *knew* the Trade District wasn't exactly a *bad* part of town, she'd always heard *stories*.

Now she felt a little ashamed of the stories she'd believed as a child, those that portrayed everyone outside the ward as devils. But she'd been sixteen when her parents had died, frozen between the fairy tales meant to keep children from wandering where they shouldn't and the advice she should have been given as she took her first steps into adulthood and the real world.

With an eight- and four-year-old to care for, it had seemed safer to keep believing in fairy stories that told her to fear the unknown.

Now, walking next to Bridget, she was even more embarrassed by the tales of her noble childhood. She'd learned that impoverished areas of the city were little more than dens of thieves and murderers, with the occasional harmless octogenarian thrown in.

Even lacking money herself hadn't changed her mind. Bridget's song proved that being born into poverty and experiencing a money shortage wasn't the same thing.

Or perhaps she was being too hard on herself. After all, it was Bridget who'd demanded she take a cab home instead of risking the Trade District's streets at night.

No, what mattered was how Bridget felt at right this moment and if Adella could fix it.

They'd been walking in silence, and Adella stopped and said, "I'm sorry I made assumptions about you, Bridget."

Her eyes went a little wide. Maybe she'd thought Adella wouldn't be the first to bring it up again. "Thank you, but you already apologized."

"Not enough. I…" Heat suffused her cheeks, and shame stabbed at her so harshly, she wanted to come back at it with defensive anger.

But she wasn't frozen in childish responses now.

She took a deep breath, willing herself to be calm. "I think…I must have assumed a criminal background…" After another deep breath, she rushed forward, speaking quickly. "Because of where you live. Or rather, because you don't live here. I don't think like that on a…a conscious level, please believe me. And if I heard someone say that, I would argue with them, but…" She lifted her arms and dropped them. "It seems such prejudices are still inside me, and it's clear I'll have to work to exorcise them."

Bridget seemed frozen between expressions. Her wide eyes held the hint of tears, her mouth twisted as if amused, and she kept frowning before relaxing again.

Adella was so afraid Bridget would run, she decided to try again, brushing past the explanation and going straight to groveling. "I'm very sorry, truly. Please don't..." Her damned throat was clogging again. She was not this needy, for the gods' sake.

"Come here, rich little idiot," Bridget said, pulling her into an embrace.

Adella chuckled against her shoulder, too relieved to be the slightest bit offended. She felt quite idiotic at the moment, even if she was no longer rich.

"Quit pleading with me not to leave," Bridget said. "I've already made that decision, and I'm not likely to change my mind." She chuckled softly. "Not until I've robbed you blind, anyway."

"Thank the gods." Adella stepped back, wiping her eyes. "I *would* be offended if you thought I had nothing worth taking, though there's less than there used to be." She coughed through a gasp, shocked at herself. That was the closest she'd come to admitting her lack of funds to anyone except her sisters and their lawyer. Her heart thundered, and she felt astonished by how frightened the admission made her.

Well, if every noble equated lack of money with criminality...

She shook the thought away as Bridget laughed and seemed to walk easier. They stopped outside the gate of her house, and her heart picked up speed for a different reason, remembering their kisses and caresses in her office. She ordered herself to push past the embarrassment of a house with no staff and almost no possessions and issue an invitation to stay. She'd already trusted Bridget with what she looked like with a splotchy complexion. She could trust her with this, too.

And Bridget's warm gaze passing over her body said her invitation would be accepted.

She opened her mouth. The words wouldn't come.

Gods and devils. All her epiphanies this day, and she was still an idiot.

Well, an idiot who could and would kiss a gorgeous woman who was giving her the come-on.

She did so, putting all the words she couldn't say into a passionate embrace. Bridget returned her vigor, drowning out Adella's internal voice that reminded her they were canoodling in the street, a definite etiquette gaffe.

Bridget pulled back slightly and pressed their foreheads together. Adella willed her to invite herself in. Maybe all the lessons she'd learned about being a good host would override her lessons on the importance of appearances. She'd let her tutors fight it out in her subconscious.

A rattle from down the street prompted Adella to step away. A carriage trundled toward them, and she couldn't bring herself to flout convention when she *knew* she'd been seen. The streets were mostly empty of traffic at this time of day, among these houses, and this carriage was the only one on the lane to ruin their embrace.

So, of course, it pulled up in front of her house.

Bridget stiffened. Adella didn't blame her for being irked by visitors, especially when she spotted the crest of the mages' guild.

Gisele. There'd be no afternoon's delight today.

"I should go," Bridget said softly.

"You don't have to," Adella's last shred of hope made her say. She sighed before Bridget could argue. "I don't blame you. Thank you for everything." She smiled. "Go before she interrogates you."

She only meant Gisele's natural inquisitiveness, but Bridget blanched, and Adella realized that was a heartless thing to say to an admitted criminal, reformed or not.

Before she could apologize, Bridget backed away. "Can we meet tomorrow morning? I can walk you to work."

Sweet and thoughtful. Adella couldn't help a grin. "Eight thirty? I'll look forward to it."

After a saucy bow, Bridget was away just as Gisele made it down the carriage step with the driver's help.

"Aw, is she leaving?" Gisele waved gratefully to her driver as he turned the cab around and left. "I was looking forward to embarrassing you."

Adella kissed her cheeks until she squealed. "There. Now who's embarrassed?" She opened the gate and walked inside.

Gisele passed her with a glare. "You're in a gross, overly enthusiastic, and tactile mood."

"True." She nearly skipped up the stairs, unlocked the door, and held it open.

Gisele's squint bloomed into a smile. "You're in love."

Adella snorted, but gods and devils, that could easily become true.

"I want details."

"Promise not to fight with Zara tonight, and you might get them."

Gisele snorted. "Not worth it. Let's talk about the murder instead."

CHAPTER SEVEN

Well," Adella said as she opened the curtains to the sitting room, and Gisele leaned far back on the settee. "What have you and the sentinels determined about…" She still couldn't say murder out loud. "What happened?"

"You're not going to like it."

"With how often I've complained about my job, you shouldn't be surprised to hear that much of what I do is listening to things I don't like." Still, she wished Gisele had some happy news to go along with Bridget's kiss.

"Juno and Cristoff are now the main suspects."

Adella turned slowly, stunned. "I can't believe that."

"It makes the most sense." Gisele took off her headdress, the ornaments jingling as she set it on the table.

"But why jump straight to them?"

"We didn't jump. And would you rather we considered you?"

Adella gave her a dark look.

She rolled her eyes. "A passerby confirmed the cleaner's story that the victim—"

"Dolores. Gods and devils, I can't control much at this moment, but Dolores Vega was no one's victim."

Gisele inclined her head. "Someone saw Dolores in her office after the cleaners did their rounds and left. You were already gone. According to the aura residue I detected in the office, that leaves Juno and Cristoff as suspects."

Adella paced the sitting room. "It can't be Juno. She would have left shortly after I did."

"No one remembers seeing her leaving."

"So many people come in and out of there every day, and Juno never makes a spectacle of herself."

"Adella—"

"Gisele, I know Juno. I've known her for over a year. She isn't a killer." She put her hands on her hips, but Gisele matched her stare for stare. "What does Cristoff say?"

"He's nowhere to be found."

Oh, that was bad. But still not conclusive. "What if someone else had gone into Dolores's office. You said a mage can mask someone's…residue."

"Not for long. Not from me."

Adella was torn between not wanting to damage her sister's self-esteem and wanting to defend her coworkers. But there was such a thing as bragging. "You are not a god, Gisele."

"I took some traces from around the room and detected no magic except my own." She leaned back on the settee, crossed her arms, then uncrossed them after a wince. No doubt she'd overdone it on the magic, but Adella was too angry to offer much sympathy.

Much.

"Do you need your tincture?" she asked, stepping toward the stairs, not wanting to argue while Gisele was in pain.

"Does that mean you believe me at last?"

Adella stopped. "Nothing you said is proof of guilt. Juno is innocent, and Cristoff may need help." With a deep breath, she tried to force herself outside the problem. That was what Dolores would tell her to do.

Along with not biting her lip.

She pulled it out from between her teeth. "Did you go to Cristoff's apartment?"

"Yes, and Juno's, too, and though we didn't encounter any essays titled, 'How I Plan to Kill My Boss,' I did sense the residue of both auras in both places."

So they had been seeing each other outside of work. If their auras lingered at Cristoff's apartment, they'd been there within the last few days. Pity the magic couldn't be more accurate than that. But none of that even hinted at guilt. "Any unidentified auras?"

"A few. The constabulary is working with the sentinels to round up any visitors Juno and Cristoff might have had, and I'll be comparing auras as they're found, probably starting tomorrow. I doubt it'll come to much. They were the only ones in that office, Del."

She sounded so impatient that Adella couldn't help another glare.

Gisele groaned. "You are actually blaming the messenger for bad news. You know that, right?"

"Because you are jumping to conclusions."

"No, I'm following clues to those conclusions." Gisele stood and rolled her head back and forth. Adella winced at the creaking sounds. She had definitely been overdoing it, but she said, "Wait," before Adella could go looking for the tincture again. "I'm sorry, okay? I know Juno's more than your assistant, and you like Cristoff, but they both have more questions to answer, him especially."

Adella put her head in her hands as she sat. "I don't know him very well, but…Juno seemed so upset." Her hair had been a mess as if she'd been tearing at it, and her face had been tight with panic and streaked with tears. "I can't imagine that was an act."

"I don't know either of them, but panic can look a lot like grief in the right light. I've seen enough people use genuine fear of getting caught to make it seem like they're upset about something bad they've done."

The sympathy in her eyes kept Adella from snapping again. Still, Gisele might be right about other people, but she was wrong about Juno.

"One of the reasons I came home early was to make sure Cristoff hadn't come here for your help," Gisele said.

"Unfortunately, no, unless he's hiding in one of the wardrobes." A cold wind seemed to blow down her spine. "You don't think…" All her earlier thoughts about checking the house for specters leaped back into mind.

For the first time, Gisele looked a little worried, too.

"Are you tapped for today?" Adella asked.

The way Gisele frowned said yes, even if she'd never admit that out loud. Much as she could push through the pain that casting magic caused, there came a point where her body would simply refuse more hurt and shut off access to her abilities. "I can manage a little flame," she said, but her words didn't have their usual zeal.

Adella lit a small candelabra. Sunshine streamed through the window in here, but most of the curtains in the house were closed, the rooms dark. "Here." She handed the candelabra to Gisele, then picked up a small log from beside the cold fireplace. They usually only had fires in the kitchen or their bedrooms, but at this moment, she was glad she'd thought to keep some wood down here for show.

"Should we leave?" Gisele asked as she followed Adella into the foyer. She might be twenty-two now, but her voice sounded much like the little girl Adella keenly remembered.

A protective urge rose within her, and she held the log like a club. "We'll take a look ourselves. Just a precaution. We're probably worried about nothing." And there were many reasons not to fetch the law. They'd scold her for calling them in without cause. They might snicker behind their hands at her empty house. She could do this herself, had done it many times.

And she was angry enough to really wallop anyone who'd sneaked in here during this already stressful day and scared her baby sister. "It shouldn't take long to search."

To search for a knife-wielding killer who had been masquerading as Dolores's aide for years. Adella shook her head. Her life was beginning to sound like cheap fiction.

Their footsteps echoed in the foyer as they crossed to the unused room across the hall. Maybe they should remove their boots? She was about to suggest it when Gisele grabbed her shoulder. "Did you hear that?"

Adella froze and listened. The silence seemed to thunder in her ears, or maybe that was her heart. There. Scratching on wood. And it was close. "Mice?" she whispered. They weren't usually so brazen in this part of the city with its plethora of rat catchers.

The sound came again. It had to be in the closed-off room before them. She pointed, and Gisele nodded, one hand up as if ready to cast. Adella crept forward, reaching for the handle.

The front door flew open behind them with a mammoth creak. Adella cried out, Gisele echoing her before grunting in pain. She sank to her knees as Adella leaped between her and a figure outlined by the light in the doorway.

It took a step.

Adella lifted the club, trying to summon a scream, but terror had taken her voice.

"What the hell is going on?" Zara's voice.

Adella sagged, her legs like rubber, and her heart going faster than a hummingbird's wings. "Oh, thank the gods."

"Why are you standing around in the foyer with a log?" Even in the light, Zara's eyes were like obsidian shards. "And why was the door unlocked? No wonder my key wasn't working. I kept locking the damn thing without knowing it. I felt like a fool." She shook a finger. "You should always lock it behind you when you…" She trailed away and looked to where Gisele was kneeling. Her tone softened at last. "Everything all right?"

"You are a fool," Gisele said. "I could have lit you on fire." She fumbled to her feet.

Zara snorted. "Again, you mean?"

Adella hastily explained before the two could get in another spat. When she'd finished, Zara insisted that Adella and Gisele wait in the kitchen while she took the light and her saber and searched the house. Adella was more than happy to let her, though she demanded regular shouts to confirm that everyone remained unhurt.

After the house had been cleared, they regrouped in the kitchen for a cup of coffee. Adella curled her fingers around her mug. The house was always cold, but the stove would soon warm this room, at least. They spent most of their evenings here, sitting at the high table that had stood in this house for generations. On really chilly nights, they sat in front of the massive fireplace at the far end of the kitchen, but it remained dark tonight, too much of a fuel-hog to be lit every day.

They chatted as Zara set out some scones she'd made the night before, along with a pot of jam from the larder. Her orderly mind had taken well to cooking, and she'd been making most of their meals since they'd let the cook go five years prior. With Adella's limited ability in the kitchen, she was fine with eating whatever Zara made. She was just happy the food was usually tasty.

As expected, Gisele grilled Adella about Bridget, and for once, Adella was happy she knew so little. She'd never been good at keeping things from the two family members she had left.

"That's all you know?" Gisele said when Adella was through. "A nightingale who lives at some bar called the Donkey?"

"The Donkey's Rest." Or that was what she remembered.

"Why were you out so late last night if that's all you talked about?" Gisele's cheeks went a bit pink after she asked the question, and she dropped her jam-slathered scone. Her eyes were delighted, and her mouth became an O of surprise. "Adella, you didn't!"

Adella felt some heat in her own cheeks and was happy she hadn't been taking a sip of coffee at the time. "We just met." The feel of Bridget kissing her returned, but she banished the thought before her face could catch fire. "Mind your own business."

Zara looked between them. "I think I know what you're talking about, but—"

"Stop right there," Adella said. "I don't need either of you commenting on my love life."

"*Love* life," Gisele said with a grin.

"Enough." Adella cleared her throat. "We talked of various things, nothing you need concern yourself about. Now." She set her cup down, hoping that was enough of a signal to change the subject. To make sure, she changed it herself. "Why are you home so early, Z?"

"Maneuvers finished early." She sounded disappointed, and she hadn't bothered to change out of her uniform when she'd been upstairs. The dark brown trousers and high-necked jacket with double buttons up the front suited her, especially with the gold epaulets to set off her tan. She'd undone the top button, allowing the left corner of the jacket to fold down and not look as if it was choking her, but she hadn't taken off the wide belt or shaken loose her dark, tied-back hair, and her saber and helmet lay within easy reach on the table.

Adella sighed as she stared at their middle sister. People said Adella didn't know how to relax, but no one was as uptight as Zara. She didn't wear her plain cap in the city, favoring the ridiculous golden helmet she was entitled to as a scout commander. Too many people saw her youthful face and didn't treat her like an officer.

And she couldn't have that. She was only twenty-six, but as Gisele liked to joke, she'd been born stuffy.

"And you aren't at work because of fatigue?" Zara asked Gisele, but she clucked her tongue without waiting for an answer. "Now, if you were in the military—"

"Someone would have lit my trousers on fire by now." Gisele squinted as if thinking. "Hang on. That was you!"

Zara's mouth turned down as she trotted out one of her favorite phrases. "If you weren't my sister…" When Gisele mouthed the words in unison, Zara puffed up even more.

"Enough," Adella said, saddened that their only conversational options seemed to be Adella's personal life and fighting. "I do not need a headache to round out this awful day. Zara, Gisele is a mage, and that's that. Gisele, no more throwing magic around." She raised her voice and stomped her boot over their chorus of accusations and arguments. "And both of you, stop antagonizing each other."

They didn't appear too chastened, but they shut up, and that seemed the best outcome to hope for.

After a moment, Zara set her mug down. "I'm sorry you lost your friend, Del."

"Thank you." Adella squeezed her hand, thankful for the words and also for the fact that if Gisele had something mocking to say, she kept it to herself. And Zara hadn't tutted over the fact that she'd left work early, so part of them was on their best behavior, it seemed.

Silence fell for a few moments before Gisele leaned back, smacking her lips noisily. "Let's all go out and have some fun."

Adella sighed yet again, about to plead exhaustion, but Zara beat her by bemoaning the cost.

Gisele huffed. "I'm not talking a five-course meal. There are some great street vendors near the constabulary on the river side of the ward." As Zara took a breath, no doubt to argue further, Gisele started counting reasons on her fingers. "It's cheap, it's safe because the thief catchers are right there, and it will cheer Adella up."

Zara shut her mouth, looking almost pained as she nodded. Gisele met Adella's eyes and raised her brows.

Adella chuckled. She couldn't pass now that these two actually agreed with each other. She nodded.

Gisele whooped. "Just give me a minute to change." She was off toward the stairs with a brightness to her step that cheered Adella even more.

She stood. "Come on, Zara."

"Why? I don't need to change."

"Yes, you do. You're stepping away from that uniform for a while, and I'm going to wear something simple."

Zara frowned and let her shoulders slump, looking eerily like Gisele for a moment. But unlike Gisele, she put the tea things away before she walked with Adella upstairs.

Bridget wanted to kick herself as she walked home. She'd promised not to leave Adella, they'd had their first tiff, and she still had a funeral to help plan for someone she'd never met.

And if anyone learned her identity, the next funeral would be hers.

And she seemed determined to admit everything to the ambassador to her former home.

Baxter would be torn between hanging his head in shame and laughing himself sick.

When that last problem had reared its head in front of Adella's house, her libido had done its best to power through. She might have agreed to stay if Adella had asked, but Gisele's arrival had squashed that. Stupid as Bridget seemed to be of late, she possessed enough reason to not spend more time in a spy hunter's presence than necessary.

Gods, she hoped it wouldn't be necessary that often.

Maybe she could avoid Adella's home until the murderer was caught. Her libido died a little at the idea. But she couldn't very well have Adella back to her shared room at the Donkey. Adella's office had seemed a promising spot for a rendezvous, but it would have another occupant now and was located in one of those "only as necessary" places.

For the devils' sake, this was getting complicated and difficult. The beginning of a relationship was supposed to be fun, not filled with the danger of execution.

As she passed some food vendors and breathed deeply, Bridget tried to tell herself not to be maudlin. She'd known she was going to come up against the problem of her past ever since she'd escaped. The lies followed her into the truth. She'd thought she could create a new past to fit the truth she was living now, but it felt like just another cover story.

She'd heard of spies getting so deep into their new lives that they began to believe those cover stories were real. They'd been waiting in position for some occurrence or signal that had taken decades to come, and when it came, they'd been too confused to act. If all they'd been doing was gathering information, they could be abducted and eventually debriefed in the empire. But if they had a job that went undone, the empire couldn't just let them go after they'd rediscovered their purpose and failed.

Baxter had only spoken of those dead spies when drunk, and even then, he wouldn't speak of all of them. Bridget suspected she'd killed one once, but she couldn't be sure. She didn't want to be sure. It was best if that particular assignment remained just like the others.

And her killing days were over.

When she reached the square, Bridget tried not to dwell on the idea that someone from her old life could be tracking her now, but the idea made her pull her coat tighter around her and scan the lengthening shadows. Well, she wouldn't be like those spies who'd forgotten who they'd been. She remembered. She was confident in her abilities.

Until now, when she seemed close to telling someone the truth.

If Baxter was still alive and the empire dragged her home to be debriefed before dying, he would probably kill her himself. "Fifty years I been in this game, ducky," he'd say, "man and boy, and thirty years a trainer, and you're the only one I helped sneak away, and you go and get yourself caught."

She'd spit in his face for recruiting her and for likely never telling the truth in all those fifty years, probably not even about her being the first he'd helped to escape. His voice would be with her the rest of her days, and she didn't even know his real name. It certainly wasn't Baxter.

Of course, he didn't know hers, either, but that had been his idea.

Caught in a wave of loneliness, Bridget had the sudden urge to hug her mother's mandolin case right there in the street. They'd loved each other, but Emma Leir had up and died, and though Bridget had been a pretty good street thief, she would have followed her mother if someone hadn't taken her in.

Pity that someone had been Baxter, who'd brought his world of lies and murder with him. Maybe that was why Bridget had grown so angry when Adella had assumed her criminal past. To Adella, criminal clearly meant thief.

If only Bridget could have stopped at being a thief.

She paused by the fountain in the square. It seemed to be business as usual now, with people hustling about their day, and cabs and carriages making the circuit. Various nightingales played their corners. Bridget craned her neck and saw Videl, Tomas, and the unknown singer from before spread out to incorporate Bridget's territory, but they wouldn't be able to save it forever. She should go take it back before some other nightingale got ideas, but she was too depressed to smile for the crowds, and the fact that she was sinking into her self-pity made her even sadder and grouchier until she felt as if she was on a playground roundabout. She had to either fight to get to the center or let herself be thrown off.

And she didn't seem capable of allowing herself to be thrown out of this mood, so she'd sink in and hopefully come out the other side.

She went back to the Donkey, ready for a good sulk in her room, which would be blessedly abandoned for a few hours more. Maybe she'd take a shift tonight in the taproom and make some coin. But that would be money she couldn't even use to escape because she was smitten with one of the worst people for an ex-spy to be lusting after.

The taproom was mostly deserted at this time of day. Serrah Nunez stepped out from the back room behind the bar and put a few bottles away. She wore a new wig, a sparkling creation done in pinks, oranges, and yellows. A topaz sunburst nestled in the braids on one side like a sandbar amid puffy swells of hair. Bridget had to stop and marvel.

Serrah Nunez lit up under the show of attention and did a slow turn, batting her heavily painted eyes when she halted again. "Well, treacle?" she asked, smiling with rose-painted lips. "What do you think?"

"Absolutely marvelous, serrah," Bridget said, meaning every word. "You're a work of art, as always. I don't know where you find the time."

Serrah Nunez waved a slender hand bearing so many rings and bracelets, it was difficult to spot any pale flesh. "One must make time for the important things in life." She sailed closer in a dress that seemed made of a great many glittery scarves, the ends fluttering as she moved. It left her shoulders bare, though her skin sparkled with some cosmetic.

Or maybe it was runoff from the wig.

"I sense a bit of sadness in you, pudding." She topped Bridget by a head and a half, but she was slenderer. Bridget suspected that if one took away all her frippery, she might nearly disappear like a long-haired cat after a bath.

When Bridget didn't respond, Serrah Nunez put a hand on her shoulder, jewelry clanging. "Whatever's the matter?"

Bridget's affliction from before struck her. She didn't want to lie. "A woman I'm interested in…her friend died today, and I'm not quite sure what to do." Not the whole truth but not wrong.

"Ah." Serrah Nunez gripped Bridget's shoulder and closed her eyes in a pained expression. "The pain of loss, how well I know it." She shook her head and nodded. "Fetch this woman, my peach. Bring her here among friends, and we will cheer her."

Bridget had to smile. All those in the Donkey's Rest were friends to Serrah Nunez. Unless they started trouble, then they were just sorry. With her mean right hook, she used all those heavy rings to devastating effect.

"I think she wants to be with family tonight, serrah, but thank you."

"Oh." She pulled Bridget into a dramatic embrace, enveloping her in a cloud of cloves, oranges, and all the spices of her homemade mulled wine. Then she held her at arm's length in an iron grip. "You're not thinking of pouting in your room?"

Bridget sighed. "How do you read minds?"

With an enigmatic, catlike smile, she steered Bridget toward the stage. "Play for me, dear little treacle, soothe yourself with song and cheer all our hearts."

The three patrons didn't seem to notice. Only the serious drinkers came in before sundown. But Bridget didn't want Serrah Nunez clattering around her all afternoon, naming her different desserts and badgering her out of her sadness.

And playing often made her feel better.

She started with a few slower songs of heartbreak or the first bloom of love. As a few more people trickled in, she had to increase the tempo just to be heard. By the time the pre-dinner crowd began to arrive, she was playing something boisterous that people could sing along with and had scored quite a few tips for the communal jar.

She'd paused to take a sip of water and rest her hands when Serrah Nunez fluttered over to her again. "A courier just left a message for you, crumble." She held out a small note sealed with wax.

Bridget opened it. "Dining at the vendors on Bond Avenue, near the constabulary on the river side of the ward," it read. "Join me?" It was signed with an A.

Adella? It had to be. Bridget had never dated anyone else who would refer to the Oligarchs' Ward as simply, the ward, or who would expect everyone to know their way around it.

Luckily, Bridget had memorized the layout of this city in case she ever had to flee.

Like she should be doing now.

Or at least, she should cut ties with a diplomat and her spy-hunting sister.

At the *very* least, she should not respond to this note.

Serrah Nunez plucked it from her hand. When Bridget tried to snatch it back, Serrah Nunez lifted a perfectly drawn eyebrow. "From your sad lover?"

"Well, not lover, not…" She'd been about to say, yet, but settled for, "Exactly."

"An invitation?" Her deep voice took on a slight purr.

"Well…" She damned her cheeks for heating up.

When Serrah Nunez offered the note back, she took Bridget's mandolin with her other hand.

"Hey!"

"Go, peaches. You must go to her when she calls." She quickly put the mandolin in its case. "Go to her in her time of need."

"But, serrah, you can't just—"

"Go to the one you love, tartlet. I will care for your instrument as if it was my own kin." She hustled Bridget toward the door with an unarguable grip on her shoulder.

"I don't—"

"You do. I see the fire in your eyes, cherries. Ah, but I do *love* love! Go."

Bridget couldn't even grab hold of anything as Serrah Nunez guided her out the door and pushed a long jacket into her arms, then grabbed her hands and pressed several coins into her palm.

"Take a cab and fly like the wind into the arms of your love."

Bridget ground her teeth at being pushed around, even from someone with seemingly good intentions. She tried to step back into the bar.

Serrah Nunez leaned close, and her breathless voice dropped to a lower tone. "Step back inside here, and I will break your arm, Bridget Leir. I love a good romance story, and you will not rob me of this one." She winked.

Bridget sighed, her anger waning. Serrah Nunez was right. It was shaping up to be a damned love story. She'd never felt drawn to anyone like she was to Adella. And it must mean something that even after spending much of the day together and having had their first fight, Adella wanted to see her again so soon.

She wasn't sure what it meant, but it was definitely something.

Gods and devils, she was doomed.

CHAPTER EIGHT

Adella breathed a little easier in the outside air. The evening wasn't as cold as she'd feared, though she was happy she'd worn woolen tights under her simple dress and a thick jacket on top. Gisele and Zara had opted for trousers, but Adella feared getting used to them and then having to force herself into her opulent gowns for work. Opulent trousers would be nice, but they didn't seem to exist. The upper classes thought them too common. She'd often wondered if the hose and ankle-length dalmatica favored mostly by noblemen was more comfortable, but it seemed like another dress cast in a slightly different shape.

A slightly plainer, straighter shape meant to flatter those without hips. If she had to deal with the length of a dress, she might as well go as fancy as possible.

Gisele bumped her with an elbow, bringing her back to the present where they sat on a low wall beside the small park that separated the two halves of Bond Avenue while Zara stood in front of a row of shops across the street.

"You're thinking about work, aren't you?" Gisele asked.

"Fashion, actually." But Adella dialed down the archness in her tone when she added, "Work fashion."

Gisele snorted.

"Anyway, I'm not the only one. Did you or did you not duck into the constabulary over there when we first arrived to check on news of…the crime?" She'd tried again to say murder but couldn't.

"I only wanted to send a message," Gisele said defensively.

"To whom?"

"Mind your own business." She laughed when Adella gave her a bump this time. "What is Z up to in front of that pie shop?"

Adella grinned as she watched the exchange. The pie man was even redder in the face than the last time she'd looked, where Zara had her hands behind her back and the demeanor of an icy statue. "She's doing delicate negotiations."

"Uh-oh," Gisele said. "What did the pie man do?"

Adella lifted an eyebrow in her best Zara impression. "Your sign, good sir, clearly advertises that each pie contains, amongst other ingredients, potatoes. In the plural. As my pie only possessed one potato, I believe a partial refund is in order."

Gisele cackled and kicked her feet like a small child. "She did not call him good sir!"

"She did. I ran away after that."

"Oh, Z." Gisele shook her head, but the words were said with affection. She and Zara might fight a good deal, but they did love each other.

Mostly.

Gisele unwrapped an empanada and began to nibble. "The eyebrow was a nice touch. She overuses that."

"She's practiced it too many times in the mirror not to use it."

"Please tell me you've actually seen that." Her eyes went wide. "And if so, why didn't you call me so I could mock her?"

Adella nodded at the empanada. "Give me a bite, and I'll answer."

Gisele held it out so that most of it was still covered by the paper wrapper.

After a sigh, Adella took the tiny bite offered. Mostly pastry, it was nevertheless warm and flaky and lovely. She might have to get one of her own. "I did see it, and I would never fetch you for the purposes of mockery." She nodded toward where the pie man had now turned purple. "Except for now, perhaps."

"Here," the pie man roared, the sound carrying across the street. He ducked back inside his shop for a moment. "Take some potatoes and be damned!" He chucked several at Zara's feet.

She regarded them coolly and said something in return.

The pie man disappeared into his shop again, and the clang of cooking implements echoed across the street. When he reemerged, he shoved a bag into Zara's arms. She bowed and turned. He watched her walk away with a murderous expression.

"Quiet," Adella said to Gisele's snickering. "She won't let you off as easily as the pie man if you laugh at her."

"What did you get, Z?" Gisele called.

Zara opened the bag. "A handful of fingerling potatoes. Seems a bit excessive." She shrugged.

"Worth more than a partial refund," Gisele said, her voice tight with barely controlled mirth.

Zara seemed not to notice. "I agree. But he seemed so upset, I thought I shouldn't argue." She looked in the bag again. "Oh." She pulled out a large metal spoon. "I don't think he meant for me to have this. Perhaps I should—"

"No," Adella and Gisele said at the same time.

Gisele hopped off the wall with a little wince. "Let me. He might throw you in his oven." She grabbed the spoon and was off before Adella could offer to go or Zara could utter something about how he wouldn't dare.

Adella patted the space beside her until Zara sat. "Potatoes aside, how was the pie?"

"Quite tasty." She nodded happily, her dark eyes twinkling, but over the pie or the victory, Adella didn't know.

A few strains of music floated down the street, and Bridget popped into Adella's mind. She sighed, trying to think of what she could say in the morning to further apologize about implying Bridget had a criminal past. Or perhaps she could use the age-old method of pretending their disagreement had never happened.

Ah well. She didn't have to worry about it now. She could enjoy her evening, and if thoughts of Bridget rose again, she could focus on the memory of toe-curling kisses.

Gisele returned swiftly. "People are dancing outside the tavern down the street. Let's get iced buns and watch."

Adella hopped down to join her, lured by the promise of dessert and desirous to flee the glares of the pie man. They bought their buns quickly before continuing down the street. The bar Gisele had spoken of sat across Bond Avenue from the constabulary, with a stone bridge spanning a dip in the little park to connect the two halves of the street. People stood all along the bridge, warming themselves by a scattering of braziers. Despite the chill in the air, the bar had the doors and windows wide open, and music and light spilled onto the street. Groups of people danced to a lively tune played by a trio of musicians just outside the bar's doors.

Adella smiled as she nibbled her bun and watched. The festival-like atmosphere was just what she needed to clear her head.

"Why don't you join them?" Gisele asked.

"What, dance by myself?" Adella asked. "Or do you feel well enough to volunteer?"

Gisele barked a laugh. "Never been a dancer, never will be." But was the pained expression that crossed her face from the aches in her body or the damage those aches caused to her spirit?

Adella shook her head and tried not to sink into the worries that usually surrounded her. "Who then?"

"Not me," Zara said with no pain or wistfulness at all. She finished her bun in three efficient bites.

"You don't have any rhythm," Gisele said.

Zara bristled. "I could dance if I wanted."

"Children, don't start," Adella said.

"Anyway," Gisele said loudly. "I've already secured you a partner, Del."

Adella frowned. "Who?" She looked in the direction of Gisele's pointing finger, picking out a figure approaching through the meager crowd. It paused near one of the braziers, and the lean body and crooked grin sparked her desire even before she fully registered who it was. "Bridget." She turned to Gisele. "How?"

"The message I sent, silly. I figured you could use a friend besides us. For dancing…or anything else."

Adella gave her a dark look, but she couldn't be angry. She barely needed Gisele's little push to shove her dessert into Zara's hands and start walking. "Hello," she said when she reached the brazier.

"Hi." Bridget cocked her head. "I'm glad I found you. Your note didn't say exactly where to meet." She craned her neck to peer around Adella. "Or was it your note? Your surprised expression makes me think otherwise."

"It was Gisele's matchmaking skills."

"Ah. And the other woman is?"

"Zara. Middle sister."

"Gods. How many beautiful women can one family have?"

Adella laughed. "Charmer. Just three, and yes, I will tell them you said that. They'll know you're trying to curry favor just so they'll approve of you, though."

Bridget ducked her head. She seemed as if she might say something else, but Adella didn't want to talk about her family. Or anything else. She'd come out to lose herself for a bit.

Perhaps Bridget wanted to do the same. "Would you like to dance?" Adella asked.

Bridget grinned as if that was something she'd been waiting to hear. "Only if I can dance with you."

After a shared chuckle, they moved into the music, blending with the other dancers into a lively reel. Adella threw her head back and laughed. She hadn't danced like this in years. Court functions and work gatherings sometimes had dancing, but it was more like courtly maneuvering, with structured steps and precise movements. This felt wild, a chance to kick and spin and turn. The night and the firelight and the music created a bubble around her, and nothing bad could get through.

Better still, Bridget whirled through the bubble with her, all flashing eyes and ringing laughs and expert hands that kept Adella's wild steps from trampling other dancers.

When the tempo changed, falling, Bridget drew her close, her arms like a stronghold as they swayed together. She wrapped one around Adella's shoulder, and the other around her waist. The lower hand crept under Adella's jacket to leave trails of fire along her lower back, even through her dress.

Adella put her hands on Bridget's hips and luxuriated in their sway. It seemed the most natural thing in the world to fall into Bridget's smoldering gaze and move even closer, letting her eyes slip closed as their lips met.

This kiss had the heat of the others, but it felt more like a slow burn and not the roar of their previous encounters. Adella lost herself in the slow, sensuous movements of Bridget's mouth, letting the music keep guiding her until everything but their points of contact disappeared.

A louder note jarred her, and Adella wanted to ignore it, but someone knocked against her, making her stumble. She turned as someone called an inebriated apology before disappearing back into the dancers.

"Come on," Bridget said, and her voice sounded a bit shaky, matching the feeling Adella discovered in her legs as they moved beyond the dancers.

They paused by a brazier, but Adella didn't need its heat. She felt warm all over, matching the fire in Bridget's eyes.

"Adella." Bridget's gaze asked what her mouth couldn't seem to manage, and Adella wanted to say yes, that she would spend the night with her, but something held her back.

She caught a glimpse of her sisters keeping a discreet distance. Ah, yes, she and Bridget had nowhere to go. But there was more than that. Adella could find somewhere, but now that they'd ventured outside the bubble, the real world came rushing back.

The world where Dolores was dead.

A gust of grief blew through her. No doubt Dolores would want her to be happy, but there was such a thing as enjoying oneself too much, too quickly after a tragedy.

"You're about to tell me you're sorry," Bridget said. "I can tell by your expression." And she sounded sad but also accepting.

Gods and devils, Adella could fall hard for her if given the chance. "I am. Sorry, that is."

Bridget kissed her forehead, the gesture so tender, it brought tears to Adella's eyes. "I won't pout, don't worry. I wouldn't be feeling very energetic after the day you've had."

Adella scoffed and nodded toward the dancing. "Was that not your idea of energetic?"

Bridget gave her a look of such undisguised lust that it caused her core to throb. "Not even close."

Oh gods, even Dolores would be shouting at her to go for it.

Someone cleared their throat behind her in a very deliberate way, and Adella knew it would be Zara before she began to turn.

Zara was staring at Bridget with the same caution she used with everyone. Before Adella could attempt an introduction, Gisele came barreling through the crowd to Zara's side. "I told you to leave them alone," Gisele said, low and through her teeth. She smiled apologetically at Bridget. "Sorry, excuse us." She tugged on Zara's arm, but she might as well have been tugging on the bridge.

"You left," Zara said to her. "So I thought I'd come say hello." She looked at Bridget again. "Hello."

Bridget's greeting was lost as Gisele said, "Two minutes. I was gone two minutes to say hi to some friends, and you're over here sticking your nose in."

"I was being polite."

"Is being polite the new code for blundering in where you're not welcome? You're such an ox, Zara."

"How dare—"

"You tactless—"

"If you weren't my sister—"

Adella grabbed one wrist apiece and squeezed. They quieted as if remembering they were in public at last. "Let's pretend we're adults," Adella said softly. Her cheeks burned as she looked at Bridget's amused smile. "Bridget Leir, this is my sister, Zara del Amanecer, and no doubt you remember Gisele."

Bridget's smile tightened a little as she bowed. "Serrahs."

Adella couldn't blame her for being a little uneasy. No doubt she worried the two would begin sniping again at a moment's notice.

A legitimate concern.

"We should be going," Adella said. Gisele and Zara both sucked in a breath, but Adella didn't care to hear a peep. She gave them another squeeze.

To their credit, they didn't say a word.

"I understand," Bridget said. "Thank you for inviting me." She ducked her head again as if remembering they'd been set up, but Gisele had the intelligence to remain quiet. "I'll see you tomorrow for our walk to the square?"

"I'm looking forward to it." She leaned in for a quick peck, her sisters be damned.

After a soft, "Good-bye," Bridget headed away through the night.

Zara and Gisele managed to look both sheepish and defiant. Again, before they could speak, Adella said, "You two are quite alike, you know." She turned her back on their looks of shock and started toward home. Their silence was so profound, she paused only long enough to make sure they were following.

❖

Bridget whistled a lively tune as she walked back to the cab stand and waited for her turn to catch a ride. Part of her was disappointed that the evening was cut short, but the rest of her was walking through the clouds.

Adella danced with the enthusiasm of a child, but the looks she'd given Bridget were anything but childlike. Bridget would dream of how her eyes darkened with desire, of the way her golden hair had caught the light, and the way her curvy body had fit into Bridget's arms. And they wouldn't even be frustrated dreams. Only… anticipatory.

If they could ever get away from Adella's sisters. The middle one stared like a thief catcher, and the younger one was actually a spy hunter. Bridget wouldn't be surprised to find out that Adella's parents had been a judge and a prison warden.

Just her luck.

"Don't get down, ducky," Baxter would have said. "Every problem has a solution."

Yes, and the best one right now seemed to be kidnapping Adella and carrying her off so they could be together on some distant shore. Something about the look on Adella's face when she'd quieted her sisters said she might be okay with that.

But not forever. No, Bridget would have to find a way to tell Adella about her past, in private, with whatever assurances she might need that Bridget was no longer a spy. And now didn't seem the right time.

"Or are you being a coward?" Baxter would ask.

She almost said no aloud. He was only in her mind, but she seemed to hear him so clearly at times. And it might be a little cowardly, but the time for admitting her former job was not right after the ambassador to the Firellian Empire had been murdered. She would wait for that event to resolve itself, wait for the murderer to be caught. It wouldn't do anyone any good to present herself as a potential suspect in Adella's eyes. Maybe she could even do a bit of poking around, help find the murderer so Adella could have some peace.

"And so you can get laid sooner, eh?"

"Shut up, Baxter," she mumbled. But that was exactly what he would say. And all right, it was partially true. She wanted to wait until the truth was revealed between them, and the sooner this whole murder business was over, the sooner they could be together without a massive lump of guilt draped over Bridget's shoulders.

She just had to stay away from Adella's sisters until then.

As she rode home in the cab, she thought it couldn't be too hard. They'd mostly see each other in the square or on Adella's walk to and from work. Her sisters wouldn't be with her for those, surely.

Hopefully.

Bridget sighed and told herself not to dwell, to remember instead the flush in Adella's pale cheeks as they'd danced, the silky feel of her dress under her jacket. Bridget imagined it clinging to her like a second skin.

The cab halting in front of the Donkey's Rest jolted her from her thoughts, but she could feel them at the back of her mind, waiting for whenever Bridget was ready for them. She waved good night to the cabbie and headed inside, still whistling. Videl was playing in the taproom, but Bridget didn't want to linger, ready to lose herself in memory again once she was alone.

She smiled at Serrah Nunez and received a wink in return. She'd no doubt have to tell the tale tomorrow. Now she bounded up the back steps to the room she shared with Videl, surprised to find a light coming from under the door. Odd. Even if Videl had come up during a break, she should have taken the candle with her.

Bridget's hackles went up, and she paused, tiptoeing the rest of the way to the door. Baxter began rumbling in her mind, but this was much more likely to be a case of a forgotten candle or even a thief than anything to do with Bridget's past. Maybe an admirer of hers or Videl's had sneaked up here to wait naked under their blankets.

She listened at the door but heard nothing. By the light around the edges, she saw it was already opened a crack. She stepped to the side to make herself less of a target and pushed it open slowly.

Someone was sitting on her bed, but this woman was clothed, and the smile she aimed at Bridget seemed a little cruel. It took a moment for her face to line up with one in Bridget's memory. The last time Bridget had seen her, she'd been a crying mess.

"Juno?" Bridget asked as she stepped into the room. "What are you doing here?"

"I need your help."

Curious, Bridget scanned the small room, but no one else waited in the shadows. "For what?"

"Getting out of Sarras."

Surprise tried to take over Bridget's mind, but her training wouldn't allow it. There was only one reason she could think of for Juno to flee the country. "You killed Dolores."

Juno cocked her head, her casual, confident air miles away from the girl who'd fallen apart in Adella's office. "You help me flee, and I won't tell anyone who you are…ducky."

She said it with Baxter's slight burr, and Bridget's insides froze.

CHAPTER NINE

Adella awoke in the morning and stretched, smiling. Her dreams had been of the hot, fulfilling variety, and to add to that pleasantness, she'd be seeing Bridget in the flesh that very morning.

Not as nice as actually waking up with her, but Adella told herself to enjoy the anticipation while it lasted.

When Zara delivered her wake-up knock, Adella was mostly done with her morning routine. "I'm up," she called from her vanity. When Zara knocked again, Adella sighed but crossed to open the door. "Do you need proof, or…" She trailed off when Zara held out a sealed note.

"I was making coffee when a messenger delivered this."

Adella's stomach shrank. Only bad news came early in the morning or late at night. She broke the wax and frowned as she read, "Sorry, can't make our walk this morning. A friend needed my help. I'll miss you. See you soon. B."

Sad news but thankfully, not tragic. Adella sighed again. She handed the note to Zara, who hadn't moved, and went back to putting her jewelry on.

"Ah," Zara said after she read it. "Sorry, Del."

"Me, too, but I suppose I should be glad she makes time for her friends when they need her."

Zara nodded. "No doubt it was an emergency."

Adella frowned at her in the mirror, curious. "What makes you say that?"

"Why else would she pass up the chance to spend time with you?"

Adella felt a rush of affection and happiness that her sister could still surprise her. "Thank you."

Zara turned the note over as if looking for clues. "Unless this friend is actually someone else she's looking to bed."

Well, there went both the surprise and affection. Adella slammed the lid of her jewelry case and glared, even though there hadn't been any malice in the words.

Zara blinked, and her eyes widened. But instead of taking back the words, she added, "If that's the case, don't worry. I will challenge her on your behalf."

That would have to do. "Thanks."

"I'd win, have no fear." She looked a little worried now, as if she knew she'd said something wrong but didn't know how to fix it.

"I have no doubt. Come on." Adella gestured for her to lead the way downstairs.

Gisele sat at the kitchen table in her robe, a mug of coffee steaming in front of her. She gave Adella a nod, all anyone could expect from her until she'd had at least one cup. Adella sat with her own mug. She tried not to let Bridget's note set a tone of disappointment for the day, but it was difficult now that Zara had opened her big mouth.

Gisele tilted her mug far back and set it down with a hollow *thunk*. She smiled at last. "Still thinking about Dolores, Del?"

Adella shrugged as she shredded the pastry Zara had put in front of her.

"Bridget canceled their walk," Zara said as she joined them with a bowl of fruit.

Gisele's eyes widened. "Why?"

Adella poured more coffee in everyone's cup, hoping they'd drink it and hush.

"Not because she's romancing someone else," Zara said brightly. "Unless she wants a beating." She looked proud, no doubt certain she'd said the right thing at last.

"Uh-huh," Gisele said slowly, glancing between them.

"She sent a note saying she's helping a friend," Adella said as she snapped a piece of apple in half. "And I'm not upset about it."

"Clearly." Gisele added sugar to her coffee and stirred, and the tinkling sound grated on Adella's nerves. "Well, if she is up to no good, I'll add some magical pain to Zara's beating."

"Gods and devils," Adella muttered as Zara began some speech about how Gisele's assistance wouldn't be necessary. "I have to go." She wasn't in any mood to listen to an argument. She waved off Zara's offer to accompany her and grabbed her cloak and reticule and fled.

Out in the cold, still air, she breathed deep. Today could still be a good day. And just because she wouldn't see Bridget this morning didn't mean they couldn't see each other at all. She kept that in mind during her walk to the Bastión. It was a pleasant, sunny day, even with the dark clouds on the northern horizon speaking of bad weather to come.

Adella entered her workplace with a cheery step, hoping to find Juno and Cristoff waiting with perfect explanations as to where they'd been. But a dark-haired man in a heavily embroidered, dark green dalmatica squeaked and leaped from behind her desk as she entered her office.

"Ambassador," he said, bowing, "I didn't expect you so early."

Adella blinked, trying to process what was happening. "What… are you…why…" Three different questions clanged in her mind and tangled on her tongue. Who was he, what was he doing in her office, and why shouldn't she arrive at the same time she did every day? But she stopped at the sight of the silver badge pinned above his right ear, just above where his long braid curled forward to hang over his shoulder.

The badge of a secondary ambassador. Just like hers.

But he'd called her ambassador, no secondary in sight.

Her veins turned to ice. She was the new ambassador to the Firellian Empire, and she didn't need to come to work for at least another hour, giving her second and their aides time to ready her calendar for the day.

The dark-haired man was staring, and when she didn't speak, he smiled nervously. "Well. I'm Jean-Carlo." He put a thin hand to his chest. "On loan from Ambassador Flores until you select your own second." The way he ducked his chin and grinned said he wouldn't mind switching departments. His handsome face had no doubt swayed many an employer. "The Mistress of Clocks is working on hiring some new aides, so—"

"Juno will be back," Adella said, her shock fading into anger. She had a sudden urge to grab this upstart's collar and throw him out of her office so everything could go back to normal. But she forced herself to take a deep breath. She would not shame Dolores's memory by being a tyrant to the staff.

Jean-Carlo had gone as still as a puppet hanging in its strings. His dark eyes were very wide in his youthful face.

"Please continue," Adella said, keeping her tone level.

His helpful smile reappeared. "I…was just arranging your calendar for the day. Perhaps you'd like your mail?" He took something off the desk and scooted carefully past her, leading the way across the hall and unlocking Dolores's office.

Adella's office.

She swallowed hard as she followed, her legs like lead. Jean-Carlo began speaking again as he flitted through the room, but she barely heard him. Her heart pounded as she stepped through the door, almost tiptoeing toward the windows, gaze locked on where the body would be.

For a moment, her imagination showed it to her again—the hand bent into a claw, the glassy eyes, the blood—but of course, there was no body. Even the rug had been changed.

Life just kept going after something like that? It didn't seem right.

When Jean-Carlo set the key on the desk with a little click, Adella came back to herself. "And the Firellian Ambassador requested a meeting this morning," he said. "What shall I tell him?"

She blinked. Wasn't she the Firellian Ambassador? Had she simply wandered into the wrong office, and this was all a glorious mistake, and Dolores was still alive?

Before she said something stupid, she realized that he meant that the ambassador *from* the empire wanted a meeting. "Fine," she said without thinking. She gasped, wishing she could take that back, completely unprepared for a meeting with a snake while in this emotional state.

"Very good, serrah," Jean-Carlo said as he strode out the door.

Adella looked around the room slowly, seeing Dolores imprinted on every surface. A knock on the open door made her jump.

Jean-Carlo breezed back inside with a nervous chuckle. "Almost forgot, serrah." He took something off the desk and held it out.

An ambassador's badge.

The very image of Dolores's.

Adella nearly leaped away when Jean-Carlo approached with it, but the part of her that could still think clearly noted how this badge gleamed like new.

And Dolores would be buried with her own badge.

"Allow me," Jean-Carlo said.

Adella stayed frozen as he reached to her hair and traded the old badge for the new one. He had steady, gentle hands, and when he stepped back to appraise his handiwork, he smiled again, meeting her eyes with a sympathetic look.

Gods and devils, she hoped she didn't look too pathetic.

"Coffee, serrah?" he asked, his voice friendly.

"Fine," she said again.

He bowed, then exited so swiftly, his dalmatica snapped about his ankles. He shut the door softly behind him.

Silence came crashing in. Adella staggered under the weight of it and dropped into one of Dolores's padded chairs.

Her chairs.

She put her head in her hands. A promotion was not supposed to feel this much like a betrayal. This should have happened years from now, when Dolores was ready to retire. They would have had a small celebration with cinnamon pastries and cups of chocolate. Adella, Juno, and Cristoff would have walked Dolores to her carriage and waved her off.

Afterward, Adella could have visited for sage advice from time to time. And she would have helped nurse Dolores through illness or injury. If it came to it, she would have welcomed Dolores into her home to live out her final years.

That lost future sat hard on her now, and she had to fight to keep from weeping. It had taken death for her to realize they'd been more like family than coworkers. Dolores had probably left Adella the contents of this office in her will. If that was true, it might not be so much of a betrayal to think of it as hers.

No, that didn't really work. These were Dolores's books and objet d'art. Adella was an intruder who could never stand upright in Dolores's shadow.

Dolores would have tutted about that thought. Adella could almost hear it.

She smoothed her skirt and stood. After another deep breath, she said, "Right. That's enough self-pity."

And now a task jumped to the forefront of her mind. Thoughts of a will reminded her that Dolores still needed someone to act as family. Her lawyer was one of many who needed to be informed of her death. To find them all, Adella would have to get to work sorting through Dolores's papers. And her mail. She had a lot of reading in her future, not the least of which were Dolores's notes on the Firellian negotiations. Adella had a meeting soon, and in Dolores's name, she would not make a horse's ass of herself.

Bridget's mind hadn't stopped racing since last night. She'd barely slept and couldn't remember getting dressed or walking to Bastión Square, but here she was. Luckily, she was used to playing her mandolin while her mind was elsewhere. It had come in handy during many an assignment.

Another part of her old life she would never escape.

Juno had killed Dolores Vega. She hadn't admitted it, but it seemed clear. And if she knew Baxter, she was a spy for the Firellian Empire, though she hadn't admitted that, either. She hadn't said much at all the night before.

After her demand to be smuggled out of the country and her threat to reveal that Bridget had been a spy, Juno only stared.

Bridget swallowed to cover her shock and breathed deep to calm her racing heart. How quickly she fell back on old tactics. "What's your timetable?"

"As soon as possible," Juno said.

"You've completed your entire objective?"

Juno smiled. Bridget had asked the same of the many spies she'd helped flee once their jobs had been done, but it seemed that Juno recalled Bridget was an *ex*-spy faster than Bridget did.

"What was your original exit strategy?" Bridget asked.

"It's unavailable. That's why I'm here." She hadn't lost her confident smile.

So something about her assignment had changed, or she'd have been able to escape as planned in the beginning. "What—"

"Stop wasting time. If your roommate catches me here, I will be forced to begin dismantling your life."

Reminding Bridget of the stakes while also putting the burden on her if something went wrong? Pure Baxter. "Follow me."

The first step was to get her down the back stairs, so Bridget led the way. They didn't speak as they waited for the hallway to the back door to clear, then scurried through the busy kitchen and out into the night. In the street, Juno stayed one step behind, no doubt with her hand on a weapon under her cloak.

She remained quiet as they turned down two streets, stopping on what the locals called Accommodation Avenue, where several hotels lined both sides of the broad lane.

Juno gripped Bridget's arm. "That one." She jutted her chin toward the Traveler's Rest, mid-priced for the district. They wouldn't attract attention there, and they wouldn't get fleas, either. "Something on the second floor by the alley. Come to the window when you're ready." She leaned in. "And don't think you're the only one who'll suffer if you turn me in." After a last, dark look, she faded back to wait in a nearby alley.

Anger burned in Bridget as she bit back an angry retort. Undoubtedly, Juno meant Adella. Baxter would have encouraged Bridget to save herself, but he wouldn't be surprised that she wasn't going to.

She waited a few moments, then went inside the Traveler's Rest. The furnishings were plain, and no one lingered in the small lobby to partake of the uncomfortable looking chairs and old broadsheets. The young clerk behind the counter didn't ask why she had wanted a room on a specific floor by the alley. She signed a false name in the registry and paid for three nights, hopefully all she would need.

When she handed over a generous tip, the young clerk didn't even look at her again, seemingly used to having guests buy some anonymity.

In the small room, she wasted no time opening the window and waving toward the alley across the street. She didn't want to give Juno any reason to begin plans for retribution. And she had no doubt that Juno's threats weren't bluffs. Baxter would have taught her better than that.

As Juno climbed on top of a refuse barrel and reached for Bridget's hand, Bridget considered lifting her, then throwing her, hoping she'd land on her head and die.

No one was that lucky. And Bridget didn't have another weapon, nor did the room have a handy armory.

She could be calm, wait for the right moment.

Then what?

Then…she'd think of something. She backed up a few steps while Juno closed the window.

"Have you figured out how to get me out of Sarras?" Juno asked.

Bridget shook her head. "The sentinels will be watching all departing travelers, and I imagine they'll have someone looking for you at the pier and the coach houses and hostlers, even if they just want to question you."

Juno nodded. "Even the fishing boats on the river won't be safe. Which is why I need you to think like the person you used to be and not a useless lump."

Bridget fought to keep her face neutral and her temper in check. She said nothing, and after a moment, Juno sighed and took her cloak off, revealing a dark, simple dress. She shook her hair loose and untied a small bag from around her waist, tossing it on the bed.

"Go back to your bar," Juno said. "Conduct yourself normally tomorrow. Then instead of returning home, purchase me a pair of dark trousers and a shirt that is a size too large, along with a simple belt and a pair of secondhand boots."

The too-large shirt would allow her to make subtle changes to her appearance on the fly, but the rest was meant to blend in with a crowd. Bridget wanted to scoff. Juno could have done her the courtesy of asking for the spy's toolkit, and Bridget would have known what she was talking about. She hadn't completely forgotten who she used to be.

"Easy," Baxter would have said. "Let her underestimate you."

Juno sat on the bed. "Return here with my purchases and report any news you may have gleaned." She lifted her eyebrows. "And for the sake of all gods and devils, have a better plan in mind."

"Yes, serrah," Bridget blurted, Baxter be damned. "Is there anything else, serrah? A warm bath for your tired feet?" She regretted the words at once, not wanting to show the depth of her loathing.

Juno only chuckled. "Don't even think of turning me in unless you want to join me, and you don't care who else suffers. Oh, and I've made contingency plans in case I…happen to die before I can escape. You'll forgive me if I don't tell you what those are." She rolled her head and sighed. "And you won't be the only one to suffer in that instance, either."

She said it so calmly. Baxter would have warned Bridget to have a care with this one. She was either a very good actress, or she didn't care whom she hurt.

Bridget also could have belted Baxter in the mouth for sending this viper into the world.

Juno dismissed her with a wave, and Bridget left via the window, so it would seem as if she'd spent the night in the hotel rather than staring at the ceiling in her own bed.

Now Bridget tried to ponder what to do as she played and sang and pretended she wasn't buried up to her neck in trouble. All the possibilities she'd considered for her own escape were useless here. They only worked for someone who *wasn't* wanted for questioning in connection to a murder.

Added to that problem was the fact that Bridget really did not want to help Juno. She'd already made the decision to come clean to Adella about her past someday. How would that go if she ended with, "Remember how your mentor was murdered, and you cried like your heart was broken? I helped the murderer escape. It was Juno, your friend and protégé. Surprise!"

Perfect.

Bridget could go to Adella, admit her former life, turn Juno in, then warn Adella to guard herself. But that would see her on the scaffold by Juno's side. The sentinels would believe they'd done the crime together, and that Bridget was just turning her coat in order to save her own skin. For that, they *might* grant her the privilege of spending the rest of her life in jail instead of hanging.

And she would still lose Adella.

Juno wouldn't wait forever. Bridget would have to either help her or set her up in some way that killed her. Either way, she needed more information, including the best way out of the city for a wanted person and the exact nature of Juno's contingency plans.

She needed to get inside Juno's former life, all while not alerting the authorities, Adella, or Adella's crime-fighting family.

Again, perfect.

CHAPTER TEN

For her meeting with the Firellian ambassador, Adella added quite a few notes to Dolores's hefty file. Maybe seeing Dolores's neat handwriting alongside her own would inspire her to be calm in the face of de Maupassant's oiliness.

No doubt a lost cause.

Dolores's notes revealed some of the concerns Adella had brought up before, though she hadn't been convinced that de Maupassant's delaying tactics promised the dire consequences Adella had predicted. Dolores thought he wanted to weary the Sarrasian ambassadors into missing some detail that would cost them later, either from a defense or a financial standpoint.

Adella wasn't sure about the finance angle, especially now that Dolores had been killed. She didn't care how certain Gisele was that no intruders had breached Dolores's office. The Firellians were sneaky enough to find a way.

And they no doubt thought Adella would be a pushover of a replacement.

They were in for a shock. She would be calm, as Dolores had taught her, but if necessary, she would be the sword of vengeance. Dolores had never been a fan of an angry retort, let alone violence, but she'd never foreseen a future where she'd been murdered, either. Adella would need more skills than those Dolores had taught her.

Plus, she'd barely made a dent in Dolores's private papers before she'd had to study up for the damned meeting, so she was aggravated from the start. She'd at least managed to send a note to Dolores's lawyer and had begun a letter to her sister.

Before much longer, Jean-Carlo came to collect her, and they walked to the meeting together. He would have been studying her notes as she'd studied Dolores's, but now, Adella wished she knew him well enough to play off him if necessary.

"How many negotiations have you attended?" she asked.

"Six as a secondary's aide, three as an ambassador's aide." He sounded confident. That was good.

"Dealing with the Kingdom of Othlan?"

"Yes, serrah. All with the abruptness and efficiency the Othlans are known for." He gave her a wry look that said he knew the Firellians would be different.

"We're going to be really outnumbered without aides of our own."

"The Mistress of Clocks said she'd commandeer two for the meeting, so we don't have to hand around the drinks ourselves." He smiled with another dollop of wry amusement, and she started to like him.

Today would not be fun, but it didn't have to be a disaster.

De Maupassant was late, but Adella was glad of that. It gave her time to have a fortifying sip of water, arrange her papers, and attempt to stop her hands shaking. The temporary aides introduced themselves as Regina and Flavio before they faded quietly into the background, but their presence made Adella feel a jot more confident.

"You're going to do fine, serrah," Jean-Carlo whispered.

She nearly snorted but coughed to cover it. "And how do you know that?"

"Because Ambassador Vega picked you as her second, and Ambassador Flores had a deep respect for her and her decisions."

And now Adella liked him even more. She didn't care if he was flattering her or not. It was what she needed to hear.

De Maupassant arrived, giving off the same oily aura as before. His words dripped with false sincerity as he heaped praises on Dolores, a "flower of Sarras plucked too soon."

It wasn't enough to merit a sword of vengeance, but she would have settled for being the hobnailed boot of anti-obsequiousness.

"Thank you," she said. "Shall we get down to it?"

His eyes went wide. "But, Ambassador, I have not been introduced to your aide." He looked to Jean-Carlo.

"My *secondary* ambassador," she said, stressing the word as Dolores used to.

"Jean-Carlo Durand, serrah," Jean-Carlo said, standing just enough to bow before sitting again.

"A Firellian name. Well, well."

Adella blinked. She hadn't thought about that, but his first name was a blend of Sarrasian and Firellian, where his last name was from the empire. She tried to fight off fear and suspicion, but it proved difficult.

Before those emotions could take hold, Jean-Carlo said, "My mother was born in the empire, serrah, but her family moved to Sarras when she was a baby. When she died in childbed, my father named me after her parents, in her honor."

Adella breathed a little easier. He'd been born here, and he wouldn't have been able to move up through the governmental ranks unless his background had been thoroughly checked.

But she would keep an eye on him. Her pledge to Bridget to not judge those outside her sphere came back to her, but this wasn't someone from the poorer districts of Sarras; this was someone with ties to the empire. They deserved a cloud of suspicion.

De Maupassant launched into a series of questions about Jean-Carlo's life—much as he'd done when he'd met Adella—and she tried not to groan. No doubt his spies had already told him everything he needed to know about everyone who worked in the Bastión before he'd ever set foot across the border.

Adella's temper grew with each question, much as she tried to tamp it down before she threw a chair or something. She made herself breathe. She needed to derail her temper, and if de Maupassant was happy feigning emotion, she could do the same.

In a gap in the chitchat, she said, "I don't wish to hurry you, Ambassador, but I still have a funeral to plan today." She made herself blink rapidly as she said it and was gratified to see Jean-Carlo take a cue from her and nod sadly.

De Maupassant couldn't ride roughshod over expressions of grief. "Of course, of course, Ambassadors, how awful of me to talk pleasantries at such a trying time. Please call on me and my staff, however we might be needed. Now." He snapped his fingers, and one of his aides pushed a leather folio in front of him and opened it. He made a show of looking it over. "Clause one hundred and four…"

The last clause he'd tried to bring up at Dolores's final meeting. Adella counted to ten. When de Maupassant was still droning after that, she made it one hundred. She decided to let him go on for a little while. If he wanted to waste his own time, so be it. She could start planning Dolores's funeral in her head.

Or she could daydream about Bridget.

A bit of guilt rose at the thought, though Dolores would have much preferred the daydream. And besides, she couldn't write many funerary plans while De Maupassant babbled. She had a hard enough time keeping her expression neutral. If she allowed herself to write, he'd quickly realize she wasn't paying attention.

"That leads me to clause fifty-eight," he said.

Another that had already been decided, but she flipped through her pages obediently. The clause fell under the trading section and was about vegetables, of all things. The empire wanted to be Sarras's only source for some vegetables that didn't grow well in their native soil. It seemed the Firellians tried to tack on a new type at every meeting. De Maupassant clearly wanted them to buy more Firellian produce so they wouldn't buy from the Othlan Kingdom. Adella would have to consult Jean-Carlo later. He'd met the Othlan ambassador, had no doubt been to the Sarrasian embassy there. He'd know what the Othlans thought of these vegetable demands.

Adella watched de Maupassant for a few moments, her temper surprisingly in check now. It was much easier to remain calm if she didn't have to pay attention enough to take notes in the moment. Dolores had simply written up her thoughts afterward. Maybe that had been the secret of her serenity.

"…and other small gourds," de Maupassant said.

Gods and devils. Better to go back to the daydream. What was Bridget doing at that moment?

Still helping her friend, perhaps. Maybe the friend was moving, though surely that wouldn't crop up at the last minute. Maybe the friend had split from a lover or had a fight with family and needed a friendly shoulder.

As long as the shoulder wasn't too friendly.

Damned Zara.

Adella and Bridget hadn't pledged themselves only to each other, but Adella had no interest in sharing, especially if it involved lying via hastily written notes.

"And of course, pumpkins," de Maupassant said with a smile.

Adella smiled in return but offered no comment. How long would he go on with no encouragement?

She turned her thoughts to the good times she'd shared with Bridget, the kisses, the dance, the many touches, and the heat in Bridget's eyes that promised more. Adella would soon admit that her family had no money, then she'd set up an evening for Zara and Gisele to be out of the house. Gisele would smirk, but she'd play along and make sure Zara did, too, though that might result in a fight.

Gods, who cared as long as Adella got to have Bridget alone? Her sisters wouldn't kill each other, and Adella could patch them up later.

"…along the river," de Maupassant said. "Clause thirty-two—"

Adella gasped, stunned. The Kingfish River was the main avenue of trade between their countries. That had to be the river he meant. Her gasp set off a coughing fit, and all eyes turned to her. An aide topped off her water, and she tried to recall what exactly de Maupassant had said. If he wanted to do something along the river, it couldn't be anything good. It passed out of the mountains of the empire and flowed into Sarras on its way to the sea. It passed through some inhospitable countryside, heavily defended areas like the one Juno called home. History said the Firellians were always trying to find a way to get an army through.

"Are you well, Ambassador?" De Maupassant's greasy countenance was all concern.

Adella nodded, seeing a way she could get him to repeat himself. "Yes, thank you. But I'm afraid my fit interrupted you. Would you mind repeating the last thing you said, so my second can make sure his notes are accurate?"

Jean-Carlo, blessed by the gods, nodded eagerly and kept his pen poised over his papers.

De Maupassant smiled gracefully. "Of course. Changes to said clause would necessitate further stopping points along the river." When he smiled, she was forced to smile back gratefully.

Damn. She still didn't know what he was talking about and couldn't give him his gourds until she knew the rest of it. Anything he wanted to do to the river would not be in Sarras's best interest. This was no doubt the concession he was trying to sneak in that Dolores had feared. He'd lulled Adella into boredom, just like Dolores had suspected, and she'd fallen for it like a fool.

And now she was doing it again by getting caught up in guilt.

"…like peonies," de Maupassant said, "or orchids, perhaps, but we can revisit that at a later date." He glanced up, and his brow pinched with concern. "Are you sure you're all right, Ambassador? You've gone quite pale."

He oozed concern that she didn't believe for a moment, but she would use it if she could. "I think not," she said, putting a hand to her mouth. "I believe I feel a cold coming on." She coughed again.

He sat well back, and a look of distaste and fear passed over his face, though she would have bet her house that it wasn't for her. He worried for his own health, then. She could use that, too.

She coughed harder and took a long drink. "I hope not. I would never forgive myself if I passed an illness to you or your aides." She coughed over his words of gratitude, pressing a handkerchief to her mouth this time, then took the water pitcher from the aide with the hand she'd been coughing into.

"Forgive me, Ambassador," she said. "Would you care for some water?" She held it across the table.

"No…thank you." He scooted back a bit. "Perhaps we should reschedule."

"Must we?" she asked, hoping she looked stricken and not as if she was barely hiding her delight.

"You clearly need rest," he said as he stood. He waved before she could follow. "No, dear Ambassador, don't get up. Do not tax yourself." He bowed hastily and moved for the door. "We can reconvene when you are well and can correspond until then."

The aides opened the door where de Maupassant's sentinel escort waited, and they were gone so fast, the aides had their notes crumpled in their arms, and de Maupassant carried his own folio.

Adella sagged in her chair. Jean-Carlo wore a little smile but offered no commentary, another point in his favor. Even after Juno returned, she might ask him to stay on her staff.

She sighed as she stood. She could use Juno's council now that they would be discussing her homeland. "Let's go to my office, and you can fill me in on what I obviously missed."

"Serrah," he said, nodding. His expression was pleasant enough, too. It didn't seem to offer commentary either. He was earning all the points that day.

When they got to Adella's office, he revealed what de Maupassant's suggested new stops along the river were. "Waystations?" Adella asked as she toyed with her pen.

"Evidently, the empire wants to build small docks along the Kingfish River." He flipped a page. "On the Firellian side but close to Sarras, near the town of…Roundtop. According to the ambassador, farmers could then bring their produce directly to the river instead of having to go to a port city."

Adella tilted her head back and forth. "The produce would be fresher." She leaned back in Dolores's chair.

No, *her* chair.

Jean-Carlo nodded as he nibbled the end of his pen, a sign of deep thought, no doubt. It gave Adella further hope that he wasn't a spy. She would have expected those engaged in espionage to break themselves of all unconscious habits.

"They'd be able to charge more for fresher goods," he said.

Adella nodded, though she didn't trust that money was de Maupassant's ultimate goal. Jean-Carlo glanced at her, but she kept her thoughts inside. Juno should have been there. Adella could have shared her suspicions with someone she trusted.

"Would you like me to draft a letter to Ambassador de Maupassant?" Jean-Carlo asked.

"Hmm." She looked to the ceiling. What could the Firellians use these new waystations for? They had to know the Sarrasians would be watching.

"Serrah?" Jean-Carlo waited, pen poised.

"Um. Right." She had to make decisions, had to tell de Maupassant something. Give him his pumpkin monopoly? Deny it? For what reason? She could put him off about these waystations, but about the rest…she couldn't very well send him a letter flatly refusing all his proposed amendments and saying it was because she didn't like his oily hair and smile and beard. She shifted paper on her desk and tried to think.

But she had no idea what to say.

Gods and devils, she was failing at this job already. A jolt of panic froze her stomach, and her responsibilities pressed down on her like a wave. She wasn't ready for this. Everyone would know it soon, and de Maupassant would laugh at her, and her career would be over.

She tried to breathe. Why did fear of failure always come on like a mad bull?

The face of her family lawyer popped into her mind. After her parents had died, she'd confessed that she wasn't ready to be the head of a household with all its responsibilities and her two young sisters under her charge.

"My dear," he'd said with a kindly look. "You won't have to do it alone, I promise."

And she wasn't alone now, either. Dolores hadn't been alone. This office didn't have the authority to approve something like waystations on its own. Dolores would consult the minister of trade and probably defense. She would have spoken to the trade minister about the vegetable monopolies too, though the minister had trusted her to make small decisions. They'd known each other well.

And they were all on the same side.

Adella breathed deep of the air that still smelled of Dolores's cologne. "Draft letters to the ministers of trade and defense," she said, a burst of confidence thawing her insides. "Give them both the relevant points of de Maupassant's proposals. Leave room at the bottom for a personal note from me. We'll wait to write de Maupassant's letter until after we hear from the ministers."

"Very good, serrah," Jean-Carlo said, a proud gleam in his eye that made her feel even better. He bowed and made a quick exit.

She leaned back and sighed. She wasn't alone. The ministers would have heard of Dolores's death. No doubt they expected to hear from Dolores's replacement soon. Adella had never been so grateful that the empire did not allow foreign agents on their soil. She wouldn't have had the rest of her government down the hall in the empire.

And if Dolores had been killed there, no doubt Adella, Juno, and Cristoff would have been murdered, too.

Thanking the gods and the devils that she was home, Adella dived back into Dolores's personal papers, jotting down funeral plans as they occurred to her and finishing the letter to Dolores's sister.

When she found a dark, leather-bound book at the back of a drawer, she paused. A journal? Oh gods, not one part of Adella wanted to invade Dolores's privacy by reading her intimate thoughts. But if it contained something about the job or any meetings Dolores was anticipating on the evening of her murder…

Swallowing the lump in her throat, Adella retrieved the book and flipped to the last entries.

Names. Addresses. A few dates with notes. Adella breathed out. A correspondence book. She chuckled at herself. Of course. Someone who wrote to people as much as Dolores had would keep a record. Adella would have to start one of her own, and she saw no reason not to use the same book. It would keep Dolores with her a little while longer.

Her heart calming, she added the current date and wrote the names of the ministers of trade and defense, certain Jean-Carlo would finish the letters she'd assigned to him that day. She should add some simple notes, so she looked more closely at Dolores's last entry for clues about the sort of things she should include.

"Elena Garza," it read and was dated the day Dolores had died. An address in Roundtop, Juno's homeland, had been copied next to the date, with the word, "received," next to it.

Juno's mother.

Adella blinked as she remembered Dolores teasing Juno about this letter. The entries above it had dates marked with, "replied," following the received dates. Some had "sent" dates first if the correspondence had begun with Dolores.

So she hadn't replied to Juno's mother. Well, what did that matter? No doubt she hadn't had time.

Before being murdered.

With another frown, Adella searched the pile of mail on the desk. The letter from Elena Garza was missing. Curious. She'd just check the rest of the office, then she could get on with her day and put this minor mystery to bed.

But the letter wasn't anywhere to be found. Others had been recorded in the book. Adella added those from the last two days, just to make sure she'd gone through everything. Still no letter from Elena Garza. She nibbled her lip. Where had it gone? Gisele would have said something if it had been on Dolores's body.

Adella looked through the desk again. Dolores hadn't gone home before she'd died, so she hadn't taken the letter somewhere else. Perhaps she'd given it to Juno after Adella had left for the day.

Then why hadn't she noted that in the damn book when she carefully noted everything else?

Something more was going on.

Juno was missing.

And de Maupassant wanted to build waystations on the river, close to Roundtop, Juno's home. Elena Garza's home.

Adella rolled her eyes at herself. Coincidences.

Or…

What if Elena had seen something, heard something? Something so important that instead of writing to her daughter Juno, she'd written to the highest-level government official she'd heard of: Juno's boss's boss, Dolores, the ambassador to the country the Garza family helped defend against.

Adella's head spun. It seemed like a lot of connections to be a coincidence. Whatever Elena Garza had written might have gotten Dolores killed. Then the murderer had stolen the letter and had either killed or kidnapped Juno.

"No, not killed, please," Adella whispered, going cold again from dread. Why kill Juno if Dolores was dead, and the letter was in the killer's possession? Adella gnawed on her lip now. Well, who said

Elena Garza had written only to Dolores? Another letter could have been waiting at Juno's home.

And Elena Garza was in danger. If she wasn't dead already. Perhaps Juno had gone there to help her, fleeing too quickly to leave a note.

Adella sat up, determined to do something. She couldn't send troops, couldn't even request a scouting mission when all she had was suppositions. But she could write her own damn letter to Elena Garza, see if she was still alive, and find out what she knew and if Juno was there.

She grabbed a pen and paper. A week or so would give her more evidence.

Her heart felt a little lighter. The barest hint of a plan was better than no plan at all.

CHAPTER ELEVEN

Bridget knew of only one way to quickly find out all she could about Juno: romantic interest. She circulated among her fellow nightingales while sighing a lot and acting shy or coy. Any other kind of interest would have been met with suspicion. Anyone she spoke with who liked Juno would try to protect her. Anyone who didn't would have too many questions, seeking malicious gossip as payment for same.

But as a potential lover, those same people would try to build Juno up or tear her down, and both approaches contained information.

"What about your noblewoman?" one singer asked. "You caused a bit of a stir when you went to her on the Bastión steps."

Bridget shrugged. "When one finds true love, all else ceases to matter." She sighed again and hoped none of this came back to Adella before she could explain.

The singer shrugged. "I don't know much. She gave me a big tip one festival day, but that's all I can remember."

Unfortunately, that was the only type of answer Bridget had received so far. She wondered how many nobles and their friends realized that no titles or history mattered to gossip magnets like the nightingales as much as the cash they left behind.

But that didn't tell Bridget anything. She hadn't considered the possibility that Juno didn't have friends or enemies. It seemed she hadn't bothered to make either among the common folk. Maybe she hadn't found a way to use street performers. Yet.

"Sloppy," Baxter would have said. Everyone who passed through the square was marked by the nightingales, and people sometimes stopped to speak with them or forgot they were there and then gossiped within earshot.

But if Juno had done neither…

Bridget cursed and tried to think of another way to gather information. Adella had mentioned another aide, the one working under Dolores. She searched her memory and found him, her ability to retain information without really listening coming in handy again.

Cristoff.

Time for a change of tactics.

She kept the hopeful lover facade while searching for Cristoff instead. She kept her target the same—her preference for women was well-known—but she hinted that Cristoff was supposed to be helping her prove her love to Juno, but he'd vanished.

She finally struck gold.

A friendly, good-looking, generous man was well remembered by a group of people who appreciated all those attributes. It helped that he'd passed through the square at least twice a day, and that he'd asked—and tipped—many a nightingale for recommendations on where to make purchases requested by his boss, Dolores Vega, the murdered ambassador, a woman of specific and expensive tastes.

Such conversations had often stretched to other matters, like Cristoff's own likes and dislikes and the places he'd frequented. The sentinels had spoken to a few nightingales already but not all of them. And there were some things they wouldn't tell the law.

Through Dolores, Cristoff appeared to have acquired a taste for the finer things in life, but he didn't have the cash his boss possessed. He'd stayed away from money lenders, but he'd begun to buy from what most people referred to as "less established dealers," code for smugglers. And some were as dangerous as the lenders.

Bridget didn't press for names. She even faked a shudder at the idea of getting involved with such people. She eagerly agreed with anyone who cautioned her to steer well clear of them. They didn't need to know that such people were her next target and that she didn't need names since she knew the goods Cristoff fancied. And she already knew that smugglers operated out of the Tides, the name given to the docks.

Gods and devils, all that water. Freezing in the river flashed through her memory, and she shuddered, her mouth going dry. She breathed deep and forced herself to relax. The smugglers wouldn't be *in* the water.

She made herself think about Cristoff again. A smuggler could be behind his disappearance—one hell of a coincidence—or they might be able to help Bridget trace his last steps. Alive or dead, he could help her find out more about Juno.

By the devils, if she could prove Juno had killed two people, she might be able to paint Juno as a maniac who told twisted lies, calling anything Juno said into question.

At the end of it all, even Baxter might not have been able to figure out what to believe. Bridget didn't know whether to be ashamed or proud of herself. That was becoming the story of her life.

By the time she'd collected her information and performed enough songs to allay suspicion, evening was upon her, and she had a shopping trip to do for Juno.

But she'd also promised to walk Adella home.

Well, Juno had told her to act as she normally would. And Juno wouldn't betray one of her few assets just because said asset was a little late.

Hopefully.

To be on the safe side, Bridget ran across the square to a row of shops to get Juno's items and paid a damn sight too much in this area of town, but the expense was worth it to be right where Adella expected when she got off work.

Adella seemed tired but happy, and Bridget repeated her vow to show her there was more to life than work. After *her* old work was no longer trying to kill her.

"Good day?" Bridget asked after they kissed their hellos. She let herself revel in the tingles that spread through her chest at even the briefest of contact.

"Yes and no." Adella smiled sheepishly. They began to stroll toward her house, and she bit her lip and played with the edges of her cloak.

Bridget sensed she was desperate to talk when she probably shouldn't. More than one target had been the same. And even though she damned Baxter and his training, Bridget needed information, and anything Adella knew might end up being relevant.

"You can talk to me," Bridget said softly. "I know what people say about nightingales being gossips, but we can keep a confidence when asked." Her teeth ached to use spy tricks, to imply that if Adella didn't speak, she was calling Bridget and her peers untrustworthy gossips…which was rather true. But it was also true that she meant what she'd said, and though that didn't excuse her behavior, it did explain it, and—

Baxter would have growled and said, "Shut up and listen. You can berate yourself later."

Luckily, Adella waited a few more moments, nibbling on her delectable lips. "Well, I was able to put the Firellian ambassador off for a bit by pulling some ministers into our discussion." She said it quickly, like a warning shot. Bridget waited for the real volley.

"He's up to something," Adella said, "and I know that's what I should be focused on. That or Dolores's funeral, which I did make some headway on." She paused.

"Good," Bridget said. "Well done."

Adella gave her a soft smile. "Not easy when I was distracted."

"By the ambassador?" Gods and devils, getting her to open up felt like pushing a cart out of the mud, but Bridget kept her face neutral.

"Oh, to hell with it. Gisele will tell me not to talk about the murder, but you're my…we're…" She blushed.

Bridget couldn't help a grin, briefly torn between having information and exploring what they were to each other. She stayed quiet.

Adella smiled brightly. "A piece of Dolores's mail has gone missing, a letter from Juno's mother in Roundtop, on the Firellian border. I think she might have seen something happening at the border and then told Dolores. Possibly. Then maybe Dolores was killed for it, and…perhaps Juno is in trouble as well. Maybe Cristoff is, too, if Juno told him." She paused after the burst of words, her smile gone as she seemed to realize how much conjecture she had with all of her use of possibly and maybe and perhaps.

At least she was imagining Juno in the thick of it, if on the wrong side of things.

Still, there was this mysterious letter. Its contents could have prompted Juno to kill Dolores. If so, Juno would have destroyed it.

Unless Dolores had hidden it.

A prize indeed.

"What do you think?" Adella asked, nerves heavy in her voice.

"You never saw the letter?"

"The contents, no, but I saw it unopened. Dolores had laughed about it. She thought Juno's mother was writing to her boss's boss to bemoan the fact that Juno doesn't write home enough."

Bridget's mind raced. Juno was a spy. Even if for some reason, her mother was living on the Sarrasian side of the border, nagging her to write home, the letter shouldn't have contained any information she would kill for. Baxter would have had Juno cut ties with her family or use them if she really was a traitor, and if she was using them...

Bridget sighed. There were too many things she didn't know.

"Does that sigh mean you think I'm right or crazy?" Adella asked. The lip biting was back.

Bridget stopped and cupped Adella's chin. "Please don't chew your lip off. It would hurt, and we wouldn't be able to kiss."

Adella's blush reappeared, and her eyes flicked to Bridget's mouth. "Perish the thought." She tilted her head up to kiss Bridget softly, sweetly, and Bridget wanted to tell her everything, but Juno's warnings rang in her ears. Juno might have other allies. All cities played host to those who'd do violence for coin, even killing a noble. Getting to know some local thugs had been one of Baxter's spy tips.

And she couldn't forget that the Sarrasian authorities would hang Juno and Bridget side by side. They would never believe someone could retire from being a spy, and Bridget couldn't expect Adella to keep such a secret from her spy-hunting sister.

They began walking again, hand-in-hand. "I don't think you're crazy," Bridget said. "You just need more information."

"Well, I'll have it soon. I wrote to Juno's mother."

Bridget's belly went cold, but she forced her voice to be calm. "What did you write?"

Adella shrugged. "I asked what was in her last letter and warned her there might be danger. I had to admit I didn't know where Juno had gone, but I said such a resourceful woman was probably safe."

Resourceful? Bridget nearly barked a laugh. "Aren't you worried such a letter makes you a target as well?"

"Are you worried about me?" She gave Bridget's hand a squeeze.

"After what happened to your predecessor? Yes."

Adella shook her head. "No one knows I wrote a letter but you, and by the time I receive a reply, Gisele will have caught the killer."

Bridget wanted to weep. Why did all the gods and devils hate her so? Maybe getting Juno out of Sarras as quickly as possible was the way to go.

Until Juno told the empire where Bridget was hiding. If they didn't know already. And whether they knew before or would find out from Juno, once they had used her, they'd do so again.

And again and again.

Until they finally killed her.

She should have let the river have her all those months ago.

"Hey," Adella said, her brows drawn. "I'm sorry if I worried you. I will be all right."

No doubt Dolores had thought the same. An earlier thought resurfaced. If Adella could put together a case against Juno with only a little prodding from Bridget, they could convince the Sarrasian authorities that Juno was lying when she eventually named Bridget a spy. It would carry a lot of weight coming from a noble.

It was one more thing she'd have to apologize for in the future, but for now, it was a plan. And during such a plan, Bridget was certain she could convince Adella to employ extra protection. Juno wasn't the only one who'd made a few friends of the thuggish persuasion.

Baxter would have been proud, the smug little shit.

Bridget kissed Adella lightly before walking again. "I am worried, but that wasn't what I was thinking about. I heard a rumor once about Cristoff. I'd forgotten it until now, but I think I should follow it up."

❖

By the time Adella got home, she was so excited, she could barely keep from jumping about. Bridget, lovely ingenious Bridget, had remembered a rumor she'd heard that Cristoff liked bootleg luxury items, the finer foods, wines, and whatever else Dolores had enjoyed but at a fraction of the cost because they were smuggled or stolen.

And she knew where the people who sold them could be found. And *those* people might be able to give them a clue as to Cristoff's whereabouts. And if they found him, they'd be closer to finding Juno, maybe even to finding the murderer.

Adella had gripped Bridget's hand and had asked about finding those people tonight, but Bridget had seemed to think it safer during the day, and Adella had bowed to her superior knowledge.

Well, Adella assumed she had superior knowledge, which was her unconscious bias at work again. She took a deep breath inside her foyer and told herself Bridget was probably using common sense. The day no doubt proved to be safer where most things were concerned.

Before they'd parted, Adella had promised to try to recall anything she could about Cristoff's preferences, and Bridget had said she'd ask around. They'd planned to meet at lunch tomorrow and formulate a plan. Adella grinned.

She was going to meet *smugglers*.

She might get to wear *trousers*.

It was all far more exciting than it had any right to be given its proximity to tragedy.

Clasping her hands, she squealed a little anyway, nearly as pleased with the idea of adventure as she'd been with the many kisses she and Bridget had exchanged on the way home.

"Is that you, Del?" Gisele called from upstairs.

"Yes." She hung her cloak up. "Want some cocoa?" Silence answered her for a few moments. "Gisele?"

"Can I have mine upstairs?" The words were softer, embarrassed, strained.

Adella told herself not to panic, to proceed normally instead of taking two steps at a time. But that was the closest Gisele would come to saying she couldn't make it down the stairs. It didn't mean she was curled up on the floor in agony. It didn't make her like Dolores, clawing at the carpet even in death.

Adella bit back a curse and forced herself to walk to Gisele's bedroom, wanting to avoid the irritated words that would follow any fussing on her part.

Gisele looked tiny sitting in the middle of her bed. Her tincture lay un-stoppered and empty by her blanket-covered knees. She had another throw across her shoulders, and she'd only taken half her hair down. Her pale, tear-stained face shone in the light of the open window. She gave a smile and a little wave, wincing as she did and clutching a handkerchief in her fist.

Adella's heart ached as she forced her own tears down, took off her boots, and climbed onto the bed.

"You'll wrinkle your gown," Gisele said.

"The devils can take my gown and iron it, too."

Gisele snickered, then sighed when Adella began taking down the rest of her hair. "I didn't lose it until I got to my dressing table. Then I knew I had enough energy to either finish my hair or climb into bed, and that was it."

Adella kept her touch gentle, guiding Gisele to lean back against her. "You chose wisely. The dressing table would be very uncomfortable to lie on."

Gisele chuckled again before uttering a small noise of pain.

Words of censure would not be welcome, so Adella bit them back. She was not Zara. This was Gisele's chosen path, her pain, her life. "Want to tell me about it?"

"I did some complicated magic, a kind used only when a murder case has run out of clues. I've only done it once before."

"You did it now for Dolores?" Guilt replaced her anger like the tide washing away footprints. "You shouldn't—"

"I didn't do it for you," Gisele said sullenly. "Well…sort of. But I would have done it anyway because it needed to be done." She shifted as if trying to turn.

Adella stopped her. "Save your energy for telling your story."

After another sigh, Gisele said, "It's called a corpse walk."

"Very cheerful name."

"Ha. Ha. Sometimes, the undertakers can't see the very small things that happened to…a body."

Adella wanted to say, "Dolores," but she didn't. She worked the last hairpin free and tried to rub some of the tension from Gisele's shoulders.

Gisele's head lolled forward. "A mage can sort of…go through a body. I don't know quite how to explain it. We look for things that shouldn't be there."

Like big knife holes, but Adella didn't say that either. "But it isn't done for every murder case?"

"The mages who can do it are few, and only some of us are willing, and we can't do it often." She shuddered, and even that small movement caused a whimper. It was no wonder even the highest agencies in Sarras only *asked* mages to ply their trade. Commanding them would be like ordering someone to step into a fire, or so Adella imagined.

She hugged Gisele gently. "I'm so sorry, Gilly."

Gisele patted her hand, but she also said, "Don't call me that. I'm not a baby."

"You'll always be my baby sister. Don't make me prove it by cuddling you more while you're too weak to resist."

"Monster."

They both chuckled, but Adella didn't make good on her threat or pull out the childhood nickname again. She braced herself before she asked, "Did you find anything?"

Gisele was quiet for a few moments, but she had to have known Adella would ask.

"I can take it," Adella said quietly, hoping that was true. "I promise, no breakdowns."

"Small damage to her wrists and feet," Gisele said quickly, as if purging the information. "The undertaker had spotted the wrists already. She'd thought it was from grappling with an attacker, but I think Dolores was bound. And the feet…"

Adella's horror was mounting, moving through her like a chill cloud. She made herself sit still, waiting.

"Small holes between her toes and under her toenails. Our sentinel liaison said he'd heard of such things before."

"Torture." Adella wasn't able to keep the shock from her words, but she kept her promise and didn't weep or become sick. Oh gods, Dolores.

"More popular in some countries than others."

"The Firellian Empire." It all came back to them. Adella forced her horror into anger, kindling it and letting it burn.

"Among others." Gisele turned her head slightly. "Don't rush to a conclusion."

"I'm not. There are far too many fingers pointed their way for any conclusion to be considered a rush." And she'd add Gisele's pain to her anger over Dolores's death, Dolores's *torture*, by the gods. Once the cold-hearted, murderous beast had been found, she'd help send them to the devils herself.

"Del?"

Adella shook herself. She gave Gisele's shoulders a final pat. "I'll bring you a cocoa." At the door, she turned to find Gisele watching her timidly, an expression she rarely wore. "I'm sorry you had to go through that, sweetheart. I thank you for it, and I don't ever want you to forget how proud I am of you, of your accomplishments."

Gisele smiled, her beauty showing through the drawn expression and the dark smudges under her eyes. She looked away and muttered, "Love you," the words smashed together and nearly lost.

Still, Adella beamed. "I love you, too." She waited until she was a few steps from the door before she added, "Gilly."

A brief squawk of protest followed her down the hall, but it had laughter in it, too, a sound Adella would no doubt need to hold on to through dark deeds to come.

CHAPTER TWELVE

Juno gave the items she'd requested a short inspection before laying them aside. "What else have you got for me?"

Bridget had been piecing a fake escape plan together all day. Juno's implication that she had other associates in the city might be true, or it might be bluster, but Bridget didn't want to take too many chances. She needed to skirt the truth. "I'm investigating smuggling as an option. Even if we can't find someone suitable to take you, smugglers know their way around officials and patrols."

Juno nodded slowly. "That might require considerable funds."

"Do you have them? I certainly don't." That was the truth, at least. Bridget did all right to live on and had a bit of money saved, but she couldn't afford to live anywhere but at the Donkey, where she got a deep discount for playing. And even then, she had to share.

Juno regarded her quietly for a few moments, and Bridget tried hard to read her expression. It was fairly closed off, but a bit of tightening around the eyes coupled with her talk of money in the first place implied that she didn't have much either.

"Are you saying you wouldn't be able to acquire the needed funds?" Juno asked with a smirk.

"I'd have to steal them, and I doubt you'd want to attract that kind of attention to someone who's…helping you."

An evil glint appeared in Juno's eye. It turned Bridget's stomach. "You walked Adella home today, did you not?"

The change of subject was no doubt meant to confuse her, maybe intimidate her, but she knew it still came back to money. "There is no way I could ask her for cash without arousing suspicion."

A slow blink said she'd managed to put Juno a little off her stride. She clearly had to hide her frustration and give herself time to set a new course. "I'm sure you could manufacture a reasonable excuse."

"You know her sister is a spy hunter?"

"What of it?"

Bridget forced a relaxed pose and shrugged when she was so tired of this dance, she could scream. "They're close. The sister would find out about any financial requests. Do you want a spy hunter becoming suspicious of her sister's new friend? She could easily follow me to you."

"Friend?" The smirk returned.

Gods, to be able to throttle her. "It's one easy step from me to you."

"Oh, all right," Juno said with a sigh. "We can leave Adella out of it. Unless you betray me, then she'll have to die."

Throttle her, pitch her out the window, and stuff her in a rain barrel for good measure. Only Bridget's vow to stop killing allowed her to keep her expression neutral.

When Juno sighed again with a touch of exasperation, Bridget thought she must have succeeded at being inexpressive. "Look into your smugglers," Juno said.

"And the cash problem?"

"Stop fishing and get out."

Bridget did so, happy to follow that order. So Juno didn't have much ready money, and she couldn't walk into a counting house using the name Juno, not with the sentinels watching for her. No doubt she had more aliases at her disposal, and now that Juno had the means to disguise herself, she might attempt to retrieve some funds under one of those names, something Bridget couldn't do for her without the appropriate identifying papers. Even with them, they looked nothing alike, and there was always a chance one of the employees would remember Juno's face.

Whatever her situation or her reasons, Juno would be slowed by a lack of money, and that was reason enough to be happy for the moment.

At the Donkey's Rest, the evening was just winding up when Bridget arrived. Videl was slated to play that night, so Bridget took a seat at the bar and nursed a gin and ginger, putting off having to go upstairs to plan and worry.

Serrah Nunez paused across from her and tapped her lacquered nails on the bar top. She wore her green and blue wig, the one bearing several enameled clips that resembled tentacles rising from the depths of her hair. "Long day, marshmallow?" She'd painted her eyelids and lips to match her wig, and the rest of her face, neck, and décolletage sparkled and shone as if dusted with crushed pearls. "Don't tell me you've had a spat with your lady love."

"No, all is well there. I walked her home tonight."

Serrah Nunez's eyes widened. "Do tell. I'm guessing last night went well, too. You rushed out this morning before I could ask."

Happy to sink into that memory, Bridget smiled. "We danced, we kissed."

Serrah Nunez put a hand to her bosom. "Oh, tell me more, treacle. You're doing my old heart a power of good."

Bridget sputtered on her drink. Serrah Nunez didn't usually discuss her age, but she hardly looked old. "You're still in the first blush of youth, serrah. I won't hear a word otherwise."

"No wonder you make all the ladies swoon, you yummy little custard cake." She winked and set another drink on the bar. "That deserves a second gin on the house. Now, tell me what's next for you and your lady."

Bridget took a sip, glad to feel normal again if only for a few moments, before she had to go from a woman beginning a romance to an ex-spy up to her neck in bother. "We're meeting for lunch tomorrow."

"Then you should have had a smile on your face from the moment you arrived."

But she couldn't smile, not when her thoughts were back to her troubles. "I have to help her with a problem, and it might get tricky." She sighed, knowing she should have said nothing, but depression and alcohol were making her chatty.

Or maybe she was getting used to just blurting things out. It was much better than never saying anything out of fear of blowing her cover.

Serrah Nunez leaned closer, bringing the scent of cloves and oranges. "Tricky how?" She radiated genuine concern.

The bar was filling up. Bridget only had to stall a few moments, and Serrah Nunez would be carried away by work. But she knew a great many people. She might be able to give Bridget a start for her smuggling investigation.

"And you can trust her," Baxter seemed to say, which was just her experience in reading people piping up.

"She's trying to find a friend of hers," Bridget said. "Someone who was caught up with smugglers. She's going to tell me all she knows tomorrow, and I'm going to the Tides to investigate."

Serrah Nunez's gaze went far away for a moment. Bridget couldn't help but smile at her sea-inspired ensemble again. Maybe that was a sign from the gods that Bridget was on the right track. "A good place to start, truffle, but don't tell me you're going on your own."

"Well, my noble lady friend is certainly not coming with me." She thought back to their conversation and frowned. Gods and devils, she hoped Adella wasn't thinking they'd go together. With all her frippery, Adella would stand out like a dog in a tree.

"Well, I've known a few smugglers in my time, even though I'm still in my first blush." Serrah Nunez winked again. "I can help you."

"Oh…great." Bridget smiled, waiting for a list of names, but a sense of dread was growing inside her. She forged ahead. "You can just tell me the names. No need to write them down or anything. I'll remember."

"No need at all, sugar. I'll come with you."

The dread reached fruition. "You're…"

"Coming with."

The wigs, the paint, the elaborate dresses? If Adella was a dog in a tree, Serrah Nunez was a horse on a roof. Bridget couldn't think of anything to say.

Serrah Nunez smiled wryly and tapped Bridget's chin with one finger. "Close your mouth, cinnamon bun. I'll dress down for the occasion." She shrugged one elegant shoulder. "In my way. I'll meet you at the corner of Market Street and the wharf at thirteen bells, just after you finish what is sure to be a delicious lunch with your delectable companion. Don't be late." She sailed away to mingle with her customers.

Bridget was still trying to catch up, wondering how long Serrah Nunez planned to stay with her tomorrow past smuggler introductions, how Adella was going to react to the news of someone else accompanying Bridget in her stead, and exactly what dressing down meant. She drained her glass in one long, burning gulp before heading upstairs to think.

And pray.

❖

Adella was distracted all the next morning. She didn't yet have a reply from the ministers of trade and defense about the threat of Firellian treachery, but the oligarchs' birthday celebration was right around the corner. Business always slowed this time of year as everyone daydreamed about having several days off in a row.

Fiddling with her pen at her desk, Adella wondered how much of the festivities she'd be able to spend with Bridget. Like food sellers and barkeeps, nightingales worked during the holidays, and Adella didn't want to deprive Bridget of the chance to earn coin. Maybe Adella could help her by putting some money in her case to get her started. Or by guilting anyone she knew who passed by.

Better the second option. She didn't have much coin to spare. Maybe that would be a good way to admit to Bridget that her family wasn't as affluent as they seemed. An offhand remark about not having much to start Bridget's tip jar could save her from a lengthy explanation.

Or it could prompt one.

Adella sighed as she sat back in her chair, tired of her pride for once. Tired of lying. Zara would say it was none of Bridget's business, but Adella hated the idea of falsehoods between them, even those of omission.

When a knock sounded on her door, she jumped a little before laughing at herself. Clearly, part of her subconscious was still lingering on murder and torture. "Come in." She didn't relax until Jean-Carlo popped his head around the door.

"A note for you, serrah." He laid it on her desk. "And the Mistress of Clocks has some potential aides to interview. Do you wish to do it personally, or shall I attend to it?"

"Let's both do it," Adella said as she cracked the wax on the note. "We both need one, after all."

He brightened, and she realized she'd as good as said she wanted to hire him full-time. Well, he was personable and seemed like a hard worker, but Juno might still come back. Adella sighed again and supposed she'd deal with that when it happened.

Like so many things lately.

She smiled and nodded, and Jean-Carlo beamed back at her. Gods, she hoped he didn't turn out to be something awful, like a Firellian spy.

Inside the Bastión? Preposterous.

"Have the candidates come in late this afternoon," she said. She might be able to focus then. He bowed and left with a spring in his step.

The note was a simple one from Dolores's lawyer, saying they'd received notice of her death and would be in touch when they had the paperwork sorted out. She was glad to see something was progressing. She hadn't yet heard from Dolores's sister, but she didn't expect that until tomorrow at the earliest since she lived in a small town outside the city. Adella wanted to settle on a date for the funeral, and she couldn't wait too long. Especially now that Gisele seemed finished with her investigation in that quarter.

Even after she heard from the sister, Adella did not look forward to having a firm date. More than anything else, it meant Dolores's life was done, marked in stone and left to history.

But weren't they all?

"Gods and devils," she muttered to herself. Her emotions were all over the room today. And she had a good deal more life to think about.

For instance, soon she'd change into the trousers she'd borrowed from Zara—accepting the risk that she might love them too much to return to gowns—and go meet Bridget and some random smugglers. She was glad Zara's trousers were there instead of Zara. She'd probably try to arrest the smugglers in the name of the oligarchs' army, even though that wasn't what an army was for.

When Adella couldn't stand the excitement any longer, she ducked out of her office, told Jean-Carlo she had some errands to run before lunch, then went into the cloakroom to change. Her hands shook as she got undressed, and she had trouble doing up the trousers and tying the shirt at the throat and wrists. She put on a short coat, then threw her cloak over all of it so no one would see her outfit as she exited the Bastión. After a deep breath to settle her nerves, she left her carefully folded gown in a cubby in the cloakroom and stepped outside wearing trousers for the first time in her memory.

She felt so…light, almost as if she wasn't wearing anything. In public.

She drew the cloak tighter around her. Her coat barely covered her backside. When she took the cloak off, everyone would be able to see it. *Bridget* would be able to see it. Her memory of how tight the trousers had looked in the mirror at home multiplied tenfold. She was curvier than Zara. What if everyone could see…everything?

Adella forced herself to move to the side of the busy Bastión steps and breathe. The trousers had been a little snug at home, but it wasn't as if she'd needed assistance to get into them. They weren't *that* tight. And now that she thought about it, her backside being admired by Bridget wouldn't be a bad thing.

With some of her confidence returned, she hurried down the steps and across the square, slowing when she reached the edge of a group who'd stopped to listen to Bridget play and sing. Another singer had joined her, a soprano whose higher tones mixed well with Bridget's deeper voice. They crooned a love song that had the audience enthralled. Adella couldn't even be jealous as they leaned close to one another and sang a tale of two lovers separated by fate. The song was so lovely, it made her stop obsessing about funerals and smugglers and her outfit.

When the lovers found each other at last in the realm of the gods, goose bumps broke out on Adella's arms, and she clapped along with everyone else. Bridget thanked the singer with a smile, but her face lit up when she met Adella's eyes. Warmth ran through her. As long as they were together, everything would be all right.

The audience and the other singer moved away, and Adella couldn't help putting her arms around Bridget's neck and pulling her into a kiss, strangers be damned. Bridget returned the kiss with a passion that sent shivers down Adella's spine. "That was beautiful," Adella said when they parted. "I'm so proud to know you."

A tinge of pink came to Bridget's cheeks, and her brows rose. "Because of the song or the kiss?"

Adella gave her another peck. "Both."

"Well, thank you." She ducked her head as she packed up her mandolin. As she straightened from her crouch, she froze and stared at Adella's legs, and a look like horror came over her face.

Adella glanced down at where her cloak stood open. Gods, her trousers were too tight, and worse, Bridget hadn't liked what she'd seen. Adella's cheeks burned as she pulled the cloak closed again and looked for somewhere to hide, but the whole damned square was open. Unless she wanted to dive into the fountain.

"So you are planning on going, I take it?" Bridget asked.

Her words barely made it through Adella's mortification, but she stopped trying to find somewhere to run and tried to understand. "What?"

"Your…unusual clothing. Well, unusual for you." She took Adella's hand, and her smile seemed apologetic. "Not that I mind something that shows off your legs. But, Adella, this could be dangerous."

Her trousers were dangerous? Was there some quality to them no one had warned her about? It was nice to hear Bridget liked her body instead of being horrified by it, but—

The words coupled with the situation and made sense at last. Going from embarrassment to relief to irritation was enough to make her head spin. "I'm coming with you to the Tides. You can't go alone. What if that was what Cristoff did only to meet with disaster?"

"Ah, you would have both of us be in danger instead."

"Yes." She worked to keep her temper in check and remember that negotiating was her job. As long as personal feelings didn't get in the way. But they always seemed to be in the way. Especially now. She took a deep breath. "Two people make a more difficult target. And if it comes to it, I can always reveal my status to any attackers.

It isn't fair, but accosting a noble attracts more attention than other crimes."

Bridget's mouth quirked up. "At least you acknowledge that it's not fair. And I will admit that being able to threaten someone with the sentinels would be a nice perk." She leaned close. "But for the sentinels to become involved, they'd have to *find* our bodies."

Adella shivered. Bridget was right. Juno and Cristoff had both been from families of rank, just a step away from nobility, and they'd vanished like early morning fog. She shook her head. "The fact remains that I cannot wait here while you go alone."

"Let's talk over food." Bridget led the way toward the side of the square where a group of vendors waited, though Adella didn't have much of an appetite. Nor would she be swayed by some treat like almonds roasted with cinnamon and sugar, no matter how delicious they smelled.

"I won't be alone," Bridget said. "Serrah Nunez, who owns the Donkey's Rest, is acquainted with"—she glanced around—"some of the people we're seeking. She's coming along."

Adella thought back to their evening at the bar, and the colorful woman sailed into memory. She scoffed. "With her coming, I needn't have bothered to change."

Bridget grinned. "She promised to tone it down. And you can put your gown back on after lunch because you don't need to come."

Adella fought the urge to stomp. The sound of her boot coming down hushed her sisters but would make her look petulant now. She lined up her arguments. "Three is even better than two."

"Adella—"

"I can walk with you or follow you. Your choice."

"Look—"

"You don't own the street. You can't stop me."

"But—"

"If it's safe enough for you and Serrah Nunez, it's safe enough for me." She tilted her head. "I can argue all day, but neither of us wants that."

Bridget sighed hugely and rubbed the bridge of her nose. Adella fought the urge to celebrate.

"You'll do as I bid?" Bridget said. "Keep quiet when I say?"

"Absolutely." Probably.

"And if I tell you to run? Even if I have to linger to cover our retreat?"

She nodded slowly. She could do that. Very probably. "I'll run for the nearest constabulary." When Bridget looked skeptical, Adella added, "I will admit that, during an altercation, I am best suited to fetching reinforcements." Almost absolutely probably.

Bridget seemed satisfied if not pleased. "Well, if you're coming, you'd better put your jewels and your ambassador's badge in your pocket until you need them to convince the thief catchers to come pull my fat out of the fire."

Adella's cheeks burned again as she did as Bridget asked. How could she have forgotten something so obvious? "Just making sure you were paying attention."

Bridget snorted a laugh. "Let's hope the constables don't accuse you of theft instead of believing your station." She kissed Adella's cheek. "Now, we should put something in our bellies to give us the energy we'll need to run for our lives."

"Cinnamon sugar almonds, just the job." Adella led the way to the cart before the smell drove her crazy.

Chapter Thirteen

They reached the wharf and Market Street just as thirteen bells tolled around town. Bridget tried to relax, but she'd never spent a lot of time in the Tides, and she was afraid they stood out. Adella had been gawking at everything. Even without the expensive cloak she now carried over her arm, she stuck out. At least they'd been able to leave the mandolin with Videl, or they would have been even more conspicuous.

Adella beamed at the bustling docks beyond the river wall and the tall masts of the ships sitting close. Those that waited their turn to dock bobbed out on the Kingfish River, far wider here then up in the mountains where Bridget had first climbed into it.

She shivered again at the memory, happy the river wall stood between them and the water. A deep breath of the cool air coming off the river calmed her and carried the faint scent of fish from the market, which sat in front of where the docks for the larger ships gave way to smaller piers where fishing boats, pleasure craft, guide boats, and sentinel launches tied up.

Someone cleared their throat, and Bridget turned. A tall, thin person leaned against the back of a warehouse with one trouser-clad leg crossed over the other at the ankle. A dark coat covered them from the neck to the knee, and when they stepped into the light, Bridget noticed that the jacket was burgundy velvet with silver buttons. A diamond broach shone from their right shoulder, and more sparkle came from the silver head of a dark wooden walking stick held in one long-fingered, beringed hand.

The rings led Bridget to peer at the face, and she couldn't help a gasp.

Serrah Nunez still wore a hint of paint around her eyes, and she'd done something to her cheeks that made her face sharper. A pair of round, blue-tinted spectacles couldn't darken the sparkle in her eyes as she smirked. She touched a hand to her forehead, just below where her short brown locks lay artfully curled. "It's been a while since I went with this look, but I've always been fluid in my dress." She shrugged and chuckled. "Among other things. Do close your mouth, pudding."

"Amazing," Bridget said, envying the ability to make any set of clothing look good. "You truly are a work of art, serrah." As Serrah Nunez waved the comment away, Bridget turned. "Adella, this is Serrah Nunez. She owns the Donkey's Rest. Serrah, Adella."

They bowed to one another. "Charmed," Serrah Nunez said. "But let's go with 'he' for the duration of our little adventure. It's how I'm known down here." He twirled the walking stick up to rest on one shoulder. "As well as a few other places."

"Whatever you say, serrah," Bridget said, as charmed as always. "One must keep some mysteries to oneself."

Serrah Nunez grinned. "Well said."

"It's wonderful to meet you," Adella said. "Thank you for keeping an eye on Bridget."

Serrah Nunez put a hand on his chest. "My pleasure, treacle. I did wonder if you would insist on coming. You two are scrumptious together." He offered his arm. Adella linked hers with it, and they began to stroll like old friends and not people currently taking the air in a place that smelled of fish and waterlogged wood.

Bridget frowned when she realized the surrounding noise of crowds, ships, and birds prevented her from hearing what they were talking about. After all, she was the common factor between them. She caught up quickly, took Adella's cloak, and grasped Adella's free hand. "What are we talking about?" she asked with a grin she hoped looked nonchalant.

Serrah Nunez gave her a knowing smile, and Adella said, "Fashion. He has some wonderful ideas about opulent trousers."

"More than anyone else, I'd wager," Bridget said, wondering what she wanted such a thing for.

Serrah Nunez winked. "It's all in where to shop."

The talk of shopping provided a nice distraction for Bridget's nerves, but she kept her eyes open. Most people on the docks went swiftly about their business. She spotted a few people lingering in the shadows of nearby warehouses. Raucous noise came from one narrow lane where the sign of a net and anchor swayed in the stiff breeze coming off the river. In the distance, large warehouses gave way to smaller buildings and shanties just before the stalls of the fish market began.

Serrah Nunez led the way to a narrow set of stairs that connected the top of the river wall to the lower docks. Bridget stumbled at the sudden sight of water. The path at the bottom of the river wall was a simple floating pier while the pillars of the high docks loomed behind them. She'd be inches from the water, a foot at most.

"Are you okay?" Adella said. Serrah Nunez had pulled ahead slightly, already walking down the narrow stairs.

"I...I'm not that comfortable with water." She swallowed, her throat tight with fear that wanted to become panic.

"I won't let you fall." Adella smiled softly, her eyes caring. "If you want to wait here—"

And send Adella into danger alone? "No, I'm...I'll be okay." She walked down with wooden legs, her hand on Adella's shoulder until they reached the pier itself.

When the pier lifted and fell slightly under their feet, Bridget clung to Adella's hand and whispered a prayer to the gods and even a promise to the devils, pledging devotion if they'd keep her out of the water.

Serrah Nunez had paused ahead, head cocked. Adella looked a little pale, and Bridget felt entirely too pleased that she wasn't the only one having trouble.

When Adella shivered, Bridget said, "Here, put this on." She swung the cloak around Adella's shoulders as they began walking again.

Adella shook her head. "The gold embroidery will give me away."

She was probably right, but it wasn't as if the people they were going to see were shy of money. Still, better to be safe than sorry. Smugglers weren't the only miscreants who made their homes down here.

And worrying about Adella was giving Bridget something to focus on besides the dark gray waters of the Kingfish River.

"Let's turn it inside out," Bridget said, draping it that way over Adella's shoulders. "We're lucky the lining is plain."

Adella looked away. "It's been replaced since my mother's time."

The sadness in her voice was no doubt from the fact that she was an orphan. Bridget sympathized. And it spoke of both sentimentality and frugality that she continued to wear a fine cloak that had belonged to someone she cared about. Bridget caressed her neck, wanting to kiss her, but some sort of fishing bird cried out, and Bridget nearly jumped out of her skin.

"It used to be silk," Adella said softly.

Whatever material it was now, it certainly wasn't silk, though the mint color was close to matching the finer exterior. And it was nicer to stare at than the people bustling about on their boats as if the water wasn't waiting hungrily to claim them. "Oh?"

"But I didn't have any silk."

"I see." Bridget frowned. Adella seemed nervous all of a sudden, not really looking at anything. Bridget squeezed her hand, wondering if the motion was still upsetting her. "We'll be all right."

Adella bit her lip. "You don't understand. I'm not—"

Serrah Nunez turned again and waited for them to catch up. "See the fishing boat near the end? With the green pilot house?"

Bridget found it easily, a small craft with one mast, the sail currently furled and the deck piled with nets. "Your contact?"

"*Tsk*. My acquaintance. Now, you don't know exactly what your friend was looking for last time he came down here, correct?"

Bridget listed off the items Cristoff was rumored to favor, those she'd discovered from the other nightingales. Adella supplied a description of him.

Serrah Nunez nodded. "Let me do the talking. I might have to spin a few tales. Just nod along, truffles." When they did so, he beamed. "That's the way."

As they approached the small vessel, Bridget let go of Adella's hand, and they nodded to each other as if reaching an understanding about not giving away more than they had to. Bridget had to admit that she'd missed this feeling of anticipation that came before a mission, when she might have to think on her feet. The damned river and Adella's presence tempered it, not just because of the possible danger but because Bridget couldn't give away how accustomed to danger she was.

And she had a stray thought that somehow, Juno was watching. The hair on the back of her neck prickled as if she could feel eyes gliding over her skin.

At their target ship, Serrah Nunez thumped the side with his walking stick, then waited, hands resting on the stick's silver head. Mere moments passed before a short woman stuck her head out of the pilot house. Her weathered face broke into a wide grin. She disappeared only to come limping around the other side. Her iron-gray hair had been tied back with a scarf, and she wore green leather trousers while a vest of the same hue covered a billowy white shirt. A hint of metal gleamed from her mouth, matching her shiny rings, necklace, and artificial left leg from the knee down.

"Pali," she cried to Serrah Nunez as she got closer. "It's been a long time." Curious brown eyes slid over Bridget and Adella. "What brings you my way?"

"Time for a chat, Ami?" Serrah Nunez asked.

Ami gave them all another once-over before she waved them ahead, and they stepped on board. Bridget breathed easier on the boat. At least it had rails keeping everyone from pitching into the water.

Ami limped around the back of the pilot house and sat on a crate, gesturing for them to find their own seats. "May I present Tin-Pin Ami," Serrah Nunez said to Adella and Bridget. "Ami, these are Sugar and Spice, my clients."

Bridget bowed when she wanted to snort. Adella seemed to be holding in a laugh of her own as she sat on another crate. Bridget stood beside her.

Ami chuckled. "You and your damn sweet tooth, Pali. What can I do for you?" She looked Serrah Nunez up and down. "You look too well to need help from a humble fisher."

"Pudding, I have never needed help from a fisher, no matter what my state, and you've never been one anyway. Nor are you humble about anything." He sat but held the walking stick in front of him, hands resting on the top. "Sugar and Spice need to speak to you about your real business."

Ami said, "I don't do that anymore," and Serrah Nunez spoke the words along with her. When she frowned, he added, "Dear Tin-Pin, you must think up another line. But you're in luck. We aren't going to ask you to do what you *don't do* anymore. We merely want some information about those who do."

Ami leaned back, staring. Bridget wondered exactly where she was from. The name Ami could come from any number of places, especially if it was short for something else. If it was even her real name. Bridget looked to Serrah Nunez, wondering just what Pali was short for.

If that was even his real name either.

The world seemed very full of falsehoods at the moment, Bridget's greater than most.

"Tell me what you want to know, and I'll tell you how much it'll cost," Ami said.

"We're looking for someone." Serrah Nunez described Cristoff and the sort of goods he favored.

Ami's expression didn't change. "What do you want him for?"

"Does it matter?"

"Well." Ami crossed her artificial leg over the other. The inside edge gleamed as if it had been sharpened. "If you want to kill him, I think it only fair that I charge more."

Adella straightened, expression darkening. Bridget put a hand on her shoulder, but Ami's eyes had already flicked in her direction. Bridget bit back an angry retort.

"Want him alive, then?" Ami asked.

Serrah Nunez remained unruffled. "Do Sugar and Spice look like killers? Do I? We are merely retracing his steps in order to speak with him."

"About what?"

Bridget was getting tired of this. She'd agreed to let Serrah Nunez take charge, but she knew how to move a conversation along, too, and she wanted to get out of here as quickly as possible. "This is a waste of time," she said, adding a bit of growl to her voice. "She knows nothing. Let's go." She took a step toward the pier. Adella half rose, expression unsure.

Serrah Nunez put up a hand. "As you can see," he said to Ami, "we are rather pressed for time."

Ami eyed Bridget with a wry smile. "You must be Spice." When Adella snorted, Ami looked her way. "Or maybe you're both a combo, huh?"

Now Adella stood, too, sighing.

"All right, all right," Ami said, putting her hands up. "I'll ask my crew if anyone knows your man. Wait here." She stepped into the pilot house again, and her head disappeared as she descended into the ship.

Serrah Nunez looked at them both with his brows up. "Is that what it looks like when you follow directions?"

Bridget felt a dash of schoolroom shame. She shook her head at the same time as Adella.

"Any more disobedience, and we shall all return home without a treat. Is that understood?"

Bridget fought a sputter and nodded with Adella, who now had a little smile.

"That's better," Serrah Nunez said, beaming as he stood, too. "Cheer up, sugar cookies, we're getting what we want." His face fell when he looked over Bridget's shoulder. "Or perhaps not."

Bridget turned to find a crossbow pointed through the pilot house window. She tensed, ready to fight, but a man holding another crossbow came around the side of the pilot house, and Tin-Pin Ami blocked the other side.

So they had more than one route belowdecks. She only hoped she'd be alive to need that information later.

Adella had never had a weapon pointed at her before. She had no idea how to react. Her lessons on protocol hadn't covered this.

And now was not the time to laugh hysterically, no matter how much she wanted to. Her stomach was far too twisted in knots.

"Sorry, Pali," Tin-Pin Ami said. "I'm going to have to ask you to step downstairs." She glanced at the bowmen. "Forcefully."

Adella looked to the sides, at the other ships, but any crew they had seemed to have vanished.

"All mine," Tin-Pin said, giving Adella a wry smile as she nodded to the other ships. "You'll get just as caught if you jump for it."

"A fleet?" Serrah Nunez asked. "You've done well for yourself."

"Yeah, I'm a regular admiral." Tin-Pin's smile seemed a little sad, but Adella doubted sentiment would slow her from…whatever this was. She gestured again. "In the pilot house and down the steps, please."

Bridget sneered. "Why should we make our murders convenient for you? By all means, kill us out here where a passing sentinel launch might see."

Adella had to fight to keep from holding her breath. This couldn't be how she died. She couldn't leave her sisters all alone.

"I don't want to hurt you, Spicey," Tin-Pin said. "A friend of mine wants a word is all, a nervous friend, and he won't be happy until he's had his word with you under guard." She frowned. "And though I don't *want* to hurt you, I will if you don't get your asses downstairs. My nervous friend can find out all he wants to know from your corpses instead."

It sounded like what Gisele had said about the corpse walk. Was one of them a mage as well? She took a deep breath to calm her nervous stomach. At the moment, it didn't matter. She needed to stay alive, and she wanted to keep everyone else alive as well.

But everyone was standing fast. She had to break the stalemate. Negotiation was her job, after all. And though the smugglers held their weapons steadily, they didn't seem eager, merely ready.

Gods and devils, how would she know what killers looked like before they did their grisly business? She told her panicky heart to be quiet and began walking forward.

Bridget whispered, "No."

Adella shook her head, ready for dissension. "I'm sure we can negotiate with this mysterious friend, yes?"

Tin-Pin nodded. "He just doesn't operate in the open." Her frown came back when she looked over Adella's shoulder.

"Come on," Adella said loudly, proud there was no warble in her voice. "Come with me." She didn't turn but heard Serrah Nunez talking softly, then felt Bridget behind her, close enough to touch, her breath going like a bellows. Adella desperately wanted to take her hand, but she had to hoard information like jewels. That was part of negotiation. She could do this. And heading downstairs was a concession she could easily make that would put her captors in a good mood.

She hoped.

Belowdecks was more spacious than she imagined, with a hallway leading into a large, comfortable common space and another short hall past that with several closed doors.

Adella stopped in the common room with Bridget and Serrah Nunez, who were both stone-faced. After taking Serrah Nunez's walking stick, Tin-Pin gestured to two padded benches that sat on either side of a wooden table. Adella sat on one side, Serrah Nunez on the other, and Bridget perched on the table itself with her legs dangling toward the rest of the room.

With a snort, Tin-Pin sat on another bench that ran along the other side of the room like a sofa. Small windows near the ceiling let in plenty of light, and Adella spied an almost hidden corridor beyond the stairs. One of the bowmen lingered there. The other had remained above.

"Coffee?" Tin-Pin asked. "Water? Something stronger?"

Before Adella could politely decline, Serrah Nunez said, "Is that a joke?"

"I'm not going to poison you."

"You'll excuse me if I don't believe you." His eyes glittered behind his spectacles.

Tin-Pin crossed her arms. "On my honor, Pali."

Serrah Nunez smiled sweetly. "Go to hell along with your honor, Ami."

"When you hear from my friend, I hope you'll change your tune."

"How long do we have to wait?" Bridget asked.

"Only a few moments, Spicey." A thump and the sound of voices came from overhead. "Or it might be right now," Tin-Pin said with a grin. "Keep your seats. He doesn't require formality."

Adella's heart began to pound again, and she tried to marshal her thoughts. She put on a placid smile as a handsome, dark-skinned man came down the stairs, his clothing similar to Tin-Pin's but finer. His black hair was cut very short, nearly shaved. He had as many rings as her, but they glittered with the occasional jewel, and two large ruby studs sparkled in his ears. He regarded everyone coolly with honey-colored eyes.

Adella waited for an introduction, but another pair of feet clomping down the stairs drew her eyes. When this person bent to look into the cabin, she shot out of her seat. "Cristoff!"

The fearful expression on his gaunt face morphed into happiness and surprise. He held out his long arms as if holding something back, and Adella froze, remembering the bowman, and the first man now had a hand on a long-bladed dagger at his waist.

Cristoff took the few steps forward and embraced Adella. "It's all right, Vincenzo. She's a coworker." He held her at arm's length, tears in his bright blue eyes. His dark hair was held back in a tight braid, and he'd exchanged his dalmatica for the trousers, shirt, and vest combo the others sported, except he'd added a hooded cloak. "You came looking for me, serrah?"

"I'm so happy you're all right," Adella said, covering his hands with hers.

Tin-Pin and the man Cristoff had named Vincenzo glanced at each other. "Coworker?" Vincenzo asked. His accent was thick, like that of someone who came from one of Sarras's coastal towns. "From the Bastión?"

"Secondary Ambassador Adella del Amanecer," Cristoff said, then his face fell. "I guess you must be the only ambassador now."

So he knew about Dolores. Because he'd killed her? Her stomach shrank, and she wished to be out of his reach but feared moving. But his tanned face was so open in grief, she couldn't believe it. "Do you know who killed Dolores?"

He shook his head sadly. "I didn't even know she was dead until I read the broadsheets about it."

Adella frowned. "But when the sentinels went to look for you the morning after she was dead, you were already missing."

His eyes widened. "Not missing, serrah. Hiding. Because someone had just tried to kill me."

CHAPTER FOURTEEN

Drinks were handed around and introductions made before they all sat to hear Cristoff's story. Adella was happy to discover that Vincenzo was not only Cristoff's smuggling contact but his romantic partner as well, even if she worried a bit about Vincenzo being a smuggler. But in the end, when Cristoff had been in danger, he'd had someone to turn to.

Even if it was a criminal.

Adella leaned against Bridget's knee and tried not to hold anyone's career against them in this room.

"I didn't see who it was," Cristoff said as he sat sipping a brandy. "I'd been out with some friends the night Dolores was murdered, and when I came home, someone was waiting for me."

"No clue about who they were?" Bridget asked. "Dress? Scent?"

He closed his eyes. "From the little I saw, it seemed as if they were wearing a black mask that covered their entire face. Dark clothing. No scent that I can recall." He took another swallow, his hands shaking. "I dropped my keys just inside my apartment door, and something…whooshed over my head." He laughed without much humor. "Being tipsy and clumsy saved my life."

Vincenzo put a hand on his knee. "Shall I tell the rest, my love?"

"Yes, thanks," Cristoff said with a sigh and a grateful look.

Adella smiled, hoping Juno was in good company, too.

"When he saw the ruffian," Vincenzo said, "Cristoff stumbled back into the hall. The assassin came at him, and Cristoff's feet caught in the hallway runner—"

This time, Cristoff's laugh had a little happiness to it. "That's sweet, Vin, but that's not what I told you. The truth is, I tripped over my own feet and rolled down the stairs."

Adella winced in sympathy. She couldn't recall him being clumsy, but his body had chosen the right time to become so.

"I made so much noise, my neighbors began peering out their doors up and down the halls. I ran outside instead of going back up to my apartment."

"Smart," Bridget said. "Your attacker had probably gone back inside."

Tin-Pin nodded. "They probably changed clothing in there, then simply walked out."

"The sentinels checked your place," Adella said, "and my sister didn't mention anything about an open or unlocked door. This intruder no doubt closed up when they left."

Cristoff stared at her for a moment before recognition lit his face. "Your sister's a mage, right?"

"Hired to investigate Dolores's death, yes. And I'm very happy she isn't investigating yours as well." That got a smile from both men. "She said a few people had been in your place, and last I heard, the sentinels were trying to match your visitors with their auras."

He frowned. "Good luck to them. I had a party two nights before. They'll have a hell of a time sorting that out."

"Don't worry. My sister is very good." Reading auras took a fraction of the effort other spells did. Gisele could get away nearly pain free. And any relief was a cause for celebration.

"I came straight here." Cristoff took Vincenzo's hand. "And we asked some of the others to detain anyone who asked for me."

"Momentarily," Vincenzo added. "Until we discovered their purpose."

"See?" Tin-Pin leaned back on her bench.

Serrah Nunez gave her a smile. "You aren't forgiven just yet, peaches."

"I never thought you would be looking for me, serrah," Cristoff said to Adella. "I am sorry for any inconvenience."

Bridget snorted, but Adella patted her knee and said to Cristoff, "No apology necessary. I'm glad you're safe. I only hope Juno is, too. She went missing after she left the Bastión on the morning of Dolores's death."

He shook his head. "I hope she didn't meet the same person I did."

"She didn't mention anyone trying to kill her the night before the murder," Bridget said. "Why didn't this masked attacker come after her then, too?"

Yes, that did seem odd.

Cristoff shrugged. "Perhaps they did, but she was in the arms of her secret lover instead of at home."

Adella sat back, stunned. "Her what?"

He smiled knowingly. "She admitted she was seeing someone but never told me who, just that she was excited about them. Of course, I never told her about my beau, either." He glanced shyly at Vincenzo, who winked.

"Embarrassed by me?" Vincenzo asked in a teasing tone.

"No, you're far too special to share."

Serrah Nunez gave a lovesick sigh, but Bridget cleared her throat. "Juno's lover," she said slowly. "Any clues?"

"She could have fled there," Adella said, still surprised by the secret love lives of the people she worked with. She'd shared some personal information with Juno, and she thought she'd earned enough trust for reciprocation. She couldn't get mired in self-pity, but perhaps Juno never saw them as more than supervisor and subordinate.

"No clues spring to mind, sorry." Cristoff smiled at Adella. "We must arrange a way to get in touch again if needed."

She shook her head, thrown into confusion again. "But…you're coming back with me, right? I can take you to my sister, and she can bring you in for the sentinels to question."

The room went quiet, with only the creaking ship and the cry of birds outside breaking the silence. Adella's mouth went dry. She'd just mentioned the authorities in a room full of criminals. She didn't know whether to be embarrassed or terrified.

She swallowed, and the small motion hurt her throat. "Gisele will make sure you're all right," she said calmly despite the ringing in her ears. "And once you tell them what happened, they can search for this mystery lover as well. And if you give them a guest list for your party, Gisele can more easily discover your attacker's aura and make sure the right person is arrested." She was on a roll, thinking of all the ways Cristoff could help, but Vincenzo leaned forward.

Bridget tensed, and Adella gave her knee another squeeze.

"Serrah," Vincenzo said, "if he turns himself in, he will be under suspicion no matter what your sister says. The sentinels will lock him up and might not be able to protect him from this masked killer."

What could be safer than jail? It didn't sound like a fun place, but they didn't let murderers wander about, did they?

She bit her lip. They absolutely did. That was where such people were *kept*. All the attacker would have to do was get themselves arrested.

"No." Adella shook her head before anyone could go on. "You underestimate my sister's influence. And mine. You're a witness, not a suspect."

Vincenzo's eyebrows rose. "I don't think the sentinel commander will take your word, serrah. She does not answer to mages or ambassadors, though I'm sure she will be unfailingly polite when she tells you she will take your recommendations under advisement."

"It's not just about me," Cristoff said before Adella could argue. "They'll want to know where I've been, and I'm terrible at lying."

Adella was about to ask why he wouldn't tell the truth, but Serrah Nunez jumped in. "They'd want to speak to Vincenzo, honey, and the smuggling would come out. A few well-bribed sentinels may turn a blind eye, but the rest wouldn't be able to ignore a few smuggling leaders thrown in their laps."

Vincenzo and Tin-Pin were watching her. They were criminals, true, but she didn't want them arrested, not after they'd helped Cristoff, who clearly trusted them more than the authorities.

Some government official she was turning out to be. Zara would be appalled.

Adella sighed. "You can give me the guest list. I'll give it to Gisele but won't mention you."

"Where did it come from, then?" Tin-Pin asked.

Adella shrugged. "Dolores's desk?"

"You would have found it already," Bridget said.

Cristoff snapped his fingers. "Her hidey-hole."

"Her what?" nearly everyone said at once.

"She had a secret space under the floorboards in your office," Cristoff said. "You never knew?"

Adella shook her head. One more thing Dolores never got to tell her. "What did she keep in there?"

"Lately? I'm not sure. It's a very small safe just under the loose board by your bookshelf. The key should have been in her desk."

"It wasn't." And that hadn't been the only thing missing. There had been the letter from Elena Garza, Juno's mother. The killer might have taken it, but what if Dolores had hidden it instead? And then had been tortured for its location?

If she hadn't given it up, Cristoff would have been the next logical person to ask.

Adella's insides went icy as a string of what-ifs ran through her mind. What if she hadn't gone out with Bridget that night, if she hadn't taken a cab home? If her sisters hadn't waited up for her, if she didn't live with a soldier and a mage…

When Bridget touched her shoulder, she looked up. Everyone was watching her. She took a deep breath, trying to put a possible near miss out of her mind. "Yes, I'll, um, I'll say I got it from the hiding… thing. Once I find it." She looked to Cristoff, unable to imagine the stress he'd gone through while looking over his shoulder. This seemed the safest place for him after all. She had the sudden urge to stay here with him, though that wasn't possible. Even after the killer was caught, she'd probably never go anywhere alone again.

Cristoff gave her a list, and she tried to think of a plausible reason it would be hidden in Dolores's secret safe. Perhaps she could say she'd found the correspondence book in there as well, and this was stuck in the pages. Or Dolores had kept a list of people Cristoff associated with. For some reason.

Gisele would never buy that.

Oh well. Adella would have to say it was none of Gisele's business and leave her to tell the sentinels any lie she wished. A promise to reveal everything after the killer was caught should suffice.

Probably.

❖

Bridget tuned out the conversation as Adella worked out a way to get in touch with Cristoff again. Serrah Nunez would keep them from making a stupid plan. Bridget fought the desire to fidget. Baxter would have reprimanded her for showing her feelings so freely. Adella seemed happy, but they hadn't uncovered anything useful about Juno. Even the fact that it had likely been Juno who'd tried to kill Cristoff wasn't much help because he hadn't seen her face.

"I'm going to stretch my legs," she said in Adella's ear. At a questioning look, Bridget gave what she hoped was a confident smile and gestured for Adella to stay put. She caught Ami's eye and nodded toward the steps.

Ami seemed amused as she followed. "What is it, Spicey?" she asked when they were on deck.

Bridget paused before saying her real name. Spicey would do for now. "What if someone wanted to move people in and out of Sarras instead of goods?"

Ami cocked her head. "I'm guessing you're not asking the way to the ticket office for the pleasure cruises?" She snorted. "Think this Juno character smuggled herself out of danger?"

Bridget shrugged. It was as good a reason as any for why she was asking.

"Possible," Ami said as she leaned against the rail. "If you know the right people."

"And who would that be?"

Ami grinned. "No one you should ask around for. People smuggling is quite different than shifting goods. It's rarely done for… altruistic purposes. I wouldn't fancy Juno's chances for survival with some of them." She raised her brows. "But how would an aide from the Bastión know who to ask? Unless Juno's secret lover is someone used to making people disappear."

Bridget thought of Cristoff and Vincenzo and snorted. "Maybe all the Bastión aides roam the docks looking for romance."

That got a grin. "I could ask around on your behalf. See if anyone's seen her. For a price."

Bridget hesitated. She didn't want to pay for information she didn't need. She knew exactly where Juno was. But if she *did* have to ultimately help her sneak away…

Or sneak away herself if Adella couldn't forgive her.

"I'd rather have names and ask my own questions," Bridget said.

Ami stared without comment.

With a sigh, Bridget retrieved several coins from her pocket and held them out. "How many names will this buy?"

Ami's gaze flicked to the money, and she *tsked*, but she spirited the coins into her vest. "More fool you. Come on." She led the way onto the pier and nodded down the line of ships. "See that cutter with stars painted on the rail?"

Bridget swallowed the lump of fear in her throat and followed, making herself listen. Ami spent several minutes nodding in this direction or the other, never looking in the same direction as Bridget. Maybe no one would notice who they were talking about.

But now that she was making herself ignore the river, Bridget had the sensation of being watched again. People moved here and there on the ships or the dock or the wall above, but no one seemed particularly interested in her. Still, she couldn't get over the itchy feeling on the back of her neck. She shifted, trying to glance around surreptitiously, but she couldn't look in every direction at once.

"What's the matter with you?" Ami asked. "You got nits?"

"Don't you feel it?" The wind seemed to be blowing in fits and starts, and sound passed strangely around her.

"What the devils are you on about, Spicey?"

Sweat dribbled down Bridget's back. The unseen eyes were getting closer. She could feel them dragging over her skin, could almost sense someone's breath on her neck. With her instincts screaming at her to act, she spun, swinging wildly.

Her blow connected with…something.

Something unseen.

It made a little grunt as a person might, and Bridget staggered back into Ami.

A man appeared as if from thick fog, and Bridget's heart leaped into her mouth. He came at them, saber in hand and his teeth set in a snarl. Bridget registered the blue uniform of the sentinels before Ami shoved her out of the way.

Bridget stumbled behind Ami, fighting to keep her balance. She managed to stay on the pier, out of the cold fingers of the river. Ami stayed low and kicked her false leg in a sweeping motion. The sharp edge tore through the sentinel's trouser leg, and he yelped, staggering to the side and falling in between the pier and the river wall.

"Get aboard," Ami said. She stood and pivoted to shear through one of the ropes tying her ship to the dock.

Bridget gawked at the man bobbing in the water. Poor devil. "Gods," she whispered. Where had he come from? She heard more cries as other sentinels popped into view along the pier. Where had they all come from?

"Get in the fucking boat," Ami yelled, and Baxter seemed to yell with her.

Serrah Nunez came around the side of the pilot house. Bridget had a moment to wonder how long he'd been standing there eavesdropping before he hauled her aboard. Ami leaned against the boat and gave it a shove before Serrah Nunez grabbed her, too, and the boat began to drift backward. Ami yelled orders to her five crew members, and they swarmed the deck. The ships to either side helped push them out, and the sail was up before Bridget fully comprehended what was going on.

They were sailing on the river, surrounded by water.

Sentinels flooded the pier, sentinels who'd been invisible. It had to be something to do with magic, an area the empire had never excelled in. But Adella often bragged about her sister's ability.

A spy-hunting sister who might be watching.

Bridget darted for the pilot house as the ship drifted farther. She met Adella coming up with Cristoff and Vincenzo. "Sentinels," Bridget said breathlessly. "And a mage."

Adella's face drained of color.

Vincenzo frowned. "They must have followed you." Accusation was heavy in his tone, and Bridget bit back the urge to snarl.

Adella rounded on him. "You don't know that. It could be a coincidence. Or something you did."

He snorted. "Ridiculous. Why would they come now?"

"Criminal activity springs to mind."

Bridget caught her shoulder just as Cristoff took Vincenzo's arm and shared a look with Bridget, one that said they had to keep these two apart.

Serrah Nunez shouting, "Enough," saved them the trouble. "Fighting among ourselves gets us nowhere. We need to get out of the crew's way." He shepherded them toward the rear of the ship and stood between Adella and Vincenzo. But his look of censure faded to one of fear when he looked behind them. "Oh shit."

Those two words quieted any mumbling. Several sentinel launches had cast off, and who knew how many more were waiting downriver.

Chapter Fifteen

Adella thought fast as everyone chattered around her. The sentinels were pursuing them, and they had to think of a way to escape before…

She shook her head, her reasoning coming back in a rush. "Wait a minute," she cried and had to repeat it before everyone fell silent. "Why are we running away?"

Everyone stared as if she'd lost her mind.

She pointed at the launches. "We've done nothing wrong, and those are servants of the same government as me."

Bridget licked her lips and cast a glance at Vincenzo. "Adella—"

"We weren't doing anything wrong when they found us," she insisted. "I can testify to that." Vincenzo's nostrils flared, and she tried to see this from his point of view, but there was only so far she could go with this group and stay fully inside the law. "If we surrender, I'm sure I can explain."

They all looked doubtful, even Bridget, and Adella's position had never felt as worthless as it did now. She fought the urge to say that she and Bridget and Serrah Nunez hadn't done anything wrong, at least, and did not deserve to be dragged into this mess.

Cristoff looked at her with a pleading expression. He wouldn't want Vincenzo to go to jail. But she didn't want to flee the country, either, or wherever this ship was currently headed. "Then what's the plan? Because we three need to get back."

Vincenzo snorted. "If it's not you they're after."

"Don't be ridiculous."

Bridget took her arm, a look of worry on her face. Right, her criminal past. But surely she hadn't done anything bad enough for the sentinels to chase her. The constabulary would be enough. No, they had to be after the smugglers.

Then why bring magic into it? "You saw their mage?" she asked Bridget.

She blinked. "No, but they were using magic."

"What form did it take?"

"Does it matter?" Vincenzo asked, but Serrah Nunez hushed him.

Bridget shook her head. "The sentinels were invisible. I've never seen the like."

Yes, that was an amazing, complicated feat, the kind of spell Gisele excelled at, the kind that wasn't cheap. "Why bring in a mage for smuggling?" Adella said. Waving at Vincenzo, she added, "No offense."

He crossed his arms. "None taken. I've said from the beginning that they're not here for us."

She let that slip past as it seemed true at the moment. Only serious crimes, those of a political nature like Dolores's murder prompted the sentinels to hire a mage. The guild's rates were exorbitant, especially for someone like Gisele.

Adella's belly was cold as her mind turned over. *Was* this her doing? Had the sentinels been tracking her because they suspected her of Dolores's murder? Preposterous. Gisele wouldn't have kept that from her.

Unless she didn't know. What if they only told Gisele they needed her for an operation that involved following a suspect? Then that suspect had led them right to Cristoff, who they wanted to question, at least. Gisele might not have known Adella was one of their targets. Gods, she was going to be so angry when she found out. If she wasn't too busy writhing in pain from the effort of bending the light around a host of sentinels.

As if to answer, a rumble like thunder came from behind them, and the sentinel launches rushed forward as if under gale winds before they returned to normal speed. A breath of air blew around

Adella, chilling her, but it was nothing like what had seemed to speed the launches.

"Devils curse all mages," Tin-Pin said as she joined them. "We'll never outrun them if they keep getting boosts of magical wind." She looked over her shoulder. "Head for the cove."

Vincenzo gave her a look before nodding toward Adella and Bridget. "Are you sure, Ami?"

"What damned choice do we have? We'll sort it out."

Adella mashed her lips together, hoping the smugglers weren't looking for a place to fight the sentinels. She couldn't let people get hurt, not when this could very well be her fault. She clenched a fist. It was up to her to make it right.

"Put us off the ship," she said. "If they want us, they can have us. Me," she amended at Bridget's worried look. She didn't really know how to swim, but... "You must have something I can float on."

Everyone began talking at once, some advocating for her safety, others arguing that she wouldn't be enough to stop the entire pursuit. Even if she was in obvious distress, it would only take one ship to rescue her.

"Adella," Bridget said softly. "The water will be too cold." She shivered as if feeling it. "You can't...not alone. But I..." She looked stricken.

She didn't want to come. Adella's heart twisted even as she told herself not to be selfish. It was simply too much to ask for Bridget to put herself in danger.

But it *hurt*.

Bridget's face fell, and she cupped Adella's cheeks. "I would cross a thousand frozen rivers for you. It's..." Her gaze flicked back toward the sentinels.

"They won't care about a few thefts." Adella winced, aware she was assuming again on all counts.

But Bridget was still pale, more fearful than offended. "It's more than that."

"What is?"

Bridget didn't respond, only looking fearful and sad and making Adella's heart race. Gods and devils, what had she done in the past she'd barely spoken of?

"I don't think we have to throw you overboard just yet," Tin-Pin said. She plucked Adella's cloak. "Still, wouldn't be a bad idea to get ready to swim. As a last resort, of course."

Bridget gave her a murderous look, but Adella hurried to take off the cloak and tried to fight her nerves. She'd seen people swimming. She'd been in a large bath. She could do this if she had to. The thought nearly made her laugh, though the situation wasn't funny at all. Still, that would be better than crying or screaming in fear.

She told herself to calm down. She wouldn't have to swim. Readying herself was only a precaution. With any luck, she'd remain ignorant forever. "Thank you," she said to Tin-Pin. The sailors began tipping some of their cargo overboard in order to gain speed. "For not throwing us out."

"Thank him," Tin-Pin said, gesturing at Serrah Nunez. "If Pali wasn't with you, you'd have gone over first." She muttered something like, "Still might," then joined her crew.

Serrah Nunez put an arm around Adella's shoulders before fear could consume her. "Stick with me, trifle. I'll get you and your lady love safely to shore."

Adella sighed. "I'm sorry I got you into this mess."

He chuckled. "It's just a little excitement to remind me of the past and make me happy I run a bar as I decline into…" He twirled his hand. "Middle age."

She stood on tiptoe to kiss his cheek and quoted from one of her favorite novels. "'A pure and noble spirit knows no age. It serves as a vital beacon unto eternity.'"

He teared up a little before he held her close. "I changed my mind, sugar. Spicey cannot have you because I'm keeping you for myself."

She laughed, all her emotions ganging up on her and making her own eyes misty.

Bridget sounded a little choked, too, when she said, "Don't make me die fighting you, serrah."

They all shared a chuckle, but Adella couldn't help noting the tension underneath, especially as the sentinels seemed closer than before, and the cold water waited below.

❖

It was hard to imagine the day going worse than it already had, but Bridget still had several scenarios in mind. And judging by Ami's warning about having to swim, at least one might come true.

Oh gods, she'd rather do almost anything else.

And despite any assurances that they would safely reach the shore, Bridget noted the way Ami kept running an eye over their group as if wondering how much trouble she could shed by throwing them overboard.

Bridget stayed close to Adella, trying to keep calm for her. Inside, she felt like a sack of knots. And not just because of the terrors of the river. The sentinels might not be after the smugglers or Adella. They could easily be on Bridget's track, especially if they'd caught Juno. Even if Juno had kept her secret, if the sentinels found one spy, they'd be looking for more.

And Adella wanted them to give themselves up. Bridget had wanted to shake her one moment and make a tearful confession the next. Adella had clearly never been arrested, let alone by Sarrasian sentinels. Even with her position and connections, she was in for a long interrogation. If by some miracle they thought Bridget was nobody special, they would still live up to their reputation for holding prisoners until they found *something* to charge them with.

She'd never experienced it personally, but she'd heard enough stories to know there must be some truth in them. And all governments were corrupt at some level. A brutish police force was just as likely as a spy ring who had been told that gathering information was now secondary to performing assassinations. She could almost hear Baxter waxing about the old days, when spies were there to protect their homeland rather than murder for its profit.

Adella's hand clasping hers brought her back to the present. She'd lost the look of suspicion she'd had when Bridget had blurted that she was more than a thief. Still, the damage had no doubt been done. It would probably eat at her like the rats rumored to infect sentinel prisons.

"We'll be okay," Adella said, words that seemed between statement and question.

"Of course," Bridget said. Adella would remain well, and that would be some comfort when the sentinels turned their mages loose on Bridget, spy hunters like Adella's sister.

Maybe it would *be* her sister, full of anger at the woman who'd been lying to her.

Bridget shook her head. She couldn't let fear about the future hobble her in the present. She squeezed Adella's hand. "I'm sure we'll be fine as long as we obey those with a more experienced hand."

That earned her a grateful smile.

Serrah Nunez came back to join them after speaking with Cristoff and Vincenzo. "Evidently," he said, "there's a cove a few bends down the river where it's possible to hide a ship if we get there fast enough. Ami has watchers and is flying a flag that lets them know we're being pursued."

Bridget and Adella glanced up at the same time, but a few colorful flags fluttered from the mast.

"Which one?" Adella asked.

Serrah Nunez shook his head and shrugged. Bridget leaned to Adella's ear. "That's more information than we need."

She frowned. "What's the harm in us knowing? Who are we going to tell?"

A sentinel interrogator, Bridget wanted to yell, but she couldn't say how she knew that, not now that her initial fear had passed. She needed Adella to trust her, at least until this ordeal was over.

And the next one.

And the one after that.

Gods and devils, they were doomed.

The launches didn't leap ahead again. Their mage must have run dry, but Bridget's nerves still sang as they approached this miracle cove. As they took a sharp bend in the river, they lost sight of the launches, and another quick bend would leave them out of sight for an even longer time. In fact, Bridget didn't spot another ship waiting ahead until they were almost on top of it.

A ship the same size and color as theirs that was slowly sailing downriver.

Bridget began to see their escape plan taking shape as they changed direction toward a deep cove between the steep cliffs of the riverbank, with only a narrow entrance betraying it. What she'd first thought were interlocking tree branches hanging over the entrance to the cove now looked like a wad of tree limbs and other detritus that had been suspended in midair.

"Take cover," Ami called.

Her curiosity piqued, Bridget took Adella's arm and followed the others to the back of the pilot house while Ami and some of the crew waited inside. Other crewmen kneeled behind the railing.

"What's happening?" Adella asked, excitement replacing the darker emotions in her voice.

Bridget gripped her hand, anxious to see what would happen, too. Before they could all wonder aloud, several loud *clacks* and *twangs* came from the cove, and ropes shot from the tree line as if from giant longbows. They arced over the ship and then *thwacked* onto the deck. The crew leaped to grab them and tied the weighted ends at various points along the front of the ship. The deck shifted alarmingly as they surged forward.

Bridget stumbled, nearly falling, but Adella held her fast, her other arm in the grip of Serrah Nunez, who held on to the pilot house with his free hand.

Bridget leaned around Adella, gawking as she traced the ropes back up to their sources in the cove and saw several huge, crossbow-like apparatuses. The ropes now led past the crossbow things and threaded through large wooden wheels lying on their sides. The wheels seemed to bear the weight of the ship so oxen could pull the ropes into the trees, hauling the ship forward alarmingly fast.

"Brace," Ami called.

Vincenzo kneeled, gesturing for them to do the same. They all grabbed one another as the boat slid up on shore and jerked to a halt. Rocks crunched against the hull before the whole ship tilted slightly to the left.

A deep shadow fell across them, and Bridget looked back as a net covered with tree limbs lowered over the cove's entrance. She could just see people splashing on the other side, securing long planks to the bottom of the net. These bore different sizes of rocks, including some realistic looking boulders that had to be made of cloth and paint.

Ami stepped into Bridget's line of sight. "That's enough grinning at our precautions, Spicey. Everybody ashore."

They helped each other off, barely getting their boots wet before they were on the rocky bank. "Extraordinary," Adella said as more people hurried down a small slope that led into the trees. They swarmed Ami's boat with new sails and cans of paint.

"It's a shame," Ami said. "I liked the green."

Adella pointed back the way they'd come. "The other ship waiting out there? A decoy?"

Ami snorted. "None of your business."

"Hey," Bridget said, frowning.

Ami frowned right back at her. "Don't get huffy at me now that I've gone to all this trouble. That *decoy* might not be carrying anyone the sentinels want, but they'll still be arrested, and I'll have to bail them out and reset this lot." She waved around. Bridget was about to retort, but Ami put up a hand. "Everyone stays quiet until we're in the camp proper, and even then, low voices."

Bridget wanted to point out that she had been the noisiest, but Serrah Nunez took her arm and one of Adella's and followed Ami up the slope and around a bend in the trees. Her heart beat a little faster when one of the crew moved close to Ami and spoke in her ear. Bridget read lips well enough to catch his as he glanced toward her.

"…do with them?"

Ami's muttered response was lost, but the man nodded gravely and hurried ahead.

Bridget looked to Serrah Nunez, who seemed a bit apprehensive, but he nodded ahead as if to suggest seeing this through or perhaps asking what choice they had. Bridget leaned across him and spoke softly. "Stay together."

Adella nodded. Her wonder had given way to a frown, and now that faded to a flash of fear before she lifted her chin. Bridget swallowed a smile at the look of placid disdain. Serrah Nunez gave another reassuring nod, and his grip tightened on Bridget's arm, a reminder of his many rings and how they'd added power to his punches at the Donkey's Rest.

They weren't helpless. They had physical prowess, Adella's position, and skills at getting out of various tight spots. Bridget took note of the people, the terrain, marking any little thing that could aid in their escape.

Should it come to that.

Adella wondered how she was supposed to stay with Bridget and Serrah Nunez if the smugglers seemed determined to separate them. So far, no one had tried, but as they emerged from the trees into a camp of tents and lean-tos, the more people she spotted.

If this turned violent, they were doomed. Perhaps they should have leaped overboard when they had the chance. Whatever the sentinels planned, it surely didn't include anything remotely close to killing her and burying her in the woods.

No, she couldn't leap to conclusions.

No matter how possible they seemed in the moment.

Tin-Pin led them to a circle of logs around a low-burning campfire and gestured for them to sit. They crammed together on one log, and Serrah Nunez's arm tensed as if he feared someone yanking them apart.

Adella glanced back for Cristoff, desperate for a friendly face who would argue for her while she argued for Bridget and Serrah Nunez, but he didn't appear. She swallowed nervously. If Vincenzo had kept him back, it was to protect him.

If only from seeing his colleague murdered. He might put up a bit of a struggle when he found out what her fate was to be—he'd seemed touched by the fact that she'd sought him out—but it wasn't as if they were friends. And he'd been happy enough to throw in his lot with criminals. He couldn't be too surprised when they began acting the part.

Patience. She couldn't let nerves get the better of her. She would remember her training. Tin-Pin stood in a circle of her fellows, talking quietly. Adella licked her lips, trying to wet her dry mouth before she whispered, "What's going to happen?"

Serrah Nunez shook his head. Bridget's jaw was set and determined, but clearly, neither of them had been in a position quite like this.

Anger wormed through her. She did not like being afraid. Or being kept waiting for negotiations to begin. "Either they know who you are, or they know who I am," she said loudly. When the smugglers turned, she hoped her face looked calmer than she felt. "Maybe both."

Serrah Nunez's arm tightened further, and Bridget made a noise that might have been exasperation or despair. Adella ignored them. Tin-Pin dismissed her fellows and approached, and grabbing someone's attention was a good start to negotiation.

She didn't waste it. "Your decoy won't fool them, especially when they don't find me aboard. They'll tear this forest apart looking for me." A slight exaggeration, but the smugglers had hidden Cristoff carefully, so they knew just how seriously the sentinels were taking the death of a noble like Dolores. The same would be true for Adella.

But she wouldn't let it get that far.

Tin-Pin tilted her head. "Do tell."

"They won't stop looking for me. Ever. You'll have to leave Sarras in order to find a place to rest your head."

"You assume a lot."

"She speaks from experience," Serrah Nunez said.

Ami smirked. "I'm not worried about how much you've seen, Pali." She gestured to a path that cut through the forest. "You're free to go."

Adella fought a gasp. Would he? He could summon help, but it would take far too long to arrive.

He dropped his arms to clasp hands with Adella and Bridget. "I must decline," he said with a smile.

Tin-Pin rolled her eyes. "They must be awfully good clients."

"I'd rather walk barefoot through glass than see love snuffed out." His smile shifted to a stony look. "And you can bet your ass I won't walk quietly, Ami."

With a sigh, Tin-Pin sat. "I don't doubt it. Between your fists, Spicey's glares, and your noble's speeches, I'll be done to death. I'll make you a deal." She gestured toward a small shelter under an overhang at the back of the camp. "You three wait in there. We'll pack up and get gone along a track you won't see. Then someone with a crossbow will let you out to make your own way back home. Good enough?"

Adella breathed easier. She nodded, and the others stayed quiet. Tin-Pin ushered them into the small, one-roomed hut, the only light coming through the cracks in the ramshackle walls. Adella sighed and held tight to Bridget, who kissed her hair and returned the strong embrace.

When Serrah Nunez's touched her back, she reached to hug him, too, but he lowered his head and whispered, "Don't relax. She definitely plans to kill us."

CHAPTER SIXTEEN

Bridget wanted to bow to Serrah Nunez's superior knowledge and experience, but Adella wanted to talk and reason everything out. Incredibly irritating, but Bridget had to give her some slack. This was all new to her, and they had to trust Adella would act without question when the time came.

Hopefully.

For the moment, Bridget left it to Serrah Nunez to explain his reasoning and looked around the small hut with the aid of some matches she found in her coat pockets, handy for lighting a lady's cigar if the situation called for it.

Not that there was much to see. The ramshackle structure had been built around an old tree stump that now had a ratty blanket thrown over it. probably so it could serve as a table or chair. An equally old blanket lay on the floor, undoubtedly someone's bed.

She peered between the boards of the walls. There did seem to be a lot of activity in the camp, but she couldn't tell if they were packing to leave or not.

"If they don't move right now, they will soon," she heard. It sounded so much like what Baxter might say that it took her a moment to realize it was Serrah Nunez speaking to Adella.

Adella's voice was calm when she replied, "And why carry out that part of their plan if they don't also intend to release us?" She tapped a beat on her thighs, belying her tone.

Serrah Nunez snorted. "Ami probably doesn't want to risk getting blood on her possessions."

"Still—"

Bridget sighed loudly. This was why spies didn't have non-spy coworkers, so they didn't have to explain when they needed to be quick. When Adella turned to her with an angry glint in her eye, Bridget shook out her match. This might be easier to hear in the semi-dark.

And it would be harder to feel Adella's glare.

"I know that in your job, Adella, motives matter as much as actions, but that is not the case here. And neither are the reasons behind Serrah Nunez's conclusion. None of us can see the future, so we have to go along with whoever has the most experience with the situation." She let that sink in for a moment. "And whatever Ami has in mind is also irrelevant. We three want to make sure each of us gets safely back to Sarras, so we need to get away and only rely on one another."

"And as quickly as possible," Serrah Nunez said, his tall shadow moving against Adella's side, comforting or mollifying. Bridget hoped it did both, and she wouldn't have to remind Adella of her pledge to follow instructions.

"Very well," Adella said softly, loosening the tight feeling in Bridget's chest. "I acknowledge your greater knowledge, serrah. What would you have us do?" The words were only a little frosty, and she had only acknowledged *Serrah Nunez's* knowledge, but Bridget could work with that.

Baxter would have reminded her, "You're not supposed to be displaying your skills at getting out of a scrape anyway."

True enough, though Adella would have so many questions after this, it would either be time for the truth or a commitment to a lifetime of lies.

"Or walk away," Baxter would say. But he would have had a knowing smile. She hadn't been able to walk away from Adella before, and she damn sure wouldn't be able to do it after they survived this.

And Serrah Nunez would thrash her if she tried.

"Well," Serrah Nunez said after the silence had stretched on. "It wouldn't take much to bash through the door or the walls, but we would certainly be noticed."

Adella moved into a sliver of light, briefly highlighting her beautiful face. "And no matter what else, Tin-Pin has made good on her promise to have someone watch us."

Bridget would have shared a look with Serrah Nunez over "what else." She was just glad Adella was going along with them even if she clearly wasn't convinced they were right.

"That might be the only part that was true," Serrah Nunez said. "Even if the rest of the crew is leaving, Ami wouldn't leave just one bowman to kill us."

Bridget nodded. The crossbow was a slow weapon to load. There would be at least three attackers, making a mad rush too difficult if they waited. She rubbed her chin, trying to think past her nerves and get into her old mindset where she could think clearly, detached.

But her eyes kept drifting back to Adella. She'd never had a true partner in any of her jobs, not someone she cared about. And even if the feelings weren't the same, she cared about Serrah Nunez, too.

Baxter wouldn't scoff at that. After all, he'd given her the keys to escape because he'd loved her like a father.

The rotten old bastard.

She shook the thought away. If she couldn't push through her feelings, she'd just have to work with them. "Adella, keep watch. Let me know if the guard moves away or if there's no one else in sight. Serrah, help me look for weaknesses in the structure, so we can quietly get out some other way."

"Right," Adella said as Serrah Nunez's shadow moved to the other side of the hut. It was only wide enough for one person to lie down and not very deep. It wouldn't take long to feel over all the boards, pressing and shifting. The rear "wall" was the dirt and rock of the back of the overhang and let out a musty smell as she passed a hand over it.

"How are we?" she asked while she searched.

"Nothing yet," Serrah Nunez said, his voice muffled from where kneeled.

Adella shifted, and bands of light played over her pale hair. "The guard is still there, but he isn't paying much attention."

Handy. Bridget stood on the stump and felt over the ceiling. In the dim light, she saw a darker spot and discovered the rough surface of a tree limb or root. She risked lighting another match and saw a root snaking through the ceiling before curling back into the earth. The smugglers had built around it, leaving a few gaps. The overhang no doubt kept out the rain. But some moisture had gotten down this far, making the root and the surrounding boards damp.

Nearly rotting them.

"Serrah," she said, waiting until he stood beside her.

He could reach the boards unaided and whistled softly. "We might be able to lift the entire ceiling here at the back." More than one board lifted just from their probing.

Bridget grinned. "Whoever sleeps here owes us for saving them from a collapsing roof in the middle of the night."

"Can we get out that way?" Adella asked.

"Tell me when the guard is looking away, and I'll see."

Adella was silent for a few moments before she said, "Now."

Bridget lifted one board from the back corner and shifted it up and over the top of its fellows, making a hole.

"Stop," Adella said, a bit too loudly, but by the way she cleared her throat, she seemed to realize that without being told. "Okay, now."

Serrah Nunez worked a board loose on the opposite end, but instead of pushing it up, he shifted it into the hut. It left Bridget's hole wide enough to get through. "Let me know the next time he checks and looks away," she said.

Adella paused another few moments. Bridget resisted the urge to prompt her, trying to remember she could only report the guard's movements, not control them.

"All right, he's looking this way. Wait, wait…now."

Bridget used the tree root to pull herself up but ran into the top of the overhang after only two feet. Dirt cascaded around her collar as she paused. Luckily, a multitude of smaller roots hung around her, shielding her from the camp. When the crossbow wielder glanced back at the hut, she froze, but he looked away again with a sigh, the crossbow resting easy in his arms.

Bridget slithered farther out of the hole, her muscles protesting. Finally, she lay along the edge of the roof, moving carefully so she didn't collapse it. The camp was a hive of activity, but Adella was right; no one seemed to be paying them much attention, and the action seemed directed toward the river rather than the back of the camp. The area of the overhang was nicely in shadow, too.

Bridget spoke between the boards beneath her. "Pass me a blanket."

After a moment, a ragged woolen corner poked out of the hole near her feet. She reached back and pulled it through slowly while someone fed it to her, keeping it from snagging. She waited for another half-assed check from the guard before she dangled the blanket over the side of the little hut, tangling it in the roots above, impaling it in several places so it would hang unaided.

Then she waited, telling herself she was one with the boards and the roots and the earth. She hadn't had to revisit this place inside herself in so long. She hated it, and she'd missed it, and the push-pull was almost enough to break her out of it again, but she made herself persist. She would only be as violent as she had to be when she set her humanity aside for a moment or two.

When the guard looked back, he did a double take, squinting into the shadows. She willed him to move closer rather than call for someone else. She'd dealt with her share of bored guards. No doubt he'd be thinking he didn't need help checking out a rogue blanket. He was younger than she'd first thought, no doubt eager to impress, and he wouldn't want anyone to call him foolish or laugh at him for panicking over loose linens.

He came closer, cradling his crossbow in one arm while he reached for the blanket. He tugged on it gently before looking upward and moving around behind it.

Bridget rolled over and fell on top of him, making his breath leave in a *whoosh*. She kept her own teeth shut as she hit his shoulder, sending pain traveling through her ribs. Her weight knocked him to the ground, and the crossbow fell. She twisted, getting behind him, locking her legs around his waist, and hooking one arm around his neck.

He thrashed, but she trusted that the blanket and the shadows would hide them. She used her other arm for leverage, and he exhaled the little air left to him. He slapped at her arms, her hands, trying for her face, but she only moved her head away. She was the earth and the trees and the shadows, unfeeling.

Soon enough, he began to still. Baxter would recommend killing him. It left one less foe at her back.

She snarled. She wasn't Baxter, didn't have to be him or anyone like him. She wasn't a shadow but a person, and she'd made her vow. When the guard slumped, she let go and laid him flat, checking to make sure his heart still beat, that he breathed. His face looked almost peaceful.

Bridget took his cap and jacket and left hers before peering out. So far, no one seemed to be paying them much attention. She ripped the blanket down and laid it over the unconscious guard before taking his crossbow and moving back to the front of the hut, sticking close to the door and keeping her face turned away from the camp.

"Is he dead?" a soft question, Adella's voice. They'd been watching.

"No," Bridget said, trying not to blame her for even asking. After all, she *could* have killed the guard. Strange circumstances would be making Adella question everything. "Get back from the door. Serrah, get ready." She waited for a murmured assent and then kept her face tilted down and the cap pulled low as she scanned the camp. When she spotted a man near Serrah Nunez's height, she waved, catching his attention.

He looked at her curiously, and she waved him over, watching him in her periphery, head turned toward the hut. When he began walking toward her, she opened the hut door, glad to see Adella had moved to the back, and Serrah Nunez was pressed against the side.

"What is it?" the man asked as he came closer.

Bridget gestured into the hut and then shrugged as if seeing something she couldn't fathom. When he reached her side, she shoved him through the door, and Serrah Nunez's fist shot out, catching him in the chin. The smuggler's head snapped back, and Serrah Nunez caught him by his jacket and yanked him fully into the hut.

Bridget shut the door and tried to look like a bored guard again while listening to some slight scuffling inside. She risked a look out the side of her eye. No one was staring this way, but a woman did cross to where the tall man had been working and looked at a few crates he'd been fiddling with. She put her hands on her hips and glanced around.

Bridget cradled the crossbow and kicked the dirt, her head down, waiting for the woman's gaze to pass over her. The woman wiped her forehead, then stomped away into the camp.

Bridget opened the door. Serrah Nunez stepped out wearing the pilfered coat. He'd tied his dark handkerchief over his hair and had taken off his spectacles. Bridget hoped no one got close enough to see that he still wore his fancy coat under the stolen one or that the handkerchief appeared to be silk.

Without a word, he walked to an unattended pile of torn sails and broken boards and bent as if sifting for something he'd lost.

"Wait there, Adella," Bridget said softly. They couldn't afford taking out anyone else. The tall man had already been missed. But they still needed a gap in the activity to get all three of them into the woods. Bridget willed those working nearby to move far enough away that they could get Adella out and rush for the forest, but she feared moving too much. Even with a crossbow, she didn't want to fight her way out. They'd be overwhelmed within moments.

When she heard Tin-Pin Ami's voice, Bridget fought the urge to freeze. She stared at the hut and tried to look like a guard who'd just heard his boss's voice and wanted to seem attentive. She didn't dare glance in that direction. She was lucky she and the guard both had short dark hair, but they didn't look alike. Gods and devils, Ami had to leave without checking on her prisoners, she had to…

Her voice came closer. Shit. Bridget rested her finger on the crossbow trigger.

"Fire!"

Bridget almost spun at the cry, but she made herself glance over her shoulder. Everyone else was looking at where a plume of smoke rose from one of the tents. A heartbeat passed before everyone ran that way.

Bridget yanked the door open. "Come on." Adella nearly shot out, and Bridget shut the door. She caught Adella's arm, turning to see if Serrah Nunez was with them as they hurried into the forest on the northern side of the camp.

He was gone.

She made herself keep walking but risked a look at where the smugglers were trying to put the fire out. She didn't see Serrah Nunez among them, and no one was raising another cry of alarm, so she kept going, praying.

Adella was already breathing hard. "Where—"

"Slow down," Bridget said. "We won't run until we're out of sight. Serrah Nunez will catch up." Gods and devils, she hoped so.

Still, when he stepped out of the trees to the south, Bridget nearly shot him. She made herself relax and look back, seeing no one, but that couldn't last forever, not once they'd noticed the guard was missing. She held the crossbow to her chest. "Run."

Serrah Nunez could have easily outpaced them, but he hooked an arm through Adella's and helped her run. She was out of breath first, but Serrah Nunez wasn't far behind. Running a bar had no doubt replaced running for his life, if indeed he ever had. And it had been months since Bridget's last dash through a forest, so a stitch began to build in her side after several minutes.

"We have…to slow down…" Serrah Nunez said. Adella had turned red in the face, but she managed to nod. Bridget slowed to a walk and looked back, but no one seemed to be following them. That was beyond good. She could barely hear over the rush of blood in her ears. She only hoped the smugglers were far more used to sailing than running. And with any luck, Ami had decided they weren't worth the effort when she could disappear before they could tell anyone about her hiding place.

Not that they were going to tell, anyway. Even Adella would have to see that most of what they'd done this day should be kept secret.

At least, Bridget hoped so.

CHAPTER SEVENTEEN

For a time, the pounding of Adella's heart and the stitch in her side distracted from the many questions she had swirling in her head, but that didn't last long. She'd envisioned a fun, slightly exciting outing to one of the seedier parts of town. She never imagined she'd be abducted by smugglers who were hiding Cristoff, being pursued by the sentinels, then being held in a camp in the woods until a time when it was more convenient for her captors to murder her.

On top of all that, she felt like she didn't know the two people with her at all. With Serrah Nunez, Adella could wave off the fact that the jovial, caring, stylish man she'd met had battered someone into unconsciousness with two quick punches before stripping his coat, dumping him on the floor, then sneaking out to presumably light the fire that had allowed them to escape.

Well, she could almost wave it off. The sudden violence had frightened her even if it had been in her best interest. But with Bridget...

As warm as she was from running, Adella still shivered at the memory of Bridget choking the guard. Her face had been so still, grimly determined, but then a look of anger had come over her features before the guard went still at last. Adella's heart had thundered, and she'd been certain the guard was dead, even after Bridget had told her he lived.

She still wasn't sure.

Had that been the work of a former thief?

Bridget had all but admitted she had greater crimes in her past, reasons the sentinels would want to keep her once they had her. Gods and devils, what had she done? The silence between them left plenty of room for her mind to wander, though building protests from her feet and back began to drown out any wilder imaginings. Her walks to and from work seemed nothing compared to this hike through the forest. She'd have to remember to spend less time behind her desk, but such practical thoughts couldn't distract her either.

Adella focused on the long walk and how they would have to get a ferry to take them back across the river or else keep walking north to Fury Bridge, which was on the other side of the city.

Her feet answered for her: they would take the ferry. She had enough pennies for all of them if they didn't have their own fare.

"Don't worry," Bridget said. "It can't be far now." Her smile was encouraging, as if she was trying to remind Adella that they were all in this together, all thinking of the future. A tightness around her eyes suggested anxiety, which was a bit alarming.

Gods, Bridget was *not* going to hurt her. They cared about each other, Adella was certain. And there was no reason to hurt her besides.

Not the most comforting thought.

But the first thought still held true. Adella took her hand and gave it a squeeze. "Thank you for getting us out of there."

Bridget's shoulders dropped a fraction, and a look of relief passed over her face. "Of course. I'd rather die than let you be harmed."

Terribly sweet. And it did delight some primal part of her to know she was well protected. She could now use phrases she'd only found in novels before: "Lay a finger on me, and my paramour will thrash you!"

Or choke you into oblivion while displaying all the emotion of a corpse.

Less delightful.

"We're going to have a long conversation," Adella said.

Bridget nodded, and the anxious look came back.

"I feel as if many things have…gone unsaid." And she was guilty of that, too, but her family's relative poverty didn't seem that big of a secret out here, after the smuggling and imprisonment and escape from would-be murderers.

Bridget nodded again and glanced around as if fearing they'd wandered into a crowded lane when they were all but alone. Serrah Nunez had strode ahead as if to give them privacy.

Adella knew they should wait, that now wasn't the time, but she couldn't leave all the secrets hanging in the air. She'd already realized hers wasn't that important, so why hesitate? "My family…" Damn, it was still hard to get out. Pride reared in her again, but she beat it down. Bridget wasn't another noble who would laugh at her financial status or ban her from parties or events. And she could clearly keep secrets.

"We…don't have much money." She rushed the words out. "When my parents died, there were death duties, money we had to pay in order to inherit our house. They were…exorbitant, and my parents had tied up quite a bit of money in various schemes that didn't pay out or won't for years." She bit her lip, feeling a pain in her chest, an ache for her parents that never really went away.

Bridget squeezed her hand now, her expression sympathetic.

Adella smiled, grateful. "Thank you for not asking why I didn't surrender the house. My lawyer suggested that on many occasions, but I know how desperate my parents had been to keep it. They loved it, spent a lot fixing it. Our name is an ancient one, and…" She chuckled softly. "They were proud of it. I am, too."

"And these death duties took all your money?"

"Nearly. There were also creditors to pay off. And the house still needed some restoration that was already in progress. I sold… almost everything to resist going further into debt. When I turned seventeen the year after they died, I took the first job that became available in the Bastión, one of the few places the nobility can work and not be sneered at for it." She shook her head. "Though things are a bit different for nobles now, especially for any offspring who aren't the heir. My sister Zara is in the army, still perfectly respectable for the nobility, but for Gisele, well, noble mages are a little harder to come by." She was rambling now, but she'd been carrying her secrets around as if they were a heavy barrel, and now that she'd opened it, everything had to come out.

"We get by with three of us working." She sighed. "At least until the next time the house needs some repair. I save most of our money for that." She looked to Bridget again to find her still sympathetic, looking away as if thoughtful, but she didn't make any suggestions, thank the gods.

"So that's why I walk everywhere and wear boots and don't reline my mother's old cloaks with silk." She lifted her arms and dropped them. "See? Nothing to admire."

Bridget's eyes widened. "You've been taking care of two children on your own since you were sixteen, you kept a roof over their heads, you made sure their noble legacy stayed intact, and you managed your finances better than your parents did? That is a *lot* to admire, Adella." She pulled them to a halt and drew Adella into her arms. "You're extraordinary."

Adella wanted to weep but managed a breathy laugh. Every one of her good feelings about Bridget reappeared and carried away her burden, making her feel lighter than she had in years. "You're the only person I've told outside my family and our lawyer."

"That makes me marvel at you even more." Bridget kissed her forehead and started them walking again with one arm around Adella's shoulders. "How old were your sisters when your parents died?"

"Eight and four."

"Gods and devils! You were more mother than sister."

Adella snorted a laugh. "To Gisele, yes. I still try to baby her, though she hates it. Zara resented that I was 'in charge' for an extended period. For a long time, she insisted our parents were coming back, and she'd get to tattle on me for bossing her around." Zara still liked to be the one giving the orders, but Adella held that back, not wanting to burden Bridget with all of her family's past at once, though they'd already spoken about some of it at the Donkey's Rest.

Gods, that had only been a few nights ago. They still had so much to learn about each other.

Like the events that had led her to her confession. She looked at Bridget, trying to give her an encouraging smile, one that said, "If I can do it, so can you."

Bridget returned her smile but said nothing. Was she missing the encouraging part on purpose? Adella kept looking at her, waiting.

Finally, Bridget sighed. "All I can say is that I care about you deeply, and I can promise that answers are coming. They were coming before, but I had a few…circumstances to deal with first. Events that involve other people and their secrets."

Adella nodded slowly, though her curiosity tripled in size as she tried to glean meaning from Bridget's words. She didn't want to reveal others' secrets. Adella could understand that, but did it mean she was tangled up again with someone from her past? Adella fought to keep from asking, but she needed a little clarity to keep walking beside the woman who knew how to choke someone so efficiently. "And once you have settled these incidents?"

"I will tell you all. And any ties to my past will remain there."

Adella had to nod, had to trust. They'd been through too much together for her to walk away, but they didn't have enough claim on each other for her to demand answers. She could wait a little longer. But she wouldn't forget, and the image of Bridget's impassive face during the bout of violence would stay with her for a long time to come.

When the trees began to thin, Bridget dumped the crossbow, saying it would garner too much attention. They passed easily through the city gates with many others, and when they finally arrived at the ferry, afternoon had faded to evening, and the tall buildings by the river cast everything in shadow. Serrah Nunez directed them toward one of the smaller ferries operated by someone he seemed to know. Adella nearly balked. She'd had enough of his confederates for one day, but in the end, she was tired, and the fare was cheap.

Still, she kept her eyes open on the ride. When they came ashore without incident, she sighed, relieved, and hustled with the others back into town and away from the Tides. They didn't even bother to go past the place where Tin-Pin had been docked before. They stayed to the south, winding between the closed stalls of the fish market.

"You don't think they'll come looking for us, do you?" Adella asked. She shivered at the thought and from the cool evening breeze that her jacket wasn't doing much to stop. She missed her mother's old cloak for more reasons than that, and it darkened her mood further.

"Ami will see that as more trouble than she's willing to take on," Serrah Nunez said, his voice so confident that Adella believed him. "Bridget and I will be back among our own friends, and attacking a noble would be like blundering into a hornet's nest. She's smarter than that." He shrugged. "Give it a few years, and I might even see her again, who knows?"

Adella couldn't tell what the thought made him feel, if anything.

At the Donkey's Rest, he gave Adella a hug and a kiss on the temple. Before they parted, he whispered, "Give her the benefit of the doubt. She's earned it." He walked to the door before she could respond. "Come visit anytime. Your drinks will always be free, crumb cake."

Adella smiled and wondered how much of her conversation with Bridget he'd heard. Or maybe he argued for understanding and handed out free drinks because he liked them. She had the sense that he'd never be so gauche as to mention her lack of money if he knew.

As for giving Bridget the benefit of the doubt...

She turned, taking in Bridget's smudged face and dirty jacket. Even for all her darker thoughts, Adella had never once imagined Bridget would abandon her in their crisis. Bridget had more than earned that faith.

Adella stood on tiptoe and kissed her firmly. When Bridget's arms went around her waist, she leaned in and returned the kiss that seemed a celebration of their continued survival. Bridget's tongue passed her lips, and she moaned, relishing the rush of heat in her core. Bridget knew her secret now. For Adella's part, nothing stood between them and a night of ecstasy, a celebration of remaining alive.

And Bridget's secrets?

For passion like this, Adella could forget them for an evening.

When they parted slightly, breathless, Adella ran a hand through Bridget's hair and kissed her jaw. "Walk me home?" Zara and Gisele would just have to go to bed early.

Bridget smiled crookedly. "Or to your office?"

Adella gasped. She hadn't considered sex in her office. It sounded a little...wicked. A thrill raced through her. "All right."

As they began walking in that direction, Bridget leaned toward her ear. "I've been dying to see what Dolores left in her hidey-hole."

It took a moment to switch her brain to a new heading after she tried to make those words fit into the evening she'd just planned. Then she remembered what Cristoff had told her about the hiding place in the floor of her old office. She grinned. Knowing what was hidden in there was almost as exciting as the prospect of sex.

Well, not really, but it was pretty damned exciting all the same. By the end of the evening, she might have enough clues to catch Dolores's murderer *and* welcome Bridget into her bed. Or to the couch in her office. Or the desk.

Or all of them.

❖

Bridget had high hopes for this hiding place of Dolores's. The sooner they riffled through it, the sooner Adella might be led to Juno, and then Bridget could confess all and accept the invitation she'd glimpsed in Adella's eyes.

Baxter would have called her a fool and told her to take what was clearly being offered and *then* confess, but she wasn't an old letch. She could wait.

"Oh yeah?" Baxter would have asked. "You'll be able to wait after she's peeled off them tight trousers? When her eyes are giving you the come-on? When she's lying naked before you with her—"

She shook her head, forcing him to shut up in her mind as she would have done in person. The old goat would have delighted in embarrassing her. But she knew that if she made love to Adella before revealing her past with Sarras's longtime enemy, the fallout would be so much worse. There was no bed large enough for the two of them and Bridget's secrets.

Night had fully fallen by the time they arrived at the Bastión. A few people still trickled out, those who'd worked a little late, and no doubt the cleaners would be inside. The ever-present door guards gave their clothing an odd look, but Adella still had her badge and her keys, and the cloakroom attendant inside recognized her.

Anticipation built in Bridget, a thrill that held more than a little fear. It was too much to hope that the hiding spot held anything as damning as a note that said, "Dear Adella, Juno killed me. Love, Dolores," but they seemed so close to the end of this particular adventure, to the end of lies.

Where Adella would have to decide whether to stay with her or go.

"No," Baxter reminded her. "She won't have to go anywhere, ducky. She could turn you in, and you'll do all the going, either fleeing the country or getting marched to the scaffold."

The thought made her stomach shift, causing a feeling between nausea and hunger. They passed someone mopping the floor, and the overpowering scent of cleaner put Bridget firmly on the side of feeling sick. The sensation only increased when Adella unlocked the door to her old office and lit a candle on the desk.

Bridget pushed through the feeling and kneeled near the bookcase. The floorboard lifted as Cristoff said it would, revealing a small safe below. Bridget swallowed. "Do you have the key?"

"I never found it." Adella bit her lip, disappointment written across her face.

Bridget hesitated to suggest picking the lock, but…oh well, the truth would come out soon anyway. "Bring the light." She rummaged in the desk and found enough to improvise some lockpicks. As she went to work with them, Adella remained silent, but Bridget could practically hear her mind turning over. Maybe the amount of questions no doubt swarming in her head would delay any peeling off of trousers or come-on looks or lying down naked.

That was for the best, even if she did want to kick herself for thinking it.

The lock clicked and turned. Bridget opened the door and leaned back, though she wanted to reach in. This had to be Adella's discovery. She was going to confess, but it was best to put Adella in the most accepting frame of mind. And that would come after the pride of discovering Juno's treachery on her own.

Adella pulled out several sheets of paper, focusing on one after she gave the others a brief glance. She frowned hard as she read.

Bridget couldn't stand more than a few moments before she whispered, "What is it?"

"A letter from Juno's mother, Elena Garza." Her voice sounded flat, as if she couldn't decide on an emotion. "An old acquaintance of hers wrote her, saying their child was looking for a job in the Bastión and heard Elena's daughter worked there in Dolores's office. She was hoping Elena could write to Juno and make an introduction." She lowered the letter. "All very proper but very confusing to Elena because her daughter had died as a child. She wrote to Dolores, curious about the woman who claims the Garza name, especially with the first name of Juno."

Bridget's heart beat so hard, she could feel it in her eyes. So the woman they both knew as Juno had taken her new identity from the dead. Fairly standard procedure in Bridget's old world. The identity already had a history in place, and in this case, the family was too far away to suspect. But a chance letter from a random acquaintance who'd lost contact before the child had died could undo the whole thing.

Bridget licked her lips. Adella still seemed too shocked to act. "Could it be a different Juno Garza?"

Adella brightened a little, then frowned, just like Bridget wanted her to. "No, she said it was her mother when she saw the letter."

A costly mistake. Bridget wanted to rub Juno's nose in it but was still hoping she would be killed rather than caught. "So…"

Adella wasn't looking at her. "She was frightened when she saw it." Her frown slipped a little. "I…I thought this letter might hold the reason why Dolores had gotten killed, and that it had put Juno in danger. I wondered if it had made her run away."

It had. And the warring expressions on Adella's face said part of her knew that, but she needed to *say* it. "Well, if the Juno you know isn't really Juno at all…"

Adella stared now, but Bridget was surely just voicing Adella's thoughts, playing Baxter for her. Adella wasn't stupid. She just didn't want to believe.

Bridget saw the moment it hit her. Her color faded to the hue of wax, and her mouth dropped open.

"She killed Dolores," Adella whispered.

Gods above, yes! Bridget made herself look doubtful. "But—"

"No." Adella stood and waved the letter like a flag. "She was *pretending* to be a dead girl, and she got caught. Dolores must have confronted her." She began to pace, turning quickly in the small space. "That nasty, duplicitous, devils-cursed…"

Bridget let her rage. Her heart ached for the pain and anger radiating off Adella like heat, but she had to see this through.

Adella rounded on her. "But why *kill* Dolores? Why not run away?"

Bridget crossed her arms and pretended to think. "I suppose it would depend on why Juno was living a false identity in the first place."

Adella pointed at her. "Exactly. She could have been running from something. A criminal past?" She clutched the paper. "She's certainly a liar and now a murderer." She snarled before stopping and taking a few breaths, eyes tightly closed.

Bridget waited, ashamed for manipulating her, but she would have gotten here eventually. Still, the nausea was back.

"Why get a job in the Bastión if you're a criminal on the run?" Adella said quietly. "In ambassadorial work, of all things? With the… Firellian…office." Her eyes opened, and they blazed with righteous anger. "She's a *spy*."

Adella felt as if her brain was on fire. She kept reliving moments with Juno, little courtesies and confidences. The way Juno had always encouraged her or listened to her ramble.

Gathering information, winning her trust. Juno knew how much Adella hated even the idea of spying.

That must have made her laugh especially hard.

Adella stalked out of the office, barely hearing Bridget hurrying to keep up.

"Don't you want to lock—"

"No." There was only one thing she wanted: to wring Juno's neck. But she didn't know where she was or how to find her, so she'd do the next best thing. She would lay all of this before Gisele, giving the sentinels a target.

When she got outside and the cold night wind tore through her jacket, she paused. The frigid air spoke of late-season snow and dampened her anger enough to think. Gisele might have seen Adella with Cristoff. Who knew what she was thinking? She'd be wondering what Adella was hiding, maybe more.

Best to set things straight, then.

"Where are we going?" Bridget asked.

"Home to get Gisele and then to the sentinels." She began to walk again. Bridget said nothing, but her worries were probably coming back to mind, too. "I won't be angry if you can't come with me." She wanted to be angry at everyone, at the whole world, but Bridget had already said that her secrets couldn't be told just yet.

"I *want* to go."

"I know." Adella made herself breathe. It wasn't hard to take Bridget's hand, reminding herself that not every relationship was built on lies. "But you can't come with us to see the sentinels. I'm not upset about that, I promise. Insisting you stay behind is my way of protecting you now."

Bridget hung her head. Adella understood. It was hard to feel helpless. She'd felt that way during their escape at times, and she sympathized with the need to do something, anything, after a shock. When she'd first read Elena Garza's note, even before she'd fully comprehended it, she'd felt as if she might leap from her own skin if she didn't move.

She walked faster as she relived that horrible realization, as she saw Dolores's body in her mind and imagined Juno torturing her, killing her for the letter still clutched in Adella's free hand. She stuffed it inside her jacket and wiped her hand on her trousers, but she couldn't get rid of the vile feeling covering this whole business. Juno had tortured and killed Adella's mentor, her friend.

Juno wasn't even her real name. She was no one, a devil, a nightmare thing.

Adella imagined her hiding in the Bastión, lurking in some dark corner like a spider until even the cleaners had left. Then she'd gone to kill Dolores and steal the letter, but Dolores had already hidden it, outsmarting the devil.

If only she'd taken steps to protect herself, too.

Adella felt tears rushing up and gritted her teeth. She couldn't afford the time to weep when she needed to act.

"Adella?" Bridget asked, her sympathy too much.

"It's all right. I'm all right. You should go." More lies.

Bridget *tsked*. "I'm not leaving you. I'll see you home."

Adella looked to the blanket of stars overhead and tried to choke down the sobs gathering like an enemy host inside her. "I don't… want to…" If she said any more, they'd escape. She braced herself for a hug or more comforting words, but Bridget squeezed her hand just shy of real pain, making her gasp.

"Then get angry," Bridget said, her voice laced with a gravelly edge. "Think about what you'll do when you find her. Think about the trials ahead of *her* now that you're on her track."

It worked, pushing back the tears with vengeance, and she felt a rush of affection for Bridget for giving her what she actually wanted instead of what someone conventional might think she needed.

Adella wanted to thank her, but a rushing shadow from the bushes on her left caught her eye. She drew breath to call out, but the shadow slammed into her before she could speak. With a grunt, she staggered into Bridget. They toppled into the lane in a tangle of limbs. Adella's chest ached as she sought to get her breath back.

The streetlamp above them winked out, turning the lane into a land of shadows. Bridget twisted free and rose. Adella heard a cry of pain that cut off abruptly. She kicked away from a darker shadow amongst all the others and tried to call through her fear, failing to make a sound beyond a wheeze.

Someone said, "No!" as the darker shadow lunged for her. She held up her hands to ward it off, but a fist rushed past them and slammed into her stomach.

Her universe became pain that roiled from the middle of her and spread all through her limbs. She folded around it, breathless again, though her throat ached with silent cries. Her ears rang, and the cold stones dug into her. Helpless, she watched the shadow come for her again.

CHAPTER EIGHTEEN

Once Bridget fought past her fear, she slipped easily into the mindset of violence. As soon as they'd been hit, she'd known it wasn't an accident. Someone was attacking them, so she'd struck out blindly, punching and kicking after the light had gone out. When one of the shadow forms had gone toward Adella, she'd called out but had been unable to stop it.

Adella had gone frighteningly quiet now as she lay in the street. Bridget lunged in that direction, just making out her pale hair in the light from the streetlamp down the lane. Someone stood between them, and she grabbed hold of them and heaved, sending them tumbling to the ground.

Another person grabbed her from behind, tearing at the material of her stolen jacket. She shrugged out of it, but another pair of hands latched on to her shoulders. She twisted and grunted, kicking back until the attacker let go, but the effort put her off balance, and she fell onto the person she'd just downed.

Bridget brought her knees up, trying to grind them into the downed attacker while getting to her feet, but someone caught her again by the left arm and wrenched it up behind her back. She cried out, pushing with the motion as the person who held her reared back. On her feet now, agony spreading through her shoulder, she tried to kick but hit nothing. The person who'd been knocked to the ground grabbed her flailing leg, and she was caught between them. When a fist plunged into her stomach, she couldn't cry out or cough, couldn't even curl around the new ache in her core because her shoulder still felt as if it was being torn from her socket.

"Get the other one," someone said.

Adella. Bridget tried to break free, to fight past the sharp pain, but her attacker twisted her arm again, and little flashes of light passed through her vision as a sickening feeling rolled across her shoulders. She couldn't hear beyond her own choking, and she couldn't make a noise.

Gods, surely someone had heard something. Someone had to be coming. By all the gods and devils, please!

Footsteps pounded nearby, and the attacker holding her arm seemed to disappear. Bridget fell forward, gasping, her arm screaming as she brought it in front of her again. The stones of the lane dug into her knees, bringing her back to herself, and she looked again for a glimpse of pale hair.

There, beyond the shuffle of shadowy feet. Adella. And she was moving.

Bridget felt a jolt of hope. Someone had come, and she wasn't going to waste the gift they'd given her. She managed to lurch upward, though her stomach ached like fire when she tried to straighten. She shuffled forward, bent double, and fell again at Adella's side.

She tried to speak but only managed a wheezing whisper. "Adella…come on." She smoothed Adella's hair, beyond relieved when Adella clasped her hands. Bridget tried to pull her up, not knowing how badly she was hurt, but they couldn't stay here to find out. Bridget's gut cried out at the effort of lifting someone to their feet, but she could only whimper at that pain.

Adella couldn't seem to straighten either, and Bridget put an arm around her shoulders. She looked about at the huge houses behind their gates. Many had candles or lamplight shining from the windows, and Bridget led Adella toward the nearest one, determined to rattle the gate until all the devils in hell took notice.

A rush of air behind her made her turn. She shoved Adella away before a shadowy form caught hold of her. She lashed out with a fist, and it connected with something soft. The person grabbing her made a strangled sound and staggered back to stand silhouetted against the faraway light. Another shadow approached and flung out a leg, kicking the attacker in the head and knocking them to the ground as solidly as if they'd been shot with an arrow.

Bridget tried to ready herself to fight, but this shadow held up its hands. "I'm here to help, serrah." A man's voice. And he wasn't attacking. That was all she cared about. She turned for Adella, who'd regained her feet. Bridget helped steady her.

"This way," the man said. He walked toward the light, and that was good enough for Bridget. If he'd come from one of the houses, she'd follow him in, take stock, and figure out what to do from there. She limped along with Adella, and to his credit, the man didn't try to touch them, not even when they came close enough to the light for her to see his features: pale face, dark hair in a tidy queue, and the dalmatica of a noble. One of Adella's class. Good.

He paused under the light, and Adella gasped, her eyes wide as she tried to straighten, wincing. "Jean-Carlo?" she whispered.

He bowed. "At your service, serrah."

Bridget breathed a little easier since Adella knew him, but he seemed to be waiting for something else. "Are you a neighbor?" Bridget asked.

"I'm Serrah del Amanecer's secondary ambassador."

They taught people how to kick someone in the head in ambassador school? Bridget almost laughed at the absurdity of the thought.

"Let's get to my house," Adella said, glancing back.

Bridget did the same. She couldn't see anything in the shadowy area of the lane, but she didn't want to wait for anyone to come after them. She continued to help Adella, each step less difficult than the last. Jean-Carlo stayed with them, walking at Bridget's side with the occasional glance over his shoulder. He seemed incredibly calm, and she kept having visions of his leg streaking out with a serpent's speed.

He followed them into Adella's house, but she pointed him toward a corner in the foyer, and he obeyed. She seemed to have recovered her breath as she locked and bolted the door, but she still held a hand to her stomach. In the dim candlelight coming from a room to the side and the back of the house, Bridget spotted a cut on her cheek, but her eyes were hard and steady.

"Stay there, Jean-Carlo," she said. "Zara! Gisele!"

Bridget stayed at Adella's side as they watched him. He might have saved them, but Adella clearly wasn't in the mood to trust anyone.

"What's going on?" Zara walked downstairs holding a lantern, and Gisele came from the back of the house to stand in the light from the next room. "Del, what happened?" Zara took Adella's face in hand, turning the cut toward the light.

"We were attacked."

Her sisters looked to Jean-Carlo, and Zara took a step toward him, though she was unarmed. Gisele's face seemed pained, but she raised her hands, muttering under her breath.

"No," Adella said. "He rescued us. I just…I don't know who to trust."

Jean-Carlo stayed calm through all this, and now he bowed again. "Wise, serrah."

Zara and Gisele began firing questions so fast, no one could answer. Bridget waved to get their attention. "We'll tell you what we can, but not yet." She inclined her head toward Jean-Carlo, not sure what Adella wanted him to know. He smiled slightly as everyone fell silent.

"Jean-Carlo, where did you learn…" Adella sighed and rubbed her stomach again. "Are you really an ambassador?"

"Among other things." He rubbed his chin. "I've worked in a few different foreign relations departments. Mostly, I work in security, moving to various offices that seem at risk from infiltration."

Bridget's belly would have gone cold if it wasn't still burning. Gisele narrowed her eyes and said, "You're a spy hunter." Clearly, they were thinking along the same lines.

He bowed again, and his eyes raked over them, but he didn't linger on Bridget, and she tried to keep her face impassive, tried not to give him a reason to look at her. Her inner Baxter was telling her to run, screaming at her, but she forced him down.

"And you're after…" Adella paused, waiting.

"I suspected Juno," he said, nodding toward the door. "And it was lucky I followed you tonight, though you managed to lose me on your little adventure this afternoon." He smiled, and Bridget wanted to shake him until he told them everything he knew.

Adella took a step forward, her eyes glinting dangerously. "How long have you known about her? Before she killed Dolores? Could you have stopped her?"

He shook his head, seeming alarmed for the first time tonight. "I was given the order to guard you after Ambassador Vega's death. I don't know when my superiors began to suspect a spy in your office."

She still scowled, and her sisters glanced at each other, no doubt burning with their own questions, but they seemed ready to act if Adella decided she wanted Jean-Carlo obliterated.

"What now?" Bridget asked quietly.

He glanced at her before looking to Adella again. "Something you did today or tonight in the Bastión prompted her to act, if those were indeed her thugs." He nodded again to the street. "The thing to do now is find her."

"Are you working with the sentinels?" Gisele asked, her dark eyes flashing.

He gave another enigmatic smile. "Sometimes."

She frowned hard, seemingly hating that answer. Bridget had to admire her tenacity.

"I want to speak to your superiors," Adella said.

"I'll see what I can do."

It wasn't a promise or a denial and was probably the best they were going to get.

"Is your commanding officer going to assign guards to our house?" Zara asked. Her hand clenched near her hip as if she was missing a weapon.

He started to smile, then ducked his head, no doubt amused by the fact that the soldier in the room thought he had anything so mundane as a commanding officer with a host of guards at their disposal. "We're certain Juno's resources don't extend to an army. Attacking two unarmed people in the street is one thing. Laying siege to a locked house with a soldier and a mage inside is another. You'll be perfectly safe, but I'll snoop around a bit outside if you don't mind. And if anything else occurs in the night, I'll tell you." He looked to Adella. "If you'll do the same?"

"We're to find you while you're snooping?" Adella asked, a sneer in her voice.

He pulled a card from his pocket. "Messages sent to this address will find their way to me."

She accepted it and looked to the door. Bridget took the hint and undid the locks and bolts so Jean-Carlo could leave. "Thanks," she said, and he gave her a nod before striding down the path to the lane. She wondered if she should go with him to examine the downed attackers, but she didn't want to rouse more of Adella's suspicions, not when she was already on edge. A nightingale didn't go about investigating the doings of spies.

When she shut the door, the questions came hard and fast again. Adella wordlessly turned for the back of the house, and everyone else trailed behind her until they were grouped around a kitchen table. Zara and Gisele laid out food and drinks and water to wash with. Adella dabbed at the cut on her cheek as she started talking. To Bridget's surprise, she told them everything, even where Cristoff could be found, though she didn't give the name of the smuggler shielding him.

When she'd finished her story, they sat quietly for a few moments. Zara went out a side door and came back with two handfuls of ice wrapped in towels, and Bridget gratefully put one to her stomach. Adella did the same, and Bridget wondered if their similar injuries meant that their attackers had meant to incapacitate and capture them rather than kill them.

"Um," Gisele said quietly, breaking the silence. She looked up sheepishly. She had dark circles under her eyes, and her shoulders stooped as if she was in pain. "The invisible sentinels showing up at the boat? That was me. I didn't know it was you they were after, Del, I swear. They said they were going to capture a suspect at the docks."

Adella sighed and put her chin in her hand. "I figured as much." She touched her sister's hand. "I'm not angry. The sentinels must have had someone watching me, and I led them to Cristoff."

Bridget ducked her head to hide a grimace. Cristoff hadn't been the only one in danger on that boat.

Gisele frowned. "I told the sentinels you couldn't be a suspect, that you'd never kill Dolores."

"Clearly, they didn't believe you," Zara said. She shrugged when Gisele glared at her. "Or they thought Adella might lead them somewhere beneficial even if she wasn't guilty. And that was what happened."

"I didn't know," Gisele said again, winding a lock of dark hair around her finger like a little kid.

"It's all right," Adella tried.

"No, it isn't." When Gisele stood, she winced and sat again. "Why would the sentinels keep something like that from me?"

"You would have told Adella," Bridget replied, while Zara snorted and said, "They couldn't trust you."

This time, Gisele stayed standing as she faced Zara down.

"Don't," Adella said, a warning in her tone that brooked no argument. "We're in deep water now. Spies and their hunters, lies and murder." She shook her head, and tears shimmered in her eyes. "A person I once cared about sending thugs to attack me in the street."

Bridget wanted to go to her, but she'd waved off her sisters, and Bridget sensed that she didn't want to break down, just as she hadn't wanted to in the lane. Bridget tried to put all her support into a look, hoping Adella would understand that she was here if needed, but inside, despair was taking hold of her. How had she thought that Juno's secrets coming to light would help ease the way to her own confession? It didn't matter that Bridget's spying days were over. Adella would see her as being just like Juno, especially after she discovered that Bridget had kept Juno's nature a secret.

Could she conceal just that fact? Or would it stay between them, an ugly little mark, an itchy scab she wouldn't be able to resist picking at? When Adella gave her a grateful look, she almost revealed all, almost dumped all of it into the sadness lingering around this table. Adella would weep, then, and rage, and maybe her sisters would tear Bridget in two, and neither piece of her would have to worry about the mountain of betrayal she was carrying into this relationship.

But it felt like Baxter had his hand over her mouth, and she couldn't speak for a few moments.

"What do we do now?" It took them all looking at her for Bridget to realize she'd said that. It must have been Baxter still working through her. A spy wouldn't be asking that sort of question.

"What can we do tonight?" Zara asked. "That man was right in that no one will want to attack the house, but we can stand watches if we're worried."

"I'd like to talk to my sentinel contacts," Gisele said bitterly. "Find out what else they're keeping from me."

"They don't report to you," Zara said.

"They owe me an explanation."

Bridget smiled at what seemed like good-natured bickering even with the anger behind the words. She wished she had a sibling or two.

Someone else to have to leave behind?

Perhaps not.

Adella made a small tired noise as she rubbed her forehead, and her sisters fell silent again. "You won't be getting one tonight, I'll wager. And neither will I." She smiled at Bridget. "Since Juno… whoever she is, isn't going to appear before us tonight for a good beating, I don't think there's much we can do besides try to sleep." She stood, wincing as she rubbed her stomach. She grabbed the lantern off the table. "I'm going to bed. You can stand watch if you want, Zara."

Bridget tried to find the right way to ask what Adella wanted her to do, but Adella took her hand and led her upstairs, deciding for them both. Behind the door of a large bedroom, Bridget hesitated as Adella set the lantern down and removed her coat. All of Bridget's former lustful imaginings came back, but they couldn't fight past her guilt… or the pain in her gut and shoulder. "Adella—"

"Please stay with me." Her back was turned, and her head drooped. "Just to sleep. I can't…" A sob stole the rest of her words.

Bridget nearly leaped for her and drew her close. They weren't in the street now. No one had to hold on to their anger or fear losing control. Bridget crushed Adella to her chest as heartbreaking sobs seemed to rip through her, shaking her from head to toe. She clung to Bridget as if to a mast during a storm, and Bridget weathered it all, murmuring that she was still here, that she wasn't leaving, even joining in with a few tears for all the chaos that remained in their lives.

But just for tonight, that chaos was locked outside the door.

When Adella's sobs eased, Bridget led her to the bed. She undressed Adella tenderly, doing her best not to look, not to see as a lover but only as a caretaker. She left Adella in her underthings and fetched the nightshirt she'd spied at the end of the bed.

After Adella put it on, she kissed Bridget gratefully. "Thank you."

Bridget kissed her back before helping her under the covers. "Thank you, too."

She snorted humorlessly. "What exactly have I done for you?"

Bridget undressed quickly, leaving on her shirt and underclothes before she doused the lantern and climbed into bed to draw Adella into her arms. "You've given me a glimpse of feelings I never thought I'd have, of a life I never imagined for myself." And it was true. She'd had lovers, but she'd never felt like this, like she could die for someone.

Like she could live for them, open and honest and as her true self.

Adella turned in her embrace and snuggled close. "We've only known each other a few days, but I...I..."

Bridget kissed her forehead. Yes, it was too early to be throwing around words like love, too early to know if what they had would even survive after this crisis was over. At the moment, it was enough to hold each other and fall asleep feeling safe.

CHAPTER NINETEEN

Adella woke in a spike of panic. It was dark, and someone's arm was wrapped around her. The people who'd attacked her and Bridget were back, and they'd caught her.

Before she could leap away, she remembered the rest of what had happened and relaxed. No one had caught her. She was in bed with Bridget, and the house was locked up tight. Zara was probably patrolling the halls. Gisele might have stayed awake, too, and Adella was tempted to give in to guilt because she hadn't also stayed awake to keep the devils at bay. But she'd been so tired, and her stomach had been aching.

As she slowly turned over, the ache reminded her that it hadn't gone anywhere. She resisted the urge to gasp and settled instead, hoping she hadn't awakened Bridget, but the slow breathing behind her now didn't change.

She was in bed with Bridget.

After all that had happened, she'd thought her libido might have abandoned her, but it stirred now. Neither of them was wearing much, and they were so close. Bridget murmured in her sleep and snuggled closer, her hand moving over Adella's hip, and her breasts pressing against Adella's back. That was enough to elicit a gasp, but she calmed as the pain in her midsection flared at even the small movement.

Turning and kissing Bridget awake seemed out of the question, not if they'd both have to contend with pain cutting through their pleasure. Pain that would remind Adella of Juno's betrayal, no less.

She wadded a bit of sheet in her fist. The woman she'd known was not Juno Garza. That was a poor dead girl whose memory did not deserve to be used by Firellian spies. Adella would have to write another letter to Elena Garza and say how sorry she was about the atrocities a devil from hell had committed while bearing her daughter's name.

Devil-Juno. That seemed fitting, like an evil presence that possessed people and turned everything around them to ash. Adella wanted to see her pay, not just for the murder and the humiliation but for being something as repulsive as a spy, burrowing into other people's lives like a tick.

Adella's face was beginning to burn with her anger, and the cut on her cheek throbbed. She forced herself to breathe. There was no hint of light coming from behind the curtains. Even if she got up, she couldn't start her day. All the people she could report Juno to were either still asleep, or they had already been informed by Jean-Carlo.

Her heart didn't know how to feel about him. He said he was on her side, but he was as much a spy as Devil-Juno. Jean-Carlo might not be his real name. He'd been good at his job, but she imagined he was good at every job he took on. He had to learn fast in his line of work: pretending to be other people. She *tsked*. At least they'd never shared any confidences, though he had given her some good counsel, had made her feel more competent in her work. She'd ask him if he'd laughed about that later with his superiors, if he'd mocked her. No doubt he would deny it, but she told herself she would read the truth in his eyes. She had to believe that.

And in Devil-Juno's eyes? Did she even want to see that creature again? No, such a monster didn't deserve a last conversation. Adella would be content to see her for the last time as she swung for her crimes.

At that, Adella had to slip out of bed. She wouldn't be able to sleep with that image in her mind. It pleased part of her and sickened another. After Devil-Juno was caught, no doubt Adella would change her mind a thousand times concerning her fate, but at the moment, vengeance was winning.

Adella slowly crossed the bedroom and found her dressing gown hanging on the back of the door where she'd left it. She eased out of the room without fetching the lamp, not wanting to wake Bridget. She paused in the hall and let her eyes adjust. Her room was nearest the staircase, and she took a few steps that way, avoiding the creakiest floorboards. The stairs were frigid against her bare feet, but she tried to ignore the feeling, especially after she saw a glow of light coming from downstairs.

As she'd thought, Zara sat awake in the kitchen. She'd lit a fire in the large hearth that at one time had been used to cook whole boars on spits but was now only for keeping them warm on the chilliest nights or when they sat up late and didn't want to gather around the high table.

Zara looked up from a book as Adella took one of the other two chairs near the hearth and put her feet on the low bench they used as a footrest. "Did something wake you?" Zara asked.

"Memories." Adella rubbed her feet together.

"You should have worn slippers."

Queen of the obvious. Adella sighed and shrugged, staring into the low fire. Maybe watching the flicker would put her back to sleep. "Are you going to bed at all tonight?"

"No, I'm used to staying up."

Adella nodded. When Zara was on patrol with her scouting unit, she was often awake and on the move for days at a time, not collapsing until she was back in town, and then she slept for a week. Adella didn't look up again until Zara stood before her, holding out a steaming mug. Adella took it with a grateful smile and breathed deeply. Hot chocolate and a warm fire. She'd be asleep in no time.

But Zara wasn't finished. She sat on the bench and pulled off her socks, revealing another pair beneath the thick outer ones. Adella tried to object around a mouth full of cocoa, but Zara ignored her and put the thicker socks on Adella's feet, giving them a quick warming rub after she did.

Queen of the kindhearted, too. Gisele would have added, when she wants to be, but Gisele wasn't here. Adella took Zara's hand and squeezed, grateful beyond belief that her sisters were still exactly who she thought they were. "Thank you."

Zara smiled bashfully and resumed her seat. "It's been quiet. That fellow said he was going to snoop around, but I haven't seen him from any of the windows."

"Like your unit, I imagine he can remain unseen when he wants to."

"An urban scout," she said with a snort. "It would mostly be blending in with other people. Sounds too easy."

"It's called a spy," Adella said, sneering at the thought.

"What good is a spy among his own people?"

Adella waved around. "You saw tonight. They walk around with their own people waiting for foreign spies to act."

"Spy *hunters*," Zara said. "That's just a different kind of soldier or a sentinel or constable."

Adella's ire rose. "It's not the same. They lie." She clutched her mug until it grew uncomfortably hot under her fingers, then held it by the handle again. Zara was staring at her as if trying to understand, and Adella almost snapped at her to look somewhere else, but that would only confuse her further, and then she'd try to stare out of the corner of her eye, which was often hilarious, but Adella was in no mood.

She sighed, hating that she was rambling in her own head. She was simply too tired to explain herself. "It's been a long day," she said quietly.

Zara nodded. "I'm very sorry about your friend. Friends. It must feel like two of them have died."

It took a moment to figure out who the second friend was, but when she realized Zara was talking about Devil-Juno, she sneered again. "She was never my friend, never real."

"In your mind, she was," Zara said in a determined tone. "And you were a friend to her, as much as you could be while still being her boss."

"Yes," Adella said between her teeth. Tears threatened again, but she blinked them away. "I was such a fool."

"You shouldn't feel foolish for being a good friend," Zara said, leaning forward until Adella had to look at her. "And trusting someone isn't a crime. She killed the friendship you had. The blame is on her, not you or the man who protected you or Dolores or anyone."

Adella stared, not expecting such insight from her quieter sister. Zara tended to see things in black and white, and this time, Adella knew she was right. And Adella had really needed to hear that from someone too stubborn to consider any other point of view.

Feeling her lip wobble, Adella reached to still it, overly conscious of making Zara uncomfortable. "I want to hug you," she said breathlessly.

Zara allowed it after their mugs were safely on the bench. She held Adella awkwardly, but she always did so, hugging as if the other person was made of delicate porcelain.

"Thank you, Zara," Adella said, rubbing her back before settling in the chair again.

"Are you going back to bed now?"

"No, I think I'll stay and watch the fire a bit longer and no doubt fall asleep in this chair."

Zara smiled. "What about Bridget?"

Adella sighed just thinking about her. "I really like her a lot. What I feel might even go beyond liking her. I liked her before all this trouble started, but she's stuck with me through everything, even with all the danger I've put her in. She's loyal and kind and lovely, and she smells really good." She was rambling again but in a better way.

"Um." Zara cleared her throat. "I meant, what if she wakes up, and you're not there?"

"Oh." Adella yawned. "She's smart. She'll know I didn't up and disappear. I'll be here when she comes looking." She stared into the flames, lost in thoughts of Bridget now.

She let her eyes stay closed after one slow blink too many, but she still heard Zara mumble, "I'm glad you like her, but if she hurts you, I'll kill her."

Ferocious but sweet all the same. Pure Zara. Adella drifted to sleep, comforted.

The sounds of people bustling around the kitchen behind her woke Adella from her slumber. She tried to sit up, and her core ached again, painfully reminding her of her adventures the night before. She sank back into her seat, and Bridget kneeled beside her.

"How are you feeling?" Bridget asked, rubbing her arm and giving her a tentative smile. Her short hair was tousled from sleep, quite a sexy look.

Adella returned the smile and glanced at Bridget's arm and midsection. "Sore. How are you kneeling there and showing me up?"

"We nightingales are used to the occasional jab to the gut. That's how they teach us in music school."

Adella *tsked* before she tried standing again, letting Bridget help her. "I'm sorry I wasn't there when you woke up," she said softly as Zara and Gisele were sitting at the kitchen table. They were talking, but Gisele's many glances out of the corner of her eye told Adella she was trying to eavesdrop as much as possible.

"That's okay. It gave me a chance to go through all your things."

Adella sputtered a laugh, then put a hand to her aching belly. "Oh! I forbid you from being glib until I feel better."

"Noted." She kissed Adella's cheek.

Adella wanted to return the gesture, but Gisele was staring now and grinning like an idiot. Zara didn't seem to be paying attention to anything but her food. The dark circles under her eyes stood out even on her tanned skin. "Do you want to get some sleep, Zara?"

She looked up and frowned as if Adella had suggested she jump off the roof. "I'm going with you when you report to the sentinels." She looked to Gisele, who nodded. "We're not letting you out of the house alone again."

Adella knew they wanted to keep her safe, but she could look after herself. Mostly. Sometimes. And she was the oldest and didn't need a nursemaid. All the arguments lined up in her mind, but the pain in her stomach seemed there specifically to remind her that she *did* need help. And when she caught Bridget's worried look, she knew no backup would be coming from that quarter.

And Bridget couldn't go to the sentinels with them.

Several emotions warred within her at that thought: anger at secrets still untold, fear that Bridget's past was more tangled than she'd thought, relief that Bridget would be out of danger's path by not being at Adella's side. When Bridget led her out of the kitchen toward the front door, Adella didn't know what to say.

"Those things I needed to do before I can tell you about my past," Bridget said quickly. "I can take care of them while you're out. And then…" A bit of redness came to her cheeks. Had her mind wandered to the same lustful place Adella's mind had gone before they'd discovered Dolores's letter?

"Then I can be honest," Bridget finished.

Adella wanted that, too, but she was a little disappointed. She supposed she should get her mind off sex for the time being since there were more important things happening…but it was something to look forward to. And complete honesty was obviously important to Bridget before becoming more intimate. It was a lovely sentiment, one Adella shared. She stood on tiptoe and kissed Bridget soundly, hinting at the rewards for honesty.

When they parted, Bridget's brows rose. "Well, thank you for the reminder that I should hurry back."

Adella grinned, more at ease than she was last night, hopeful now that night had given way to day. She could move forward instead of stewing in her own thoughts or seeking comfort from everyone else. Anger still lurked inside her, fanned by lingering pain, but she could work with it instead of sinking into it and letting it consume her.

And if the night brought despairing thoughts again, she would take comfort in the fact that the dawn was never far away.

As she strode away from Adella's house, Bridget wished she could have made last night linger. Not the attack, obviously, or the getting punched or the arm wrenching that still made her shoulder feel as if it was full of broken glass, but the part where she'd cuddled against Adella, locking out all the bad things in life.

When she'd woken up alone, she thought she'd dreamed everything but had no explanation for the enormous bed she'd found herself in until memory had come rushing back. With a chuckle, she'd considered searching the blankets and pillows to make sure she hadn't simply misplaced Adella in the absurdly large bed. Then she'd tripped over a nightstand on her way to where the sunlight peeked around a curtain and had thrown it open.

Adella hadn't been in the room, and Bridget had worried she'd overslept and that Adella and her sisters had gone to the sentinels without saying good-bye. A suspicious part of her had wondered if that was on purpose. If Gisele the spy hunter suspected her, they'd be back with a host of sentinels to arrest her, and…

She'd made herself breathe. She'd been able to put those fears to one side when she'd been a spy, but now that she was trying to live as her real self, it was all too much. But she'd managed to find her center, point out to her overactive imagination that it was barely dawn, dress, and go downstairs to discover Adella adorably asleep in a chair before a large hearth on the far side of the kitchen.

All through their hurried breakfast, she'd fought her nerves. She'd been so grateful when Adella didn't expect her to join them on their sentinel quest. She'd been wondering what she should do when it had hit her. She could get rid of Juno, then whisk Adella away before whatever plan Juno had to unmask Bridget as a spy could be put into place.

And her vow not to…dispose of anyone?

It would just have to wait.

The thought had kept turning over in her mind until she couldn't wait to get out of the house. Adella was safe from Juno's thugs now that she and her sisters had their guard up. Bridget could deal with anyone who got in her way now. Then after Juno was dealt with, Bridget would tell Adella about her past and that Juno tried to blackmail her, but she'd refused to help a spy.

She'd have to fudge the timeline a bit. That gave her pause. Adella would not like that Bridget had known about Juno for a while now, but Bridget could tinker with that. A tiny lie wouldn't be important, not with her past out of the way.

Baxter would be giving her a flat, knowing look, but she would have told him to keep his mouth shut. She had a plan now, one that could work. If she removed Juno, she'd have the freedom to do as she wanted.

"Remove her," Baxter would have said with a cat's smile. "Isn't that a pretty way to say it, ducky?"

Bridget shoved her hands in her pockets as she walked. The wind was picking up, and the first few flakes of snow were falling, soon to turn the streets pristine. She'd already passed the place where she thought she and Adella had been attacked, but there was nothing to mark it. Jean-Carlo had cleared away any bodies he might have made, or someone had done it for him.

"At least you thought the word bodies that time," Baxter would have said. "Even if you're still not saying the words you really mean."

She told him to be quiet. He was a part of her, and she needed all the parts of herself to be on board with this plan.

The…disposal plan.

Bridget sighed at herself. Killing. She was thinking about killing someone, killing Juno. Killing, ending, snuffing out like a candle.

"Murder," Baxter purred.

Bridget rubbed her forehead and muttered at him to shut up, causing a couple walking ahead to glance over their shoulders, then hurry along. Bridget held in a curse. She was getting closer to the Trade District, and there were more people out walking. The richer Oligarch's Ward would be teeming with carriages soon, and Bridget hoped Adella and her sisters would splurge on a cab. She was happier losing herself in more crowded streets. She kept her eyes open for anyone paying too much attention to her, but Juno couldn't have planned for her every move, and she was certain she would have seen anyone following her from Adella's house in the daylight. If Juno had assigned someone to watch the house all evening, Bridget hoped they'd frozen their ass off.

Or that Jean-Carlo had…dispatched them.

Baxter would have roared with laughter at that. Even though the old bastard had agreed that she needed to flee from a job that had become more assassin than spy. Maybe she'd think of her current goal as one last job, one that was on the side of justice for once.

Maybe that would help her forget when it was over. She could always make her vow again.

She paused several streets away from the hotel where she'd left Juno. She didn't want to go back to the Donkey's Rest, not wanting to drag Serrah Nunez or anyone else further into this. If Juno had watchers, she would have definitely set some there. Bridget scanned the streets for anyone loitering as she walked slowly toward the back of the hotel, aiming for the alley below Juno's room.

As the day grew lighter, more people ventured out, even with the dusting of snow. Few lingered, giving Bridget a better chance of spotting any guards, but she couldn't move too slowly either, or she'd attract attention. The last thing she needed was some constable thinking she was casing the local businesses to pull off a quick theft.

Whenever she saw anyone waiting in a doorway or under an awning, she paused, ducking out of sight and waiting until they moved or took a different direction.

Would Juno even still be at the hotel? If she was sending people after Adella and Bridget, then surely, she would have abandoned that hiding place. Unless the thugs hadn't really been after Bridget, too. If Juno had found out that Adella and Bridget had gone to see the smugglers, had sailed off with them, maybe Juno thought Bridget was running for it, that Adella was seeing her off. Or Juno could have thought they were seeking allies. Either way, Juno would have made good on her threat to hurt Adella if Bridget didn't obey.

And Bridget hadn't gone to see her yesterday at all, disobeying in one way, at least. Bridget gritted her teeth as she moved closer to the hotel. Baxter would have told her to stop thinking herself into a quagmire and get more damned information. And the hotel was a good place to start.

After turning down two more streets to avoid people who didn't seem in a hurry to get anywhere, she'd almost reached the alley. She paused on another side street that went by the alley in question before turning a corner. No one waited in the alley unless they were crouching behind a stack of boxes. And no one could stay that way for long in this weather.

Satisfied, she scanned the other streets again, seeing no one at all on this narrow little lane. She paused on a stoop and blew on her hands to warm them, shifting slightly to limber up so she could climb those crates and get to the window quickly. She tried to find the quiet, violent place inside her, but her nerves were jangling like discordant bells.

When a hand closed over her arm, she nearly shrieked, her heart in her mouth as she whirled.

CHAPTER TWENTY

After a few hours, Adella understood a little of why the smugglers, Serrah Nunez, and Bridget had seemed disinclined to work with the sentinels. Even for non-criminals, it seemed a massive waste of time. The aide they'd spoken with at headquarters had led them to a nicely appointed waiting room where they'd sat for nearly an hour in order to speak to a lieutenant Gisele had worked with before. She'd tried to hurry things along, but she hadn't known anyone higher up in the command chain. Adella told the lieutenant about Devil-Juno and had showed him the letter and told him about a spy in the Bastión.

He hadn't seemed to know quite what to do, so he'd handed them over to a sergeant who'd led them to a waiting room to see a captain. When Adella had politely asked how long they could expect to wait this time, the sergeant had huffed and said the captain would be free when he was free and nothing could hurry them.

Adella's tank of civility had almost run dry, and she'd wished for Bridget's ability to choke someone at that moment.

Finally, the captain had deigned to see them, but he'd been so welcoming and jovial that Adella had forgotten her ire for a moment and had laid all before him.

He had stared for a few moments, left his office to have a word with someone else, then a different lieutenant than the first had come in and led them to a different, larger, even more nicely appointed sitting room in a different building. They hadn't seen the captain again.

When they were alone, Adella had been so stunned that she'd stared at the door for several minutes. She turned to Zara, who shrugged.

"Don't look at me. This isn't the army. They have their own way of doing things." She poked a pillow. "Mainly sitting, looks like." She only had a little sneer as she said it.

Gisele seemed embarrassed. She'd clearly been hoping her work with the sentinels rated more than this waiting room merry-go-round, but she was a hired weapon, after all. Adella couldn't be angry. She'd tried throwing her title around, both as a member of one of Sarras's oldest noble families and as the ambassador to the Firellian Empire. The sentinels had seemed impressed, but they still hadn't known what to do with her. Part of her couldn't blame them. She was here without an appointment. But she still resented becoming lost in the halls of bureaucracy.

"I wonder who we'll get to see this time," Adella said. Hell, she wouldn't be surprised if they'd been left in here to die surrounded by gilded chairs, padded sofas, and tables that shone with so much polish, the current of air from the opening door should have sent the silver tea set gliding across the surface.

More tea. Or possibly coffee. She wished she'd eaten more breakfast. They'd been supplied with endless cups of coffee or tea, but she dreaded drinking any more, or she'd have to go in search of the facilities, and with her luck, that would be the only moment the next officer could see her, and she'd be out of luck for that whole day. Or maybe when their next guide arrived, they'd be shown through a door with a bright light, only to discover they'd been hustled out the back of the building.

"At least our news is important enough to get us referred this far," Zara said, but her sigh belied any optimism in her words.

"Or the others just had no idea what to do with us," Gisele said.

Adella nodded. They had verified a traitor and had discovered the identity of Dolores's murderer, but no one seemed to know quite what to do. Maybe that was why people like Jean-Carlo existed: to take care of pesky little problems like spies.

Still, Adella sighed. She'd hoped they'd be rushed into some kind of war room where there would be maps of the city, and everyone would be discussing what their next steps should be to hunt every spy in Sarras. Instead, they had an endless parade of porcelain cups and one time, something that looked like a cookie but had the texture and taste of a paving stone.

Maybe she and Bridget had actually been killed the night before, and this was an elaborate trick by some mischievous devil in hell.

"Maybe we should have brought a bribe," Gisele said.

Zara's jaw dropped, and she made a sound of disgust. Gisele smirked, clearly seeing a way to end her embarrassment and boredom by provoking their sister.

"Don't start," Adella said before Zara could begin an affronted speech.

"What else is there to do?" Gisele said.

"Turn us all invisible, and we can sneak in," Adella said, lifting an eyebrow to cow Gisele back into silence.

Gisele ducked her head. At least Adella was still good at some things. And she needed to get her thoughts in order about what to say if someone asked her about the smugglers…if anyone really spoke to her at all. She planned to downplay her role in that entire smuggling business. Not that she'd lie. *Most* of it would be true. She and Bridget hadn't known where Cristoff was when they'd set out to find clues. Then they'd gotten caught in something they hadn't really understood. She was only going to omit how they'd escaped by violent means and say they'd managed to sneak away.

And if someone insisted on knowing who her compatriots were, well, she had an icy stare of her own that could match anyone's.

"What if we're going to see an oligarch?" Gisele said quietly.

Adella and Zara glanced at each other, and Adella saw her own shock reflected in Zara's face. Oh shit. Her icy stare wasn't that good. "Do you…I can't see why." Her mind raced. She'd only ever seen them at large gatherings and had been hurried through the odd receiving line. As old and noble as her family was, they hadn't contributed to many of the oligarchs' schemes because they didn't have the money. Gods and devils, the oligarchs might even know her family lacked the cash to enact change.

Now she was all the more nervous. She strode to a larger mirror on the wall and straightened her jewels, tucking away a strand of hair that had come slightly loose in all her pacing.

Zara joined her. She'd worn her ridiculous gold helmet and her even more ridiculous dress uniform with the golden, lace-like spaulders covering her shoulders and extending up her neck like a choker. It didn't make any sense as armor, but Adella recognized that the dress pieces were like her jewels and dresses and badge. They were a show of wealth, and that was a show of strength in Sarras.

Even if it was a bit of a lie on their part.

Even Gisele was done up in her full mage gear: her ornate black robe with its high collar and sleeves that extended over her hands, her highly tooled gloves, and her headpiece with its long, dangling ornaments. Her elaborate hairdo of curls rivaled Adella's.

They were as ready for the oligarchs as they would ever be.

Finally, an even fancier officer arrived, something like a colonel, if Adella's memory served. That was higher than they'd seen yet. She led them up a staircase and down a hallway with carpet so thick, it almost felt like walking on sand. A museum-like hush dominated this corridor. No one bustled about, and all the highly polished doors stood shut, as if they were ornaments between the oil paintings of military figures.

The colonel opened a door at the end of the corridor and motioned them through. Adella squared her shoulders as she marched in, cloaked in her dignity and ready with a courtly bow.

No one waited inside the large office. Adella nearly stumbled to a halt in front of a mammoth desk. She turned, but the colonel had shut the door behind her, leaving Adella and her sisters alone.

So they were to wait? Again? Adella closed her eyes and counted slowly to ten. She should have expected this. If their first lieutenant had made them wait, why wouldn't the oligarchs?

She didn't bother to hide her exasperated sigh as she sat in one of the plush armchairs in front of the desk. The window had a fantastic view of the Bastión and the small park that sat behind it. Zara wandered over to look out while Gisele sank into the other chair and slumped.

Adella wanted to whisper at her to sit up in case an oligarch should burst in and find a grown woman sitting like a child, but she didn't have it in her to scold. She even fidgeted with her gown. It was usually one of her favorites, icy blue and without so much fullness in the skirt as her others, but the bodice and corset and layers felt very restrictive. She knew she should have never worn trousers. They were too much of a departure from all this bulk.

She would have worn one of her plainer, off-work dresses if she'd known how much she was going to be waiting today. She could have changed just before coming in here. Or would she have bothered? If clothing and jewels were a weapon of sorts among the nobility of the Bastión, they didn't seem to mean a hell of a lot in the sentinels' headquarters.

But if she was going to meet an oligarch…

She frowned at the desk, at the bookshelves with only a few sparse ornaments. This wasn't what she expected of an oligarch's private office. The desk was almost bare and shone so brightly, Adella could see her reflection. It didn't look like anyone ever worked in here.

She stood and moved behind the desk so she could see the nameplate fixed to the surface. She froze, her mouth open. "Supreme Commander Mila Morena-Torres," she read.

Zara hurried to her side. "Are you serious?"

"Wait," Gisele said. "It's not an oligarch?"

But was it better or worse? Adella set aside any protocols for oligarchs and fought to dig out one for the supreme commander of the sentinels, someone she'd never met. *She* was probably in the room with the maps and the plans for attack. Or maybe she was assembling some kind of squad.

Gods and devils, were they going to be part of some operation? Did she want that?

Her heart beating fast now, Adella tried to think her way through this, to figure out what was going on. There was no need for her to report to the supreme commander. There had been no need for her to see an oligarch, either. She'd just jumped there because of her station, but what were they doing here?

Because of her role in the sentinels' failure to capture the smugglers and Cristoff?

Adella put a hand to her chest and counted her breaths this time. There was no reason to panic. She just needed more information. She glanced at the closed door and reached for one of the desk drawers.

"Adella!" Zara said, shock clear in her voice.

"What?"

Zara stepped in front of her. "Don't you dare."

"What do you care? You're not in the sentinels," Gisele said, sitting up.

"It's *wrong*."

Adella supposed she was right. She'd spent too much time associating with criminals and sneaking around offices lately. Zara was still glaring, so Adella took a step back. Gisele bit her lip as she remained seated, but her expression seemed caught between shock and amusement.

Adella crossed her arms. "I am tired of having my time wasted."

"Then why haven't you left?" a new voice asked from the corner of the room.

Adella grabbed hold of Zara's arm, the attack of the night before rushing back. She looked to the side of the room where a woman had entered from a door that looked like every other part of the wall. Adella calmed as she took in the blue uniform with braided epaulets that told her the newcomer was the commander they were waiting for.

The rest of the uniform seemed as plain as every other sentinel's, and she wore her iron-gray hair very short, defying convention. After noticing that, Adella wasn't surprised to see that she wore no jewelry, though her rank permitted it. Even Zara wore earrings when not in the field.

"Mila Morena-Torres," she said as she strode across the room. Her features were pointed and severe, her words clipped, and her voice deep as if raw from shouting at those under her command. When she stopped at the desk and gave them a small bow, Adella was surprised to see that her hazel eyes had laughter lines in the corners.

Adella bowed, her sisters following suit. "Supreme Commander."

"Commander will do." A tiny smile tugged at the corners of her thin lips. "Or Mila if we're feeling very comfortable."

Adella wanted to say, "We are not," but she simply inclined her head.

"Please." The commander gestured to the chairs, including the one behind the desk.

Adella tried to fight her blush as she sat in the large chair. Getting caught complaining had stolen some of the wind from her sails, but she perched on the very edge of the chair and let her corset hold her upright. Zara nearly ran for the chair beside Gisele.

Morena-Torres stayed standing, and Adella wondered if that was a power move until she stepped to lean against the wall near the window with one leg crossing the other at the ankle. "Well, you haven't left, so I'm guessing what you have to tell me is important."

After a deep breath, Adella began to launch into her discovery of the letter and the attack for the third time that day, but the commander held up a hand.

"I've been given those particulars already," she said, but before Adella could bark back, she held out a hand. "May I see the letter."

"Of course." She slipped it out of her reticule—also for the third time that day—and handed it over.

Morena-Torres scanned it quickly and set it on the desk before resuming her relaxed position. "I'm sorry you've been through so much trouble today." She put a hand to the front of her impeccably pressed uniform. "I wanted to hear some of the story from your own lips, but duties kept pulling me one way or another." She smirked. "Next time I get visitors, I'll supply them with a junior officer to yell at while they wait."

Adella didn't want to return the humor in her look, but it was a little funny. And at least the commander hadn't offered to supply more drawers to look through. "What would you like to know?"

"Tell me about this Juno, about the person you thought you knew."

Adella paused, surprised at the burst of sadness inside her. Zara had been right. It felt as if that Juno had died. She began speaking before the feeling could overwhelm her. "We met when I first came to work in Dolores Vega's office." She stumbled for a bit, but then it was like someone had opened a bottle, and the words came flowing out. She'd met Juno when she'd been working as a clerk, just before she'd been hired as an ambassadorial aide. They'd gotten along so well that when Dolores had hired Adella to replace the secondary ambassador after his death, Adella had known she'd wanted Juno as her own aide.

She talked about how kind and supportive Juno was, how great a listener, an incredible confidant, but part of how Adella had gotten the job as secondary ambassador stuck in her mind. She couldn't recall just how her predecessor had died. They hadn't been close, as Adella had worked more with Dolores. An accident?

A murder?

The words dried up in her throat. She looked at the commander and saw her grim thoughts there, too. "She killed him, the man who had the job before me."

Morena-Torres said nothing.

Adella nodded to herself. "She stuck to me when she saw how much Dolores liked me, and then she became my aide. I would have picked her to be my secondary one day after Dolores retired." Her heart hurt, and she was glad her stomach was mostly empty as bile burned the back of her throat.

"But that letter caused her to move more quickly than anticipated," the commander said. "If she'd found it before you did, no doubt she would have tried to stay where she was and become the secondary ambassador, maybe even getting your job one day." She shrugged. "Or so I think."

The room seemed to be spinning. Adella grabbed the desk. One of her sisters whispered her name, but she couldn't look. "Did you… already suspect her somehow? Jean-Carlo…was he already watching her before she murdered Dolores?"

Commander Morena-Torres sighed and leaned her head toward the window. She looked outside for a few heartbeats before waving lazily. "I don't often work directly with the counterintelligence agency you're referencing. The sentinels are more about discovering the truth than working around it. We chase down major criminals." She focused on Adella again with lightning quickness. "Like smugglers."

Adella didn't bother to try for a blank expression. She was already frightened and sickened. Any changes would give the commander more to read. And she didn't bother to argue that they had more than enough things to worry about already. She remembered Vincenzo's words about the commander politely hearing her recommendations on how to treat smugglers before completely dismissing them.

"My sister is usually not involved in cases like smuggling," Gisele said. "I, however, am frequently hired to be part of such operations, so I can answer any questions you may have about that." She didn't bat an eye or glance at Adella. Her face was impassive, almost serene, as if she was trying to assure the commander that she had an answer for everything.

Whether those answers would be the truth or not was anyone's guess. But Gisele could also respond to any questions with the fact that no one had told her she was part of an operation that was hunting her sister. Adella had heard her say before that mages couldn't operate to their full capacity unless they had all available information.

Whether *that* was true or not was also anyone's guess.

Morena-Torres's smirk was back, but it disappeared quickly, and she focused on Adella again, who wondered just what quagmire she'd wandered into. She didn't know much about Sarras's counterintelligence capabilities. Well, that wasn't completely accurate. She didn't know *anything* about Sarras's counterintelligence capabilities, except that they existed, if she could believe the commander. And she knew that her coming here would be seen as picking a side between squabbling government bodies, but she hadn't even known where to find the counterintelligence people.

Except...she still had Jean-Carlo's card. She hadn't recognized the address in the Trade District, but she bet they wouldn't have ushered her through a million well-appointed waiting rooms to get to Jean-Carlo. He'd have found her. But she didn't have any information he was currently lacking. She'd have been wasting his time.

As she was beginning to suspect she was wasting her own right now. All she'd wanted to do was report what she'd discovered and find out what the sentinels planned to do about Devil-Juno.

"How are you going to find her?" Adella asked.

Morena-Torres cocked her head. "I'm sorry you've become caught up in this trouble, Serrah del Amanecer, and I'm happy you seem to detest spies as much as I do. You'll be happy to know your part in it is over." She straightened as if she might dismiss them.

Adella's ire rose again. No way was she leaving without knowing anything, not after having been kept in the dark for so long, not after everything she and Bridget had been through. And she might not be a spy hunter or a sentinel, but she knew a source of information that no one else had access to. She looked the commander in the eye. "It may seem like I'm not well-placed for gathering information. I'm an ambassador who's not even allowed into the country she negotiates with."

She stood, casting off fear and doubt and anger as much as she did when entering the negotiation room. "But mine is an ancient and noble family, and though the days of private armies and blood-feuds and duels at dawn are over, I have the right and the duty to pursue someone who has taken advantage of my good nature, who has cast doubt on my name and that of my family. I will hunt her on my own if I have to, and my cries for justice will ring so loudly, they will resonate in the oligarchs' ears."

Morena-Torres had the decency to stand up straight during Adella's speech, but something about her stance and the set of her face said that Adella's impassioned words would get her nowhere, that even though a noble's path to the oligarchs might be shorter than others', it wouldn't stop the sentinels from forbidding Adella to interfere with the law.

As it probably should be.

And as Adella expected.

So before the commander could reply, Adella offered the one way she could actually help. "Also, I'm sure the Firellian ambassador is refusing to grant you an audience, as he is entitled to do under diplomatic law. I would also guess he has threatened to withdraw to his own country should you press him, which could serve as an unofficial declaration of hostilities with Sarras's most volatile neighbor."

The commander blinked, frowning slightly.

Adella resisted the urge to smile. "Whereas, I, as his fellow ambassador, have the right to request a meeting which he cannot deny, under the treaty between Sarras and the Firellian Empire, without making a similar declaration." She kept her smile soft, modest. The sentinels might ignore her or chase her on the docks, and this counterintelligence agency might plant spies in her midst, but none of that changed who she was: someone who knew diplomatic law backward and forward. She'd been trained by the best, and it was high time she started making Dolores proud.

Commander Morena-Torres sighed, and Adella knew two things, she'd been right about the Firellian ambassador, and she'd scored a victory.

"You and your sisters cannot hunt Juno through the streets like some slighted knight of old," the commander said firmly.

Adella gave a grudging nod, trying to look disappointed, though she hadn't wanted to do that in the first place. But it gave the commander something to forbid her from doing, which in her experience, people in power loved to do.

"But we could use your help with the ambassador."

Adella bowed slightly, graciously. "It will be my pleasure, Commander."

CHAPTER TWENTY-ONE

Jean-Carlo blocked Bridget's punch and took a step back, fists raised as if ready for a brawl, but he didn't attack. He waited with a calm look on his face.

Bridget took a few moments to wrestle her heart out of her throat before she could speak. "What in the devils' names are you doing grabbing my arm from behind like that? I almost..." She was about to say she would have killed him, but with the skills she suspected he had, it wouldn't have been easy. She could still see him kicking one of the shadowy attackers in the head the night before. She didn't even know if she could stretch her leg that far.

He gave another of those damnable bows. "My apologies, serrah."

"Don't give me those bullshit manners. What the hell are you doing here?"

He quirked an eyebrow, and she hesitated. With his job as a spy hunter out in the open, he had much more of a right to be here than she did. She was still supposed to be a nightingale, not a spy hunter.

Or a spy.

"Did you follow me?" she asked, trying to find out how much he knew about her, how long he'd had her under surveillance. If he or his cronies had discovered her former job, it could even now be winging its way to Adella's ears.

And to the ears of those who'd see her hanged for it.

At this point, she didn't know which fate would be worse. The latter would only be the end of her life. The former would be the end of her dream to become something besides her past and the end of what was fast becoming love. The death of hope was so much harder to contemplate.

Jean-Carlo seemed in no hurry to answer.

She couldn't blame him. If he was anything like who she used to be, he wouldn't be in the habit of giving up secrets. She put her hands on her hips. "Are you going to tell me to go home, or are we doing this together? Juno tried to have Adella killed. I'm not going to wait around for someone else to take care of her."

He regarded her quietly for a moment, his head tilting slightly as if he was weighing his options.

She tried not to seethe, thinking. Having a witness would make her eventual confession to Adella more difficult, but Adella didn't trust Jean-Carlo. Bridget should be able to talk around anything he might say.

More than that, her thoughts of a few moments ago caught up to her. She loved Adella. She hadn't dared think it before, but the words rang true. A future without Adella seemed beyond bleak, and if that wasn't love, Bridget didn't know what was.

Even Baxter might have shed a tear.

"Do you really think she's in there?" Jean-Carlo asked, nodding toward the hotel.

"If you didn't think so, too, you wouldn't be here."

That got a little smile and a shrug. "You met Juno at the Bastión, did you not? She knows what you look like?"

But she could shrug, too, not giving him a damn thing.

He gave her a wider smile now. "She's never seen me. I can walk in the front door and find out if she's still there or not."

"So do it. I'll wait here and make sure she doesn't bolt out the side." Like hell. The minute he was gone, she was up and through that window.

He stared as if trying to read her mind, but she made sure her expression stayed blank. She thanked the gods he couldn't actually see her thoughts. If the Sarrasians had developed that power, the Firellians damn sure would have known about it.

After another sigh, Jean-Carlo left. As soon as he was out of sight, she ran for the window. At least his sudden appearance had given her adrenaline a boost. She was up the crates in a moment, then grabbed hold of the windowsill. She pulled upward, trying to peer in, but she didn't want to dangle too long, or her arms would give out. Her strained shoulder was already complaining loudly. She didn't see anyone on the bed or in the open armoire on the opposite side of it. She pulled herself up farther, her arms shaking. She had not missed this part of spying, by the gods.

When she got a knee on the sill, she breathed easier, but she still had to hurry before someone came down the alley. Juno wasn't there, but she might have left some clues behind. Better to find them without Jean-Carlo looking on.

Bridget got out her pocketknife and tried to get a better look at the window lock, hoping she could force it rather than break the glass.

No need to bother. Juno had left it unlocked.

Very careless, even for someone who might be inexperienced. Bridget didn't buy it. Even if Juno had abandoned this room for good, she wouldn't have left the window unlocked. What would be the point? Bridget peered into the room again and saw a shadow against the wall by the door. Not large enough to be a person. She shifted to let in more light. It looked like a chair, but there was something in the seat, a familiar shape.

A crossbow?

Yes. Loaded and ready, and now that she stared, she saw a string going from it to the doorknob. Aha. Juno had fled out the window and had left a trap behind her. Luckily, Bridget had gotten here before the cleaners.

Well, Jean-Carlo would be getting there first.

Bridget cursed. She had to stop him. Adella wouldn't believe her innocence if his corpse was part of her story. She slid the window open and dove inside, somersaulting as her hands connected with the floor.

Something *whooshed* over her head. Another trap? She kept rolling and heard a footstep behind her. With a push, she came up on her feet on the other side of the bed and pulled her knife again. The crossbow would have to wait.

Two people, little more than shadows in the dim light, stood between her and the window. They must have been hiding to the sides, and she'd rolled right into their ambush. By their bulk, they couldn't be Juno. More of her hires? Whoever they were, they didn't seem so keen on approaching now that she had a knife in hand.

After a glance at each other, one lunged for her around the foot of the bed. She slashed at his hand, and he pulled up short, but she gave ground as the other clambered across the mattress. There was nowhere to go, nothing else to use to fight them.

Not quite true.

As the second thug touched the floor on her side of the bed, she grabbed the top of the armoire from the side and yanked, bringing her feet off the floor for extra weight. It pitched forward, and the second thug tried to dash away, but it caught his hip, knocking him down before it fell on top of him. He cried out in pain. Bridget jumped on the back of the armoire for good measure, then stepped onto the bed. The thug grunted, but his mate didn't even reach for him, coming for Bridget again and swinging with something that gleamed in the light.

She tried to duck back, but the mattress buckled slightly, and a line of pain flared across her shin as his weapon sliced into her. Staggering, she reached for the wall to steady herself while kicking with her wounded leg to drive the thug back. She had to get the hell off this bed.

With one leg wounded and the other foot fighting to get tangled in the blankets, she gave up walking and dropped to bounce away from another attack. The bedframe cracked, but she found her feet on the side. Her gut and shoulder still ached, and now her leg felt as if it had been seared on a grill. She faced off with the thug, and his knife seemed so much larger than hers. If she could dive out the window…

The doorknob rattled and turned.

The crossbow.

"Jean-Carlo, don't," she cried.

The thug lunged. She tried to knock his arm away, but his other fist came up in a swing. She ducked, her head to the side, and his attack whistled past her ear. With a grunt, she strained against his armed hand with hers as he tried to push his attack rather than pull back. She took a lesson from last night and punched him in the gut.

As he wheezed and backed off a step, the door flew in. The crossbow twanged. A small cry came from the hall before Jean-Carlo appeared with a murderous look on his face, one hand over a streaming wound on his arm.

Bridget's thug backed toward the window, his knife swinging her way, then toward Jean-Carlo. The thug under the armoire pulled himself forward and received a kick to the face for his effort. The other ran for Jean-Carlo while his foot was off the ground, but he only pivoted and swung his foot up and across, kicking the thug in the jaw.

Mere seconds and they were both down. Wherever he was from, they taught more than spy craft.

He glared at Bridget. "You might have warned me."

"I did." She rolled up her trouser leg to get a look at her wound. It was oozing, not streaming, but she needed to put something on it.

"You said, 'don't.' Nothing that implies a crossbow."

She stuck her knife through one of the sheets, then pulled on it, tearing off a hasty bandage. "I'm sorry if I didn't have time for a soliloquy while someone was trying to carve my face off."

"If you had time to call my name, you had time to say crossbow."

She put her hands on her hips. "Do you want a bandage for your arm, or do you want to grouse at me? You don't get both."

Still frowning, he shrugged out of his coat and let her rip open the sleeve of his shirt to see his wound. Luckily, the bolt hadn't stuck in him, but it had dug quite deeply into the outside of his arm as it flew past.

"You're lucky you're fast," she said. His wound seemed deeper than hers, so she put a folded piece of cloth on it before tying the bandage around.

He mumbled something about being even faster when he knew exactly what he was up against. She pulled the bandage hard, making him grunt. She didn't bother pretending to apologize.

"Why don't you sit while I search?" She lit a candle from the bedside table and began to look around.

The abused bedsprings groaned as he obeyed. "What are you looking for?"

"I won't know until I find it." Both thugs only had a few coins in their pockets. She pocketed them to pay for her pain and suffering.

"How did you know Juno was here?" he asked.

Bridget held the candle near the floor to look in the tipped-over armoire, but it was as empty as she'd suspected. "Are we going to play that game where we each answer a question for a question?"

"No."

"Then in the vernacular of the streets, I ain't telling you shit."

He snorted. "You're no mere nightingale."

"Mere?" She sneered. "Playing and singing are talents, chum, and they're even more impressive when you can do both at the same time." She moved to search the nightstand near him.

"And you have more talents still." His calm look was back, but she had no doubt he could leap into action as needed.

The nightstand drawer seemed empty, but she shoved her hand into the back to be sure. "You have more talents than a *mere* ambassador, but I'm not judging you."

He made another derisive noise, but as she touched something in the side of the drawer, she stopped paying attention to him. The object was small and thin, hard and jagged. She tried to get her fingertips around it, but it seemed stuck in the wood. She considered leaving it and coming back once she was alone.

"What have you found?" Jean-Carlo asked.

Damned observant kick-happy ambassadors. "I don't know." She wiggled the drawer until she could pull it out. Then she brought the candle close. "Some kind of metal." She pried it out of the wood with her knife. It stained her fingers blue. "It's a nib off a pen." She held it close to the candle. "Probably broken when someone jammed a pen into the drawer too quickly." She turned it over and over, thinking. "It has to be Juno's. Otherwise…"

She looked at Jean-Carlo. "The ink would be dry," they said at the same time.

Juno had done some writing lately, and Bridget could guess why. Juno either knew Bridget had betrayed her or didn't care either way; she'd written to someone telling them Bridget was an ex-spy. Or more likely, she'd claimed Bridget as her confederate and probably Dolores's murderer and maybe even a devil in human shape.

Bridget straightened, mind racing. Juno would have written to Adella for sure. Who else? No, who else didn't matter at the moment. Bridget had to intercept that one letter. Juno no doubt knew it would be too easy for Bridget to take a letter from Adella's house. She would write to Adella at the Bastión.

Bridget took a step toward the door.

Jean-Carlo stood in front of her.

She backed up. Her pulse raced, her leg, shoulder, and stomach ached, and her body felt alight with nerves. Part of her wanted to try going through him, but he was very fast with those feet, and she didn't have the time.

"Please," she said between her teeth.

His face remained stoic. "I'm going to need a little more than please."

She took a deep breath. "You're right. I am more than a nightingale. I'm a woman in love." She breathed a humorless laugh to hear it come out like that. "I don't mean to sound like a novel, but it's true. I have to protect Adella, even from myself. I have to be the one to tell her the truth about who I am."

His eyebrows rose. "And that's why you want to dash out of here? To tell her the truth?"

"Before she reads whatever Juno has written about a life that is behind me. Adella has to hear it from me first. I don't know where Juno has gone. I'll leave that to you. But it's clear she plans to take me down with her. Please, Jean-Carlo. Adella is too important to me. I can't lose her without a fight."

His mouth twisted to the side, and he sighed. "All right." He stepped out of the way.

Bridget blinked a few times, hardly able to believe that worked. She started toward the door. "Thanks, really, you—"

"Thank me by letting me be the second person you tell the truth to. I *insist*."

She promised nothing. She didn't have the time or the energy to think past her current mission.

Just like Baxter had taught her.

Adella tried not to fidget too much as she waited for Ambassador Lancel de Maupassant. Before she'd come to this meeting, she'd collected the reports from the ministers of trade and defense. Her suspicions about the Firellians planning something at the border weren't unwarranted. The defense minister thought it very possible. To his thinking, an aggressive move from the empire was imminent. Even the minister of trade also thought that the new docks the Firellians wanted to build on the Kingfish River weren't just for produce.

First spying, then acts that could lead to war? How she wished Dolores was with her now.

Adella took a deep breath and tried to remember her training. Dolores would counsel her to be calm and cagey. When the door opened, and de Maupassant entered—thankfully without aides, as requested—Adella's training faded away. Dolores had believed in her for a reason. And right now, she preferred to be bold.

She didn't return his bow, didn't even wait for him to sit before she said, "You put a spy in my office."

He blinked slowly, sinking into his chair. "Opening negotiations with insults? Perhaps I should retreat until you're in a better mood."

Oh, she was in a mood, was she? He hadn't seen anything yet. She passed over Elena Garza's letter and let him read before she said, "You remember Juno."

He flicked the letter onto the table. "I don't really pay attention to your aides. And anyway, any mistakes your government made in their hiring practices have nothing to do with me."

She wondered if the sentinels would forgive her for knocking his teeth in. She had a feeling Commander Morena-Torres might. She decided to switch tactics. "Why do you want to build new docks along the Kingfish River?"

He tapped his leather folio. "Are we finally getting to the treaty? Let me see." He made a show of turning the pages. "Ah, to guarantee the freshness of produce."

"Or better movement of troops."

He sat back with a sigh. "Your people are too suspicious, Ambassador."

Her temples burned. "I hate spies." She could almost feel Dolores chiding her for making this personal. She expected him to deny it again, but he leaned forward.

"I would never guess from the company you keep."

Her belly went cold while her face heated. With a deep breath, she resisted grabbing his hair and slamming his face into the table. She wouldn't want her hands to get covered in oil. "Your spy Juno isn't going to keep anyone's company much longer."

He smiled and sat back. It wasn't just a confident smile. He always looked like a smug lizard, but this was something more, an I-know-more-than-you smile.

Because Juno had already gotten away?

She'd managed to report to him?

Or…could it be…there were more spies to be discovered?

"Who?" she said, hoping it didn't sound as strangled as she felt.

He sniffed and toyed with his beard. "I don't know what you—"

Her fingernails dug into the table as she leaned forward. "Who are the spies?"

"I know of no spies. The river stops are for produce. Are we going to speak of anything else, or should I go?"

Adella fought to breathe. In her heart, she'd known this would be a waste of time, but she'd wanted to throw her knowledge in this bastard's face. She'd had a fantasy about him crumbling and admitting everything. A stupid, childish fantasy. She wanted to tear from the room and tell his sentinel escort to arrest him and wring every bit of information they could from him.

A definitive act of aggression against his country.

Even with that thought, she almost said, "To the devils with it," and shouted for de Maupassant's escort, but the door opened before she could speak again. Adella shot to her feet, expecting attack, ready for it, but it was the defense minister.

She frowned, wondering if she'd forgotten something. He gave her an apologetic smile and straightened his dark blue dalmatica as if looking for something to do with his hands. His long gray hair was a bit disheveled on one side, the braids looking as if they'd been picked at.

Before she could wonder what had made him so nervous, he cleared his throat and spoke to de Maupassant. "Ambassador, you are to go with the sentinels now."

De Maupassant frowned. Adella nearly whooped even as she wondered what was going on.

"Your aides and belongings are being collected," the minister said. "You and your entourage will be escorted from the city by the sentinels, and then the army will escort you to the Firellian border."

"What is this?" de Maupassant said, turning his glare on Adella.

"I…" She couldn't think of anything to say. She was as lost as he appeared to be.

"Is this a declaration of war?" he asked.

"This way, Ambassador," the minister said, holding the door wider. One of the sentinels stepped inside, and it seemed clear that if de Maupassant didn't leave under his own power, he'd be carried out.

Adella wanted to ask why, but she didn't want to seem clueless to the Firellians, nor could she be seen arguing with someone from her own government. But as de Maupassant stood, she couldn't let him go without one more question. "Who are the spies?" she asked.

He glared as he came around the table, heading for the door.

"Who are they?"

"Ambassador," the minister said, getting in her way. "Please."

"Who?" Her anger was back, and she nearly shoved the minster, but de Maupassant was out the door without answering. She banged her fist on the table. "Minister, what the hell is going on?"

He regarded her sadly. "I'm sorry, Ambassador, but Sarras will not require you to negotiate with the Firellian Empire any longer."

So it was war? She took a step back, not knowing how to feel. "When will I—"

"We'll let you know." He gave her a nod that seemed meant to be encouraging, but she took no comfort from it. "It may be some time before you are called upon again."

Adella pushed past him, heading for her office. She needed a quiet place to think, to process, to wonder what in the all the gods' names she was going to do now.

CHAPTER TWENTY-TWO

Adella had been pacing around her office for several minutes. It hadn't helped. She'd locked her door in case any other disasters thought to barge in, but no one had even knocked. She finally sat at her desk and picked up her pen to write, but she had no idea who'd she'd write…or even what she'd say.

Dear Ministers, are we going to war? If so, why? Yours, Adella.

She didn't think that would get her very far. She supposed that if someone felt she was owed an explanation, they'd give her one. As it was, Zara would probably know what was going on before she did.

And what had the minister meant when he'd said it would be some time before she was called on again? Had she just lost her job? Was everyone too cowardly to say it outright? Maybe she could find something else in another department.

Or was she tainted because she'd been working with a spy?

Adella rubbed her temples, determined not to cry yet again. She couldn't think about war or her job or money or anything else at the moment, not when there was the possibility of more spies to consider. De Maupassant could have been toying with her. It was possible he didn't know about any Firellian spies at all. He could have been as in the dark about that part of his government as she was about hers. Still, caution dictated thinking about everyone she knew, the *company she kept* that he'd referred to.

Serrah Nunez seemed a likely candidate with his nefarious contacts and ready fists, but besides the fact that Adella liked him, she didn't actually *know* him. No one could accuse them of keeping company together.

She picked up the stack of mail she'd nearly tripped over when she'd first come into the office. Swiftly, she shuffled it into a pile, tapping the edges against her desk until the letters were even. Orderly office, orderly mind. At least, that was the idea. Maybe if she avoided thinking about which of her friends and acquaintances could be spies, the answer would come to her.

With a sigh, she shuffled the mail again, moving the larger letters to the bottom of the stack. Where was Bridget now? Had she accomplished the tasks that would finally allow her to speak about her past? Maybe she'd have some ideas about who could be a spy if she knew people who were keeping dark secrets.

Or because she was used to keeping such secrets herself.

The image of her choking the smuggler came to mind again. It had flashed through Adella's memory several times since her meeting with de Maupassant. She'd told herself to quit thinking of it, but it kept rising up like bile. Why? And why had Adella assumed Bridget's secrets must be dark?

The thoughts kept tumbling block by block.

On the boat, Bridget had been terrified of being caught by the sentinels, much more so than the others. They'd spoken about prison and had seemed anxious, fearful, even, but none had approached the look of horror on Bridget's face. The future Bridget had glimpsed hadn't involved prison.

She'd been in fear for her life.

Another block in place. But what they were building was... unspeakable.

Also on the boat, Adella had tried to reassure Bridget that the sentinels wouldn't care about some petty crimes. Bridget had looked heartsick when she'd replied, "It's more than that."

Another block. An image she hadn't wanted to see.

I would never guess from the company you keep.

"Oh gods," Adella whispered. She began to tremble. It couldn't be true. Bridget had saved Adella's life, had held her when she'd cried about Dolores, about Juno, about all of it. Bridget could not have sat and listened to all her ranting about spies so casually if...

She was one.

Adella tried to make her mind go back, think again, reevaluate, but she'd created a picture. She couldn't tear it up just like that, couldn't forget it existed. The mail scattered from her nerveless fingers. She had to do something. Get up, pace, run, fling herself out the window. Something.

She had to find Bridget.

Adella planted her hands on the desk and stood, her head bowed as she tried to catch her breath.

One letter stared at her from the pile. She recognized the handwriting.

❖

Bridget hurried through the streets as fast as she could without attracting too much attention. With any luck, Adella would still be at the sentinel headquarters or maybe back at home. It was getting on in the day. She and her sisters were probably making dinner plans. Bridget would join them soon enough, take Adella somewhere they could be alone, and explain.

Oh, it was going to be a nightmare. Bridget tried to think of the best way to phrase her explanation. She could make it sound better without lying. Couldn't she?

"How does one dress up the words, 'I'm a spy'?" Baxter would ask.

Gods and devils, she didn't know. But Adella could rage at her in private, attack her if necessary. Bridget could take it. She even deserved it for keeping quiet this long. Was there anything she could hold back, or should she let it all out at once? All at once was no doubt best. A bitter pill was better as a single dose.

Adella's sisters were going to kill her.

Well, maybe she deserved that, too. Her hands were not stainless, and she'd never been held to account for all the deeds she'd done.

"First things first," Baxter would remind her.

Right, she had to get the letter.

The side entrance to the Bastión was as guarded as the main entrance, though it was a lot less grand, just a heavy-looking door set in a swath of stone. It had no handle, and Bridget bet the only way it opened was if the sentinels standing on either side knocked, maybe even knocked in code. They wouldn't have to bother if they'd let the cleaners and maintenance people come in the front, but she couldn't complain. This snobbery worked in her favor.

It was easy enough to hide and wait until someone dressed in overalls and a cap passed her by, and then she grabbed them, and put them to sleep as she had the man in the smugglers' camp. After a quick check to make sure they lived, she stripped the overalls and cap, then waited the short time until dusk.

She still felt partially frozen when she fell in behind a group of similarly dressed people in the gloom. At least it had dampened some of her nerves. She prayed Adella was comfortable at home.

When she saw that the sentinels did have a secret knock for the door, she nearly shook her head. Some things in the world were still as she expected.

Inside, the group of cleaners turned into a side room. Bridget peeked in behind them, spotting racks of supplies. The woman watching this side of the door was not a sentinel but some bored looking security guard who peered at them sleepily by the light of a lantern.

Time to add a little excitement to her life.

Though not much.

Bridget grabbed a bottle of cleaner off one of the shelves and brought it closer to the lantern as if trying to read the label. Moving quickly, she feigned a stumble and dropped it at the guard's feet.

The crash of breaking glass made everyone freeze as if caught in amber. Bridget did the same, staring at the guard's soiled trousers with mock horror.

"Idiot!" the guard shouted, and the tumult began.

Getting away was as easy as shouting, "I'll get some water," and then she was sprinting down the hallway and up a flight of stairs. She passed the W.C. sign and kept going, nearly scoffing at how well this was going. She didn't take off her disguise until she reached Adella's office door. If possible, she was going to walk right out the front as if she had every right to be here. In her experience, no one checked the faces of those leaving.

After looking up and down the hall, she picked the lock and went inside. All was dark, as she'd hoped, though the curtains on the windows hadn't been drawn. The meager light helped her find the desk but wouldn't let her see to search. She struck a match and lit an oil lamp on the front of the desk where she stood, happy to see that someone had piled the mail as if for her perusal.

"I already found it."

Bridget froze at the sound of Adella's voice. She turned slowly, praying she was dreaming, but Adella sat on a chair to the side of the window. She had a few sheets of paper in hand. Bridget swallowed, desperate to be rid of the taste of her own heart.

"I was sitting in the dark, watching the city, thinking," Adella said. "About you. And here you are." Her voice was flat, but her hand closed as she spoke, making the paper crackle like flames.

Bridget shivered. She had to say something, but what, what, what? She thought up a thousand excuses, discarded a thousand more. Should she lead with, "I love you," or would that only make this worse? "I wanted to tell you myself," she said, not much more than a whisper, but a devil had her by the throat. "I was going to tell you tonight."

"After you secured this?" Adella seemed in a daze as she stood, clutching the paper so hard, Bridget was surprised the ink didn't drip like blood.

"In my own words."

"Your words?" Adella frowned. "Your words?" She looked around as if seeing her office for the first time. A shadow seemed to fall over her face, and she snarled. "Your words are *shit*!" She put a hand behind the chair and flung it, sending it toppling, skidding to rest at Bridget's feet. "You are a *liar* and a *spy*, Bridget Leir, and you deserve to be flayed in hell!" She was nearly panting, slightly bent as if she might rush. Her hair was loose around her shoulders, and her eyes blazed, making her seem like a crazed spirit.

Bridget held up her hands, part of her wondering if the yelling had attracted attention and the other parts hating herself for worrying about that now. "I am not a spy anymore, Adella. Please, listen to me. That was my old life. I gave it up when I came here, and then Juno dragged me—"

"She didn't have to drag you hard, did she, Bridget?" Adella spat the name before her eyes widened. "Oh, I am sorry. That's not your real name, is it? We haven't actually been introduced."

Anger flared through Bridget now, at herself, at Juno, but also at Adella, who seemed to be believing whatever Juno—a woman she now detested—had written rather than anything Bridget had ever said. "That is my name. I decided long ago that I was going to live my life honestly."

"Honestly?" Adella brayed a laugh that had no humor in it. "How dare you even say that word?"

Bridget fought to calm down, fought to breathe. Tears spilled from her eyes, but she let them go. "I don't know what she told you. I never met her before that morning in your office. I don't know how she recognized me. I left everything behind when I left the empire."

Adella made a noise of disgust and turned away, but Bridget kept talking.

"I became a spy in childhood, when the Firellian spymaster took me in. My mother was dead, and he cared about me. He trained me. I followed orders. I protected the empire until they wanted to use their spies as assassins. Then he helped me flee. I love him. I hate him. I never experienced a pure emotion until I met you."

Adella whirled, her own cheeks damp, but she still bared her teeth as she pointed at Bridget. "Don't."

"It's the truth. I know you can't tell the difference right now between that and a lie." She choked back a sob, swallowing it as if it were a stone. "I couldn't tell the difference for a long time, either, and I'm so sorry you got pulled into this. I only ever wanted to show you…" She swallowed again. "I didn't want your work to consume you like it did me."

With a look of disgust, Adella rocked back on her heels. "I don't kill people for work."

"And I didn't want to," Bridget snarled back. "That's why I left." She rolled her lips under, mashing them together, searching for a sense of calm that had fled, unattainable now. "I had nothing to do with the woman who called herself Juno. I had nothing to do with Dolores. But I am happy I was here for all of it, happy you didn't have to go through it alone."

Adella's eyes narrowed. "Am I supposed to be grateful?"

"No! You're supposed to see that I love you."

"Stop." She shut her eyes.

"I tried to protect you."

"Stop." She put her hands over her ears like a child.

"Loving you is the truest thing I've ever done in my whole life."

"*Stop!*" Adella began to weep as she sank to the ground.

Bridget moved toward her, determined to gather her into her arms, but Adella slammed the balled-up letter between them. Bridget pulled up short.

"This…won't be the only copy," Adella said with a shaky voice. "She'll have written…to the sentinels. And…no matter how I feel…I don't want you to die." She closed her eyes so hard, the skin turned white in her reddened face.

"Adella," Bridget said, her heart breaking.

"Go," Adella said. "Leave before they come for you."

No, no, no! This wasn't supposed to be this way. "Come with me. I'll get us away from here so I can explain properly. Then you can decide what you want, but come with me now."

"I can't." It was little more than a whisper, but it might as well have been a shout.

And it wasn't the only sound. Someone was shouting in another part of the building.

Adella lifted her tear-stained face. "Bridget, go, please."

It felt like ripping open her own chest, but Bridget turned and fled.

CHAPTER TWENTY-THREE

Adella felt as if she had acid running through her veins. Her face burned while her body felt cold to the core, and she wanted to run as fast as she could, but she didn't have the energy to move. She'd never felt so much all at once, so many different emotions coursing through her that she barely began to embrace one before the next crashed over her in a wave.

All surrounding Bridget.

The name went round and round in Adella's head along with Bridget's lovely face and lying lips and promises of the heart that didn't mean a damned thing.

She'd never felt like such a fool.

When the sentinels came to collect her, Adella went with them eagerly, happy to be led. It didn't occur to her that her hair was down and her face was a mess until she was sitting in the same headquarters she'd been in earlier. A lifetime ago.

She had no memory of how she'd gotten here, of how many people had seen her in the street. She kept thinking of Devil-Juno's letter that had detailed a long relationship with Bridget, how they'd been comrades from the start, with Bridget coming into Adella's life at the right moment to distract her. Devil-Juno said Dolores's murder was Bridget's idea, and that Bridget was supposed to help her escape but had betrayed her because Devil-Juno was a rival Bridget longed to be rid of.

The funny thing was, Adella knew those were lies. Too many things didn't make sense. But that didn't matter. The heart of the letter confirmed what Adella already knew: Bridget was a spy for the Firellian Empire.

Oh, based on what Bridget had said, how she'd acted, it was more truthful to think of her as an ex-spy, but that didn't matter. How could a person who'd embraced such deception in the past ever live truthfully? And Bridget had known from the start what Adella did for a living, where she worked, how it would look to the government if Adella was known to have a spy—ex or not—as a confidant, a friend, a lover. Bridget had known all that, and she hadn't walked away. She'd put her own pleasure over what was best for them both. Adella would have been hurt if Bridget had refused to see her again after they'd met, but she wouldn't be *here*, in the sentinel headquarters, feeling as if she'd been ripped in half.

One other thing rang true. Bridget had known Juno was a spy. Bridget probably hadn't known it when they'd met, but she'd found out somehow after Dolores had been killed. Adella was even willing to give Bridget a little credit for helping to uncover Devil-Juno's crimes, but that ultimately didn't matter either. Bridget had listened to Adella worry for Juno, pray for her, try to find her to make sure she was safe. Bridget had embraced her through those feelings with a liar's heart.

Her tearful face and strained voice played through Adella's mind. She hadn't laughed at Adella or called her a fool. She'd wept and lamented and claimed that she loved…

Adella made a fist. No, she couldn't afford charitable thoughts at the moment, never mind anything greater. She would simply admit that Bridget hadn't wanted her to be hurt, but that also didn't matter. Bridget had still kept a secret that she wouldn't have had to keep if she'd left Adella alone in the first place.

Her thoughts kept going around even after one of the sentinels came in. It wasn't the commander or any of the officers she'd seen that day. And now that she looked, the room wasn't like any of the waiting rooms she'd occupied either. There was the mirror she'd seen her disheveled state in, but only two, straight-backed, hard wooden chairs and a bare wooden table took up any space. The walls and carpet were drab gray, with no pictures or decoration or pattern.

This probably meant something, but she was too exhausted to speculate. Maybe later, she'd figure it out.

The officer introduced himself, but she didn't listen. He seemed a very nondescript sort of person. His uniform held no markings of rank, and his skin was slightly sallow as if he drank too much. His bald head shone, and his eyes were so gray, they nearly faded into the rest of the room. His questions were simple, mostly to do with dates and locations. She answered woodenly, trying not to weep again as he kept saying Bridget, Bridget, Bridget. Even when he used Serrah Leir, it didn't help because it all meant the same horrible, lying, devil-ridden person.

Adella only hesitated once, when it came to Cristoff's current location. She admitted that she'd met him on a ship, that the ship had been manned by smugglers, but she claimed not to know any names, referring to Tin-Pin Ami and Vincenzo only as captains of their boats. She didn't owe Tin-Pin a damned thing, but any talk of her might lead the sentinels to Cristoff, and Adella wanted to protect him as one of the few people who hadn't betrayed her. If he wanted to quietly disappear, she saw no reason why he shouldn't.

When she was asked to speculate about Devil-Juno's where-abouts, Adella could only shrug and say, "She was never who I thought she was. How can I guess about someone I don't know?" When the interrogator insisted, she began listing places in the city where anyone might go for shelter: hotels, taverns, bunkhouses, rooms to let. She listed some charitable institutions that took in the destitute, but she didn't know where those places were located. After a minute, he held up a hand to stop her.

"We know Bridget Leir lived at a tavern called the Donkey's Rest. Do you know of any reason she might return there?"

Adella blinked. "Because she lives there?"

The smile he gave her was pitying, and she wanted to kick him. "Now that her secret has been revealed, she will undoubtedly try to flee the city, not return to a place she's been known to frequent. Unless she has a reason to stay behind?"

Adella had to shrug again. She had no idea what Bridget might do. Except lie. Anger began to build, and the circular thoughts from before revived like the unstoppable tide. She clenched her fists, but that wouldn't stop them. Only…

Deeper parts of her mind supplied an answer to the last question, and she seized it and clung on before the tide could drown her again. "Her mother's mandolin."

Part of her was aghast. No matter what, she was no betrayer of confidences, and she'd suspected how important Bridget's mother had been to her. If that hadn't also been a lie. Adella sensed it hadn't been, just as she could pick through all their conversations and recognize the truths.

The interrogator seemed neither heartened nor saddened by the news, but she thought she saw a gleam in his eyes as he nodded and asked if there was anything else.

They were going to set a trap for Bridget using her mother's mandolin. She felt a burst of guilt that was quickly swamped by anger. Bridget deserved everything coming to her.

Oh, her subconscious seemed to say with a questioning tone. Then why had she let Bridget get away in the first place?

She couldn't answer that, didn't want to answer. When the interrogator stood, she nearly leaped from her seat, relieved to be on the move again. He told her she might have to answer more questions at a later date, but she didn't care about later dates; there was only the pain of now.

A group of sentinels escorted her through the streets and toward her house. They told her she wasn't allowed to leave home again until they came to collect her, and they posted guards at the front and rear doors to make sure she did as she was told.

Adella made it in the door and out of their sight before she collapsed. When her sisters embraced her, she cried into their shoulders, unable to answer questions except in fits and starts. They bundled her into the kitchen and put her in front of the fire, but she couldn't accept anything they tried to give her until she'd cried herself out again.

Anger should have been waiting when she was done, just as it had the last time, but guilt leaped upon her instead. She'd told the sentinels about the mandolin. She'd told Bridget to escape, then laid a trap for her.

When Adella told this to her sisters, they went quiet, looking at each other as they sat on the bench facing her. Adella looked between them. "What?"

Gisele worried at her lip as Adella often did. "You feel bad about doing that?"

"Why should she?" Zara asked, a growl in her voice.

"Because she wants Bridget to live," Gisele said.

Zara frowned. "Why? She's a liar and a spy."

Gisele stood. "Because Adella is in love with her!"

The crackle of the fire filled the silence for a few moments. Adella stared as they voiced her feelings, but that last declaration... no. Or could she be...

Gods and devils, it was true. Bridget's lies wouldn't hurt this bad if that wasn't true. And the fact that Zara seemed incapable of arguing only proved it.

"You have to warn her, Del," Gisele said.

Zara shook her head. "She deserves to be punished."

"Not killed." Gisele crossed her arms.

"She betrayed this country."

"She never betrayed Adella."

Adella pounded her boot on the floor, and the crack seemed as loud as thunder. Gisele and Zara fell silent, but Adella's mind continued to argue with itself. She'd saved Bridget once, and she still didn't want her to die.

But Sarras hunted and arrested spies for a reason. And now that Sarras had declared hostilities against the Firellian Empire, it was even more important that they rooted all spies out of their country. That included ex-spies who might find their former allegiances returning during war.

If Bridget fled Sarras, however, that wouldn't matter anyway. She would no longer be the Sarrasians' problem, and she'd live.

To return to the empire and report any secrets she'd gleaned? No matter what Bridget had said about hating her former life, she might return to it if left with nowhere else to go.

Adella put her head in her hands. Her country or her love? Only a devil would invent such a choice because whatever she picked, she was damned.

When she lifted her head, Zara and Gisele were watching her, waiting, still with her no matter what she decided. Strangely enough, her next thought was of her last meeting with de Maupassant. If he'd known about Bridget, he'd all but given her up with that line about the company Adella kept. He might as well have stated that his country had turned its back on its former spy. Then the defense minister had come in and told Adella that she was no longer needed. Years of service suspended, maybe even over. She'd been relegated to another waiting room as endless as those in the sentinel headquarters.

She loved Bridget, and she was really starting to hate politics. "I'll warn her."

Gisele smiled in triumph but to her credit, didn't gloat. Zara sighed loudly but didn't censure, another credit.

"I don't forgive her," Adella said. "But I don't want her to die."

"Let me get my saber," Zara said, heading toward the stairs.

"I'll get some heavy cloaks," Gisele added, going for the closet.

Adella stared after them for a moment before she shook off her shock and moved. "Wait a moment. You two aren't coming."

Gisele peeked out of the closet, and Zara paused on the stairs. They glanced at each other again before both made a noise of derision, and they went about their tasks.

"No," Adella said, stomping again. When they ignored her, she moved into the foyer and stood in front of the door. "I forbid it."

Zara returned quickly, buckling her sword belt as she came down. "You're going to have a hard time sneaking out *and* guarding that door."

Adella ground her teeth. "It's too dangerous."

With a flat look, Zara pointed to the blade now on her hip, then at Adella's weaponless state.

"That's not..." Adella rubbed her temples. "You have your careers to think of."

Gisele whipped a cloak around her shoulders before handing one to Zara. "If you can turn your career to shit, I don't see why we can't do the same."

"Don't swear," Adella said automatically. "And stop—"

"Are you going to wear that?" Gisele asked, gesturing to Adella's gown. "I wouldn't."

"And put your hair up under a dark cap," Zara said. "Seriously, Del, make a small effort to not get caught."

She gaped at them for a few seconds before hurrying upstairs. They were right that she was wearing the wrong clothes, but they were wrong if they thought they were coming with her. She changed into a plain, dark blue dress and put on some thick wool leggings. A dark jacket and cap completed her sneakiest outfit, and she stomped downstairs again, sitting on the lowest step to put her boots on over thick socks.

"Before you order us to stay home again," Gisele said, "how are you planning to sneak past the guards?"

Adella didn't look up. "I'll...go out a window."

"Then you'll need me to lower you," Zara said. "As the only windows on the sides of the house, where there are no guards, are one story up." Before Adella could agree *just* to the fact that she would have to be lowered, Zara added, "And I'll have to come with you so I can help you back up, too."

"And the sentinels might still see you," Gisele said, tapping her chin. "Unless you have someone with you who can bend the light around you, making you invisible. That and going out the side of the house should ensure we stay unnoticed."

Gods and devils, they were both good points. And now that the time had come to depart, she really didn't want to go alone. She owed it to them to do so, however, just as she had never woken them up when she'd heard a noise in the night and had gone to search for intruders or evil spirits.

As they helped her to her feet, she had to acknowledge that they weren't children any longer. Zara was taller than her and had been for some time. And Gisele was often in pain, but she wasn't delicate, especially in spirit.

"I...can't ask..." Tears threatened Adella again, and she breathed deep to banish them.

Gisele and Zara shared another look, and Adella didn't much like this new camaraderie between them, especially their secret communication. "You don't have to ask," they said at nearly the same time.

When they glanced at each other again, this time with annoyance, Adella breathed a laugh, happy they would always be exactly who she thought they were.

CHAPTER TWENTY-FOUR

Bridget knew the Donkey's Rest would be watched. She wasn't stupid, but she'd already had to leave the only woman she'd ever loved. She couldn't leave her mandolin behind, too. She'd managed to save it once when fleeing her spying days. She could do it again.

First things first. She had to clear the Donkey of some of its watchers. She paid for a pen and paper at a nearby inn, then wrote a quick note reporting herself at the docks near the fish market, close enough for those stationed near the Donkey to be called to investigate, but far enough away that she should be able to get in and out before they returned.

She also reported herself as being armed, possibly with hostages, so the sentinels would *have* to go look. And she signed the note Jean-Carlo, with no idea if that would carry any weight, but she would take what she could get. Anything to hurry this along so she wouldn't be consumed by the image of Adella's anguished face.

Bridget made herself stop right there. She'd have plenty of time for regrets once she got away.

She paid the eldest child of the innkeepers to take the note to the nearest sentinel station. Gathering a disguise was as easy as stealing a hat from a nearby table, and then she left, settling in an alley near the Donkey to wait.

She barely felt the cold, even without the sun to warm her. The snow from earlier had abated, leaving a light crust on the moonlit ground that made it look as if the world was covered in icing sugar. Serrah Nunez probably loved it.

Bridget sighed. There was someone else she'd never see again. Best to sneak past her and Videl and anyone else. She could protect everyone that way.

No, she wouldn't think about that either.

She made her mind go quiet, falling back on old habits. Escaping them seemed impossible. When a large number of people left the Donkey and the area around it at once, it was time to move.

Slipping into the bustling kitchen was as easy as ever. They always left the back door open as the inside was like a furnace. All it took to hide her face was a large box she could peer over the top of as she carried it. Once through the turbulent kitchen, she set the box by the back stairs and ascended slowly, keeping near the wall to avoid any creaks. When a step squeaked behind her, she kept going as if she belonged there, but the faint scent of cloves and oranges brought her to a halt.

"Really, treacle?" Serrah Nunez asked. "Without a by-your-leave?"

Bridget forced her feelings down but couldn't turn. "Please, serrah, don't…"

"Don't what?" A closer step creaked now. "Don't ask what the sentinels want? Don't beg you to stay? Don't say good-bye?" She was close enough to sense as she leaned toward Bridget's ear. "Don't get rid of the sentinel waiting upstairs to catch your darling little posterior?"

Bridget breathed through a small laugh that wanted to become a sob. "You can do that one."

Serrah Nunez sailed around her like a glittery pink cloud. She smiled over her shoulder. "Take your box into the kitchen and wait."

Bridget obeyed, and Serrah Nunez came down moments later with a man in uniform. She clutched his arm and hurried him toward the back door, saying, "I saw a prowler out back. Oh, please catch him. I'm so terribly frightened."

"Which way did they go?" he asked, his chest stuck out in a picture of heroic concern.

"This way." She led him out the door while trembling as if she might faint from fright.

With a smile, Bridget wondered what the sentinels had told her. No matter, she supposed, though Serrah Nunez was clearly taking whatever it was better than Adella.

"But we're not thinking about her, are we?" Baxter asked.

Absolutely not.

Bridget slipped upstairs again. The sentinel had thoughtfully left a glowing lantern on the landing outside Bridget's room, and she took it in, setting it on the dresser. Videl's side of the room was as untidy as ever, but thankfully, she was out, and Bridget only had to grab her mandolin from under the bed and—

The large window opened with a bang. Bridget leaped over her bed to get away from it as a dark shadow rolled through much as she had earlier.

Exactly as she had earlier.

Juno straightened and shrugged out of a snow-dusted cloak. "Finally! Waiting on the roof for you was cold work." She pulled a long dagger from her belt.

Bridget wasn't interested in hearing more. Or fighting. Getting away was all that mattered. Even though her Baxter-ish side wanted to kick Juno's ass.

Bridget shoved the bed, sending the light frame sliding toward Juno. When she hopped out of the way, Bridget darted for the door, mandolin case in hand. She heard a rush of air, and her right foot shot out from under her. She managed to turn as she lost her balance, falling to one knee on the wad of Videl's clothes Juno had thrown.

Bridget raised her mandolin case as Juno lunged. The dagger *thunked* into the wood. Bridget pushed up and forward, ignoring the pain in her leg and shoulder and stomach and now her knee. She used the case as a shield, grimacing when the dagger ground against it again. Juno staggered back from the force. But Bridget couldn't turn and run, or Juno would be on her, and if she took the fight into the hall, any remaining sentinels might discover them.

"What are you waiting around here for?" Bridget asked. Maybe she could convince Juno to flee Sarras. There'd be time to track her down and take revenge later. Or not. "If you escape town—"

"There is no escape from this fucking town." Juno began to circle.

Bridget mirrored her. "Try harder."

"If I'm going to die, I'm taking you with me."

Shit. If she could force Juno alone into the hall, maybe she could lock the door and go out the window. "Well, that attitude won't get you very far."

Juno barked a laugh. "Droll until the end. No wonder Baxter sang your praises right up until the day he died."

Bridget hesitated, her mind stuttering.

Juno sprang, dagger flashing. A slice of pain spread along Bridget's fingers. She kept in a cry as she swung the case up and out, the heavy end clunking against Juno's legs, sending her stumbling back with a grunt.

"Liar," Bridget said, swinging the case to the side this time, but Juno ducked under and gouged Bridget's leg above the other cut. She hissed in pain and let go of the case, thumping Juno's head. With a gasp of pain, Juno flattened and rolled away, coming up ready.

"Go to hell and find out." Juno lunged again.

Bridget grabbed the case and swung it wildly, but it was proving a shitty weapon. And her fingers were bleeding, making her grip slide. Juno would cut her down one slice at a time.

Maybe then, Adella would believe how sorry she was.

Juno stabbed the case, but an agonizing sensation tore through Bridget's knee at the same time. She sucked in a lungful of air as the accompanying crack from her leg vibrated through her. Juno had kicked her. She fell, dropping the case. With a grunt, she grabbed Juno's arms as the dagger descended.

Juno pressed forward. Bridget strained against her. A sound came from the right, and Juno glanced back. Bridget shoved while Juno leaned to the side. The combined movement kept Juno's head out of range of someone's kicking leg, but the boot still grazed her shoulder.

Jean-Carlo. Bridget had a chance.

As Juno cried out, Bridget whacked her knee with the side of a fist. Juno staggered, and another kick landed on her hand, sending the dagger to the floor. Cursing through the pain, Bridget grabbed the dagger and pushed up again, trapping Juno against the sill of the open window.

Juno gripped the frame with one hand, forced to sit on the sill as she leaned away from the blade pressed against her neck. She held her injured hand against her chest. Her eyes flashed with fear. She was finished.

Bridget breathed with her for a moment. "I told Baxter I never wanted to kill again."

Juno swallowed, and the blade dimpled her pale throat. "Break your promise," she whispered. "Or keep it. He won't care. He's dead."

It was tempting, and she'd planned to do it earlier, but she'd also told Adella that her old life was behind her. She couldn't lie again, even if Adella would never know it.

"I…" Gods and devils, if anyone deserved death, it was Juno. Adella might even agree. But a promise was a promise. Would Baxter be proud or not?

Bridget stepped away. "I won't."

Juno sneered and stayed on the sill. "Doesn't matter. You're as dead as I am." She shook her head as if Bridget was far stupider than she could fathom. "And Adella? She's dead, too. Your whole kingdom is."

Bridget snarled and took a step, but Jean-Carlo put out a hand to stop her, then grabbed a wad of Juno's jacket in his fist. "Why's that?" he asked.

Her sneer faded a little in the face of his calm expression. "Because our army will crush yours," she said after a moment.

He cocked his head. "Yeah, that's what I thought." He shoved her hard.

Juno sailed out the window as if she'd been launched from a catapult and dropped silently into the gloom.

All four stories down to the frozen stones below.

Bridget's heart thundered as she looked out. Juno lay like a broken doll in the bar's back garden. Bridget looked to Jean-Carlo, shocked at his action, his cool demeanor, and the fact that he hadn't used his feet to dispatch her.

He also now stood between Bridget and the door.

"Why did you do that?" she asked.

He shrugged. "That was for the crossbow as much as anything else." She drew back, and something in her expression made him roll his eyes. "If she knew anything, she wasn't going to admit it. I can always tell. And sometimes, killing an enemy is the job." He put his hands on his hips. "I don't think you'll be the same as her. You look like a person who's ready to talk."

Bridget stood and breathed. And bled. She didn't know what to think, what to say, except that the prospect of getting arrested did sound better now that she was exhausted and wounded. Finally, she shrugged, too. "That's why I quit the spy game. Because killing people was going to be just another part of the job."

He smirked. "See? Ready to talk."

She wanted to smack him now, for more reasons than just to crack his bravado. She had to get past him, or she'd dishonor Adella's wish that she stay alive. "What now?"

He gestured toward the door. "The sentinels are downstairs. Would you like to be delivered to them conscious or unconscious?"

She had to chuckle. "Being carried sounds pretty good right now."

He had the decency to smile. She tensed, ready to rush him, but a creak came from the hall. He turned, face expectant as if he hoped to see his backup. Bridget took a step, glancing at the door.

No one stood there.

She stopped, frowning. He did the same.

Bridget held her breath.

When Jean-Carlo's head jerked to the side as if he'd taken a hard punch, Bridget nearly cried out. He dropped like a stone and lay still. Bridget continued to stare when Zara appeared from nowhere, her blade lifted as if ready to bash Jean-Carlo with the pommel again.

"What?" Bridget whispered. She thought her jaw couldn't drop any more, but when Adella and Gisele walked in, she could have sworn it hit the floor.

Adella's insides burned at the look of hope on Bridget's face. She wanted to lash out, scream, weep, and throw herself into Bridget's arms all at once. Thankfully, Zara spoke before she had a chance to do anything. "We'd better bind those wounds quickly, or you won't get very far."

"Where am I going?" Bridget asked as Zara took clothing from one of the beds and ripped it up for bandages.

"Away from here." Adella heard the anger in her own words, making it sound as if she'd only come here to throw Bridget out of Sarras personally. "To live," she added. For some insane reason, she didn't want Bridget to leave angry at her, no matter how she felt herself.

Good thing they didn't have time to explore anyone's feelings.

Adella turned to where Gisele leaned against the wall. "How are you?"

Gisele's face was pinched, but she nodded. She'd only kept up the invisibility until they were out of sight of the house, and then she'd used it again to get them into the Donkey, but anyone could see the toll it took.

Adella touched her arm. "We can find another way to disguise—"

"I'm helping." Gisele pushed off the wall.

A noise from the hall made everyone turn, Zara stepping forward with a hand on her saber. When Serrah Nunez walked into the room, Adella moved in front of Zara to prevent anything hasty. Adella wouldn't have recognized Serrah Nunez if she'd only ever seen her in the clothing from the docks. Even now, with a closer view of her painted face, Adella could hardly believe it.

"Well, well, puddings," Serrah Nunez said with a smile. "Isn't tonight full of surprises?"

"Where's your protector?" Bridget asked.

"Alas, knocked down in an alley by the prowler he sought to catch." She shrugged. "Or that's what I'll tell him when he comes to."

Adella didn't know what they were speaking about, but she didn't care now that it seemed taken care of. "We have to get Bridget out of the city."

Serrah Nunez winked. "I guessed. I won't ask. And I've already been thinking. Where was it you arranged to get word to Cristoff?"

Adella drew back. "You want the smugglers to take her?"

"Don't they still want to kill us from last time?" Bridget asked. Even Zara and Gisele seemed incredulous, and they'd only heard about it.

"Tin-Pin might, but Vincenzo has no right to be angry, and I'm betting young Cristoff feels badly enough about putting Adella in danger that he can talk Vincenzo around. Plus, since Cristoff has escaped detection for now, it's because Vincenzo has a good place to hide him. Now, do you want to argue, or shall I go ahead and see what I can arrange?"

Adella had to admire her efficiency.

And they didn't have another plan.

"We'll follow more cautiously," Adella said.

"*We* will?" Bridget asked. Covered in bloodstained bandages and limping, and she still didn't want help? Adella didn't know whether to admire that or just kick her.

Serrah Nunez gave Adella a questioning look, but Adella only supplied the name of a tavern in the Tides. "I'll do what I can to clear a path for you," Serrah Nunez said.

Gisele sighed. "Appreciated. Not bumping into people is the hardest part." She gestured for everyone but Serrah Nunez to come close. When she began to chant, the words seemed to slide around in Adella's brain before departing, and as before, she couldn't recall a single syllable. Bridget began to speak but broke off quickly, and Adella knew they were seeing the same thing. The air around them shivered and became coated in rainbows and shifting patterns of light and dark, what being inside a prism must be like. Since the other three were within the spell, Adella could still see them, but it was clear that Serrah Nunez could not.

Her eyes went wide, and she backed away slowly. "Yes, I see… or rather, I don't. I'll meet you there." She went out in a flurry of colorful skirts.

"Slowly," Gisele said. "Too quickly and you'll break the spell."

They began moving together at a frustrating pace. Zara took the lead, Adella followed, Gisele came next, and Bridget brought up the rear. Adella was happy Bridget wasn't right behind her. Accidentally brushing against her would have set off another tumult of emotion.

Serrah Nunez had made good on her promise to clear a path. No one waited on the stairs, and the cooks and servers seemed busy on the other side of the kitchen. Like before, they hugged the wall, and Gisele waited until they were out the door and down the street, out of sight before she dropped the spell.

She leaned on her knees, breathing hard, a sheen on her forehead. Adella fought the urge to fuss over her again. Zara held her up instead and still managed to glare at Bridget. Adella felt some satisfaction from the fact that Zara would cheerily punch Bridget in the face if asked.

Bridget kept looking Adella's way from the side of her eye. Adella could let her go now. She'd made up for telling the sentinels about the mandolin. Bridget could finish escaping by herself. But she looked so damned forlorn, not to mention bedraggled and bandaged, with only her mother's mandolin for company.

"Are you..." Adella couldn't finish asking if Bridget was all right. She could see by the bandages that the answer was no. And she wasn't interested in hearing more bravado.

After a deep breath, Adella tried something else. "Do you need money?"

Bridget blinked before smiling softly. "No, thanks. I have a little, and I can earn more."

Adella nodded at her injured hand. "You can't play until that heals. I suppose..." She stopped again. She'd been about to say that Bridget could always go back to her old job or become a hired killer, but Bridget wouldn't, perhaps couldn't, do either. Adella knew that as she'd known the truth from the lies in Devil-Juno's letter.

Anger warred with sadness again, and Adella clenched a fist to silence them both.

"Let's go," Gisele said.

After yet another deep breath, Adella repressed the urge to ask if Gisele was sure. She was going to get heartburn from forcing so many emotions down.

Zara helped Gisele limp along, and Bridget had to go easy, too, making them a sorry-looking team. Still, Adella didn't think it an accident when she and Bridget pulled slightly ahead.

"The Juno imposter is dead," Bridget said softly.

Adella gasped and stared, not expecting that.

"Jean-Carlo killed her." Bridget glanced her way. "I couldn't do it, not after promising you that I've changed."

Adella tried to think through the sudden ringing in her ears. How the hell was she supposed to feel about all that?

The smuggler Bridget had choked came to mind. She really had left him alive.

Because she'd changed.

Adella shook her head. Bridget had stopped killing, maybe, but she still knew how to lie. Adella couldn't let herself forget that.

"Thank you for telling me." She bit her lip. If they were admitting things, maybe it was better to send Bridget away angry. "I told the sentinels about your mother's mandolin."

Bridget stared now. "You did? Then why did you come and—"

"I didn't mean to tell them." She lowered her voice. "I was in shock and being asked so many questions, and it just came out." Well, shit, maybe she *couldn't* handle Bridget's disappointment or anger. "I'm sorry."

To Adella's relief, Bridget waved the words away. "Don't worry about it. They were probably going to watch the Donkey anyway. I'm sorry you had to go through an interrogation. Did they…they didn't hurt you?"

"Of course not." The very idea shocked her.

Bridget shook her head. "No *of course* to it. The sentinels don't have a very friendly reputation in many countries, not just the empire."

Adella closed her mouth. It had been on the tip of her tongue to defend anything Sarrasian against the opinions of a Firellian. But Bridget didn't like any government bodies very much.

And Adella was beginning to share that opinion.

They walked for a long while in silence, avoiding large groups of people and sticking to the shadows when they could, a proper group of criminals. The idea that Bridget was about to disappear forever kept careening through Adella's head along with all the emotions. She wanted to see the back of her and hated the very idea of it, all at once like everything else. The plane of her thoughts had become a place she didn't recognize.

As the odors of the docks grew stronger, signaling they were nearing the end of their journey, Adella knew she had to forgive Bridget. She didn't have to let go of her anger or any of the other negative emotions, but she could push them away and deal with them later, heartburn be damned. Here, now, she had to send Bridget away as unburdened by guilt as she could.

After all, she wanted Bridget to *live*.

And they loved each other. That was one truth among the lies.

The sign of the tavern came into view. They paused well away from a streetlight, and Zara went inside to find Serrah Nunez. Gisele leaned against a nearby wall, and Adella moved a few steps away with Bridget.

She had her mouth open to say the words that would let Bridget shed some guilt, but Bridget said, "Come with me," sending Adella into a tizzy once again.

She swallowed a laugh at the sheer absurdity. "How did you know what I was going to say?"

Bridget blinked. "I didn't."

"But you assumed I had forgiven you enough that you could ask me to come with you again?"

Tears sprang to Bridget's eyes, sparkling in the gloom. "You forgive me?"

Adella cupped her own cheeks, fighting down tears. This conversation was far more backward than she intended. "I do. And no, I can't come with you."

"Please—"

Adella stepped forward and kissed her, their tears mingling as Bridget embraced her so tightly, it stole her breath away.

That was fine. Each breath was too painful at the moment.

When they broke apart, Adella put a finger to Bridget's lips to be sure she got the first word this time. "I love you, Bridget Leir. I still want to punch you, and I can't say that I trust you, but I know that what we had was real."

Bridget pressed their foreheads together. "Then come with me and let me earn your trust again."

"I can't."

"You can punch me all you want."

Adella breathed a laugh so close to being a sob that she had to swallow it. "There will be questions about tonight, and I can't leave my sisters to answer them alone." Even if she was tempted to go for an hour, a day, a few weeks, a lifetime. "I can talk our way out of danger, no matter what you and the other experienced criminals believe."

That got her a little smile.

"But I don't know if I can keep you from the noose," Adella said, the thought more painful than any before. "So you have to go, and I must stay."

Bridget let go and stepped back, wiping her face. "Well, that's… incredibly shitty." She smiled hopefully. "Maybe someday—"

Adella shook her head, unwilling to let that thought into her heart. "Leave someday to itself. Today isn't finished yet."

When Serrah Nunez emerged, she had directions to Vincenzo's ship. They headed quietly toward the docks. Bridget told them of her ruse in sending the sentinels to the fish market, but any tumult from that appeared to have died down. Hopefully, no one would think to look in a place they'd just searched. Adella had to admire the ingenuity, even if events had seemed to work out this way on their own.

Serrah Nunez hallooed the ship, then went on board. When Cristoff came out a moment later, he led a grumpy Vincenzo, who seemed cowed enough to let Cristoff do the talking. When Cristoff embraced Adella, he gave Vincenzo a dirty look, and she guessed there had been more than a few words between them about Vincenzo allowing Tin-Pin room to do away with Adella.

Good.

Then Serrah Nunez was hugging Bridget, and it was time. Adella had often wondered what it would be like to pause her life, turn the hourglass on its side, and she'd never wished for that ability more than now. If she could only exist in this one moment where she'd suspended her anger just a little longer…

Bridget stood in front of her, then, eyes repeating the earlier question.

Adella drew her close, repeating her earlier answer with the desperateness of her embrace.

Vincenzo said something to Cristoff, and then he was tugging Bridget along, onto the ship, and they sailed away along the dark water.

Adella watched until the ship passed out of the moonlight and into shadow.

CHAPTER TWENTY-FIVE

Bridget couldn't help but compare this journey down the river with her last two. Both times, she'd been fleeing, and here she went again. Like the first time, she wouldn't be able to go back. Unlike the first time, she desperately wanted to.

Yesterday, she'd been terrified of the sentinels, and that hadn't changed, but now she suffered a worse fate: losing Adella. She'd never see that sweet face again, never hold those comforting hands or feel that warm embrace.

She'd never care for someone so much ever again. And no one would care for her, not with her past in the way. Gods and devils, she was doomed.

Bridget put her head in her hands. The dock was long lost to shadow, but she'd been staring in that direction, hoping to burn Adella's face into her mind. All her fears since meeting Adella played through her head. Losing Adella forever had always taken center stage. Greater than the fear of her own death, she'd been scared that Adella would find out who she'd been. But now she realized that it wasn't really the confession that had worried her. It was Adella's reaction, the image of her walking away. The reveal of the truth had gone worse than Bridget had anticipated, but the culmination of her fears had been the same.

She'd lost Adella.

The only person she had ever met who always put others before herself, who had made sure Bridget escaped even after the world's most painful revelation.

What was death compared to that?

Bridget couldn't stand still. She rocked back and forth, holding on to the rail so all this feeling wouldn't fling her overboard. Even the threat of drowning didn't scare her in the shadow of what she'd lost. What would Baxter say? She couldn't imagine. He wouldn't come to her. Even if he still lived, Juno's words had killed him in Bridget's mind.

That was a boon in some ways. She was free.

But adrift.

She'd need a new voice of wisdom. Unless she finally filled that role herself and used what she'd actually learned from her fucked-up past and the visions of her miserable-looking future. What conclusions could she draw about her situation?

Easy. She could not lose Adella.

Bridget put a hand over her mouth. That was it. If she hated what her life had become, what it looked to be, she could change it. She'd done it before. She'd run from her life, and she realized now she was still running. It was time to stop, time to declare that love, that Adella was worth whatever else might come.

She would not let Adella face the sentinels without her. They would have each other right up until the end, and no one could take that away from them. Not the sentinels, or the empire, or any other force in the world.

Forget Baxter being proud. Bridget could be proud of herself.

She marched to where Vincenzo and Cristoff stood near the mast. "Take me back."

It was hard to read their expressions in the moonlight, but she could tell by their lack of responses that they thought her stupid or insane.

"Have you lost your mind?" Vincenzo asked after a moment.

One question answered. "Adella doesn't know what awaits her in a true interrogation. I need to save her from that."

Cristoff gasped before shaking his head. "They wouldn't dare. Her family—"

"No doubt has a lot less sway than they used to," Bridget said, thinking of their lack of money. "And anyway, aren't you from a noble family?"

"A minor one."

"And you have a healthy fear of being arrested."

Cristoff took Vincenzo's arm, but he shook his head slower than before as if doubting his own words.

Vincenzo stepped in front of him. "I won't put Cristoff in danger."

Bridget's anger mixed with fear until it felt as if she had some vile sludge running through her veins. She'd made her decision, but she couldn't enact it. She couldn't force the boat to shore. There had to be another way.

She looked at the silvery river. It had been so cold coming down from the mountains in the empire. It had nearly taken her life while she sang, "Break Not My Heart, O Lady Fair," to time how long she could stay in the freezing water. But the river had robbed her of thought and tried to drown her with a surprisingly gentle hand.

It still haunted her dreams.

How far was it to shore now?

It didn't matter. Dreams or not, she could make it. She would do anything to fix her lady's broken heart.

Resolved, terrified, Bridget shoved her mother's mandolin into Cristoff's arms. It didn't deserve a dunking, and she wanted to think of it being free, no matter what happened to her. A piece of her mother would continue to exist, and the pieces of her that had never been a spy would exist, too.

As Cristoff sputtered a question, Bridget handed all her money to Vincenzo. "Please look after that mandolin for me. Someday, Adella might like it."

"What are you doing?" Cristoff asked, fear and concern in his voice.

Bridget smiled. Before doing something stupid and probably insane, it was nice to know someone cared. "Being proud of myself."

She took the deepest breath in her entire life, stepped onto the rail, and dove into the liquid silver.

Adella and her sisters had managed to sneak back into their house without being caught, but Adella knew their ordeal wasn't going to end there. Her relief at Bridget's escape managed to cut through her sense of dread enough that she was able to enjoy a cup of coffee as the light of dawn filtered through the kitchen windows. All her other emotions were still muted, buried under exhaustion, and she hoped she'd soon be able to sleep for a week. Perhaps after work, she could…

But she didn't have work anymore. The minister of defense had all but dismissed her. Well, that was cause for celebration at the moment, was it not? She could go to bed straightaway as long as no one came—

Three hard knocks rapped on the front door. Adella looked at her sisters. Gisele was wide-eyed. Zara frowned deeply. Adella hoped she looked as fresh-faced as they still did, but she doubted it. As she stood, she wished she was ten years younger so she could at least feel ninety years old instead of one hundred.

A harsh clanging sound echoed from the front door as someone pulled the bell, and the knocks came again. Adella gestured for her sisters to stay put as she crossed into the hall and called, "Coming." She straightened and stuck her chin out and tried for a regal expression that said confidence.

Failing that, she'd settle for an exhausted one that said she no longer gave a shit.

Supreme Commander Mila Morena-Torres waited on her stoop, a few grim-faced sentinels surrounding her, one with his hand still on the bell. No wonder they'd rung and knocked so aggressively. Adella bet no one kept the commander waiting.

Though maybe if they had, she'd be more sympathetic to those forced to wait in her headquarters.

Adella smiled and hoped it didn't look too much like a grimace. "Commander, how lovely." She stood aside. "Won't you come in and join us for the first coffee of the day?"

Morena-Torres's smile didn't reach her eyes. "No, thank you, serrah. I'd like all of you to come with me instead." She held her hand toward the road as if inviting Adella into her parlor.

A sliver of dread oozed through Adella's exhaustion, turning her innards to ice. "If we need to speak, surely we can do so in the comfort of my kitchen." Part of her was appalled by the suggestion.

True, she didn't want to go with the commander, but she also didn't invite people into her home lest they see how little furniture and comforts remained.

But after losing Bridget and her job, she didn't really care about that at the moment.

The gods were not without a sense of humor.

But Morena-Torres seemed to be. Her smile disappeared, and she seemed to give up any pretext of friendliness. "Now, Serrah del Amanecer. You and your sisters will come with me."

At least the commander had come for them herself. Adella supposed that was a compliment. She glanced back to where her sisters had ignored her instructions and now stood in the hall. Gisele still leaned on Zara, but by the steadfast look in their eyes, they'd fight if Adella ordered them to.

And they'd die.

"Get your cloaks," Adella said. While they were all alive, she could keep them that way. "And one for me. Quickly." She thanked all the gods and even the devils as they obeyed without argument.

Adella linked arms with her sisters as they walked through the streets, but the sentinels crowded far too close for conversation. By the way Gisele clung to Adella's arm, she was in pain, but Adella fought back the urge to ask about that or to give her any sympathy. Gisele wouldn't want the sentinels to know that she was tapped as far as magic was concerned.

The streets were cold but clear, and few people were out to see three nobles being escorted to the sentinel headquarters. Adella was gratified by that. She hadn't cared if the commander saw the sparseness of her home, but she still had some pride left.

In the sentinel headquarters, they were separated, but Adella had suspected they might be. She gave Zara and Gisele a reassuring squeeze and tried to look confident as Commander Morena-Torres led her to one of the plain-looking rooms Adella had been questioned in before.

She avoided looking in the mirror, not wanting to see any dark circles or new wrinkles, and sat while the commander took the other chair. "Are we being charged with a crime?" she asked before the commander could say anything.

Morena-Torres tilted her head. "Should you be?"

Adella was not going to fall for that. "I'd like my lawyer present if that's the case." She'd only ever seen her family lawyer for business dealings, but he'd have more knowledge about this sort of thing than she did. Or he'd know someone to call upon. She wasn't even certain lawyers were allowed in these sorts of interrogations—she'd been too dazed to ask last time—but some of them defended criminals.

Was she a criminal?

The thought almost made her burst into hysterical laughter. She was so far from a criminal that she didn't even know how to behave if charged with a crime.

Morena-Torres sat back in her chair, seeming far too relaxed for a commander again. "We failed to apprehend Bridget Leir last night. But you already know that."

Adella said nothing, too relieved and too saddened to show either expression.

"One of my sentinels was injured, as was a spy hunter. And the spy known as Juno was killed."

Adella wanted to say, "Good," but she was still trying to figure out the protocol here. Dolores had taught her that frosty silence was the path to take when she didn't know what would be best received.

Morena-Torres's eyebrows rose. "Nothing to say? Not even a denial of knowledge?"

"How are the two people who were injured?" It had been hard to see Zara hit Jean-Carlo, but he was owed a little pain for lying.

"What if I said they'll never be the same? That they may die from their injuries?"

That did hurt a little, and she couldn't remain silent. "I'll help if I can."

Morena-Torres sat forward. "And why should you feel responsible?"

Damn. "Juno used to work for me."

"And Bridget Leir was your lover."

With their bodies, no, she'd never had that privilege, but in their hearts…emotions welled in Adella's chest, and she had to look down, certain they would show on her face. But maybe it was time for that.

"She lied to me," Adella said quietly. That was true, but Adella missed her all the same.

"Then why did you help her escape?"

"Who says I did?"

Morena-Torres sighed. "Really, serrah, if you keep me going around in circles, I may have to resort to tactics that cut to the heart of the matter."

The fear on the smugglers' faces came to mind. Adella frowned, happy her anger hadn't deserted her. "You think you can get away with torturing a noble?"

"Torture? Really, I don't know where you could have gotten such an idea." Morena-Torres smiled without humor again. "I think you've been spending too much time with criminals." Her eyes were hard.

Adella racked her brain for something to say that would get her and her sisters out of here. She was certain they were being as stubborn as she was, though maybe with a little more anger. If she confessed, perhaps she could convince Morena-Torres that her sisters were either blameless or had been compelled into action. She met the commander's eyes and waited.

Morena-Torres sighed as if she didn't like what she was about to say, about to do. Utter bullshit. "Don't worry, serrah, we're not going to get out the thumbscrews or put you on the rack. What we will do is go through your entire life, your contacts, your accounts, and see if you have any other spies hiding in your household. And though we try hard to avoid it, such investigations always wind up going public." She sighed again.

Adella could have happily hit her with a chair. A dozen thoughts flashed through her mind at once: all the time and effort she'd put into keeping up appearances, all her worries while sewing new trim on old gowns or giving the minimum at charitable events, even her relief that very morning that few people had seen her on the streets with the sentinels. She'd tried too hard and sacrificed too much for all her labors to simply be undone.

But this morning, she hadn't cared if the commander saw inside her house.

That was because of exhaustion. Once she'd had some sleep, she would have been mortified.

Truly? She'd invited Bridget in, and it hadn't mattered.

But that was Bridget, who cared for her, loved her. She'd said Adella was amazing for keeping her family together after their parents had died, for keeping her sisters safe in their ancestral home.

That stuck in Adella's mind. It *had* been quite a feat, much more than she'd realized. People with far more money had accomplished far less.

Gods, had she been proud for the wrong reasons all this time?

Adella smiled softly, her feelings quiet for once. "Go ahead and tell everyone, Commander. We've got nothing to hide."

When Morena-Torres frowned, Adella gave her a brighter look, betting Bridget would have been proud, too.

A sharp rap on the door made Morena-Torres turn and call, "Come," very sharply. Adella repressed another smile. One of the officers hurried in and had a word in the commander's ear. She gave Adella a satisfied, cat-like smile and stood. "You and your sisters can go."

Adella stood, relieved, but that sliver of dread had become a plank that sat atop her chest, robbing her of air. She couldn't help asking, "Why?"

"You can stay if you want," Morena-Torres said with a shrug. "But now that we've got Bridget Leir, we don't need you."

Adella had to hold on to the table to avoid collapsing as every emotion from last night returned, bringing a hundred more with them.

CHAPTER TWENTY-SIX

They'd given her a change of clothes, but Bridget was still cold. The Kingfish River hadn't felt as freezing during her late-night swim as it had been when she'd escaped the empire, but it had come damned close. When she'd finally reached shore, she'd been surprised to find all her limbs still intact and made of flesh, not shards of ice.

On the walk through Sarras, her wet clothing had felt like frozen skins weighing her down, tripling her exhaustion. She'd shivered so much that her teeth had chattered like castanets in her head. Every time she'd forgotten where she'd been going or why, she'd stopped in a doorway to get out of the wind, and the answer had come floating from the depths of her brain.

She couldn't lose Adella.

Then she'd pointed herself in the direction of the sentinels' headquarters and had kept going.

A shuffle through a homeless camp under a footbridge had provided a few moments by a fire in an ancient looking brazier. Many people there had been awake, no doubt preferring to sleep during the relative warmth of the day. They'd asked questions she couldn't answer, clucking over her wet clothes and bandages. When one had thrown a tattered blanket over her shoulders, she'd promised its return.

The skies had lightened shortly after, and she'd blinked at them with bleary eyes. She'd gotten lost again or turned around and had been about to turn in the direction of the Donkey's Rest and her bed when she'd remembered that she hadn't yet met her objective.

She couldn't lose Adella.

Even if she hadn't been quite sure who that was.

A beautiful face and figure had come to her like the light at the end of a long tunnel, and she'd stumbled the right way again.

The iron fence surrounding the sentinels' headquarters had two people guarding the gate, and Bridget had laughed to see them standing nearly sideways in midair before she'd realized her head had fallen toward her right shoulder. Had she been sleepwalking? She'd hoped her dreams had been nice.

The guards had glanced at one another before telling her to push off. They'd said something about this not being a homeless camp and had threatened her with the constabulary. She'd wanted to laugh in their faces and tell them just how much trouble they'd be in if they let her get away, but she'd been too tired.

"I'm Bridget Leir," she'd managed. "Ex-spy for the Firellian Empire." Then she'd shoved the blanket at one of them. "Please see this returned to an actual homeless camp."

Then she'd fallen over.

She'd smiled before actually passing out, pleased the bastards were having to carry her at last.

When she'd woken up, she'd been in the same room she currently occupied, a windowless box of a cell, though the iron-banded door had a slit in the bottom, and a little light filtered in, enough for her to find a bucket in the corner and nothing else. She'd been wearing a clean—and gods be praised, dry—shirt and trousers, and her hand and leg felt freshly bandaged. At least the cold had numbed the pain, but it slowly came back angry.

She prayed to the gods now that her arrival had ensured Adella's release, having no doubt the sentinels had already brought Adella and her sisters in for questioning. She rubbed her shoulders as she sat against the cold stone and wished she hadn't given that blanket back. It probably wouldn't have survived the delousing powder she smelled on her skin and hair. Bugs might have been the only things holding it together.

It had been a very thoughtful gesture, though. If she ever saw the sun again before heading to the scaffold, she'd have to see that the blanket's owner and their cronies got a meal and a bed.

Sighing, Bridget let her head thump against the wall. She'd done everything she could to avoid losing Adella. She could go to her grave knowing she'd done the right thing. Adella would be sad, even with all the lies, but she could mourn properly rather than wondering forever if Bridget had truly loved her.

This would prove it.

But gods and devils, it was going to be a long, boring, uncomfortable wait.

At last, they came for her and led her to a nondescript little room and not the shriek-filled, blood-soaked torture chamber she was expecting. But the locale didn't matter. A middle-aged woman with short gray hair, a sharp face, and penetrating hazel eyes sat across from her at a table. A man stood near another door on the opposite side of the room, and he watched her like a statue, but she bet he wouldn't be slow to go after the truncheon on his hip.

"Sit," the woman at the table said.

Bridget frowned, not happy to be treated like a dog, but that was better than being flogged. She sat, and the guard who'd brought her in stood in front of the door she'd come through.

The golden epaulets on the woman's uniform said she was someone important, maybe even the commander herself, but she didn't bow or offer an introduction. "You've had quite a few defenders today, scads of people vouching for your good character, telling us that the woman posing as Juno lied about your helping her."

Bridget blinked, not expecting that. Then she smiled, imagining Adella as one of those people who still cared about her, cared to find out the truth.

"So," the commander said, "tell me who you are besides"—she glanced at a piece of paper—"brave, loyal, kindhearted, and noble." She smirked. "I notice honest isn't on here."

Bridget sighed. "I wasn't trained for honesty." She wanted to lean her arms on the table, lay her head down, and take a nap, but she also didn't want to be beaten before the torture. Something in her still wanted to lie, to deny and dodge and put on an act where she begged for mercy. With another sigh, she told that part of her to be quiet. Baxter was dead, and she hadn't lost Adella, and it was time for the truth.

"I began training to be a spy when I was a child. My mother had just died, and the only thing I had left of her was her mandolin. A man named Baxter took me in." She managed a smile as the floodgates of memory swung open. "I loved him, and I hated him."

Bridget talked for hours. People came and went, but she didn't note the faces. When someone asked a question, she answered it. When she asked for water, they provided it, even giving her bread and cheese at one point, which she chewed during pauses in her story. She left nothing out, reminding them with every piece of information that her knowledge was out-of-date. She gave them the protocols used when a spy went missing so they might know what to expect from the empire after Juno's loss. She gave them everything. It was only when someone asked for another pen that she noticed one of the new people was writing at one end of the table.

Good, maybe she wouldn't have to tell this story more than once.

She named everyone she could think of, cited every job she'd done, and finished the story of her career with her escape.

"Why leave?" the commander asked as she popped a bit of cheese in her mouth.

"I didn't want to become a killer for the empire. Baxter had sold me on the idea that what we did as spies allowed us to better defend ourselves. Assassination just made us…bloody."

The commander shrugged. "Why not kill your enemies before they can kill you?"

Bridget watched her without comment. That was exactly what she'd expected someone with such a high position to say. Bridget only hoped the commander would believe her even if fleeing a life of murder wasn't something the commander would do.

"I couldn't do it," Bridget finally said. "I didn't have the stomach for assassination."

The commander made a note. She probably thought Bridget a coward. Oh well.

Then came her time in Sarras, and she could smile for real as she spoke about Adella. It was hard to admit all the secrets she'd kept, but she tried to put all her feelings into words. Maybe they'd let Adella read this part after Bridget had been executed? The thought gave her hope, and she omitted nothing, stressing that Adella had not known of Bridget's life as a spy. Pure selfishness hadn't allowed her to break from Adella before they'd fallen in love. Desperate need hadn't allowed that breakup after their feelings had developed. Rather than changing her, love had brought out the person she'd always wanted to be.

Gods, she hoped they would show Adella that part, at least. But if she asked, they might deny her just to torture her, and she didn't want that.

The commander prompted her to speed through a bit of the romance to get back to Juno and Dolores's murder, but Bridget wouldn't be hurried. The love story needed to be written down, too.

Finally, after recounting her cold walk through predawn Sarras, she was done.

The commander stared at her for a few moments. Bridget stared back, letting all her emotions play freely on her features, not holding anything back. She was still exhausted, but it was warm in this room, and she felt free. After fighting the desire to purge for so long, it felt nice to give in, to let everything out.

"I really detest your kind," the commander said, her expression slightly bored, as if she was talking about not liking a certain kind of cake or décor. She gestured to the papers. "In spite of all this, you're going to hang. You know that, right?"

When Bridget said nothing, the commander nodded at the guard, and he tugged her to her feet. If she'd still been a spy who'd been captured, she would have said something saucy like, "No kiss good night?" Now she only smiled tiredly as the guard escorted her from the room. In the dark of her cell, she curled up on the bare floor, using her arm as a pillow and slept for a thousand years.

As she paced the floor away at home, Adella was at once desperate to see Bridget and glad they were nowhere near each other. Bridget had heroically, romantically come back to the city to free Adella from the sentinels' clutches; she was sure of that. It was the only way Bridget would have been caught. It was the most kindhearted, noblest thing anyone had ever done for her.

On the other hand, Bridget had undone all the work it had taken to make sure she avoided capture. It was the stupidest, most pigheaded thing anyone had ever done. Period.

Heroic, romantic, pigheaded, kindhearted, noble, and stupid. It was difficult to believe one body could contain so many traits. And since Adella still worried for her and missed her desperately, they had to be in love.

Falling in love in only a handful of days? She never would have believed it of herself. It was the kind of story that happened in novels set during a war, when there wasn't time for long walks, sighing copiously, holding hands, and shy glances over lavish dinners. But she and Bridget hadn't had much time, either. After Dolores had been murdered, things sort of tumbled along until…

Here they were, a mere week and a half since they'd first met. And Bridget had spent most of that time in jail.

The sound of the door opening had Adella running for the foyer. Zara came in, her cloak damp, but whether with rain or snow Adella didn't know. In the week since Bridget had turned herself in, Adella had mostly stayed home, writing letters to everyone she knew who could help spare Bridget's life. She'd barely even looked out the windows.

"Well?" she asked as Zara hung the cloak up. "Any news?"

Zara shook her head and frowned. "I was on maneuvers all day and didn't hear anything about Bridget. My squad will be marching out soon."

Gods and devils. The oligarchs and minsters had to be worried that the Firellians were massing or on the move if they were sending the scouts. Adella gripped Zara's arm. "Oh, Zara, you…I can't…" It was too much to worry about.

Zara patted her hand with a sympathetic smile. "Don't worry about me, Del. I've been in the field before. Let's focus on Bridget." Her face darkened a moment. She still had plenty to say about her personal plans for Bridget, and nearly all of them involved some kind of duel.

Her being out in the field might be the best thing if Bridget was spared. Then Zara couldn't give her "a damn good hiding."

But Adella didn't want her to go, didn't want anyone else she cared about to be somewhere she couldn't find them. She balled her hands into fists and recited the mantra she hadn't had to use for Zara in ages: it was her life, her decisions. Adella would probably always use the same words for Gisele. But at least her career left her freer with her movement than Zara.

If only those movements didn't cost her pain.

Adella stomped back into the kitchen, away from all these worries. She was always concerned for her sisters, but her new worries for Bridget seemed to make all the others boil to the surface as well.

She sat at the kitchen table and looked over her list of all the people she'd written to, ambassadors, ministers, nobles, everyone who had any sway. Her main argument had been that, during these troubling times with the empire, what better asset could Sarras desire than an ex-spy and the fount of information she provided?

She'd left out the circumstances under which she and Bridget had met, leaving her personal reasons hazy as to why she argued on an ex-spy's behalf. No doubt the truth would come out eventually, but ever since her house had been visited by sentinels, she'd ceased to care what the neighbors thought.

Maybe she was just too tired. She envisioned waking up in the spring in a state of absolute mortification.

Zara bustled around the kitchen, setting out some things for dinner. Adella went through her lists and notes again, though she could have recited most of what she'd written by heart. She'd gotten a lovely, encouraging note from Serrah Nunez, who'd informed her that even Cristoff had come out of hiding to speak on Bridget's behalf. Adella wondered what Vincenzo thought about that. She'd have to find out if Cristoff was also being held by the sentinels. Another letter campaign could be in her future.

She'd hired a criminal lawyer for Bridget, too, though Bridget hadn't been up before a magistrate or anyone the lawyer had been accustomed to dealing with. The latest report held better news. The lawyer would finally be able to *meet* Bridget tomorrow.

Maybe.

Adella leaned her forehead on her palm. The lawyer's bill would be coming soon. She could dip into the all-important house repair fund or sell some of her jewelry. Maybe Serrah Nunez could take up a collection at the bar.

When the front door banged again, Adella went to slip off her seat, but Zara put a hand on her shoulder. "It'll be Gisele. Anyone else would knock."

Unless they were being attacked. Ah well, she didn't want to go running toward that anyway.

Gisele came into the kitchen, her mouth open to speak, but Zara said, "Did you lock the door behind you?"

Gisele frowned hard but turned and marched away. She came back a moment later. "It's locked. Okay?" she said with a teenager's petulance. At least she'd done it. Zara mumbled something, and Gisele stuck her tongue out.

"Children," Adella said firmly. "Enough."

Gisele sat to peel off her gloves. "I stopped by the Bastión to pick up your personal mail, Del." She handed over a stack of paper.

"Thank you." Hope fluttered through Adella's heart as it did with every new letter. She'd received replies from almost everyone, though most had been from aides or secretaries thanking her for the letter and promising a response soon.

The *thwap* of another stack of paper landing on the table got her attention. She looked up at Gisele's grin. "What's this?"

"Just a different sort of magic I managed to work," Gisele said. "I got a copy of Bridget's confession."

Adella stared at the stack of paper, all her emotions paused, the world going still. "How?"

"I may have played on the guilt of my sentinel contact for keeping me out of the loop." She waved casually. "And I may have flirted a bit."

Zara made a disapproving noise, but Gisele ignored her.

Adella continued to stare. "I…do I want to read it?" She was mostly asking herself, but Gisele nodded emphatically. Adella couldn't help giving her a look, her cheeks heating as she thought about what might be in there. "You read it?"

"I'm only human." When Zara made another tutting noise, Gisele bristled. "Just read the damn thing."

"Don't swear," Adella whispered, but she pulled the stack of paper closer. She didn't want to read it here, not while being watched, so she took it to her bedroom and sat at her vanity, taking a deep breath before she began.

Gods and devils, there was so much feeling in these pages, it had to be a word-for-word account. Adella imagined Bridget in one of those featureless rooms, pouring her emotions out. Adella cried for Bridget's upbringing, finally understanding some of the things Bridget had tried to tell her. Her feelings for this Baxter person swung between admiration and disgust as much as Bridget's seemed to, and she nearly held her breath during Bridget's escape.

When she got to the part about their time together, she read slower, rereading some parts over and over as Bridget's feelings spread across the page as if someone had opened her heart and used blood instead of ink. When her vision blurred with tears, Adella dashed them away and forced herself to keep reading, desperate to consume every word, every reassurance she'd been missing.

She had wanted to save Bridget before, but she hadn't known if she'd be able to trust her again.

Now…now…

At the end of the story, Adella put her head down and wept, both for their past and their future. Bridget couldn't have known Adella was going to see this. She'd had no reason to confess it all unless she just wanted someone to know the truth.

Gods, Adella had to save her.

After wiping her face, she ran downstairs, determined to get back to work. She seized the mail and her list. There had to be some people she hadn't yet written to, some information she didn't have. She flipped through the new letters, and one name stopped her. Flora Vega, Dolores's sister.

"Del, are you all right?" Zara asked.

Adella held Flora Vega's letter and tried to decide just how she felt. "I will be, once I find a way to save her."

She began reading the letter, and a flood of memories came back. She'd been so ignorant when she'd written to Dolores's sister. Ignorant and happy. Flora wrote how nice it was of Adella to write to her personally and how she was looking forward to meeting Adella at the funeral.

Gods and devils, the funeral. She'd completely forgotten. And it was only a few days away. Adella stared in shock that wanted to become horror, but she was too tired, too emotionally drained. She couldn't even find the energy for a few more tears. How would that look at Dolores's gravesite? "I would weep for my dear friend and mentor, but I'm too exhausted trying to keep my ex-spy lover from the noose."

"What is it?" Gisele asked quietly.

"Dolores Vega's funeral is in three days."

Zara and Gisele both said something about going with her. She nodded, grateful. Maybe if they cried, no one would notice her nodding off between them.

Flora Vega's letter finished by saying she'd heard from Dolores's lawyer and thanked Adella for seeing to all of Dolores's affairs so quickly. She would be moving into Dolores's townhouse in the city, but she didn't mention what would happen to their country home. Maybe she'd sell it. The thought would have appalled Adella before, but it seemed the height of good sense now. She looked around the well-loved kitchen but thought about the taxes and repairs and bats in the slowly rotting attic. Maybe it would be a good idea to get away from all the ghosts once and for all.

Even if it made her parents weep in the land of the gods.

With a sigh, Adella put away Flora's letter, happy someone would be getting some use out of Dolores's house and money. The thought of lawyers made another missive catch her eye. Dolores's lawyer had written her, too. She opened it, hoping they'd only thank her and not try to sell her their services.

She read it once, again, a third time. With her heart beating like thunder, she stood and read it again. Her sisters fired questions at her, but she couldn't hear them over the fire in her veins.

Dolores's sister might have gotten the townhouse and some of the money, but a huge chunk of it had just come Adella's way.

Triumphant and fierce, she slid the paper around so Gisele and Zara could read it. When they looked at her again, shocked, she nodded. "Tomorrow, we're going to the bank, and then we're going to grease some palms." She folded the paper. "But tonight, we're going out to dinner."

If pleas wouldn't work to free Bridget, Adella would see what some old-fashioned bribes could do. There was more than enough for that and the house and to give her some much-needed time off before she found another job.

And by all the gods, she was going to buy some opulent damned trousers.

CHAPTER TWENTY-SEVEN

Bridget awakened from the deepest sleep she'd ever experienced with no idea of the time or date. A bowl of some soggy, lumpy oats sat just inside her cell door. It had all the taste and consistency of paste, but she ate it. What else would the sentinels do with her? She supposed she should be happy that so far, they hadn't done much *to* her.

When they hauled her to the interrogation room a second time, she'd been nearly as worried as during her first trip. In the commander's place was a sallow, bored-looking man who asked for her story again.

She sighed but told it.

He asked some follow-up questions which she'd already answered.

She answered them again.

She ate and drank everything given to her, knowing they wouldn't bother to poison her. If they wanted to give her drugs to make her more talkative, more fool them. She hadn't held anything back.

When the sallow man suggested that any gaps in her story might result in Adella's arrest, Bridget bristled. "Adella is innocent. She didn't know about my past. As for the events that happened in Sarras, Juno Garza, or whatever the hell her name is, was at fault."

"And your escape from custody?" he asked. "Serrah del Amanecer and her sisters took part in that, and two people were wounded."

Bridget fought to keep her cool. "Put that on my shoulders."

He stared with gray, watery eyes. "That's not how law works."

"Make it work." She crossed her arms. "Or would you like me to stop cooperating?"

He mimicked her pose. "That implies you haven't told us your entire story."

Well, shit. But she didn't let despair catch her. There was always another card to play. "I can continue to advise you about what's happening in the empire. I can interpret their actions, give you a host of possibilities for any movement."

"Until you're hanged, you mean."

Now that she wasn't so tired, that threat did make fear creep through her innards. But she nodded. "Or I could keep silent until you hang me."

His smile was tired and resigned, as if their positions were reversed. "Maybe you can, maybe not." He nodded at the guard to take her from the room.

Bridget kept her breathing deep and even. Here came the torture. She tried to recall Baxter's instructions on how to go elsewhere in her mind, resisting pain, but she couldn't help tensing, and her mind jabbered that she had to fight and flee before the agony began.

When they let her back into her cell, she couldn't believe her good fortune. She stayed awake for hours, certain they were going to surprise her at any moment with multiple instruments of pain.

Nothing.

Confused, she finally nodded off only to be startled awake when someone opened the door. She shook her head as they pulled her to her feet, trying to fight through her grogginess, but several nightmares were still with her, and fear surrounded her like a cloak.

Still no torture. Only the same room with the same interrogator and the same questions. Except she was a damn sight sleepier. Still, she answered him, then went back to her cell. When she was next startled awake, she did the whole thing again. Then again. She lost count of how many times she'd either just gone to sleep or had been pulled from oblivion and hustled down the hall to tell the same story, too tired to think straight. At one point, she begged for sleep, but she couldn't determine if the words were actually leaving her mouth or if they were a dream. The room began to spin, billowed by the rush of air every time the interrogator opened his lips. Someone shook her awake again and again, but they couldn't stop the room from spinning.

"Let go." Adella's voice. "I've got you."

❖

Bridget woke up in her cell again. Her body ached as if she'd been beaten, but she couldn't find any bruises in the meager light. Though nowhere near well-rested, she felt better than she had in…

Hours? Days? Weeks?

Had Adella been there? Surely that part had been a dream, but she took some comfort in it.

She ate the lumpy oat mush when it came again, and moments later, when a tingly feeling spread all through her limbs, she wasn't even surprised.

Drugs. She was almost looking forward to them, curious.

When they brought her to the interrogation room, she felt drunk but without the sleepiness that usually accompanied alcohol. She squinted at the interrogator, trying to determine if it was the same one. "Hey…" She had to stop and marvel at how slurred her speech sounded. "Are you the same guy, or do they have a stable of unhealthy-looking questioners to draw on?"

He didn't respond to that, merely making notes in a folio.

"Hey." She tried to wave to get his attention, but her arms felt like lead. "If you're going to torture me, can you do it now while I'm drugged?" She laughed, but it sounded as if she was half braying and half wheezing.

He finally looked up, and she thought he might share in her marvelous joke, but he only started on the damn questions again. She didn't really want to answer them, but the answers just kept falling out of her mouth, often with new commentary about how she thought of this person or that, but no one in the room seemed to appreciate her monumental wit.

When she reached Adella's part of the story, she wept and tried to be poetic about Adella's beauty and grace and spirit, but the interrogator kept interrupting her, and she couldn't stop her responses to the new questions. He wouldn't go back to let her praise Adella more, even though she tried saying, "hey," and "but," and "I wasn't finished."

That felt a bit like torture.

They soon dumped her in her cell again, and she watched the ceiling ripple and bend. She wished she'd been able to hallucinate Adella again before falling asleep.

When Bridget woke the next time, her eyes were crusty with grit, and her mouth felt as if she'd been sucking on an old burlap bag. And she was beyond angry. If they were going to hang her, they should fucking get on with it. She'd no longer believe anything they had to say about whether Adella would be charged with a crime. She didn't think anything she said or did could change their intentions, and unless they were going to let her see Adella, they could shove their threats up their asses.

She went to the interview room ready for a fight, and the commander waited for her again, the sallow interrogator nowhere in sight. Maybe Bridget had hallucinated him, too.

The commander did not look happy. "I can't save you much longer, Bridget."

"I prefer Serrah Leir to you."

The commander raised an eyebrow. "I'll take your preferences into consideration when you start telling me the truth."

Bridget felt a rush of heat up her neck to her head, and she gritted her teeth in anger. "Everything I've told you is the truth."

With a dramatic sigh, the commander shook her head. "If this is how you want to go to your grave, that's up to you."

So they were going to hang her at last. The reality of it was a little less of a relief than it had been in her cell. "Can I see Adella one last time?"

"If you answer our questions truthfully."

"I already have." Bridget tried to keep from screaming, knowing it would get her nowhere. "Which points are you confused about?"

"Those we can't verify."

Bridget tried not to sneer. "I can't verify things for you, not from in here. Hell, probably not from out there." She nodded to the door she'd never been through. "And it sounds like you wouldn't believe me even if I went back to the empire and made sure I have all my facts straight."

The commander fired off a few more questions, some more in-depth than before—like the current placement of spies, some of the Firellian defenses, any invasion plans—and Bridget had to admit that she didn't know the answers.

"Do you want me to speculate?" Bridget asked. "I can try, but though I knew the Firellian spymaster, I wasn't living in his head. I don't know everything he knew or even if he was privy to everything you're asking about."

"I think you know more than you're saying. Damned spies. The lot of you deserve to be killed." Her voice rose at the end, and her eyes blazed, and Bridget was certain more than one person had crumbled beneath that gaze.

But Bridget had nothing more to give. As she repeated that, her sense of anger and fear was rising. The commander kept barking accusations, and Bridget came to a place where she was ready to leap over the table, leading with her fists, so they'd hurry up with the punishment.

A glint on the commander's brow stopped Bridget before she could move. Sweat? This room was warmer than the cell but still fairly cool. No, the commander was working herself into a lather. Angry, yes, and impatient, but that didn't seem enough to warrant sweat from the icicle of a woman Bridget had first met.

She was anxious, maybe even nervous.

Maybe running out of time.

For what?

Bridget would have to watch her closely.

Calmly, she answered the questions again, denying that she'd left anything out, that she knew anything more, and each response seemed to make the commander angrier. At last, the commander stood, knotted her fist in Bridget's shirt, and hauled her upright. The guards stiffened, shuffling closer. Bridget forced herself to stay relaxed and let her arms hang at her sides. The commander's eyes were bloodshot as she screamed in Bridget's face, calling her every filthy name in the book.

When that didn't work, she started on Adella.

Bridget clenched her jaw until it ached, letting the grinding sound of her teeth fill her head. She wanted so badly to swing at the commander's head or gut. She could get a really nice shot in; the commander was wide open.

Bridget didn't need Baxter to tell her this was a trap. But as the slander against Adella continued, she had to fight harder than ever to keep still. The edges of her vision were tinged in red. She had a fist balled and ready, and she finally couldn't resist—

The door Bridget had never been through opened. The air seemed to be sucked out of the room. The commander dropped her back into the chair. She breathed deeply, and the roar that had begun in her ears subsided.

A blond, dark-eyed man she'd never seen before entered, giving the commander a censuring look. He smiled at Bridget, bowing, and his deep yellow dalmatica seemed far out of place when compared to the sentinels' dark uniforms. "Serrah Leir," he said. "My name is Horatio Diaz. I'm your lawyer."

Bridget nearly laughed. What trick was this?

Dark red spots bloomed in the commander's cheeks, and she stared at Horatio Diaz as if she could melt him with her gaze.

He returned her stare. "Serrah Leir will be coming with me." He handed over a sheaf of papers.

The commander snatched them from his hand, not even bothering to look. Maybe she already knew what they said, but Bridget wished she'd say something, give some clue so Bridget would know how to feel.

She had a lawyer? A real one? What the hell was going on?

"Get her out of my sight," the commander said, the words low and ragged.

Horatio Diaz gestured for Bridget to come with him, and she responded to the urgency in his face by obeying as quickly as she could. He shushed her when she started to speak in the hallway, and she let him take her elbow and lead her up staircases and through better appointed rooms. At each turn, she expected the trap to gain shape. They were going to get her hopes up only to dash them. Each door opened would lead back to her cell. This was another form of torture like the lack of sleep and the drugs and whatever else had happened in the hours, days, weeks, since she'd been here.

The cold outside hit her like a slap. How far were the sentinels going to go with this ruse? Two of them stood outside the door, but they didn't grab her and force her back inside. She felt hollow as Horatio Diaz came to a stop at last. He swung a coat around her shoulders and the thin shirt the sentinels had provided.

"Thanks," Bridget mumbled, all she was able to get out. "I'm… this…" She glanced around as he led her farther into a plain square that stood between three stout buildings. No gallows in sight.

"You're quite welcome, but your release isn't down to me." He nodded across the square where two people waited.

Adella, fresh and beautiful in a sky-blue cloak. No, it couldn't be. This was a dream, another hallucination. Bridget's insides felt like water, but she wished them into ice. She couldn't fall for this trick, couldn't believe. There was no way.

Then Adella was crushing her in an embrace, and if she was going to die, she wanted it to be at that moment.

Adella kissed her quickly. "I love you, Bridget Leir. And I am trying to trust you. I'm so glad you're safe."

Bridget held Adella's tear-stained cheeks and kissed her in between saying, "How?" over and over.

Adella glanced over her shoulder. "We're not quite done yet."

Bridget followed her gaze, and it took her a moment to recognize the man in the dark suit with a bandage peeking out from under his cap and a horrible bruise down the side of his face. "Jean-Carlo?" she whispered.

"Your minder, though he used the word handler. I told him you're not a dog, but…" She shrugged, her blue eyes still swimming with tears, but she'd never looked lovelier. "You're to be Sarras's expert informer on the Firellian Empire, reporting to Jean-Carlo whenever he wishes your opinion or information, an essential resource now that hostilities have begun between our two countries." A cloud passed over her features. "And I should warn you, he's very angry about being struck in the head while trying to arrest you."

Bridget breathed a laugh. "He can be as angry as he wants. As long as I can see you, I don't care about anything else."

CHAPTER TWENTY-EIGHT

The day of Dolores's funeral was sunny, warmer than the last few days had been and entirely too cheerful for the occasion. But Adella told herself that Dolores would have liked it. As she'd gotten older, Dolores had begun to loathe the cold.

Adella tried to put that thought out of her mind, too, as the coffin slowly disappeared into the ground. Quite a few people had shown up, and the presiding priestess had assured them all that Dolores would spend eternity in the realm of the gods. Adella thought so, too, but like most people, she doubted priests or priestesses could simply know this. Swearing by the gods and the occasional prayer was one thing, but actually believing in their power or the power of their "earthly interpreters" was quite another. They were a quaint holdover that would no doubt fade away.

Like Dolores's memory.

Adella sighed, brushing at a few stray tears. She couldn't distract herself from sadness for long. She tried to focus on the fact that Dolores would have loved her outfit as well. A shopping trip with Serrah Nunez had yielded blue velvet trousers with a vine and leaf design embroidered on the outside of both legs in silver thread. Her tight jacket had a bit of silver at the collar, as did the lace of her shirt cuffs, which spilled out of the jacket sleeves and over her hands.

She hoped to start a new trend among the nobility. Dolores would have liked that, too.

Gisele and Zara stood at her sides, both in the full regalia of their offices. They'd taken her hand or laid their arms over her shoulders at different times. Luckily, they hadn't had to weep for her, though she hadn't collapsed in a heap, either. It was a relief to finally give Dolores the farewell she deserved.

Dolores's sister had said hello before the funeral and now she nodded good-bye as the first shovelful of dirt fell on Dolores's grave, bringing the ceremony to the end.

Adella tugged on her sisters' arms, wanting to get away before anyone could drag her into conversation. Now that her family had money, they seemed to be in everyone's good graces again, especially after she'd bribed a few officials to secure Bridget's release. If she was willing to give cash away, there were more than a few people willing to take it.

If only Bridget was as free as she'd hoped. She wasn't allowed to leave Adella's house yet and would be under Jean-Carlo's watchful eye much of the time. He'd seemed quite agitated when he'd visited their house for the first time after Bridget's release.

He'd informed Adella that he would be Bridget's new supervisor, or handler, as he'd kept saying. When he'd laid eyes on Zara, his bruised face had tightened even further. So he'd discovered that she'd been the one to knock him unconscious in Bridget's old room at the Donkey's Rest.

Adella had looked between them, unsure quite what to say. Zara hadn't backed down from his challenging stare, and both of them had seemed as tense as vipers. And Gisele had been in the kitchen, no doubt listening. She argued with Zara on almost every point, but Adella had no doubt that she would throw herself into any fight on Zara's side.

Before anyone had a chance to move, Adella had asked a question that had popped into her head when she'd found out Jean-Carlo wasn't who he'd pretended to be. "Did you laugh at me?" She'd wondered the same about Juno, if these spies took pleasure in deceiving others, or if they simply regarded it as another part of the job.

Jean-Carlo and Zara blinked at her in surprise, just as she'd hoped. They'd had to forget their antagonism long enough to wonder what the hell she was talking about.

"Zara," Adella had said, "wait for me in the kitchen, please."

Zara's light touch to her arm had let her know that help was only a shout away. She had smiled, but standing there in the foyer of her own house after all she'd been able to accomplish, she'd never felt safer.

"I beg your pardon, serrah," Jean-Carlo had said when they were alone. "Laugh at you?"

She'd stared at him, hoping it conveyed a sense of challenge, too. "When you were acting as my second. My nerves, my hesitance at my first diplomatic meeting without Dolores. Did you get a chuckle from that once you were alone because I was depending on you while having no idea who you really were?"

He'd frowned, looking pained, but was that because of feeling or injury? "No, serrah," he'd said, shifting slightly as if uncomfortable. "I thought you did a fine job. I wouldn't…mock you."

"You were so cheerful," she'd said, "so helpful. I thought that if Juno didn't come back, I'd ask you to stay on."

His smile had seemed a little pleased, a little sad. "Thank you, serrah. And it was nice to be cheerful for a time. I so rarely get the opportunity."

She'd regarded him for a few moments. She couldn't hold on to her animosity for spies and their ilk, not if she was ever to trust Bridget again, but she was finding her anger hard to let go of. Still, she'd felt sorry for him, for what Zara had been forced to do. And he had saved her life at least once and had taken revenge on Devil-Juno.

"You can be cheerful when you're here," she'd said. "Or embrace your true demeanor, whatever that may be outside your…job."

His healthy eye had gone wide. The other had seemed a little too swollen to follow. "When I'm here? How do you mean?"

"Minding Bridget. Handling her, though I still hate that word. You'll need somewhere to meet, and I'm sure you'll want to simply clap eyes on her on occasion. We can't have you hanging from the windowsills trying to get a peek inside."

He'd swallowed and blinked, and she'd wondered if she'd caught him off guard. The thought had pleased her more than a little. She'd liked the idea of surprising someone who no doubt thought they'd seen everything. "Very generous, serrah."

She'd nodded, hoping she'd bought some goodwill for Bridget, too, but that wasn't the only reason she'd invited him in. She seemed to have gotten a taste for peeling back the layers of spies.

Now, as she and her sisters took a carriage back home, Adella didn't quite know how to feel. Bridget was at home. No matter who else was there, Bridget would no doubt be there for a long time to come. After they'd freed her from prison yesterday, she'd slept all afternoon and all night. This morning before the funeral, she'd seemed much recovered, though a trifle thinner than before. Every time Adella saw her, she remembered the confession she'd read, the lovely things Bridget had said, the way her feelings had danced across the page.

It made it hard to hold on to her anger. Not that she was trying to do so. Well, she didn't think she was. No, she wanted to forgive and forget and trust, but…

"How long is Bridget going to be in the spare room?" Zara asked as the carriage rattled along the cobbled streets.

Adella sat back at the forward question. It disarmed her enough to ask a question that had been going around in her head along with issues of trust. "Do you think I should ask her to my bed? So soon?"

"Why not?" Gisele said while Zara frowned.

"She…well…" Adella sighed. "I don't know if I forgive her."

"I could still duel her," Zara said. "If that would make things better."

Adella was surprised enough to snort a laugh. "I don't think that would help."

"What would?" Gisele asked.

Remembering that Gisele had read the confession, too, and no doubt hoped for a happy ending, Adella *tsked*. "Can we not all be so involved in my love life, please?"

Gisele smiled softly. "You still love her."

And that was true. Adella brushed past hope and fear and thought of the way Bridget moved so confidently, of the way she danced, played, sang, kissed. She thought of all the promise in Bridget's eyes that had so far gone unfulfilled.

Gods, she still wanted Bridget. The warm, tingly feelings passing through her said her body would call her a liar if her mind tried to deny it. But she didn't want to deny it. She wanted to draw a line under this part of their lives, a way to move on, start fresh.

See if their hasty feelings of love could become permanent.

Judging by the confession, Adella was the only person Bridget had ever loved. And Bridget could be the one Adella would love forever. Was there a more wonderful way to celebrate that than for them to hold each other, kiss each other, touch and taste each other?

The thoughts brought more heat to her face, and she knew she was blushing, but there was nowhere to hide. "I'll think about it," she mumbled, knowing she'd already thought of an answer, but she did not want to speak about it with her sisters.

Gisele looked out the window and smiled. Zara continued to stare as if that wasn't a satisfactory answer.

Adella glared. "I'm not telling you anything else, Zara."

"But you didn't answer my question."

Adella bristled as Gisele looked at Zara in surprise. "And I don't intend to!"

"Why are you getting angry? I only wanted to know how long Bridget will be staying with us."

Adella thought back on her words and sputtered a laugh. Gisele joined in, and they both nearly collapsed in laughter while Zara frowned at them. Finally, realization dawned on Zara's face. "I was asking how long she was going to stay, and you thought I was asking if you were going to have sex with her. That's why you said all that." She beamed as if beyond proud at herself.

It started the laughing all over again, but this time, Zara joined in.

When they reached the house, Adella nearly ran in, her mind and body on fire. In the last moments in the carriage, she'd decided to wait until evening to invite Bridget into her bed, but now she couldn't wait to see if Bridget would even agree to such a thing. She needed to hear Bridget's feelings, if too much had happened between them on her side, or if...

Instead of getting tangled in her thoughts, she rushed to the kitchen and found Bridget tuning her newly recovered mandolin at the table. "Hello. How was—"

"Where's Jean-Carlo?" Adella blurted.

"Um, he left." She sighed. "Said he'd be watching as usual."

Adella nodded and fought the urge to pace and wring her hands. Why in the name of all the gods was she so nervous? Bridget was watching her curiously. She began to speak but hesitated, unable to imagine having a serious conversation while Zara and Gisele were puttering around the kitchen making coffee.

Right. First things first.

Her mind falling somewhat back into orderliness, Adella asked, "Can we have a word in private?"

"Of course."

Adella led the way past where Zara and Gisele were standing near the foyer, both of them looking as if they didn't know where to go, one frowning, the other grinning. Adella waved them into the kitchen and led Bridget upstairs, the only place they could really speak in private.

And since she hadn't refurnished most of the rooms, her bedroom seemed the obvious choice.

Yes, speaking privately, that was what she wanted. It wasn't because the muscles in her core had tightened like bowstrings, making her ache.

She turned when Bridget shut the door, but words deserted her as she looked into those deep blue eyes. Bridget's short hair was tousled, as if she'd been running her hands through it. Adella wanted to do the same. She took a step forward but stopped, needing to ask, needing to hear, needing…

Surprised to find tears waiting on the answer, she asked impatiently, "Will you please kiss me already?"

Surprise lit Bridget's face, but then it darkened with desire, and she was pressed against Adella as if she'd started there. Their kisses were fast and hurried, greedy, as if they were still in a race for their lives. Adella didn't want it any other way. All her hesitant thoughts and questions fled, and Bridget didn't seem to need words either as she wrapped her arms around Adella's waist and pulled her close.

Adella moaned as Bridget moved from kissing her lips to her neck. She divested Adella of her jacket and shirt with a skillful touch that seemed like magic, and then she ran her hands over the velvet trousers to cup Adella's backside.

She left off kissing Adella's neck and shoulders long enough to grin. "I like these trousers." She kissed Adella again, sucking at her bottom lip. "But if they don't come off easily, you're going to need a new pair."

"Yes, gods, yes."

Adella gasped as Bridget lifted her. She wrapped her legs around Bridget's waist, and they stumbled to the bed. Adella lost herself in sensation, but she was still mindful enough to know that yes, she wanted Bridget to stay. In her house, in her bed, in her life. She would hold on to happiness for as long as she could. Beyond money, beyond pride, beyond duty, that was all they could hope for.

And it was enough.

About the Author

Barbara Ann Wright writes fantasy and science fiction novels when not hoarding glitter. She has been a finalist in the *Foreword Review* Book of the Year Awards, the Goldie Awards, and the Lambda Literary Awards. Her first novel, *The Pyramid Waltz*, was one of *Tor.com's* Reviewer's Choice books of 2012 and made *BookRiot's* 100 Must-Read Sci-Fi Fantasy Novels by Female Authors. *Lady of Stone*, the prequel to *The Pyramid Waltz*, was recommended on *Syfy.com*. Her work has won five Rainbow Awards.

Books Available from Bold Strokes Books

Coming to Life on South High by Lee Patton. Twenty-one-year-old gay virgin Gabe Rafferty's first adult decade unfolds as an unpredictable journey into sex, love, and livelihood. (978-1-63555-906-4)

Fleur d'Lies by MJ Williamz. For rookie cop DJ Sander, being true to what you believe is the only way to live…and one way to die. (978-1-63555-854-8)

Guarding Evelyn by Erin Zak. Can TV actress Evelyn Glass prove her love for Alden Ryan means more to her than fame before it's too late? (978-1-63555-841-8)

Love's Falling Star by B.D. Grayson. For country music megastar Lochlan Paige, can love conquer her fear of losing the one thing she's worked so hard to protect? (978-1-63555-873-9)

Love's Truth by C.A. Popovich. Can Lynette and Barb make love work when unhealed wounds of betrayed trust and a secret could change everything? (978-1-63555-755-8)

Next Exit Home by Dena Blake. Home may be where the heart is, but for Harper Sims and Addison Foster, is the journey back worth the pain? (978-1-63555-727-5)

Not Broken by Lyn Hemphill. Falling in love is hard enough—even more so for Rose who's carrying her ex's baby. (978-1-63555-869-2)

The Noble and the Nightingale by Barbara Ann Wright. Two women on opposite sides of empires at war risk all for a chance at love. (978-1-63555-812-8)

What a Tangled Web by Melissa Brayden. Clementine Monroe has the chance to buy the café she's managed for years, but Madison LeGrange swoops in and buys it first. Now Clementine is forced to work for the enemy and ignore her former crush. (978-1-63555-749-7)

A Far Better Thing by JD Wilburn. When needs of her family and wants of her heart clash, Cass Halliburton is faced with the ultimate sacrifice. (978-1-63555-834-0)

Body Language by Renee Roman. When Mika offers to provide Jen erotic tutoring, will sex drive them into a deeper relationship or tear them apart? (978-1-63555-800-5)

Carrie and Hope by Joy Argento. For Carrie and Hope loss brings them together but secrets and fear may tear them apart. (978-1-63555-827-2)

Death's Prelude by David S. Pederson. In this prequel to the Detective Heath Barrington Mystery series, Heath discovers that first love changes you forever and drives you to become the person you're destined to be. (978-1-63555-786-2)

Ice Queen by Gun Brooke. School counselor Aislin Kennedy wants to help standoffish CEO Susanna Durr and her troubled teenage daughter become closer—even if it means risking her own heart in the process. (978-1-63555-721-3)

Masquerade by Anne Shade. In 1925 Harlem, New York, a notorious gangster sets her sights on seducing Celine, and new lovers Dinah and Celine are forced to risk their hearts, and lives, for love. (978-1-63555-831-9)

Royal Family by Jenny Frame. Loss has defined both Clay's and Katya's lives, but guarding their hearts may prove to be the biggest heartbreak of all. (978-1-63555-745-9)

Share the Moon by Toni Logan. Three best friends, an inherited vineyard and a resident ghost come together for fun, romance and a touch of magic. (978-1-63555-844-9)

Spirit of the Law by Carsen Taite. Attorney Owen Lassiter will do almost anything to put a murderer behind bars, but can she get past her reluctance to rely on unconventional help from the alluring Summer Byrne and keep from falling in love in the process? (978-1-63555-766-4)

The Devil Incarnate by Ali Vali. Cain Casey has so much to live for, but enemies who lurk in the shadows threaten to unravel it all. (978-1-63555-534-9)

His Brother's Viscount by Stephanie Lake. Hector Somerville wants to rekindle his illicit love affair with Viscount Wentworth, but he must overcome one problem: Wentworth still loves Hector's brother. (978-1-63555-805-0)

Journey to Cash by Ashley Bartlett. Cash Braddock thought everything was great, but it looks like her history is about to become her right now. Which is a real bummer. (978-1-63555-464-9)

Liberty Bay by Karis Walsh. Wren Lindley's life is mired in tradition and untouched by trends until social media star Gina Strickland introduces an irresistible electricity into her off-the-grid world. (978-1-63555-816-6)

Scent by Kris Bryant. Nico Marshall has been burned by women in the past wanting her for her money. This time, she's determined to win Sophia Sweet over with her charm. (978-1-63555-780-0)

Shadows of Steel by Suzie Clarke. As their worlds collide and their choices come back to haunt them, Rachel and Claire must figure out how to stay together and most of all, stay alive. (978-1-63555-810-4)

The Clinch by Nicole Disney. Eden Bauer overcame a difficult past to become a world champion mixed martial artist, but now rising star and dreamy bad girl Brooklyn Shaw is a threat both to Eden's title and her heart. (978-1-63555-820-3)

The Last First Kiss by Julie Cannon. Kelly Newsome is so ready for a tropical island vacation, but she never expects to meet the woman who could give her her last first kiss. (978-1-63555-768-8)

The Mandolin Lunch by Missouri Vaun. Despite their immediate attraction, everything about Garet Allen says short-term, and Tess Hill refuses to consider anything less than forever. (978-1-63555-566-0)

Thor: Daughter of Asgard by Genevieve McCluer. When Hannah Olsen finds out she's the reincarnation of Thor, she's thrown into a world of magic and intrigue, unexpected attraction, and a mystery she's got to unravel. (978-1-63555-814-2)

Veterinary Technician by Nancy Wheelton. When a stable of horses is threatened Val and Ronnie must work together against the odds to save them, and maybe even themselves along the way. (978-1-63555-839-5)

16 Steps to Forever by Georgia Beers. Can Brooke Sullivan and Macy Carr find themselves by finding each other? (978-1-63555-762-6)

All I Want for Christmas by Georgia Beers, Maggie Cummings, Fiona Riley. The Christmas season sparks passion and love in these stories by award winning authors Georgia Beers, Maggie Cummings, and Fiona Riley. (978-1-63555-764-0)

From the Woods by Charlotte Greene. When Fiona goes backpacking in a protected wilderness, the last thing she expects is to be fighting for her life. (978-1-63555-793-0)

Heart of the Storm by Nicole Stiling. For Juliet Mitchell and Sienna Bennett a forbidden attraction definitely isn't worth upending the life they've worked so hard for. Is it? (978-1-63555-789-3)

If You Dare by Sandy Lowe. For Lauren West and Emma Prescott, following their passions is easy. Following their hearts, though? That's almost impossible. (978-1-63555-654-4)

Love Changes Everything by Jaime Maddox. For Samantha Brooks and Kirby Fielding, no matter how careful their plans, love will change everything. (978-1-63555-835-7)

Not This Time by MA Binfield. Flung back into each other's lives, can former bandmates Sophia and Madison have a second chance at romance? (978-1-63555-798-5)

The Dubious Gift of Dragon Blood by J. Marshall Freeman. One day Crispin is a lonely high school student—the next he is fighting a war in a land ruled by dragons, his otherworldly boyfriend at his side. (978-1-63555-725-1)

The Found Jar by Jaycie Morrison. Fear keeps Emily Harris trapped in her emotionally vacant life; can she find the courage to let Beck Reynolds guide her toward love? (978-1-63555-825-8)

Aurora by Emma L McGeown. After a traumatic accident, Elena Ricci is stricken with amnesia leaving her with no recollection of the last eight years, including her wife and son. (978-1-63555-824-1)

Avenging Avery by Sheri Lewis Wohl. Revenge against a vengeful vampire unites Isa Meyer and Jeni Denton, but it's love that heals them. (978-1-63555-622-3)

Bulletproof by Maggie Cummings. For Dylan Prescott and Briana Logan, the complicated NYC criminal justice system doesn't leave room for love, but where the heart is concerned, no one is bulletproof. (978-1-63555-771-8)

Her Lady to Love by Jane Walsh. A shy wallflower joins forces with the most popular woman in Regency London on a quest to catch a husband, only to discover a wild passion for each other that far eclipses their interest for the Marriage Mart. (978-1-63555-809-8)

No Regrets by Joy Argento. For Jodi and Beth, the possibility of losing their future will force them to decide what is really important. (978-1-63555-751-0)

The Holiday Treatment by Elle Spencer. Who doesn't want a gay Christmas movie? Holly Hudson asks herself that question and discovers that happy endings aren't only for the movies. (978-1-63555-660-5)

Too Good to be True by Leigh Hays. Can the promise of love survive the realities of life for Madison and Jen, or is it too good to be true? (978-1-63555-715-2)

Treacherous Seas by Radclyffe. When the choice comes down to the lives of her officers against the promise she made to her wife, Reese Conlon puts everything she cares about on the line. (978-1-63555-778-7)

Two to Tangle by Melissa Brayden. Ryan Jacks has been a player all her life, but the new chef at Tangle Valley Vineyard changes everything. If only she wasn't off the menu. (978-1-63555-747-3)

When Sparks Fly by Annie McDonald. Will the devastating incident that first brought Dr. Daniella Waveny and hockey coach Luca McCaffrey together on frozen ice now force them apart, or will their secrets and fears thaw enough for them to create sparks? (978-1-63555-782-4)